BENEATH THE DOOR

THE CHRYSALIS SAGA BOOK ONE

HOLLY JANE

To every single person who's once been told they can't accomplish their dreams; **you can.**

To my Alpha and Beta readers: your time and feedback have been invaluable to me to grow both personally and professionally.

To my editor Haley, who I'm sure spent many hours tearing out her hair over my bad language habits.

To my family and friends, who patiently let me hunch over my laptop for hours and pretend the world doesn't exist for a few hours every day.

To Ryan and my animals, who keep me sane (kind of).

Finally, to everyone who at some point has lost a part of themselves along the way; **it'll be OK.**

-I-

The door rattles on its hinges, shaking everything around it. Behind the heavy metal exterior, I hear cries and wails. They progress from the sorrowful howling of a child to angry screeching to pure roaring hatred. The door vibrates in time with the bangs as tiny fists pound the other side. It increases in intensity until the entire house feels like it's shaking on its foundations.

Despite the noise, I hear my parents continue their day upstairs idly. My mother busies herself with reheating the beef casserole leftovers from the last party. I hear my father opening his new "Wine of the Month Club" delivery. Two people that had fallen out of love many years ago exchange small talk as they continue about their business, calmly ignoring the commotion from the old wooden stairs leading down to the cellar.

I think for a moment about calling through the metal prison and trying to calm the situation down. I was anxious, rooted to the ground I stood by my horror and fear.

No. I couldn't. It's against the rules... I'm not even supposed to be down here.

Despite the heavy-duty locks installed way before we'd ever lived here as a family, I worry they will break off, and the anger will be unleashed. The air is cold and musty.

I swallow, turn on my heels and head back up the rickety steps before they notice I'm gone. Beneath me, the screams continue until it feels as if they reverberate through the entire house, reducing everything to its very core.

-2-

"What kind of weirdo name is *Terin?*" the tallest girl in the class sneers. She towers over me by a good few inches and she knows it. She stands close so she can purposely glare down with an eyebrow of mirth raised like she could squash me.

Sarah is framed on either side by two of her lackeys with similar half up, half down hairstyles and wrists adorned with plastic bracelets. For twelve-year-olds, they look so grown up.

Heated embarrassment spreads across my face. "It's a family name," I mumble. "My mum's grandmother was called Terin." "Sounds like terrapin." The girl shrugs. "You *do* look a bit pinched in the face. Do you wallow in smelly water?"

"She's a bit spotty too," one of the other girls' cackles. I think her name's Alice. She's usually always on Sarah and Alexa's side. They join in unison in high-pitched screeches that reach across the playground. My brother's already waiting for me across the quad with his own pinched look and glares at my three personal torturers. He waits for the girls to leave for home with a final cackle and let me go free.

"You should have pushed the big one over," he says hotly after I finally trail over. "Those gangly legs wouldn't have saved her. Her brother's in my class... I could punch him for you if you want?"

"I told you before: we both end up getting into trouble when you attack people at school that are mean to me. Besides, it's Sarah, not her brother."

"I can't hit her though, can I? Her brother's fair game though. Face full of acne. It'll make you feel better." He shrugs.

"What's the point?" I mutter. "They're not worth getting into trouble over." Self-consciously, I try to hide the broken button on the front of my blazer with its collar, the school crest decorating the side of it. Mum would kill me if she had to arrange for it to be sewn on again.

If it wasn't the girls at school giving me a hard time, it was the public-school kids on the side of the corner shop throwing 'rich girl' insults my way. Seeing my face drop towards the row of shops in the distance, Jared nudges me to follow him down the longer route around the old church.

"You need to start standing up for yourself more." he says. "Just shut up about it, Jared."

"*Terrapin*," he muses quietly. "That's a new one." Before I can move to punch him in the ribs, he grins and dances out of my way, tauntingly draping an arm over my skinny shoulders next to his broad-ened fifteen-year-old ones. Regardless of his trouble making a couple of school years above me, his own blazer is spotless, only marred by the slackened tie and crumpled shirt. He still lets me hit him lightly in the kidneys, something I imagine he didn't let his friends get away with.

"I thought all of this would have ended in primary school. Cruel girls and stupid cliques, I mean," I whisper miserably.

"Nope. Welcome to Year 7." He grins, cheerily sliding his hands back into his pockets. No one at school ever messes with Jared Coiler. He was the funny one. No one dares to bully or beat up the funny one.

The longer route takes an extra ten minutes, but we reach the house before the overcast clouds begin to pull together. Our white house was one of the bigger ones on our street, fully detached with beautifully kept pine green hedges which shielded everything beyond the electric gate from the view of the street. Jared silently holds open the side gate, letting me slip in first.

"The gardener's changed the flowers again; Mum won't be happy," I mumble to myself.

"Hm…" Jared says, pushing open the sleek, black door. As usual, the house is quiet. At this time of day, Mum would be busy practising or tutoring music students in her study. Dad was probably in his own space working.

Jared hangs his jacket and kicks off his shoes by the door, slouching upstairs with his bag without another word to me. I sigh and do the same, putting his shoes on the allocated rack along with my own. It's a massive house from somewhere in the 1800s, and our mother's immensely proud of everything from the original beams, which are still well polished and stable, to the white and black staircase that winds down from the second and third floors to the entrance hall. Every part of the house is spotless, but it's the interior that she really takes pride in.

The décor changes every year depending on her mood and muse at the time. She was currently in a minimal, neutral colour phase, which naturally meant all rooms had to suit her expectations – including Jared's and my bedrooms.

Everything had its place in this house, including my brother and I.

We're called back downstairs just before six for an earlier dinner before Dad's conference call with the CoilerTech execs. He combs through a wad of papers in front of him with a slight frown. Regardless of his youngish face, he was a middle-aged corporate father with casual and formal suits for every occasion. Even at mealtimes, he was wearing a light blue shirt with the cuffs rolled slightly to expose an expensive-looking watch that he always had a habit of glancing at every so often.

"Eat your vegetables, Jared," our mother sighs into her bowl of steamed broccoli and lentils, which exudes just as much excitement as she does. Somehow, they're the same shade as her smartly fitted dress. I idly wonder if she plans these things ahead of time.

"I didn't realise eating my vegetables benefited your image in any way," Jared replies coolly. I know this defiant mood well, which makes my stomach hurt with anxiety. I blur my vision down towards my dinner and try to count my peas.

When I eventually glance up, she flashes a look at my father, who simply returns a dark one, papers momentarily forgotten. He clears his throat and turns to me, where I can fully see the vein that pops out of the side of his forehead despite the calm persona he's trying to sell.

"Terin," he booms. "How was school today? I hear you've gone up a class in History?"

The steamed chicken catches in my windpipe, and I nod quickly. "The teacher read my work out to the whole class," I say, a little proud. "She says it was the best one today." My Dad smiles, though the vein is still there from the obvious annoyance of my brother. I glance over at Jared, who simply looks bored. The vegetables still lie forgotten.

I catch my brother's eye and pointedly glance down at the plate and back up to him. *It's not worth it*; I try to communicate – *just do what they say*.

"Jared, my son," my father says, though it's evident he's losing interest in having a quiet family dinner. "Listen to your mother – finish that plate, or you're going straight to bed."

"I'm fifteen, Dad," Jared states seriously. His outward defiance flattens me with the awkwardness of how he was managing to stay calm.

"You're under my roof, boy." The vein is more prominent than ever, I can practically see it pulsing. "Time's getting on anyway; they need to wash tonight," Mum interjects. She clutches her wine glass and drains it quickly to stack the rest of the plates. They clink loudly against her rings and bracelets. I wince at the harsh sound.

"It's never too late in life for vegetables," my father insists. He slides his chair across the varnished wooden floor, and the sound of scraping loudly fills the room. "Come on, Jared. I won't ask again." He picks up his fork, stabs some of the greenery, and waves it in his face until it's pushed against his nose like a dog.

My dinner lays forgotten before me. I'm suddenly very interested in my nails. My mother sighs again under her breath and takes the opportunity to pour herself another small helping from the bottle since we were going nowhere anytime soon.

Jared looks up at my father with such a similar expression to the one I've seen on Dad's face so many times, despite their physical differences. Jared's unruly hair was light brown with a reddish hue, blessed with Grandma's button nose and a preference for baggy clothes. Dad, a well-polished businessman with not a facial hair out of place and the attitude to go with it. In a lot of ways, they were very similar while also being total strangers at the same time.

"Come on, Jay," I press gently. "Or they'll be no pudding after."

"Pudding rights have already gone," Dad says, still waving the fork. "But you still have the chance to get out of a smack, lad." "I'm... not feeling too good," Jared says as he eventually weighs his chances. I can still see the signs of wanting to argue further. His cheeks are red, but he glances towards me again, holding his tongue and nodding once in reassurance. He waits for an agonising few seconds before he takes the fork from our father's hand and forces the greenery into his mouth, shuddering as he swallows.

I can't help but visibly relax and breathe normally. Another incident was averted. The room fills with oxygen again. Inhale, exhale. It wasn't going to happen today.

"Well, that's that. We'll have pudding tomorrow night instead. Terin – upstairs. I'll be with you in a minute." Our mother rises and drains the last dregs of her second liquid helping.

"Jared – help your mother. Then go get in your bath," Dad mutters and rises, buttoning his blazer. The vein of embarrassment still shining as a badge of irritation, he escapes from the dining room in the direction of his office.

I walk slowly up the steps to my bedroom, half hoping my brother will catch up before returning to his own. It's Mum who trots behind me in her heels, following me into my room and straight into the ensuite to start running the bath.

"I can wash myself, you know," I complain loudly.

She snorts, grabbing a couple of clean towels from the side. "You can't rinse your hair out properly. I can't have you going to school looking greasy and unwashed. They'll talk."

I decide not to point out that I was already off to an awkward start in secondary school with my name being Terin, so my appearance wouldn't matter much. I slip out of my clothes and into the hot water as soon as it was filled and patiently let her pull my long auburn hair from the water and begin to detangle it.

She potters around with deciding what shampoo and conditioner we were going to use today. Some of the most prestigious products we had, were gifts from various music critics, companies, and designers she was still in contact with. Technically Mum is retired, but she was a complete powerhouse in the industry, plucked from a less than ideal childhood in a bohemian family with no money, working herself hard with her skill with an old, battered piano to where she was now.

"Georgia says they're going to Brighton for their summer holiday this year," I say as she lathers the concoction into my hair that smells of citrus. She shudders.

"Can't imagine why; there's only fish and chip shops there. Maybe the odd retail outlet."

"Which part did you live in again? Do your parents still live there?"

"I'm unsure," she says carefully. "They prefer not to travel to London really. Why all the questions this evening, madam?" She bops my nose with a handful of bubbles, and I giggle.

"What are we going to do for your thirteenth birthday? Dad was wondering if you wanted to go to Canary Wharf with him for his next meeting. You can sit in his office and order his staff around all day if you'd like. I'm sure he'd take you to the West End afterwards and you could see *The Lion King*."

I muse the idea – I'd been to the theatre show at least twice during its current run, but I wanted to do something a little different this year.

"Maybe the zoo or something?" I say, a little shyly. "There are some new exhibits I want to see."

Mum's nose wrinkles. She seizes the conditioner bottle and goes to work on lathering my scalp and working the mixture through the waist-length auburn strands. It takes ages to dry but cutting it was out of the question, according to her.

"It could be a whole family day out," I prompt further. "Me, you, Dad, and Jared... it would be fun. We never do anything altogether anymore."

"There's a lot of planning involved in that, Terin, and a lot of things to be mindful of. It's your birthday – don't you want to be the centre of attention?" She finishes with my hair and my reply is drowned out by the jug of water that's dripped over my skull. With my hands, I squeeze my eyes shut and keep my face as dry as possible. She grabs a sponge and tugs out my arms and legs to scrub. The bathwater begins to turn a shade of blue from the mixture of the hair and body products. "So, what do you think?" I say again, keeping my tone light and breezy after she finishes scrubbing under my nails and inspecting their length.

"About what?" "About the zoo, Mum." She sighs dramatically and rolls her eyes. "I'll suggest it to Dad, but I know he had his heart set on showing you around the company. It'll be yours one day, little miss. Don't you forget it."

"On my birthday though?" I say flatly. "Can't he take Jared instead? He's three years older; he'll be running it before I will." "Enough," she warns quietly, and I have enough sense to keep my mouth shut and keep my comments to myself. When I'm out of the bath and towelled dry, she sits me on the pink leather chair in front of my dressing table and combs carefully through all of my hair, humming under her breath as she moves. I know the tune without even having to ask. It's one of her famous classical sets from some musical she helped to orchestrate years ago. I'd been brought up on it and knew it like I knew the sound of running water.

I move my fingers across the polished wood, imagining that I'm the one on centre stage at the Royal Albert and I'm the *one* that thousands of people have come to watch play. My eyes close, and my fingers drift over the wood as I imagine the keys laid out before me. I itched to touch mum's new grand piano – but she insisted I practice more on my own first.

I'm brought out of my imagination when we hear a door slam in the distance and the sound of my Dad's raised voice somewhere downstairs. There's a muffled retort from Jared and a bang from another door. I feel as if it shakes the walls – which is impossible. Maybe I'm the one shaking.

"Tell Dad it's fine; I'll go to work with him," I say quietly. My fingers are still moving across the wood, but my mind is elsewhere.

"If you're sure," she says, giving my hair one last brush before letting it fall through her manicured nails like silk. "You'll have a wonderful day, sweetheart. I just know you'll come back full of beans! Dad might even take you to the West End afterwards." She winks; her false eyelashes touch the bottom of her perfectly made-up cheeks and even post-bath, nothing is out of place on her. The woman was powerfully untouchable.

"Bedtime," she prompts and prods the brush into my back. I pull back the wispy curtains of the four-poster bed and slide under newly made sheets. She leans down to peck me on the forehead and whispers goodnight. My eyes are already beginning to close, and the sheets are starting to pull me down into unconsciousness.

"Are you going to say goodnight to Jared too?" I murmur sleepily as she turns off the dressing table lamp and heads to the doorway.

She pauses and says, "He's getting a little old for that now..." and closes the door with a final click.

-3-

The cellar was almost the third child in the house.

We were inadvertently taught to *fear* it growing up. The structure was initially built to sustain a family against German bombs from the second world war, so the thickened walls, floor, ceiling, and reinforced steel door would be more than enough to protect someone for a little while. Supposedly it's still kitted out with non-perishable food, blankets and has working plumbing, but I'd never been down there before. The threat of this punishment was enough to keep me in line.

The cellar was more for Jared than anyone else in the family. Mum once explained that being downstairs on his own calms him down when he's having one of his rage fits or when he's been really naughty. I wasn't sure if that was true, but to just *hear* the squeak of the basement door open at the top of the stairs was enough motivation to run back to my bedroom like a child and hide.

I had my questions about the cellar, but Jared never wants to talk about it. He's escorted down there usually by our father and appears a day or two later, keeping his head down and behaving for a little while before something sets him off, and the cycle begins again.

This morning was no different really, breakfast was a quiet affair with a sullen looking Jared picking thoughtfully at his egg, having only just appeared from a recent trip downstairs.

"We're going to be getting some help around the house," Dad announces. "Someone to help cook, clean, tidy; all the bits your mother doesn't have time to do." He reaches over, and they religiously clasp hands and smile at one another over slices of grapefruit and Greek yoghurt. I get the feeling it's more for our benefit than actual solidarity.

"Right, so run by what this has to do with us?" Jared mutters. He pushes his food to the side and yawns, stretching to draw it out to annoy our parents. He's had another growth spurt in the last few weeks and towers over me a little more. His shoulders have changed the most in such a short time, and they jut out and harden further in line with his sharp cheekbones.

"It means behave yourself," Mum says. "You too, Terin; I don't want to hear from this woman that I've raised impolite brats. We each have a role in this family--"

"What's mine?" Jared chuckles under his breath, but no one's laughing.

"To not cause trouble," Dad warns, watching Jared carefully as he takes another bite of grapefruit. "Be a vegetable. Do what I'm told, got it." He mock salutes, earning a warning nudge from me. Apprehension flares up in my stomach.

"He's just joking," I say quickly.

"He better be or he knows what'll happen otherwise," Dad says coolly, ignoring me, and Jared's face pales slightly. He moves his gaze down to stare at the fruit in his bowl and stays quiet until the dishes are being cleaned away. I remember the sounds of childlike fists pounding against that reinforced steel door and shudder.

An early summer heat had begun to descend on London, which was a rarity for April. The outside is painfully muggy compared to the cool interior of the house, that I have to close the curtains first in the music room before daily piano practice. Despite the heat, school stays just as chilly for me as Sarah and her crew decide to try and sneak printed photos of terrapins in my school bag at every opportunity.

"Look – the family resemblance!" They cackle loudly when I go to pack up my books for the next lesson, the pictures tumbling out across the floor. Blushing and wondering when this nightmare will end, I scramble to squash away the paper amphibians.

Soon enough, my thirteenth birthday rolls around the day after the half-term holidays begin. After waking up extra early, I find a new giant teddy bear in my bedroom, poised precariously in front of my dressing table with a massive bow around his neck. I turn my head to notice Dad peering around the door with a large smile.

"I love him. Thank you!" I say as I wrap my arms around my stuffed friend. He's so huge and squishy that my skinny limbs can't quite get around his huge frame. I hear the chuckle from the doorway.

"I take it that you like him then. I was worried you were getting too old for teddies."

"He's perfect. Maybe I'll scare Jared with him before we leave today. I don't think he's ever gotten over his fear of bears, you know."

Dad made a face. "Probably not the best idea, sweetheart. He's in one of his moods. You can show him later."

I can only nod. Jared in a mood meant arguments and hostility. Dad doesn't mention whether he's in his room or downstairs.

I skip over this detail for the time being. "Thanks again, Dad."

He smiles and nods. "You're welcome. Now, you need to paste your best stern look on. We're going up to the office, and I'm counting on you to boss around some of my employees and whip them into shape. Think you can do that for your old Dad?" I nod and try to arrange my face in my best impression of him. He chuckles and pats me on the back, leading me out of the bedroom and down to the foyer.

I'd never visited my father's office in Canary Wharf or understood the family business in any capacity. All I knew was that CoilerTech made a lot of money, we lived in a big house, and went to private schools with the other rich kids – although they were still just as mean as I imagined normal school kids were.

But for the first time ever, I am allowed to climb into the front seat of his new Mercedes and marvel at the roof that folded neatly into a panel in the back of the car with just a flick of a button.

I feel like royalty as he drives with the top down into central London. The city is packed with tourists and the morning is already pretty hot, despite the recent showers that the adults grumbled about. I wave to the tour buses, the taxis, and the passers-by on the streets as we head down by the Thames. I try not to burn with smugness as they glance in our direction and marvel at the shiny car gliding past the overpacked red buses.

We pull into a large car park that overlooks the river. The area is framed by neatly planted trees encased in wooden beams that trail from the double doors down to the private docks at the bottom of the large garden area. There are a few boats tied up to the moorings, but

I don't know if we actually own any of them. The only other people around are either walking to their cars from the building or a couple of workers trimming hedges in the far distance.

The car roof begins to unfold and connect back to the overheard rims, and I glance upwards to see the words "CoilerTech" emblazoned on the side of the tall, black building in large, silver letters.

"Welcome to the empire, little miss," Dad says, placing a hand on my shoulder to steer me towards the front doors. They open automatically to welcome us, and we're greeted by a man in a maroon suit and a smile. He's middle-aged and probably a little older than my father, but he still inclines his head and reaches out to take his suit jacket.

"Mr Coiler, good to see you. And who's this little lady?"

"Terin," I say. "I'm thirteen today."

"Thirteen years old," he pretends to gasp. "Is this your first day of work, young lady? Are you here to chair the business meetings this morning?"

I grin, and Dad pats me on top of the head. "She's here to see what kind of business she'll be running one day." He winks conspiratorially at me, and I wink back. I walk happily next to him through the building with my head held high as he introduces me to various employees. Everyone seems to have a smile for me and compliments on how beautiful and like my mother I am.

Still, I have a nagging feeling in the pit of my stomach called Jared. Have none of these people ever met him before? How did they greet him? Aside from his stubbornness, they looked nothing alike.

"We're very proud," he says over and over, pulling me along.

When we reach his office, it's the largest one, right on the top floor. It overlooks the rest of the gardens surrounding the building.

The Thames stretches out for miles in both directions, and I try to pick out various landmarks. The Millennium Eye or Elizabeth Tower. There were hundreds of antlike figures moving around the harbour, shopping in the distance.

"Great view here, eh?" Dad says. "A lot better than sitting in that stuffy music room all day, I'll bet."

"It's way more fun." I smile.

He nods in approval. "Listen, I need to head into this meeting, Terin, but feel free to make yourself comfortable. The TV is on in the corner, and my assistant is just in the next room if you need anything, OK? She'll be in to check on you in a bit."

I nod confidently and perch on the edge of the huge leather sofa in the corner and pick up the nearest reading material to appear grown up and intelligent – *The Times*. He chuckles, ruffles my long hair, and grabs a smart-looking manila folder to leave with.

As soon as he's headed back down the corridor to the glass elevators, I wander over to his intimidatingly dark brown desk and sit in his chair. I spin the seat around for a little while and pretend to type on his computer and compose emails to people I didn't know but surely would one day oversee.

I had no idea what I would do here when I was older. But it would sure as hell beat playing the piano.

I notice there are a couple of framed photos on the side of the surface. One was slightly sun damaged but shows a team of men grinning from ear to ear as my dad, in the centre, proudly holds up a rugby ball with his university's name on it. The next photo was of my mother at one of her concerts as she's mid bow and roses are being thrown across the stage to her.

The third was me. It wasn't anything special, just a photo of me playing in a paddling pool years ago. My hair was long and red, even then. I'm grinning and laughing about something. There's a stray leg in the background from someone who's walked off camera. My brother, I assumed from the small portion of swimming trunks I could identify.

My eyes move to the notepad by the keyboard. Just some usual business scribblings about 'fiscal' and 'end of year GP' accompanied by strings of numbers and dates. What caught my attention was Jared's name scribbled haphazardly in the margins above the words; 'behaviour modification' and 'fits', followed by a mobile number.

This made me feel uneasy; I knew Jared's behaviour could sometimes be patchy. He argued with our parents often and rarely came out of his room. I'd learned about sex education at school, and he fit classically into the mid-teenager stage, meaning his body was changing. He would be moody with hormones like any typical teenager his age.

When my father does finally return an hour later, we spend another hour or two in his office and parade around the building to talk to people. When it's time to leave, they say goodbye and wave politely at me. My Dad's scribbles are pushed to the back of my mind and soon forgotten about.

"So, what does your business do again?" I enquire as we exit the building into the car park.

"When you come and work for me, I'll let you in on all the industry secrets!" he promises.

"You won't even give me a hint?"

"Now is not the time. One day." He winks conspiratorially.

He takes me out for a late lunch at a local patisserie--where I'm allowed to pick any pastries and snacks I want--before we head to the West End for an early showing of *The Lion King*, as promised. Dad knows it so well by this time that he mumbles along the words to the show with me as we crane our necks up at the stage from the front rows. After the production, a couple of the cast peek out to the lobby to shake his hand and chat with him while I stand shyly by his side, star-struck and barely able to stammer out a 'hello'.

We leave the theatre and grab a quick dinner before climbing back into the Mercedes while I gush nonstop about the day. He patiently lets me ramble, interjecting questions at just the right times to show he's listening. All the rare singular attention on me just spurs on the verbal diarrhoea.

He parks the Mercedes in the new extension to our large white exterior, and we head up the gravel path to the front door to find it slightly ajar. My father immediately frowns and gently prods the door open. Inside, the lights are on, but the house is silent aside from the huge antique clock that stands by the security panel on the wall.

I see immediately that my mother is sitting at the bottom of the stairs, hands wound together on top of her knees. She says nothing when we enter. I wriggle out of my coat and stop dead only when I notice the flash of pink against her midnight blue dress.

"Your hand, Mum! It's all red and blistered." Even under the coverings of a roughly wrapped bandage, the skin was pickled and crimson through the material, which must be incredibly painful. However, her face doesn't betray any sign of discomfort.

"I burned it on the hob," she snaps and glares meaningfully at my father, who gazes back, face empty and blank. There are no words between them for a few seconds, and my heart hammers with anxiety against my velvet dress. The room feels cold.

"Time for bed, Terin," he says firmly, and the look in his eyes tells me there's no point in arguing with him.

-4-

The morning that we are due to start the next school term, Jared and I are called downstairs. It's the first time I've seen him in days; whether he'd been confined to his room or the cellar, I'm not sure. I can barely contain my happiness seeing him descend the curved stairs ahead of me, so I skip to try and catch up.

The conservatory was used to entertain guests in, so Jared and I were rarely allowed to sit in there. It's filled with modern angular sculptures and a giant cream-coloured sofa that curves into the corner to join onto a mini fridge. The glass panels overlook the expansive, clean-cut garden that slopes gently down to the woodland trail entrance at the bottom.

Mum sits in her wicker egg chair with her reading glasses and a new light green manicure that matches the five-day-old cloth covering her hand. She's pouring over some of her tutorial work while Dad sits on the opposite side of the room with a textbook on employment law. They both glance up in unison as we enter, the smell of freshly ground coffee beans and cinnamon rolls strong.

"Finally, I've been calling you both for ages!" Mum says. "We've chosen a housekeeper we like the look of and interviewed her."

"She'll be arriving this evening to meet you both," Dad interjects. "No bad attitudes. Clean clothes and smiles, please."

Jared is quiet. I try to catch his eye and gauge how he feels about this whole ridiculous housekeeper thing. His eyes remain lazily locked to a squirrel out in the garden, not making an effort to engage anyone or comment. I desperately want to ask him what had happened when Dad and I returned home that night.

The walk to school later that morning is just as quiet. Jared moves a little faster than me the whole way. Whenever I hurry to catch up with him, he moves quicker until we are both in a near sprint towards the school gates.

"Terrapin's all sweaty!" Alice, Sarah, and Alexa cackle upon seeing my reddened face on arrival. Aside from some teachers huddled under the canopy by the front doors, only a few other kids besides us were dotted around this early before the morning bell. Moodily, I ignore them and sulk off to the library to find a quiet space to read and get my breath back. Jared has long since disappeared to find his tutor room without so much of a glance of concern back at me.

When the bell rings, I'm already sitting in my usual seat at the edge of class in my own year group. Georgia throws down her bag next to the desk and takes the seat beside me.

"You know they're calling you Terrapin now?" She raises a pale eyebrow that disappears into the same shade of soft blonde hair; it's almost translucent. Two silk bows pull back her French plaits and frame her face on either side, making her look grown up. I feel like a misshapen rock next to my best friend.

"I heard. I don't think they know how to spell it."

"No," she agrees. "They tried in the toilets already, but it's all rubbed off now."

I can only groan in response. "They need to be stopped."

"They're the most popular kids in the year. It's basic school hierarchy." Georgia shrugs. It was easy to not be bothered when you were beautiful and confident.

As we settle in to listen to Mrs Thistle's lecture on *Of Mice and Men*, my mind drifts back to under a week ago at my father's office. I'd been thinking on and off about his hastily scribbled note. Behaviour modification for Jared?

I allow myself a split second to imagine what that would be like. No weird goings on with him. No fits of rage, a sudden burst of strength or loss of where he was. No dark sneer when he gives me wrist burns for the fun of it. Would he still be my same brother if they took all that away from him? He was a good person deep down, especially when he was away from our parents.

Still, I guess they knew what was best for him.

"Another rough day?" Jared comments surprisingly when I join him at the school gate as soon as the end-of-day bell rings. He looks more relaxed than this morning; hands lightly rested in the pockets of his trousers and his tie half pulled down. A few girls in his year whisper and swoon as they walk past, but he doesn't seem to take any notice of them.

"Hierarchy is an outdated concept," I say despairingly.

"If you say so." He cracks a confused smile and rolls his eyes. "God, Terin, you're so weird sometimes."

Regardless of the insult, I smile back at him, and we grin together awkwardly. We start slowly walking back home, taking the long route again. I swallow down the urge to ask him the questions I really want to; there's no point in breaking his good mood now. I was sure whatever happened to Mum was an accident anyway.

Instead, I shyly begin to tell him about the few ideas I had for a writing assignment for English, elated when he 'oohhed' and 'aahhed' in the right places to spur me on. Whether or not he was really interested or just being kind for my benefit, I didn't really care. I had my brother back.

By the time we reach home, our parents are both downstairs and dressed neatly for the arrival of the new housekeeper. After we're ushered upstairs to get washed and changed, we're poised at the foot of the winding stairs like a pair of porcelain dolls, awaiting her arrival.

Her name is Mrs. Greenslade, I soon find out. She's a small petite woman with an old-fashioned pinned pinafore and dress that reaches down from her chest to her knees. Her speckled grey hair is pulled up into a tight bun and accompanied by silver hair clips. She's obviously a lot older than my parents, but I shudder as I imagine her as a mother––with such a stern and unforgiving expression. Her eyes are a shade of gunmetal, and I struggle to find any warmth inside them when she speaks.

"You'll address me as *Mrs.* Greenslade or *madam*," she instructs us after we're pulled downstairs into the living room. "I will make it plain now, children, that I am *not* here to be bossed around by you, I am here to look after the daily workings of the home. If you have games or books left out when I'm cleaning, well, that's too bad." Her raised eyebrow suggested just precisely what would happen with those items. "You will eat what you're given, and I will serve meals at the same time each day. If you don't wake up or come downstairs on time, there won't be any leftovers to heat up and eat later on."

Jared opens his mouth to make a comment but subsequently shuts it again, seeing our father's dangerous look. I smile sweetly and tell her I'm pleased to make her acquaintance, and I hope she'll find it homely here.

I pad down the hallway towards my room after Mrs. Greenslade's welcome dinner of meat, vegetables and potatoes. It's only early evening, but my parents have invited her to the conservatory for after-dinner drinks, which gives me a little extra time before I'm marched to bed. Maybe I'd even start scribbling story ideas in my workbook.

I hear music floating down the hall from Jared's room. There are basslines and instruments shockingly different from the classical scores I have to listen to. There's no sign of a piano in sight, just drums and electric guitars that scream in time to the hurried lyrics that spill from the cracked open door. I find that I like it.

Jared's room was strictly off limits to me most of the time, unless I knocked first. It's smaller than my own, and his wallpaper and carpet is darker than mine, but the décor still screams of my mother's obsession to uniform every room in the house under her interior vision.

Peering through the ajar door, I realise the music is coming from something on his laptop. He's sat cross-legged on his bed, staring into the corner of the room, a crease of worry on his forehead. Hearing the door creak open further, he jumps and sees me staring from the doorway.

"Oh. Just you," he says rudely.

"I wanted to say hello." I lick my lips nervously. "Do Mum and Dad know you have this kind of music?"

"Nope." he grins. "You're their little music goblin; they don't care what I listen to."

"Lucky," I pout. "Where did you get those CDs from?"

"I have my sources." He winks and taps his nose. He gets up to change a disc for another one from a pile stacked next to his stereo. Each album cover was darker than the last, with band names in a font I can't even read properly. A new song replaces the last. Another heavy track with lots of drums and screaming. I still hover in the doorway nervously at the threshold of his private sanctum, protected only by the wonky 'no girls allowed' poster on the door. I wonder idly how he managed to get that design choice past our mother.

"Just come in already. Stop *gawking* at me."

I jump excitedly at the rare honour. I close the door behind me and skip over to the bed to sit on the edge. He moves his socked feet over to give me room.

"It's been ages since you let me in here," I say in awe as I gaze at his collection of model planes suspended from the ceiling. There's a pile of expensive-looking toys from years of birthdays and Christmases that are gathering dust over by his old wooden chest. He makes a noncommittal noise under his breath.

"You never wanted to play with any of this?" I walk across the room and approach the pile. Even from afar, I could sense the sudden change in energy over him.

"I never wanted to play with anything from *them*," he says eventually. I don't need clarity on who he's talking about. His chin sticks out defiantly; lips pushed together like a sullen child.

"They care about you," I say loyally. Jared scowls and narrows his eyes.

"They shove me in a cellar when they can't be bothered with me. You're an idiot for thinking otherwise," he says hotly. A few moments pass by, and he can see the hurt on my face, so his features relax slightly, and he pats the space in the bed next to him. I approach slowly and sit down again.

"What happened with you and Mum the other day?" The words tumble from my mouth before I have a chance to stop them. Even with his back turned, I can see the stiffness reach from his waist to his skinny shoulders. He shrugs, saying nothing.

"It looks like she was burned," I continue, unable to stop the verbal assault now.

He flinches. "I don't really know. I get mad, and stuff happens."

This confuses me. "Did *you* burn her?"

"Of course not, idiot," he says. "She stupidly burned herself. Probably annoyed because I made her drop her favourite wine."

"What did you do?"

"She knows not to make me angry." I think he blushes partly from shame and partly from embarrassment. "They know I'm different; they want me to behave. Pretend I'm normal."

"You *are* normal; you're my brother."

"Hmm," he replies. He moves his fingers absent mindedly over the tower of CDs by his bed again, muttering something under his breath along in time to the music.

"They say you're naughty and give them hell," I mumble. My cheeks flush with the awkwardness of the conversation. I love Jared but somehow feel like I'm betraying my mother and father. "Have you ever tried... you know... not getting so angry?"

"Shut up, Terin," Jared mutters. His expression flashes darkly. I think I imagine it, but the room begins to fill with dry heat that builds with each passing second. It almost seems like it's radiating from *him*, although his body hasn't moved an inch.

I try and look for the source – were his clothes draped over the heaters again? Once he'd stolen a lighter from Dad's office during one of our dare games and held it too close to his sheets, setting his own bed alight and earning himself a few days in the cellar. But there was no sign of the device now. Even outside of his window, the trees move wildly in the breeze under an overcast sky. No sunshine whatsoever.

Above us, the air around his model planes begins to shake and wave. Slowly, before my very eyes, his planes start to melt with every passing second. Paint flakes, plastic bucks under the strain. Until they resemble nothing more than lumps of debris on strings. Is... Is he doing this?

Unable to voice any thought – any feeling, besides shock and awe. I can only stare at my brother, who gazes steadily back at me with darkened eyes—a shiver curls from the base of my spine to my head.

-5-

I go to bed that night, both confused and terrified.

I know what I saw – I'd *felt* the swell of the inferno of heat on my skin. It had appeared and faded away so suddenly that the ruined planes were the only evidence of the energy being there in the first place.

I don't know what to make of it all. Jared is weird, very weird. But he isn't some kind of supernatural *thing*. There must be a simple excuse for what I witnessed. Temporary aneurysm of sorts. Overactive imagination. Hell, maybe I was in some sort of dream.

The look in his eyes filled me with fear at the time. The dark brown hues almost looked more maroon than ever. No. It was a trick of the light. I'd heard of spontaneous combustion in people before – perhaps this was an environmental version of the phenomenon. I had a bumper book of weird occurrences and miracles on my bookshelf, filled with unexplainable things. Maybe even if I asked mum or dad, they'd be able to offer me a good explanation. In the meantime, I'd try and forget about it. Put it to the back of my mind.

Mrs. Greenslade, true to her threat, indeed makes sure that she cleans every part of the house that our mother directs her to – thankfully, not including our bedrooms.

The woman, small as she was, moves with the speed of a charging bull from one room to another, rubber gloves and cleaning materials in hand. She polishes the surfaces, cooks the meals, fluffs the textiles, and waxes the floors – seemingly taking enjoyment at the sight of my brother slipping across the hall as he runs late to school on several occasions.

I try on a few attempts to try and get to know this woman and if she does have any children my age that could come around and visit. But she squashes that notion flat by saying, "Don't be silly, girl. I don't have children and never will!" With a curl of her lip.

After that, I try and avoid her as much as possible.

Mrs. Greenslade's cooking is better than our mother's but includes a lot of fruits and vegetables that we hadn't even heard of. Her favourite keyword is *organic* – which pleases my mother to no end. Soon enough, they were sharing recipes and nutritional facts in idle conversation. For someone who had no interest in children, the older woman has many ideas about how to make them eat food they didn't want to.

"It's avocado," she says, overshadowing me at the table. "Go ahead and eat it; it's very good for you."

"I don't like the texture," I complain. The green mush was smashed across my morning toast, turning browner by each passing minute. It reminds me of the last time I had the flu and had to have a permanent tissue shoved into my nose. Across the table from me, Jared has the same expression.

"If she doesn't wanna eat it, she doesn't have to. I'm not going to either." He pushes his plate away and pulls his juice closer. Regardless of the gloweing look he receives from both the housekeeper and our mother; he looks calm.

"Jared, Terin..." our mother begins.

"No, no," Mrs. Greenslade says. "It's OK, Helen; if they don't want to eat, then they don't have to." She pulls both plates from the glass table and subsequently tips them in the bin, moving to place them in the dishwasher.

"I'll have normal toast with butter," Jared says. "Terin likes jam."

A cold smile crosses the housekeeper's face. "My dears, breakfast is over. You had the opportunity to have something nutritious and filling, now that time has passed. You'd better get ready for school now, the both of you." "That's the rules, kids," our mother affirms softly from behind her morning fruit and granola bowl. The latest gossip column magazine is open in front of her; she grazes the glossy pages with a manicured nail and looks between my brother and me. "You'll get what you're given from poor Mrs. Greenslade and will be grateful for it or go without."

My stomach rumbles, but I'm more curious than anything. I watch Jared carefully out of the corner of my eye. Sure enough, he looks angry, but there is no sign of the swelling heat I had felt in his room before. There is no stench of melting plastic or pile of ruined toys or furniture in the room.

I had definitely imagined the whole thing. How could I not? It was stupid to think otherwise.

My timetable was easy enough today that I could enjoy the double block of Biology with Georgia in peace – knowing that Sarah, Alexa and Alice would be in Drama, leaving me at least two hours of relaxation before enduring more amphibian insults in the quad. It's spitting lightly when Jared and I leave the house, so we walk to school quickly and try to ignore the hunger pangs, too famished to even complain about Mrs. Greenslade to one another in moody silence.

"How are you getting on with your story assignment?" Georgia asks. We sat in the usual seats in the middle of one of the science classrooms. I watch her fingers move across her perfect page of notes copied from the board and glance down at my own rough handiwork.

"Not good. I don't really know what I want to do with it," I say, pulling our assigned petri dish closer and began to sprinkle the soil with watercress seeds. She launches into her plot, and I patiently listen to her with slight interest as we work.

I suppose if I was truly stuck, I could write about my brother being some kind of secret, super soldier with an unexplainable ability to manipulate heat, energy, or whatever.

"I could always write about my parents locking my brother in our cellar." I shrug nonchalantly.

"Little dark and morbid for me, but sounds exciting," she says, clearly thinking I'm joking.

"Morning, class." Our biology teacher, Mr. Stammers, enters and smiles briefly at the rest of the room, throwing down his neat pile of binders on his desk. He takes one of the board pens and scribbles 'Evolution' towards the top.

"The topic for this next term involves looking at the natural cycle of life and how living organisms adapt and grow to continue procreating," he says. "Can anyone explain to me what evolution means?"

Georgia's hand shoots up, and he indicates in her direction. "Evolution means the natural process of changing to suit the environment. Like how land creatures originally came from the sea and grew the ability to walk."

"Very good," he nods. "Evolution is an incredible process, and everyone in this room would not be sitting here today if our cellular ancestors hadn't spent hundreds of thousands of years continuously changing," he holds up his hand. "Our thumbs, for instance, evolved to this state to help us use tools. Who gets all wrinkly in the bath if they've been sat in it for ages?"

The class murmurs and nods in agreement.

"Evolution," he says again, strolling back and forth slowly. "Our skin becomes wrinkled when exposed to water for a long time, to enable us to use grip. Although they look like we've aged about 50 years, those wrinkles have a definitive point to them. Even as you are all sitting here today, we continue to be altered on a microscopic cellular level. It'll take a very long time for it to be obvious, but our children, grandchildren, and so on will continue this."

"Is that why we don't need our appendix anymore?" Someone towards the back of the class pipes up. "I had mine removed when I was younger."

Mr Stammers nods. "Aside from the theory our appendix might protect certain bacteria, it's not part of our usual digestive system.

Plant-eating vertebrates still depend on it heavily to assist with their digestive tract, but ours functions perfectly without input. Once upon a time, we did use this. Now, it's the most commonly known useless organ for our contemporary species."

"My Mum had her Gall Bladder removed, is that useless too?" someone else offers.

"Gall Bladders are slightly different," the teacher replies. "Although we can live without it, it still provides a function to store bile created by the liver and is secreted into the small intestine to help break down food."

"What if everyone had their gallbladders removed right now?" Georgia asks. "Would we eventually stop having children with Gall Bladders?"

"Possibly," Mr Stammers shrugs. "It would take a very long time, but the body adapts to what it's given in its environment. If our bodies decide that we would have a better survival rate if we only ate vegetables, for example, the mechanism of natural selection would ensure that certain genetic mutations would occur, ensuring our survival and reproduction rate. Perhaps we'd eventually lose our canine teeth to tear and process meat."

"A natural mutation?" I mutter. It was louder than I thought because Mr Stammers glances at me and smiles excitedly.

"Natural selection and adaption will always be the future of our species. Charles Darwin dedicated a big chunk of his work to this theory, which is still very much used today. It's how certain insects and arachnids develop pre-cognitive senses, how giraffes have long necks to reach the tops of trees, and how cheetah can blend into the savannah's environment."

"Because they changed?" I ask.

"Over hundreds and thousands of years, everything has changed," he affirms, gesturing to the classroom. "And in a thousand years from now, humans may have changed too."

When Jared and I return home in the afternoon, our parents are both downstairs in an online meeting with a business associate. Mrs. Greenslade ensures they aren't disturbed by the rest of the house as she stalks downstairs like an army general. Dinner was another odd mix of vegetables in mashed potatoes with homemade fish cakes that still had little bones in them as the main portion. Jared and I eat quietly without a word to the housekeeper as she watches and nods in approval. I was glad to escape to my room in silence.

Darwin's theory quietly races around my head. The more I think about it, the more it blows my mind that humans would one day be capable of things we didn't even dream existed in this day and age. It was a long shot, but I wonder about my brother and whether his cells differed from the rest of ours.

There's a loud, sudden commotion in the entrance hall that I can hear all the way from my room. A screeching sound tears down the large house's barren silence, stopping my heart in my chest.

Homework abandoned, I fling myself to my feet and follow the sounds to the top of the winding staircase. I can hear my heartbeat in the soles of my feet as they slap against the cool floor.

At the bottom of the stairs, Mrs. Greenslade lies in a pale heap on the polished hardwood floor, screaming at the top of her lungs. Her hair bun is askew, and her face is red from embarrassment. She's glaring up the stairs towards me. There's a movement behind my field of vision, and I see Jared pressed against the far wall, hands wrapped around his knees. Trembling uncontrollably.

"Devil boy!" she screams again, clutching herself and pointing towards us. "You *pushed* me!"

My parents rush into the entrance hall from my father's adjoining office and follow her accusatory glare upwards. The momentary silence is shattered when they try and calm down the housekeeper with clipped tones.

"There must be some misunderstanding here," my father tries to reason. He crouches next to the woman in his pressed work trousers, soothing words flicking fast from his mouth.

I peel my eyes away and turn slowly to Jared, face in a mask of horror.

"It was a mistake," I call downstairs, mainly to my parents. "He wouldn't...." I'm glancing back and forth between her and the boy shaking nearby. He doesn't look so tall and old to me now. He seems like a lost child who doesn't know where he is. He looks at me, and his eyes are almost as dark as the charcoal curtains that line the French windows.

His arms are covered in scratches, and I almost turn back to accuse her of hurting him, but I notice he's doing it to himself. He repeatedly scratches his forearms red raw until dots of blood appear on the pale skin. He doesn't stop, regardless of how painful and angry the skin looks. I force myself to look at him.

"What did you do?" I hiss quietly. He continues the picking and says nothing. I'm not even sure he hears me or even realises what's going on. The swelling heat tingles in the air around him again – nowhere near as intense as it was before in his bedroom. It was enough to cause me to draw back and not touch him.

"This is a mistake!" I call down again. "She must have fallen or tripped or something! Look how slippery these floors are!" I desperately sweep my barefoot across the surface wood, cackling airily like the girls in my class would, without a care in the world. "Liar!" she screams, clutching at her uniform. "He wants me dead – you should have seen the look in his eyes! What a little psychopath! That boy's got some bloody demons inside him!"

"Let's get you on your feet and talk about this...." Mum rushes to try and take an arm. Mrs. Greenslade snatches it away and uses the coat rack to help herself to her feet. A swell of bruising is beginning to appear on the side of her face.

"Let's get you sat down with a coffee; we'll talk about this and––" Mum tries again.

"I'm not ever coming back to this place!" Mrs. Greenslade snaps. Tearing down her coat and bag from the stand, she throws the door open and disappears without another word to any of us.

A tense silence dawns on the house as the door closes behind her. We're all frozen to the spot aside from Jared, who's still wincing from scratching and muttering under his breath.

"Go – Helen!" Dad commands, but she's already out of the door and chasing after the ex-housekeeper. I see my father's eyes flash towards the first floor. He ascends the stairs slowly, a livid expression trained on Jared, who does nothing to defend himself.

Terrified and not wanting to see his rage, I turn and run back to my bedroom to cower under my sheets to block out the screams of Jared being dragged back down to the cellar.

There's nothing I can do to protect him. Nothing I can say to defend his actions. I'm powerless.

-6-

Despite her cutthroat nature, Mrs Greenslade does not return to the house.

It wasn't for lack of trying. I overhear my father leave voicemails on her phone to resolve the situation and offer more money for her services, but she doesn't call back. Her marigolds and cleaning equipment lay untouched in the entrance hall.

Mum and Dad stop speaking to one another the day after she leaves, and they both busy themselves with work and activities. Now that she has no choice but to take over the household chores and cooking again, Mum rushes back and forth and barks orders at me to help. Neither of them bring up the subject of my brother in front of me, and frankly, I was scared to.

What the hell is going on? I want to ask my parents and come clean about what I'd witnessed as well, but even approaching the subject of Jared and the strange events that seem to surround him was taboo.

After the spectacle, he spends the following week at the bottom of the house. It's the longest time in my living memory that he'd been down there. After the first initial protests and bangs, he'd gone quiet after the first couple of days. I hope he's still alive.

It was an unspoken rule that when Jared was locked in the cellar, I was not to go downstairs and try and let him out. It was his punishment time to think about what he'd done wrong. I knew they still fed him, only opening the door to shove meals and water inside, and he had a plumbing system down there. But aside from that, he's entirely isolated from the rest of the world.

Jared's 'funny turns' were more than just that of a typical teenager's mood swing; I was sure of it. Not with the things I'd seen and experienced in my short life so far. I just didn't understand what or why.

The school is no sanctuary either. Between them, Sarah, Alice, and Alexa had worked out the correct way to spell Terrapin and had scribbled it across my exercise book in English after it'd been left on the shelf for marking.

The teacher hands me back my work and frowns. "Really, Terin, you're getting a bit old for scribbling over your work now. Get it all rubbed off before I see it again." She moves onto the next desk as I flick open the pages, frowning.

Across the top of every page – the word was scrawled maliciously into the paper in pencil so hard; it made dents in the other pages. I could barely decipher my notes and comments through the blurry tears that appear suddenly. A couple fall before I have a chance to catch them and land on the paper.

"You OK?" Georgia murmurs next to me. Her golden eyebrows knitted together, pouring over her own flawless work.

"I'm fine," I snap and grab my rubber to begin the arduous process of rubbing their graffiti out while trying to block out the girl's quiet taunts from the back of the room.

***

Dinner has been quiet, like every other meal recently, but I have no appetite to finish it.

"No leftovers for you, then," Mum snaps and grabs the bowl of spaghetti from me. Mrs. Gleenslade's lessons obviously still resonate with her.

I decide to go to bed earlier than usual with the excuse that I wasn't feeling well and slump upstairs slowly to prove it.

I wake after a few hours of tossing and turning. The silk sheets feel like they're restricting me; the tendrils of the bed hangings join in, leering over me as I struggle out of their grasp. I don't know if I'm fully awake or asleep, but I manage to tear off the bedding and collapse onto the carpet, breathing heavily.

The room is dark; the clock reads between two and three in the morning. The only sounds I can hear are my own rapid breaths and the sound of the wind and rain howling against the double glazing.

Blearily, I head out into the hallway and stumble along the first floor until I hit the winding stairs, illuminated by the swaying of the trees in the moonlight from the roof arch. I can see the house pretty clearly in the darkness and successfully avoid the furniture and corners of the walls that jut outwards.

Letting my legs lead me, they walk me confidently to the wooden door off the corner from the pantry entrance. I reach for the handle more confidently than I feel, and it swings open easily.

There's a total lack of light at the bottom of the stairs, where there is a small concrete landing before the cellar door sits silently. Again, my eyes quickly adjust to the point where I could make out the outlines of every step that led downwards. My legs move of their own accord, taking each step at a time to test out the squeakiness of the metal frame before moving my feet onto the next. Satisfied that I won't wake up the house with the sounds of my night-time escapade, my bare feet land on the cool surface of the concrete.

The landing is tiny and contains only a couple of old cardboard boxes and pallets stacked in the corner. Now that I was older, I could easily define where the normal structure of the room ended and where the reinforced walls began around the edges of the metal door. Was the door always this scary looking? I hadn't dared to come down here in years, really... ever since the first time they decided this was the best place to keep him during these 'bouts'. Even now, I feel the creeping fingers of the dark grasp my bare arms and legs, trying to pull me closer. The air down here feels different somehow. Sharper.

"Jared?" I whisper. The storm outside sounds louder somehow, despite the lack of a window. The wind whistles loudly, and there's a loud dripping from the overhang of the roof gutter.

The silence from within the cellar door makes me wonder if he was back safely in his bedroom after all, but I hear a shuffling a few seconds later and a confused; "Terin?" he replies.

"You're still in there?" I breathe. Relief sweeps over me, temporarily eradicating the darkness and terror for a minute. I don't know if I'm happy that he doesn't sound hurt like I imagined or if I'm still worried that he sounds too different than usual. Still, I can feel his presence behind the door, enabling me to breathe deeply."

"Can you breathe any quieter – you sound like a serial killer out there," he complains. "And, of course, I'm still in here. I can't exactly let myself out, can I?"

He sounds so close that my heart skips with joy. "It's the middle of the night. They don't know I'm down here."

"You woke me up," he grumbles. "They took my phone, so I can't tell you exactly what time or day it is."

"You don't have a window? A clock?"

"Nobody uses this room, but... well, me, really. They haven't exactly furnished it to perfection. And a window would be pretty useless in a converted war bunker, wouldn't it? Come on, Terin," he tries to joke, but even I can hear the strain in his voice. I wonder what it was like to experience no natural light for several days, no ability to even tell the time of day except for relying on a body clock. The realisation makes me feel sick, I want to throw up, but I manage to breathe slowly and keep it down.

"I was worried about you. I think I had a nightmare. You were there, and you were hurt or something." The details were hazy; I don't want to think about it too much. My pulse quickens just thinking about the shadows behind my eyes.

There are a few beats of silence in which the storm fills with the steady rhythms of rain against the house. I'm shaking a little from the cold. The very bottom of the house was always naturally cooler in temperature. I wonder if he was cold in there.

"You were in mine too, I think. That's pretty weird," he mutters eventually, and I nod, allowing myself to slip down outside the door and curl up with my arms around my legs. His breath moves down too, so we were both on the floor with just the door between us.

"Do you think anyone else locks up their kids in their cellars when they get too out of hand?" I say.

He chuckles. "I'd like to know what crappy parenting book they got this from."

"The same one that suggested they should name me close to an Amphibian," I mutter darkly.

"Still getting trouble from that girl and her sidekicks?"

"Like you wouldn't believe."

He makes a noise in his throat. "I did offer to knock out her brother for you. You could always go directly to the source and punch her in the face too, you know."

"I don't fancy landing myself in this cellar for starting fights at school." We both laugh, a harsh sound that pierces the air until I stop and remember it wasn't a funny situation at all. It isn't a joke. It's real, and my brother's a prisoner.

"Is the housekeeper really gone now?" he asks.

"She's not coming back. Dad keeps trying to call, but she's not picking up. I don't think it'll work out the way they want."

"Oh, that's good," he replies, not sounding as glad as I thought he would be.

"How are your arms? They were all scratched and bloody." It wasn't easy to forget the image burned in my head. His eyes glazed as he digs his fingernails into his skin repeatedly until they bled.

He pauses. "They're fine. There are some old plasters and stuff down here, so I just put some on and left them alone. They're just scratches."

"Did you know you were doing it to yourself?" I whisper.

There's a pregnant pause. I know he hasn't fallen asleep because I can still hear him breathing, likely wondering how to answer.

"Sometimes I have no choice when I get like that," he says slowly. "I lose control, and I need to try and regain it again. Hurting myself kind of helps me weirdly control myself."

"Were you out of control when you burned Mum? When you melted your ceiling planes and pushed Mrs. Greenslade down the stairs?" I don't mean to sound so accusatory, but there was no way of sugar coating his actions. Again, he takes a few moments to breathe before answering.

"I can't control myself when I'm too emotional. I don't know what it is or what I am, but things happen by burning, melting, or whatever other weird crap happens. All I know is that all it takes is for one comment to set me off, and *BAM*, I'm seeing red and pushing the stupid woman down the stairs."

"What did she say to you?" I say quietly.

"God, I don't even know. Something about me being nasty and conniving. The next thing I know, I have her by the throat, and my arm is latched onto hers, and I'm *willing* for her to get hurt and suddenly, I can feel her skin burning under mine..." his voice breaks off. I wonder if he's trying not to cry. "I didn't even mean to push her; I just wanted to get her away from me because I couldn't stop what I was doing." There's a sniff and another pause, then a loud sigh.

"It wasn't your fault; you weren't in your right mind."

"I felt like I was. I felt like I was enjoying it until I realised what was happening," he says, barely a whisper.

I try to change tactics. "Have you tried to melt down this door?"

"Of course. I can only get about as far as making the handle really hot, and I have to stop because it's so draining. I really am sorry about what happened, Ter. I didn't mean for all this; I know it scared you."I open my mouth to answer and can only reply with a nod which he can't see. My throat is tight, desperate to push the sobs out of my chest and into the open. I can only manage brief gulps of air into my lungs, barely taking in the oxygen it needs. I wonder if Mrs. Greenslade felt similar when he had his hand around her throat.

"Go back to bed, Terin," he says softly.

"I can't," I say with a small gasp. It feels like there's been an elephant that's been sitting on my chest for days, sucking out every inch of happiness and safety from me. Even now, I feel breathless, and my skin tingles with several different sensations – from the cold air on my skin to my burning forehead to the energy that I could feel in the air. I feel like I'm losing control of the usual boring reality of day-to-day life. Like everything around me is evolving, moving up onto land and leaving me behind in the sea without legs.

"Calm down," he says. "You're getting yourself worked up."

"What's going to happen to you?" I say quietly. I feel him try and open his mouth to explain, but it closes again and whatever those words he was going to say die on his lips. I know deep down he's just as much at a loss as I am.

"I don't know," he murmurs bitterly and falls quiet. With nothing to offer and no source of hope, I sit silently and listen to the reassuring sounds of his breathing from beneath the door.

-7-

J ared emerges a week later, bleary-eyed and exhausted.

A few months pass without incident as he keeps his head down and his concentration on his upcoming GCSEs. Aside from walking to and from school and the odd meal, he keeps mostly to himself in his room.

It's the end of July when I finally get the courage to approach my father in his study. I rasp my knuckle on his chestnut varnished door before I can stop myself.

He glances up to the door opening and does a double take when he catches sight of the glittery knee-length cocktail dress with a little black jacket and matching shoes.

"Good lord, it's your mother's Summer shindig tonight?" He runs his hands through his tousled hair. He's still wearing his suit from a meeting that morning, and the circles around his eyes are unlike him. His office smells of wood and furniture polish with an air of lemon. Stacks of folders and papers are spread haphazardly around the room.

"It's a day early since a lot of her friends couldn't make it tomorrow," I mutter and tug at the dress self-consciously. It wasn't that I didn't enjoy the way it sparkles in the overhead sconces – but a public celebration in the house didn't feel right after recent events.

"Dad," I begin, trembling with anxiety that I hope wasn't in my voice. "Can we talk about something? But I need you not to get mad at me, OK?"

"Can it wait? I need to get these papers across to the office by the morning. Then the contract hopefully gets signed by the afternoon, and if all goes well, some lucky little girl gets her new piano." He winks; the distraction was easy to see.

I pause; I'm still shaking slightly. "I need to talk about it. It's important."

He nods and lets his pen sit on top of his paperwork. He gives me his full attention smiling patiently.

"Well," I say. I try to visualise myself as a confident older teenager worthy of an adult conversation. "I want to talk about why Jared is... special and why he has his... turns. Do you *know* exactly what kind of things he can do?" I try to emphasise my words, so I don't have to mention 'superpower' or 'ability' out loud. It was ridiculous. I can't believe I'm trying to have this conversation with my father.

It was as if all of the air was sucked from the room. He sits at his desk, his face turning every shade of puce imaginable, but he sits still with his smile and doesn't move. The paperwork lies forgotten, so at least I know he's heard me.

"This isn't the time," he says firmly after a brief pause. I want to ask when *a good time would be,* but the dark look on his face warns me to shut my mouth and never speak this aloud again.

"So, you do know! Is he sick? Is there something wrong with him?"

"That's none of your business," he snaps, and every word is pronounced carefully with poisonous precision. The smile of my usual daddy is gone and replaced with a strange stony look of someone barely recognisable to me. I take an involuntary step back. Is this how Jared typically sees our father?

"But Dad – he can *make* things *happen*. I don't get it – why can't we all talk about it? You and Mum have obviously seen it before––"

"Go out and watch the fireworks, Terin," he suggests with an air of finality. The dark look is gone quickly and replaced by another smile, forced and empty. His attention goes back toward the wad of work in front of him. The vein is back on his forehead, popping outwards in unspoken frustration, daring me to continue.

I nod and deflate, sensing it was no time to try and bargain for some violin alongside my regular music studies either and decide to head outside with the rest of the gathering. It was my mother's annual July summer gathering and one of many seasonal parties she liked to throw over the year. As per tradition, distant family relations and industry colleagues flooded our house. Instead of everyday quiet dinners, most guests bring gift bottles of the most expensive sickly alcohol they could muster, and a hired chef takes over the kitchen with his team.

Struggling to put my father's face out of my mind and the feeling I'd really crossed a line, I wander through the second living room and trail through the dining area and conservatory until I join up with the rest of the crowd. Even in the humid evening air – they're all wearing their best suits and dresses, standing precariously on the manicured grass with new stilettos and patented shoes.

A couple of attendees manage to grab me on the way past, to compliment my dress and my apparent fast mastery of some of the complex symphonies my mother had me practising nonstop recently. I struggle to recognise many faces; there are a couple of distant relations that stop for a quick hug. All of them stink of alcohol, and as they try and speak to me, their words are more slurred and difficult to understand as the evening goes on. I feel disconnected, dreamlike.

It's easy to find my mother – she's the figure standing alone by the trees with a champagne flute in hand, overlooking her gathering like a queen. I manage to slide away from the guests' insistent hands and approach her at the garden's edge.

"Aunt Frances is an embarrassment," my mother says. "Look at her! Barely five minutes widowed, and she's all over your father's business partner like a praying mantis with the size of those claws! At least she isn't stealing cutlery again, I suppose. Bloody klepto, she is."

"If you hate these people, why do you bother hosting these events?" I wonder aloud. She makes a sharp hissing sound to indicate that I should keep my voice down, regardless of the loud, jolly conversation all around us.

"It's about the image, my dear," she continues. "As it may disappoint you to realise, there's no way you can retain a suitable stance in society by sitting in your room all day!" Her eyes flicker towards the top of the house, where Jared's window is dark. I follow her gaze, but nothing moves behind the glass.

She makes a sound of annoyance at the back of her throat. "I wish your brother saw fit to try and make this a *solid* family event."

I decide not to point out that my father was also holed up in his room with his work, and no one in our immediate family had spoken to one another in weeks.

"You know Jared hates these sorts of things, Mum. He's not comfortable with big groups of strangers." I pause, wondering if I was pushing my luck if I asked my mother the same taboo question here and now. She snorts. "We all have to do things we don't like sometimes. Take this, will you? The fireworks are about to start." She shoves that empty glass at me and wanders over to the team of technicians she's hired, directing them on how they should do their jobs to her liking. I stand alone for a few moments in the dark before turning and tossing the empty flute into the nearest bush with a frown.

I return to the house quickly, and as soon as the French doors slide shut behind me, the muffled bangs of the fireworks begin. I head back to my room and wonder about my chances of my parents buying me a violin. Slim to none, I supposed. Mum was especially keen for me to continue with her legacy, and Dad was passionate about giving it all up as soon as possible to join him at CoilerTech after my GCSEs and A-Levels.

I head up the main staircase and hear cries from the floor above. I know it's Jared's voice instantly, but there's an agonising edge to it. I'm moving, heart pounding in my ears and fly up the rest of the stairs two at a time. I turn down the hallway towards the east of the building to where our bedrooms are.

"Stop wailing – grow up, boy!" my dad's voice is raised. I turn the corner to see that he's dragging Jared out of his room by his arms. My brother clings to his leg and kicks out with the rest of his limbs. He's crying out, completely out of touch with reality. His eyes are dark and glazed again, seemingly unconnected with everything around him.

"Not again! Don't you dare embarrass us!" my father roars as he takes Jared roughly by the shoulder and pries him off his expensive trousers. I see Jared flailing and convulsing. His lips are moving, but nothing but cries come out from them. I instinctively step forwards to try and help.

"It's an *attack*, Dad. He's burning up!" I say desperately. Despite the heat radiating from his skin, I feel only a cold stab of fear that I will lose my brother soon: one way or another."I could have bloody told you that," he hisses and shoves past me. "For God's sake, Terin – stop being so damn gormless and *help me*. And be *careful,* he's already struck me." True to his word, a deep scratch runs from under his eye and across his cheek. Blood had already splattered down to the collar of his white shirt. The wound looks squishy and blackened. Jared had burned him.

"Jared," I whisper and wrap my arms around him. He's shivering and red hot at the same time. He's trembling. "What's wrong? Is it the fireworks? Dad, I think he's having a fit or a seizure or something. They said at school to call an ambulance and to keep them in the dark room with no lights or curtains open."

"*I'm* about to have a bloody fit in a minute," he growls. He glances out of the window towards the garden. The fireworks were in the middle of a grand finale which illuminates the house in an array of rainbow colours that bounce off all three of us as we look at one another.

"The guests will be coming back into the house soon, help me get him downstairs. We can't have them hearing him screaming in his bedroom like a banshee."

"What happened?" I push. "We shouldn't move him – we don't know if he's hurt."

"Terin – *grab a bloody leg and get moving!*" Dad roars, pushing me over to his other side. Jared's black eyes land on me – I don't know if he registers it's actually me or not.

"You'll be OK," I lie and try to smile through my tears. Whether or not it will calm him down inside, I don't know. "Come on, stop struggling, Jare. You're gonna be fine."

Obediently and too scared to say no, I take Jared's fitting legs, and we rush him awkwardly down the hallway towards the stairs. Jared lashes out with both hands, narrowly avoiding me – but sears a burn mark into the side of the paintwork of the walls. Beneath him, we're leaving uninterrupted blackened drag marks along the floor from where his naked feet had connected with the carpet.

I can feel my hands hurting – whether it was from trying to hold on tightly or the force of the heat under his clothes transferring to my skin, I wasn't sure.

When we reach the archway to the living areas, he kicks out suddenly, and we both lose our grip and fall across one another. Jared skids across the marble floor, and Dad roughly grabs him by the ankles to anchor his hold.

"His head Terin – grab him tighter, you silly girl!" he snarls and drags my brother the length of the kitchen and passes the pantry to the downstairs entrance, where we try to navigate him down the metal steps. I'm sobbing. My hands are sticky with sweat and scratches from scraping past so many surfaces on the way down.

Our father kicks open the heavy cellar door and effortlessly yanks him inside. I'm too shaken up to follow. A few moments later, my father reappears and shuts it behind him with an all too familiar clang. There's a huge grey key he takes from his pocket, making sure the door is locked firmly before replacing it back into his jacket. His face is a terrifying mask of fury.

Dad and I both stand panting, staring at the metal surface in our ruined formal wear. Aside from the wound on his cheek, his shirt is frayed and blackened in a few random places. I glance down to see my own dress torn in a couple of areas. My hands were still hurting, a little more red than usual, but there were no signs of stereotypical flaking or blistered skin from his ability. We were lucky we weren't seriously injured.

It takes a few minutes, but the wails and cries begin again. It's a horrible, aching sound of betrayal. Another few moments before the banging starts, the door vibrates the outer shell of the concrete entrance in a manner I hadn't seen before. Still, the structure holds.

"We should call someone to check him out in case he's hurt. Surely Mum's got some doctor friends upstairs somewhere?"

"No," my father replies, still eyeing the door with a newly found wariness I'd never seen on his face before. I realise he's probably just as much in the dark as I am about all this.

I swallow and whisper, "What if he chokes on his tongue or something and dies in there?"

"Karma," my father mutters and heads back upstairs without another look back, leaving me alone in the dark with an intense feeling of guilt inside me.

-8-

"Sit down my dear; why not in that armchair over there?" the man gestures to the one opposite his, divided by a round footstool with a tray of two hot drinks on the top. I wasn't much of a tea person, but I was trembling from shock and exhaustion.

He doesn't look like a stereotypical doctor despite the ancient lab coat that hangs on the door of a shelving unit in the corner of his office. The room is filled with plants, some of which were housed in glass cases and others sat on the sill, soaking in the winter rays of the chilly sun from the October afternoon air.

Three months had passed since the party. It'd been twelve long weeks of contractors and workmen fixing the floors, walls and stairs Jared managed to burn during his last fit. He was back to being sub-dued, quiet, sullen. He still talks to me, we laugh and joke, ignoring the obvious elephant in the room and pretending none of it was happening, at least to and from school anyway. Twelve weeks of an uneasy peace.

And now the worst again had happened.

I realise that I'm freezing – was that why I was trembling? He sees me clutching my hands and rubbing them together and gets up to flick on an electric radiator by our chairs.

"You will settle down in a moment, Terin. Do you mind if I call you Terin? I find Miss Coiler much too formal for a situation like this." He cracks a smile across his withered face. He can't be more than sixty, but despite the wrinkles of time, he moves with graceful energy around the room as he gathers a notepad and a pen and returns to his seat. The more he speaks, his accent sounds mid-European.

"Polish," he answers suddenly. "You're trying to work out where I was born?"

"Cool." Was all I could manage.

"Your mind is like a book across your face." He continues, indicating with his pen as he opens his notebook on his lap. Tiny oval-shaped spectacles appear from the side of his seat and perch on the edge of his nose.

"I was just thinking how different this room is to my house. We don't have plants or plush blankets or anything soft and homely, really-ly."

"Sounds very modern," he comments. "But not everyone appreciates the more contemporary tastes, do they?"

I shake my head, fingers still wringing together in my lap despite the blast of warm air filling the room. I think about the past few hours that have led to this moment. I want to cry and throw up. I want to go home and hide.

"Why am I here?" I blurt out.

"I suppose that depends on what you want to talk about today," the doctor says kindly. His dark blue eyes are suddenly illuminated by the stray rays of sun that shine briefly from behind a cloud. Regardless of the statuesque pose, he waits patiently for me to answer, and I can't tell if it's a genuine look of interest to understand my opinion or if it was the same blank look my parents wore when they talked to one another.

"I... don't know where to begin."

"Then that's OK; there's absolutely no pressure on you to answer or say anything here today. I just wanted to sit here and meet with you." He takes a long sip of his tea and offers a pack of lotus biscuits on his table. I shake my head and decline, but he raises his eyebrows and smiles, offering the pack again. I tear it open and shove the sugary biscuit into my mouth.

"Do you feel better? You were looking green."

"Yeah, thank you," I say, in between sips of my own tea. The drink fills me with warmth, and I relax back on the chair a little more. I try not to think of my brother being whisked away into a similar room by other Doctors. I hope they're treating him as nicely as me.

"Where's Jared?"

"Down the hall," the doctor replies. "Just next to the bathrooms. He is chatting to one of my colleagues about what happened today. The sooner we can understand Jared, the sooner we can help him overcome whatever is bothering him."

I try not to laugh, imagining my brother having his very own heart-to-heart over biscuits and tea. There's no way he would be honest with complete strangers about his feelings or his condition. I pause my train of thought, concentrating on the doctor before me again. How much of my thinking did I really show on my face?

I would give anything for the morning to have never happened. The episodes were getting worse with time, more serious. He was being forced to spend more time in the cellar than above it. He's now white and weakly looking, despite the slight push he gave me and the promise that he will be OK whenever I nag him.

"Do you want me to take you to see him when we are done here?" That smile returns, but its warmth does nothing to ease my anxiety. The corners of my eyes sting, and my palms are sweaty.

"He didn't mean to hurt anyone," I say too quickly, but the shiver through my body gives me away. I expect Dr. Richterson's expression to change to a triumphant one, but it says neutral and stoic. He makes no move to call security on my brother or demand he be locked away.

"Stabbing another classmate is a very serious issue," he says gently. "We only want to help Jared to ensure he doesn't hurt himself or anyone else."

"It was just with a pencil," I choke, and tears fill my eyes. "Sarah makes my life a living hell. She calls me stupid names with her best friends, and I have to endure their taunting every day at school!"

"How did you feel about hearing about what happened?"

"Pretty crappy," I sniff, frustrated and furious at the injustice of everything. I know what the obvious answer is, of course. I can still hear the shrill ring of the ambulance. The sight of the girl lifted into the vehicle is embedded into my brain. Even at a distance from across the quad, I could see that she was dotted in blood and crying uncontrollably as one of the teachers had tried to soothe her in the back before the doors swung shut.

I could still feel the judgemental gazes of my classmate's eyes on the back of my head, along with the rest of the school. It was no secret that Jared Coiler was crazy when pushed around, and they wanted to know if crazy ran in the family. They wanted something new to gossip about.

"He knows she bullies me. He saw her corner me in the quad with her friends, and he just didn't think. He could have just... walked away," I breathe. The sting of shame grabs me inside, and the tears fall down my cheeks. I roughly wipe them away. The doctor sees enough sense to leave me to my thoughts for a few moments as he scribbles something down on his papers with a beautiful maroon pen. I long to reach out and touch the shiny engraving down the side. The doctor catches me looking and smiles.

"My own brother gave this to me years ago."

"You have a brother too?"

He nods. "We were completely different, chalk and cheese. He loved his philosophy, and I loved being creative.... I want to help your brother, Terin."

I nod slowly, feeling my resolve wane. I'm suddenly exhausted and feel the weight of the universe on my small shoulders. I want to tell him everything – from the beginning. But my mouth dries up, and I can see the clock on the wall ticking closer to the end of the hour session he'd spoken to my father about.

"Jared... is special," I say finally. "He's very particular. He likes his things tidied in a certain way. He gets upset easily. He has these... *fits*. Things... happen when he's upset."

I wonder just how much this doctor knew. I want to get the secret out and blurt out everything. The constant fear and confusion. The anxiety. The obvious lack of understanding and disgust from our parents.

"I see. Does that scare you?"

I frown, the pit of my stomach clenches. "Jared would never hurt me. We're close. But it's scary seeing how he'll react to things sometimes."

"What sort of situations?"

I struggle to summon something to mind, and after a few seconds of squeezing my eyes shut to think, I reply. "A kid shoved him in the corridor one day at school when he was walking past. I saw it happen. The way Jared turned to look at the kid was just...." I shiver involuntarily, and the man doesn't press me any further on the memory.

"Jared is in trouble, isn't he?" I ask quietly. My fists clench, and my brows furrow, but I'm determined to keep eye contact with the doctor, who blinks back at me in surprise.

"Jared is unwell," he says kindly. "It is my job to see what we can do to make him better, and I am not typically a quitter. If you feel up to it, Terin, I have only a few more questions before the session ends. Will you help me, help him?" It takes me a fraction of a second to nod in acceptance. I would do anything for my brother.

The hour passes by quickly after another round of tea and biscuits. Soon enough, we are saying goodbye, and I am escorted back to the waiting room where my father sits, stony-faced and his ear pressed into his mobile.

"You'd better send over some flowers to the parents," he mutters, barely registering my arrival into the seat next to him. "Suitable ones. None of the usual rubbish. We'll need to do a personalised card too. Yes, yes. Well, ideally out of the media as much as possible." He glances quickly at me and lowers his voice. "No, it's damaging for everyone.

Helen's in agreement." He ends the call without saying goodbye, slipping it back into his overcoat.

He puts his arm around the back of my chair and flashes me a quick smile, the stern look long gone, and suddenly, I ache for just a basic, soothing fatherly embrace.

We hadn't spoken any more about our conversation the night of the summer party. He'd been trying to avoid being alone with me, excusing himself from rooms using work as an excuse. There was no way he'd be able to keep sweeping this under the carpet for much longer.

"Is Jared in trouble?" I whisper.

"He stabbed an innocent girl with a pencil multiple times in front of the whole school," he replies slowly. "He's not walking away from this easily, Terin. You won't be able to understand this fully at your age, but your brother's unpredictable and dangerous."

"But he's still my brother *and* your son," I say. Even after the few months that'd passed since the party, the wound on his cheek was still in the process of trying to heal and close properly. The skin looks pinker and mismatched with the rest of his face.

"Which is why we need to protect our family as much as possible," Dad says gravely. "And that means I think you and Jared will be separated at home for the time being. Just until we get this worked out in the long run. You are not to be alone with him."

"Dad, what does that even mean?" I hiss and move out of his arms in horror. He averts my eyes to the corner of the room.

"It means," he says firmly. "You will listen to your mother and me and obey everything we tell you to do. You are not allowed to seek him out. Do you understand me, Terin?"

I try to conjure up an image of a typical day in the house. My parents doing their own thing, me playing my piano and Jared just… not there. It seemed wrong and alien. Everything about this whole situation was wrong. I was torn between cursing Sarah under my breath for goading him into seeing red by publicly trying to humiliate me in the middle of the quad during lunch and the shock of my parents' suggestion.

"I don't think you can do that, Dad. We live together!"

"It's not a request," he says. "It's a rule. Jared will be moved downstairs for the moment until we can talk properly with the doctors and work out a plan––"

"This is stupid."

"Tell that to the parents of the poor little injured girl, who are threatening to sue us," he snaps. Again, his face looks entirely different from the firm and stable presence I always knew him to be. I fight the urge to find my brother in this scary community hospital and take him far away from here.

I seethe quietly, looking down at my feet.

His mobile rings impatiently, two or three times in a row. He glances down at it with a frown and mutters, "it's your bloody mother again." And steps out of the room to take it. I see him gesture animatedly in the car park outside and imagine my mother at home is probably mirroring the same evident frustration.

I sit still. Drained, achy, and exhausted, and wait for my father and brother to return.

The ride home is silent. Not one word is exchanged between them. I continue to stare at my trainers and avoid them both. I was surprised after our conversation that Dad hadn't demanded he find his own ride home, but I am thankful that Jared was free of the private clinic. I try not to feel guilty about being honest with Dr. Richterson.

Everything was snowballing quietly around me. Our seemingly perfect little life in the heights of Chelsea with our large house was a scam. I glance across to Jared, who's glaring out of the window, his face blank. I try to imagine a world without my big brother looking out for me, and it fills me with such fear that I have to bite my lip from screaming.

"You'd better go to your room, Terin," Dad says as soon as we pull into the driveway.

"What if I don't want to?"

"It's non-negotiable," he insists firmly, eyes piercing into me in the rear-view mirror. The car falls silent beneath us. When would I be allowed to see my brother properly again? Was he *really* such a danger to me as my parents insisted?

I swallow and unclip my seat belt, diving to the side to throw my arms around Jared, who stiffens up momentarily before relaxing. He pushes his arms around me and chokes out a soft, "It's gonna be OK."

"Off him, now!" my father roars and turns in his seat to swat me over the head. I barely feel his hand through the sobs and my tears that rumble through my body. At some point, my Dad's hands are around my waist and physically dragging me from the car, into the house.

Jared's eyes are the only thing I can focus on. They shine almost jet black against the shadow of the rear seat of the car. His hands clench and unclench on his lap, practically glowing several shades of molten. He's crying and mouthing something I can't hear. But it looks suspiciously like, "I'm sorry."

-9-

We'd been split for one week so far.

I feel numb inside. Like he'd literally been broken apart from my body and stuffed into a cabinet or dark corner somewhere. I could still feel his presence in the house, no doubt probably moved downstairs to the cellar for a more permanent stay while our parents figured out what to do with him. I was scared for him, a constant state of terror that he really was dangerous, versus the fact he was my teenage older brother, and this was ridiculous. Abuse, even.

Over the past few days, I'd tried to start several unsuccessful conversations about him, all of which were shot down as soon as they'd begun. Or stopped dead with flimsy excuses of 'late meetings' and 'not now, I'm working'. Neither of them seemed to care.

Should I call someone? Mum seldom even spoke with her relatives down in Brighton and my Dad's side of the family were not a tight knit bunch. Georgia's own Dad seemed nice and responsible enough, but he was good friends with my parents. No way would he take me seriously. They'd think I was mentally disturbed if I tried to tell her what was really going on. As a last-ditch effort, I could always call the police anonymously or one of those helplines they advertised.

Could I betray my own parents like that?

"Are you feeling, OK?" Georgia murmurs in my ear. I jump in my seat at the proximity of her voice. We were in second-period English,

"I've got a lot of crap on my mind," I say.

She nods. "I heard from one of the TA's discussing in the staff room that they're sending work home for Jared. Is he in a lot of trouble? Sarah's back to school next week by the way. Might be best to avoid her for few days if you can. Her family is still super angry."

I manage to slip off during third and fourth periods to one of the toilets on the ground floor in the Art block. Thinking about Jared makes my chest hurt and the pain gradually builds until I can barely breathe, standing against the wall of sinks. My fingers tremble against the surface of the ceramic, barely registering the coolness against my sweaty skin – was I coming down with something?

I tear myself away from the mirror to splash some cool water on my face and try to breathe. In and out. Slowly. Gain control of myself. Panic attacks are normal.

The door of the bathroom swings open and closes somewhere behind me. I ignore them and continue to splash myself with the water, repeating my little mantra over and over again in my head. The next thing I know, the side of my face explodes in pain and I'm sprawling onto the wet tiles below me.

"What th−−" I begin, but someone kicks me in the gut which kills my words. Pain scorches through my abdomen and again in the back, when another foot stamps down on the middle of my spine.

I manage to open my eyes enough to see the matching hairdos of Alice and Alexa gazing piteously down at me. They giggle, laughing at some unspoken sick joke and kick me again. Lower back and shoulder. They were wearing little pointed flat shoes with a soft triangular tip that really hurts when it collides with me.

"Stop!" I beg and curl into a ball. Another kick, another laugh.

"Little message from Sarah," Alexa practically sings. "She's looking forward to coming back and seeing you again. After you know, your freak of a brother stabbed her."

"Where is the little psycho case today, Terin? He's definitely not here to protect you now." Alice sighs dramatically and leans down to grab a fistful of my hair. I wince, trying not to scream or cry or call for help. I need to make myself as small as possible and pretend this wasn't happening.

Alexa takes a handful on the opposite side and they both tug enthusiastically, trying to tear out the strands from the base of the scalp. I open my mouth to yell, and someone smacks me hard across the face and again when I collapse to the floor. My face crunches against the tiles.

"Not so tough now," Alexa sneers. "Not without big brother, rich daddy, and best friend to help you out. God, you're pathetic *Terrapin*."

"She's nothing but a smelly, washed out, greasy old amphibian."

"Greasy is definitely right. Look at her, all covered in water on the sticky bathroom floor."

"She must feel right at home," Alice cackles and her friend joins in. Their cruel voices reverberate around the room, making it sound as if there's an entire group of them humiliating me.

Let them, I think to myself. *Let them kill me, I really don't care.*

"Poor little loser. Her brother's on track to be a serial killer. Isn't that right, Terrapin? I heard that he'd been beheading hedgehogs and cats in the street and stringing them up on telephone poles."

"Not... true..." I whisper. Another kick. Another wave of pain courses through me. It was pathetic really. Jared knew that standing up for me would always get him in trouble and he didn't hesitate when Sarah was being cruel in the quad. I can't even repay the favour. I'm too weak to stand against them and fight back.

"Oh, look – she's crying!"

"Sad little baby Terrapin."

A bell rings from the corridor, signalling end of the period. Soon enough the toilets would be flooded by students on their way to lunch and would no doubt find us. The girls lean back and grin nastily down towards me and I wonder if the ordeal really was over or not. When I try to lean up slowly to get to my feet, a foot lands on my chest and forces me back down again.

My head connects with the floor, more painfully than last time. Red hot anger begins to swell through my organs, to my veins and arteries – circulating around the body. How dare these bullies *think* they could just go ahead and control someone this way?

I'm on my feet suddenly. It all happens so quick that I'm unable to really register what is happening or how I manage to stand up – I can only tell that I'm livid and I can barely feel the bruises or my sore scalp anymore.

Alexa scowls and tries to slap me. Surprisingly, my hand snaps to catch her wrist and manages to hold her easily when she attempts to wriggle out of my grasp. Alice tries to push me away, but my other arm easily swats her back and seizes her wrist too. They both gape at me, each trying to tear away from my grip which only increases in intensity.

I can feel the room around me. Every movement of water dripping from old taps, every dust molecule that lands on the surface of the clouded window lights. My skin prickles with a renewed energy I don't know I had. Everything tingles in tune to the electricity in the air and before my brain can catch up with my body, both girls scream and jump backwards.

On their skinny wrists, are raw red marks where I've had them both so tightly, painfully inflamed and shiny against the gloom of the bathroom lights. I stare back down at my own hands which were just as normal and pale as they'd always been. Maybe more so from the shock of the whole encounter.

Alice and Alexa stare at me, for once lost for words as we try and decipher what had just happened. One moment I was a crumpled ball on the floor, the next I was able to restrain them both using only two hands.

"Crazy weirdo freak," one of them whispers and flees from the bathroom with the other in tow, leaving me alone and suddenly very afraid.

The rest of the school day passes by in a blur after I take myself to the medical room. I'm summoned to the headmaster's office and told off for fighting in the bathrooms after a complaint from the girls. It was easier to stay quiet rather than fight my side of the story, especially when I wasn't sure exactly what that was. They'd called my mother to notify her of my three-day suspension from school and made me sit by the reception waiting area to be collected while someone gathered up my things into my school bag.

"Fighting in the bathroom like alley cats," Mum scowls into the steering wheel on the ride home. "For God's sake Terin, what were you thinking? Who was it?"

"I don't want to talk about it," I say firmly into my lap. And that was that.

After a tensely quiet dinner, Dad excuses himself with a mutter of, "Can I trust you to get these into the dishwasher Terin?" He disappears in the direction of his study with my mother in tow.

As soon as the machine was loaded and whirs away quietly in the huge empty kitchen, I slouch across the house in the direction of the stairs with the intent of going to bed early. It wasn't as if there was anyone around who wanted to spend any time with me, so what was the point? I briefly entertain the idea of sneaking downstairs to see if Jared's awake, but I'm in enough trouble already.

I'm so wrapped up in my own loneliness and isolation, that I barely hear my father speak from the cracked door of his room as I pass.

"It's very out of character for her."

"She won't tell me who it was, I don't suppose you manage to get anything?"

"No. It's not her fault.... She's grown up seeing him act like that, thinking it's normal and OK to throw your weight around."

"It was totally embarrassing, Richard. The teachers must think we can barely control them after being called there twice this month!" Mum paused, I can imagine her jewelled hands to her face, barely able to stand the thought of being judged by all the other mothers.

"Christ, Helen, I think he needs to go," my father says softly and I can hear him pacing back and forth around the large rectangle-shaped office. It's more or less a beige and brown carbon copy of his space at work. A few scattered family photos and nothing more. Peering through the crack, I can see my mother staring at an old baby photo of Jared, nibbling at the corners of her lips like she usually did when faced with a problem.

"What will they think of us? What will we tell everyone?"

"I don't know. Boarding school perhaps. It's not totally insane – everyone knows I came from that background. My father used to be on the board at Chiltern, you remember? Maybe we can sponsor a kid under our names, cover our tracks a little."

She sighs, it's a tired sound that all emotion had already been drained away. "I didn't want it to come to this...."

"No, neither did I," Dad says. "But this is becoming dangerous, and we need to take our safety into consideration. He hasn't hurt Terin yet but you and I both know that the cellar won't hold him forever."

She swallows and holds up her hands. "I don't want to hear any more of this Richard."

"But that doesn't mean he won't. Obviously he has some sort of lack of impulse control when it comes to his... ability. It's taking him over Helen. We need to face the facts here."

"What facts?" She laughs with mirth. "Where did you see this in any of the parenting books? When was this explained to us at the prenatal appointments?"

He makes a face. "We signed a nondisclosure agreement, we agreed to participate in the trials."

"If I'd known it'd come to this, I'd have just let him go," Mum cuts across sharply. Her words stab the air with intent and for the second time, her hands fly to her mouth in disbelief. Whether it was some sort of regret or embarrassment, I don't know. Dad's face crumples in a way I'd never seen before and he nods slowly, moving his hand over his whole face.

"I know," he agrees. "I know. Richterson suggested we let the boy study with him instead. Understand it more."

"This means we will have to explain to the school and to the social workers."

He shrugs. "One difficult conversation of honesty won't do any harm for a lifetime of security. If the Richtersons can help, I say we go ahead and do it. We have nothing left to lose."

"It's just... wrong," she whispers and I wonder if she feels the tug of motherhood goading her to protect her son.

"The whole situation is wrong," my father says grimly. "But we have put up with this as long as we can – longer than most, if the situation were public."

"And what do we tell Terin?"

"I'm unsure how much she really knows. She's so pure and I don't want this to affect or destroy her spirit. But she is starting to ask difficult questions now."

"She's getting to a similar age. She's struggling."

"Perhaps it's better to happen now rather than later on, when she understands more," he says finally.

"Fine," my mother says flatly after a few minutes of silence. There's a clink as she picks up the wine glass from his desk. "Go and make the call."

-10-

C linical trials? Nondisclosure agreement? What the *hell* had happened before Jared was born?

The day after the conversation overheard between my parents, Dad went back on his original threat. Jared and are allowed to spend time with one another. *Supervised.*

As much as it surprised me, they must know they just couldn't keep him downstairs indefinitely. I'm still filled with anxiety. No way was this over. I have a strong feeling that things were going to get much worse before they got better.

It was unfair of them to blame him for *my* actions. *I* was the one who had a fight in the girl's toilets and hurt Alice and Alexa. *I* was just as guilty for losing my cool and allowing it to happen. I was the one who could barely stand up for myself, nursing a black eye and multiple bruises on my tummy and an upgraded week suspension from school after refusing to apologise for my part.

"Really, Terin," Mum hissed when she yanks up my shirt to assess the damage. "This is ridiculous!"

"I didn't do anything, Mum," I had said with a deep blush of embarrassment. It was bad enough I was in the dark about the Jared thing. But I was now facing the very real possibility that my fight had awakened a similar freaky ability inside me. It was the only explanation for their burned raw wrists and my will to suddenly overpower them.

The last thing I need was for my mother to find out what *really* happened and start asking questions.

"The marks on those girls say otherwise," Mum snaps. "They've been suspended for fighting too."

"Good," I mutter.

Her face contorts into an ugly scowl, far from the grace of poise of the famous Helen Coiler. "You're all *incredibly* lucky to keep your places in that school! Honestly, between you and your bloody brother, I *dread* to imagine what the teachers must think."

My school suspension leads nicely into the start of the half term holiday, so I don't have to go back and face Sarah's return or the rest of the school. Yet.

It was suggested by my father that Jared attends home tutor sessions with Dr. Richterson and his wife. I didn't know the extent of the relationship the man had with my parents, but he seemed kind enough during my brief chat with him and I was definitely sure Jared would prefer it to school. The only downside was that now the holidays had begun, he was required to go to the doctor's house every day and study with them between 8am and 4pm.

The most important thing was that Jared was away from our home during the day and away from our parents, which he was happier about. As much I as miss him, perhaps this time away would even begin to heal his relationship with our parents. Maybe. Miracles *did* happen.

We're standing outside a small townhouse that sits on the apex of old concrete stairs and twisted metal handrails. There's a couple of neglected potted plants that lay dead in the entrance, either side of the front door and a couple of old Christmas decorations in the window which were either left up from last year or two months early this year. Through the window, I see stacks of haphazardly balanced books on shelves and a mug of grey tea on the sill.

Both sides of the house are connected to the next one and the next in a reoccurring line that runs all the way down the street to the petrol station in the distance. I gaze in curiosity at how cramped everything was from the neighbour's windows that seems too close together, to the rows of identical concrete stairs and rusted railings. I don't understand. Our house had always seemed too big for four people, but these homes seemed too *small* for anyone.

"Close your mouth, idiot," Jared mutters beside me and keeps his hands in his pockets. He's nervous for some reason and doesn't want to look at me in the eyes. I try to wrap my hand around his arm, but he moves easily out of my grasp.

I want to ask him why Dad and I were visiting the Richtersons with him today. I'm paranoid that my father somehow knows about the weird episode in the school toilets and wants to send me here too for evaluation. Am I going just as crazy as my brother? Was it beginning to happen to me too, whatever it was?

Dad presses his finger to the doorbell, which chimes sweetly throughout the house. The door swings open to reveal the pair of elderly doctors in the threshold who greet us happily.

Together, Dr. Gina and Doug Richterson wear identical beige and white clothing. Gina herself in a knee length dress, chiffon scarf, and smart black shoes, while her husband wears his white jacket over his tennis shirt and trousers. They smile at us warmly and invite us into the home that smells strongly of home baking and cinnamon.

Jared, apparently already at home, takes off his jacket and shoes respectfully at the door – something I'd never seen him do before – and pads off through to the kitchen. Determined not to spoil the politeness, I do the same and follow him.

Despite the unkempt appearance outside, the house is warm and welcoming with books almost on every surface and old medical certificates proudly displayed on the walls. In contrast with our own eggshell walls and boring furniture, the Richtersons' house had bright wallpaper and comfortable squashy furniture. There was an old dog bed in the corner, but no sign of any inhabitant snoozing inside.

Jared takes a seat at the wooden kitchen table to the side of the room and flicks open a Spiderman comic that sits on a pile of old magazines. Without prompt, Gina brings over a steaming mug of hot chocolate for him and sets it down. She gestures to me.

"What'll it be, lovey?" she offers. There's a small hint of a European accent but not the same as her husband's Polish undertones. "Uh, tea please. With two sugars and milk," I mumble and watch as she retreats to the other side of the room to grab another cup.

My Dad and Doug are talking in the adjoined living room where the older man is showing him the new sound system they'd had installed recently. They lower their voices and speak in hushed tones on a few occasions and glance over to us conspiratorially.

"There you go," Gina says kindly and sets the tea in front of me and takes a seat on the opposite side of the table. I don't know why I'm feeling so shy all of a sudden; I can barely look her in the eyes and say thank you.

"So... do you guys teach Jared proper subjects when he's here? Like school?" I ask.

Gina smiles. "My husband and I have a special interest in a few things we believe Jared might be keen in exploring. How are you getting on with the assignment?" She switches her attention to him. Jared shrugs, his eyes still on the magazine but I can see the cogs turning in his brain. "Trying to get my head around some of the longer terms, but I think I'm understanding. I've got some good ideas of what I'm going to put in it."

My eyebrows rose, it was the first time he'd ever taken an interest in his schoolwork.

"Good." Gina nods and her eyes sparkle. I notice that there's nothing in them that I can sense as suspicious. But the way the old woman looks at my brother – he's like a son to her. We sip our drinks and I wonder what my own mother would think of that.

"Why don't you show Terin your space, Jared?" Dad calls. "Let the adults catch up, huh?" It was the nicest tone I'd heard him use with my brother and I wonder if it's for the benefit of the Richtersons. Jared shrugs, nonplussed, and gets up from the table. I follow him quickly through the house to where he stops by a doorway framed with old beams and follows the route downstairs.

I worry that he's leading me to another dark room like the cellar at home – but we turn on the lower landing, where the stairs are still covered in soft carpet, and I'm stood in a different kind of basement.

The room was covered in posters and artwork – from the likes that I'd never seen at home. A comfortable bed lies in the corner along with a pile of folded laundry, fresh sheets, and a desk sits in the opposite side. There's no natural light, but the room is painted in a bright yellow and there's a laptop and TV on top of a set of drawers.

I see his favourite slippers over by the bed as the penny drops as I recall the recent conversation between my parents. *"Christ Helen, I think he needs to go."*

"You live here," I accused.

"I've been slowly moving in I guess."

"You're joking?"

"They think they can help me," he says thoughtfully. "And I think I need help. I'm not gonna get anywhere living at home."

"*We're* your family," I say defensively, but even the words sound too practised and out of order, in my own head. He raises an eyebrow and stares at me.

"We're a family as long as no one is a freak of nature," he says. "And I'm a freak of something. Mum and Dad don't want to admit that, and I don't wanna talk to them about it either."

"Then talk to me!" I press and move closer. "I'm supposed to be your sister!"

"Look – it's done, Ter. I'm living here now."

"I'll move with you!" I say quickly. Desperately.

The eyebrow rose again, mocking me. "You're their little musical prodigy. You're being groomed to take over the company one day instead of me and you're going to continue to be their little girl however long they want you there for."

I expect him to sound bitter, but there's nothing hostile there. Just tiredness and deflation.

Guilt rises up in my stomach so quickly, I want to vomit all over his nice new carpet. It was as if someone had plunged their hands into my stomach and ripped my organs into the chilly Autumn air.

"But I don't want any of that! Are you leaving me because you're jealous?" I huff. He turns red and moves across the room. I worry that I hit a nerve, so I try to make amends by feigning interest in some of his band posters and books.

"What sort of things do you learn here?" I change tact.

"Science mostly. Biology and chemistry. They both used to work in a lab or whatever, so they've got some cool stories. I doubt our parents will have much to do with me from now on though."

"Maybe they think it's the best thing for you?" I say stiffly. He laughs.

I can hear the sounds of the adults talking in the kitchen upstairs, but the voices are too muffled to decipher what the conversation is. I turn to ask Jared what he thinks, but he's turned on his new television and is sprawled out on the bed.

Clearly, I was the only odd one out, always kept in the dark.

"How long are you gonna live here for?" I say, barely a whisper. I surprise myself at how much my voice cracks with the effort of keeping in my tears and how unfairly short our recent reunification was.

He glances at me. "Today was actually the last day of bringing my stuff over. Dad's got the rest in the boot. He didn't want you officially seeing him kick me out and be the bad guy I imagine."

"T-Today? Why didn't you tell me this sooner? Is that why I'm here too?"

He looks uncomfortable. "We agreed it might be easier for you to come over and see the place. A clean break you know?"

"*Who agreed*? Nobody even bothered to tell me that you were moving out at fifteen!"

"Almost sixteen," he prods. "Think of this place like a private boarding school. I get to live my life away from home and *them*. I can do whatever I want to without being shoved in that damn cellar all the time." There's an air of hope to his words and I hope it's not a white lie for my benefit. I nod enthusiastically through my tears. Upstairs, the sounds of chairs scraping on the kitchen floor remind us of this limited time.

"I'll get you out of here," I whisper. "Tell me how."

"I'll get myself out one day when the time's right," he says steadily. "The man and his wife are both really nice which isn't the worst thing ever. Maybe this will be a good thing."

"Oh Jared, don't go hurting people again."

"I'm not," he scowls defensively. "But if they get in my way, I can't control it. You know I can't."

"Have you tried?" I ask desperately. Tears cling to the sides of my eyelashes. "Have you tried not hurting anybody when *it happens*." He recoils away from me as if it's a foreign concept.

"They're going to suppress me," he says, surprisingly calm. "I heard Mum and Dad talk to them about it the first time we came here. That's why I have my own room. They think they can control me. Control *it*, I guess."

"How? We don't even know or understand what it is." I hiss. Hesitation fills me. Do I tell him now about the conversation I'd overheard or for his own sanity or keep it to myself? The secret world of pre disclosure agreements and tests.

"I dunno. Medicines mostly. Of course, I'd rather stay with you, Ter, so don't even look at me like that. Being here is my best shot at figuring out who and what I am. I need this chance," he says. He suddenly looks older, wearier. It's the first time I consider the possibility that he might be as afraid of his own ability, as me.

Keep it to myself, I decide. It wouldn't change anything now, especially when I didn't understand what it all means myself.

"Hopefully it will work, and you can come home really soon." I try to stay positive and upbeat, having trouble arranging my tone to match. I expect Jared to snap at me for being naïve, but he smiles kindly. His face falls a few moments later and his brow furrows together.

"I started changing and feeling different when I hit puberty – probably around your age. People will try to tell you it's just normal hormones and growing up, but I *changed* Terin. Everything about me felt weird. There's no telling it will happen to you but... just watch yourself."

"You don't know *if* it'll happen to me." I say quickly.

"You don't know that it won't."

"What should I do then?" I'm beginning to shake. There wasn't enough time to tell him everything.

"Be careful," he says seriously. His amber eyes shine with an emotion I can't figure out. "Stay obedient, play that bloody piano, and do what they say. When you can, get away and stay far from them. OK?"

"When?"

"You'll need to figure that out yourself," he says impatiently. We hear the sounds of feet crossing the house, signifying that the adults were done with their business. "I don't know when they'll let you come back here to see me but don't be an idiot and keep your head down."

We turn and my father lightly trots down the stairs into Jared's new space. He stands casually with his hands in his pockets and doesn't regard my brother at all.

"Time to go sweetheart," he says jovially and turns as an afterthought to Jared. "I'll leave the rest of your things upstairs for you to collect."

"Great," Jared says blankly.

I want to turn around and scream at both of them for being so ridiculous and that I didn't want our family to be ruined and split up. I want to lock all three of them in a room together and throw away the key and force them to get on with each other and accept Jared for what he was. Whatever *that* is.

But I recall what Jared has said to me and keep my mouth shut. I give him one last look before approaching my father, who puts his hand forcibly on my back and guides me back up to the entrance.

"Bye, Dad," Jared mutters.

-II-

Six months pass along with a lonely Christmas. Every room in the house dwarfs me in its mammoth space until I can't breathe. The colossal weight of loneliness sits on my chest as the days pass, daring me to wriggle, scream, do anything.

I'd only been allowed to speak to Jared over the phone. Visits were out of the question until he was settled in properly. Or that's what I was told by my father anyway. Jared sounds OK from the chats we do manage to have. He tells me a little bit about the research on genetics the Richterson's are doing. He was proud that he hadn't had a fit in a while after being 'suppressed'. They were proud of him too.

Sarah and her gang had been quieter over the past half year as well after I was allowed to return back to school following my unfair expulsion. Seeing me in the corridors or in the quad, all three turn in the opposite direction and walk the other way. They don't torment me or write insults in my textbooks anymore. It's as if I simply didn't exist.

But there was something bigger on my mind.

It was like something had awakened inside me since the school bathroom incident. The air feels crisper. The sound of silence in the house, louder somehow. The surface of my skin prickles uncomfortably as if my nerve endings were firing of their own free will. Morning, noon and night.

It's almost like being able to taste TV static on the tip of my tongue, but that's impossible.

I shake my head as I prepare to start my piano practice. No. I'm fine.

My fingers are flying over the keys, but I can barely hear the sounds that are coming from them. I sigh and rearrange my fingers to my starting pose and try again. The music sounds just as stilted and devoid of all emotion as it did two hours before, when I first tried the new piece. I reset the stereo to the beginning of the track one more time.

Mum wants me to try another big ballad from another of her theatre productions, but I shyly suggest that I want to find my own piece and learn it from scratch instead. She had sighed and rolled her eyes but conceded to let me have a go. I had rifled through her joint expansive library of music to find the perfect song to match my frame of mind, which ended up being a dark gothic piece from the early 1900's. It was the moodiest thing I'd ever played, but it fit.

"Breathe," I whisper to myself to try to find that zen space of my conscious that I could sit safely in.

I let my vision relax over the sheet music and try to imagine that I'm feeling for the notes instead. My fingers easily find the corresponding keys, I'm hitting the majority of the notes confidently. The song fills the room with its heavy tone, I'm not even looking at the printed pages anymore. I'm feeling my way through the fog with nothing but my hands and my brain deciphering the next steps.

There it is again. I can feel the strange energy present. Inside me somehow? Now that my hands were busy and my motor skills were taken up with their jobs, it leaves me time to wonder more about myself. Was this feeling just a normal stage in puberty?

I finish the song with a swift flourish, nothing fancy. My fingers tingle with the effort of being tapped so roughly against the keys while I was distracted but looking at the clock, I realise almost an hour has gone by already. The energy fades into the back of my mind with the disappearing concentration and my practice was done for the day.

This afternoon is the official opening of a project my mother had been working on, with some big important music producers in London. She'd helped them compose an entire score for a theatre play in between tutoring her own music students. For her sake, I try to inject some enthusiasm and support into my face when I slip on new clothes in front of my mirror, but my expression is nothing. Just blank. A stranger, far removed from my happier former self is staring back at me.

"Are you going to be sick? You've gone pale." Dad glances into the rear-view mirror. "Hold on, we're nearly there." He pulls into the car into a quiet car park near the Palladium Theatre while I clutch myself together, wincing.

Thankfully, we'd arrived earlier than expected and the queues aren't too bad, so we are able to drift through admission and security quickly.

Mum grabs my shoulder and indicates to the toilet sign at the top of the stairs. Obediently, I follow the hems of her cream-layered dress.

"Crap," I whisper. It's marginally more than a whisper — it's a horrified, choking sound that slips out of my mouth before I have a chance to stop it. Outside the cubicle, Mum knocks on the flimsy plastic door.

"Terin? We're going to miss the start of the play. What on earth are you doing in there?"

"I'm fine, I'm fine. I just... have a bad tummy. Can I meet you in there?"

She huffs and I can almost hear her glare at her expensive gold watch. "Yes, yes fine. We're in Box 2 – don't be long darling. Dad wants you to meet with Mr. Sanders." She walks off with the rich sounds of heels clicking on the marbled floor of the ladies' toilets. When she leaves, I can only hear the low hum of the extractor fan on the walls, and I know I'm alone again.

I gulp and stare back down. I'm shaking as I scrutinize the small droplets of blood inside my knickers. I'd had enough biology lessons at school to know exactly what the dull burning was in my pelvis area was, without freaking out at least.

Jared's warning was still fresh in my mind. Although he'd insisted that his weirdness took on a whole new level when he hit puberty, there was no *definitive* that I'd develop weird powers too. This wasn't one of his weird sci-fi comics, he was just an anomaly. Since the school incident, nothing else strange happened to me.

Everything is going to be fine.

I clean myself up thoroughly as best as I can and grab fistfuls of quilted tissue to stick them in my underwear. Luckily, I'm wearing a long dress and tights and the theatre will already be partially darkened by this point.

I flush the toilet, grab my little shoulder bag, and head over to the wall of large sinks. I gaze at myself carefully for a little while as I look for signs of visible change. I don't feel any different––which is good––and my chest is still near flat, so I don't need to go out of my way to hide anything yet.

Perhaps everything will be OK and nothing else would happen.

Maybe I'd stay normal. I knew that my parents loved me no matter what. Maybe there is a lot more between them and my brother than I thought, and I'd misread the whole situation. Perhaps he really is a danger to us, and the cellar had been the best option for dealing with him at the time.

Yes, everything is going to be fine. I breathe slowly and I feel better. No signs of fever or a temperature. My eyes were the same cerulean blue as they've always been. I am not going to have a strange fit or suddenly start changing the environment or melting anything.

I am going to be OK.

There's a helpful usher in a neat uniform who shows me to the private staircase, after I exit the ladies' toilets. He's kind, funny and most of all – normal, which makes me wish I could spend the evening helping him with his tasks that he cheerfully chats to me about. I'm quiet with shame and wish I could be anyone but myself right now. I feel like I've committed a murder and the dirt was on me for everyone to see.

I can run, I think to myself. *I can just get out of those double doors and run for it. But could I do that to my parents and betray them like that? Would I want to?*

Swallowing, I head into Box 2 and take the only seat between my father and the famed Mr. Sanders. My father pats my shoulders affectionately and smiles.

"There's my little girl! Here, Terin – meet an acquaintance of mine from the Royal College; Mr. Sanders was the musical director at Oxford University. Terin's been dying to meet you, Ted."

Ted Sanders is a plain man with a thinning head of silver hair, thin rimmed glasses and a little on the pudgy side, but he extends his hand and I take it politely and tell him it's nice to meet him.

"I've been hearing a lot about you, Miss Coiler – a real piano prodigy I hear? Just like your mother. Yes, I would have thought it'd run in the family," he glances up at my father. "Does your son have any interest in music too?"

"Jared's taken up his studies at a boarding school in Switzerland," my father laughs, without missing a beat. "Something to do with modern history. Smart mind, but the boy's as tone deaf as they come." The men and my mother chortle together. I try to focus on the actors onstage, seething quietly.

"So, Terin," Ted Sanders turns to me again. "Are you going to continue piano after secondary school? I know a few professors who'd be interested in meeting with the esteemed daughter of Helen Coiler!"

"I haven't really thought about it," I say politely. How could I look so far ahead when my days could be possibly numbered? The false pretence of safety when I came out of the bathroom, dwindles away and I'm left with a cold feeling inside my stomach. I think of Jared spending his teenage years in a strange house with no real family or friends around him and I feel sick.

Was that going to happen to me too? Were my parents going to abandon me under the pretence of help?

My father nudges my side and speaks for me. "She's mentioned that she'd like to look at the possibility of playing for the Royal Philharmonic one day. Of course, Helen and I are going to support her every step of the way." He's still smiling but for the first time ever, I catch a strange air of control in his words. Ted doesn't seem to have the same opinion as me, he nods blindly and enthusiastically.

I turn to him in my seat and smile shyly. "I'm actually interested in studying abroad at university more than anything else. The possibility of experiencing new countries and cultures is really appealing and I'd love to travel."

Ted nods in approval. "There's some fantastic music programs in Europe and the US. I'm pretty sure I've got a book of contacts somewhere. Do let me know if you'd like me to make an introduction, young Terin."

"We will of course think about such a generous offer." Dad nods. "That would be beyond out of this world," I breathe. For a moment, the world seems a little bit easier to function within. "I can't wait."

The play lasts for two or three hours – but I'm barely watching anyone on the stage. This portly, small man had given me an incredible opportunity and lifeline. As much as I would miss home, the possibility of moving as far away as possible and living my own life – even *if* something did happen to me – would be so *easy*. I wouldn't have to fear anything or hide.

Most importantly I could try to take Jared with me somehow.

"Good to hear that Ted's doing well," Dad says over dinner that night. Steamed rice, fish and vegetables that are grey in colour and just as bland and flavourless. He seems to think too after he takes a bite and makes a face. "Christ Helen, isn't it time we hired another cook?"

"Yes well," Mum scowls and no doubt recalls the Greenslade incident. "It hasn't been the right time to hire anyone else really."

"Time to change that. I'll put an ad out in the morning on the way to work. Are you coming with me tomorrow, Terin? I need your opinion on a couple of apprentices I'm looking to take on?"

The question catches me off guard. I hastily swallow my mouthful. "I'm sorry, what?"

"*Pardon me*?" Mother corrects with a frown.

"It's apprentice day tomorrow," Dad teases. "You always have a keen eye for good workers when we sit down and look through CV's together."

I hesitate and the fork of my next mouthful hovers uncertainly over my plate. "I was actually thinking of going to see if I was allowed to visit Jared tomorrow. You know, since it's the sixteenth of March and everything."

He blinks slowly. "And today's the fifteenth and the day after tomorrow – the seventeenth!"

"Jared's birthday," Mum says quietly. The table is plunged into an awkward silence that's only broken by the sound of cutlery on ceramic. This continues on until everyone's finished their meals and Mum shoves a teapot on the table for after dinner drinks.

"I'll give the Richtersons a call and we'll perhaps see if he's free for a visit," Dad says vaguely. "Why don't you come on down to the office with me and in the morning and we'll have some lunch at the pizza place you like so much? The one that overlooks the river."

"Cartelli's," Mum interjects. "Did you know it was started up by a teenager originally? Linda down the club knows the family, she was positively raving about their homemade bread the other day!"

"Linda *would*, she's become the size of a bungalow after her fourth child was it?"

"Fifth. But yes, she's been stealing towels from the spa again it seems," Mum sneers and they chuckle together in unison. I look between them both and wonder how long it's been since they connected like this. I try to rack my brain to remember the last time they'd seemed so comfortable with one another and found nothing.

I guess it'd been only a matter of time before the black sheep of the family was removed and for the *curse* to be lifted. I feel sick at the notion.

"We should catch a film this coming weekend," Dad muses. "Since it's we're all in."

"We could even do some shopping. I'd been dying to check out that new boutique down in Knightsbridge."

"Sound good to you, my little flower?" Dad turns to me with a grin and a wink, looking so hopeful that I can't bear the thought of turning him down. I send silent apologies to Jared and that I would hopefully see him soon after all.

"Sure thing," I say, a little deflated.

-12-

A huge banner hangs from the entrance hall archway with my brother and father shaking hands below it. Grins frozen for the photographer that snaps a couple of dynamic shots. It was the first inkling I had to point towards this being a dream. I'd never really seen them touch.

I don't recognise any of the well-dressed faces that mill around me, delicately holding drinks in posh looking flutes. The sound of a piano spills into the background – an array of melodies that I could feel my fingers wanting to relay if they got the chance during the evening. My parents usually hire a professional pianist for posh parties and low and behold, a middle-aged gentleman is sitting on my favourite leather seat, his fingers dancing across the polished keys that are illuminated from the golden lights in the conservatory.

The spacious rooms are filled with people chatting in small groups and pretending to laugh at each other's jokes. I stare at each of them in turn, trying to grab the attention of several waiters floating around the guests with pretentious food on trays.

"For God's sake, Terin – stand up tall, will you?" My mother appears next to me, drowning in her own plumes of perfume. She was wearing the earrings that were bought for her last Christmas. Secretly, I knew deep down that she hates them, but they were expensive and cost nearly as much as the cocktail dress.

"What even is the point in all this?" I mutter. I feel her blanche next to me, head whipping around to ensure none of the guests could hear our whispered conversation. She adopts a fake smile and greets a man and his lady friend as they enter the room from the glass conservatory and help themselves to the flutes on the side.

"You know I'm not a fan of your father's business events," she concedes and swallows her own drink a little quicker than usual. "But it's important to your father and to Jared, it's important to show a united family front in front of potential investors."

"God forbid we do anything else." I cast her a look and open my mouth to make a scathing comment about their abandonment of my brother, but she's already disappeared.

I see my father surrounded by waspy business associates. But it's Jared, they're more interested in. It's his welcoming home party after all.

"I hear you've been in Switzerland!" I hear an older man say as I wander past. "Something about history?"

"Dabbling in different things really," Jared replies politely. If he sees me walking past, he's ignoring me. He's been ignoring me all evening to the point where I wondered if we were still brother and sister anymore. "Most recently, biological engineering."

"Fascinating," his partner replies. "I have worked with someone in the field before. Phillips, I think his name was. Some rather radical ideas in the industry, but trend setting, no doubt."

The sound of the piano grows louder – to the point where I feel like I can't hear my own heartbeat over the keys hammering against the wood. Moving through the crowd and trying to swallow down a cough and a splutter, I manage to slip through the crowd to the bar area at the corner of the dining room where the majority of the party guests are congregating.

"To my son!" my father, who's a little drunk by this point, proclaims, clapping the shoulders of the tall, lanky teenager beside him. I'm confused. It's like the last few years never happened. I was a little disappointed that Jared, in all his suspicion, agreed to this party on his behalf. Why is everyone acting so normal?

With every mention of the boy and his latest achievements in his apparent European education, he keeps enthusiastically clapping the boy across the shoulders, to the point where Jared deliberately takes two steps away to avoid another cuff.

My eyes fall upon the grand piano to the right of him – now empty from whoever butchered the songs before. I can feel my fingers long to run themselves over the meticulously cared for keys.

"I would like to invite you all to raise your glasses," my father booms around the room, his voice bounces off the contemporarily decorated grey and white walls. "For my son – Jared Coiler. He will begin a prestigious apprenticeship in philosophy – starting from when he finishes boarding school this year." Without waiting for anyone else, he drains his glass and holds it proudly above his head to the cheers and approval of everyone around me. My mother appears at his side with her well-practised smile. Ever the loyal wife and perfect hostess with the picture-perfect family.

All three of them smile at each other and I'm left in the middle of the crowd, wondering what the hell I could be missing. I had to look away from the sickening family scene. When I finally manage to regain some composure, I stand back at full height and my eyes fall on the sight before me.

The grand piano is now on fire. Huge yellow and orange flames spill from the expensive dark wood – spreading quickly along the flammable surface and completely enveloping the entire thing within seconds. The blaze licks and spits at the edges as the flare grows more intense; the heat in the room feels like it rises by about a thousand degrees.

"I'm going to destroy everything he's ever built," Jared's voice says suddenly. I blink and he appears in front of me. Everyone else is gone. His good-looking boyish grin transforms into a cold, calculated look. I take a step back.

"I'm dreaming," I realise, a distorted muffled sounds falls from my lips. The flames feel hot on my face, I'm sweating in a matter of seconds. Jared still looks calm and collected.

I jolt awake in my bed, coughing and spluttering until my lungs scream in protest. The moonlight spills across the floor and despite the chilly night air that pools in from the open window, I'm left with a foreboding feeling that stays with me as I try to get back to sleep.

It's another morning of music practice, overseen by my new tutor. Mr. Sanders had taken It upon himself to coach me in music theory and future college applications, at a fee of course. My parents were all too happy to oblige.

"Beautiful," Ted Sanders approves as he paces the length of the grand piano. I wonder if he's noticed me shake my head away from my daydream stupor and land back in reality again. We are in the downstairs living room, and he closes his eyes and mutters, "Really, just marvellous." He leers over my back in a move that feels a bit lecherous, but I push down the nausea and smile sweetly as I finish the last few notes.

My mother and father clap demurely in the doorway to the conservatory. The huge glass doors are open, the smell of fresh oranges breezes in from the air outside as one of the caterers prepares freshly squeezed juice. I can see them setting up the tables and chairs outside for brunch for the four of us with beautifully decorated tablecloths and matching napkins.

Dad coughs lightly to turn my attention back to Ted and quietly closes the cream curtains, bringing me back to reality.

Ted Sanders claps too, his face is a mask of excitement, and he turns to my parents. "Really, you must start enrolling her in universities now. You know how competitive the courses are, Helen."

"We've sat down and mapped out the best music programs in the country. I think Terin's got her heart set on studying abroad though."

"Well," my father cuts in. "We've still yet to discuss semantics. It would be better if she could stay as local as possible, rather than study in Timbuctoo!"

I snort. "Daddy, Julliard is the best school in the world for this program. It's not a million miles away!"

"New York," he clarifies. "What if your old dad gets too old and needs help getting the paper, hmm? Your mother studied at the Royal Academy of Music, that's just a mere train ride or two away!"

I try and calm myself, the last thing I wanted was for Ted Sanders to see his little music prodigy lose her cool like a petulant child. I turn my attention to him instead.

"You mentioned a couple of times that you have contacts in the US?"

"Why yes." He nods predictably. "I know the music professors are Yale and Berkley. I'm sure they'd be more than happy to owe me a favour and have a discussion with Terin. In truth though with her talent, I'd see no reason why she shouldn't aim all the way and *try* for Julliard. Test the waters!"

It was hard not to smirk in triumph as he said the exact words I'd wanted him to. My parents glance at each other uneasily. My father's eyes flicker to me.

"I wonder if the spread is ready yet? Helen, why don't you take Ted through to the conservatory and show him the wisteria? It's grown especially well this year; if I recall correctly, you mentioned you'd like to take a few clippings home?"

My mother takes Ted's arm and loyally leads him through the house. When their voices disappear into the extension, my father sighs and slips his hands into the trousers of his day suit. He wanders across the room to the French windows and gazes at the painting of mum and her concert above it.

"I just wish you'd take up my offer, my girl," he says sorrowfully. "You know I need a good head to run the business. Your mother has no brain for the corporate side of things. You take after me mostly – despite your skill with the piano." My body clenches and I wonder what the best way out of this argument we would surely have, is going to be.

"Taking over the business should have been Jared's right, not mine," I say carefully. "He'll be disappointed to know that he's been overlooked." It was a dangerous gamble to play as we barely mention my brother's name in the household anymore, but I don't mention how much I see him in my dreams.

My eyes are tearing up. I blink them away quickly to try to force him out of my mind and swallow the pain. I force my facial expression to stay neutral and hold my father's gaze steady.

"Yes, well, Jared's business head is fine," he says, playing the game. "But you know better than I that he would be vastly unpredictable. During his last home-schooling report, he ended up with lower than average scores."

"He's not allowed to go to a proper school anymore," I argue, more hotly than I'd intended. "Which is why he does worse. You allow that elderly pair of doctors to teach him, so he gets bored and lonely."

"He's unpredictable," my father repeats. "I can't have that sort of behaviour sully the name of the business and the empire I've spent so long building. But you Terin, you can really take the company places. I'd really like for you to be a part of that. Sure, you can go away and study the piano and be apart of some of the best musical programs in the world. But I would like your word that you'll be back here; ready to take over from me by the time you're thirty."

I let his words settle for a moment. "I have no interest in running the company, Daddy. I'm sorry. I want to be out there in the world, making my own money and my own legacy. Like you did."

A look of irritation passes across his placid face and in the light of the summer sun outside, he looks like the most grotesque thing in the large, bright room. I take an involuntary step back from the piano.

"I've tried to be kind to you, I know in some ways you are just as fragile as your brother. But I really must insist, Terin. I will happily pay for your music education for the decade or so. I will support you on your tours, your recitals, and your career. But by the time your thirtieth birthday rolls around, I would like you to be here in London, suited and ready for taking over." His voice is no longer covered in honey, and he finishes with a hard look. "Or I will not be contributing a penny to your future and neither with your mother."

I think about my perfectly executed plan of escape that was slowly ripping itself to shreds in front of my eyes. My many months of hours and hours of endless practice and loyally lapping up to Ted Sanders. Of sitting with my mother and discussing musical history and endless tests.

I'd been an idiot to think he would let me go so easily and fly away from his giant cage, without an ultimatum and a promise that one day, I'd be caged again. I feel angry tears cling to the sides of my eyes and for the first time, see the controlling figure that my brother had felt for so many years. In all his devilish glory.

And I stare back at my father with as much defiance as I can muster. There's an energy that's gathering in the air and I feel so much more confident than I was a moment before.

Outside, there is a streak of lightning that pierces across the sky. A rumble of thunder precedes it. My father and I are momentarily interrupted by the flash that fills the room.

The garden darkens, threatening the incoming storm.

-13-

Days turn into weeks after my father's soft threat and nothing further was said about the ultimatum. The same could be said for Jared. I officially turned sixteen last week and had not seen my brother in the flesh for three years. There was always some problem, some excuse in the way for why I couldn't visit. Another bribery gift bought for me to keep my mouth shut and stop complaining, all the while they brag loudly to anyone who would listen that their son is abroad at boarding school and how proud they are.

Other girls my age are at the local shopping centre, roaming around Camden Town. They are off taking daytrips to the seaside with their friends while they watched local boys with interest. They are obsessed with makeup and chart music, following the latest Kardashian exploit. Maybe they even had boyfriends or girlfriends. Georgia has had her fair share of boys in our year interested in her, but she is totally devoted to her studies, having learned that she really likes to write and create worlds. She's found her niche. Her love for something bigger.

"I'm not going crazy," I whisper to myself. The mirror image of me was slightly distorted in the fogged glass from the hot shower I just emerged from. I imagine the image of me nodding in agreement, maybe smiling kindly and offering some words of advice. Not the cool silence from the wide-eyed girl that stares back at me in fear.

"I'm not," I answer my own question. There's a small clock on the far wall of my bathroom, with a couple of cartoon characters that dangle from the hands. As the time moves along, they move along with it – forever jingling out of their own control. Like me and Jared. Totally out of our depth.

I am becoming too emotional again. Unstable. My skin feels too prickly against the soft cotton of the towel, I rub my bare forearms that tingle in the air with the pricks of thousands of small electrical bursts. There's something at the corner of my mind that feels different to my own self again. I've been referring to it as 'my other consciousness' for over a year now. No matter what I do – I can't seem to make it go away or fade. It's there, in the corner of my mind, almost as if watching me and everything I do. When I'm angry; it's angry with me. When I'm sad, it's devastated times one hundred.

Jesus, I really am crazy.

I stare hard at the clock, willing time to stop spiralling out of control. For everything to go back to as it was before.

The clock shudders and the hands stop moving. The characters judder to a halt and there's an acid chemical smell in the air as shards of melted battery liquid slowly cascades from the clock and begins trailing down the wall.

The consciousness at the corner of my mind fades away as quickly as it had arrived, along with my despair. I'm back in the world again.

It was time to face up to it. I was somehow changing into a freak of nature.

Would I be condemned to the cellar too?

"I want to see Jared." I say suddenly on the eleventh of December. It's almost like I'd uttered the worst of all bad words and my father instantly goes stiff behind his morning paper. My mother rolls her eyes and drops the melon slice back into her bowl. She gives me a hard look as if to say; *'why upset us so early in the day?'*

"He's busy with his studies, Terin," she says airily. "You know this. The good doctor keeps him busy, helping with his research."

"Right," I reply and keep my voice steady. "But I'm sure the good doctor and his wife wouldn't mind if Jared has some time off to go *bowling* with us? Anything! Maybe Christmas this year even? He's spent the last three Christmases there alone."

It's almost laughable. Our home's professionally decorated rooms gleam with hundreds of tiny lights and trinkets. There are at least three beautifully embellished trees on the ground floor with further smaller ones that lined the spiral staircases to the two upper levels of the house. The theme this year was '20th Century Glamour' and my mum had spent a lot of money on heavy drapes from the ceiling and the bannister, right down to the shade of gold glitter on the cupcakes at this year's planned dinner. There were only three of us living here and no one enjoys it.

"Will Mr. Sanders be attending this year?" my father cuts across me and glances at my mother.

"He's scoping out a school in Australia," I snap. "Now about my request--"

"Careful, Terin," he waggles his finger and sets down the paper. "You may be sixteen now, but you're still living under my roof. I'll only tolerate so much lip from you, girl."

I smile sweetly after a well-practised inner breath. I'm definitely not going to get the answers I wanted here.

"What time do the celebrations start?" I ask softly. "I want to get to the music store before it closes."

"Whatever for?" Mother sighs "You have a stack of music you haven't even played yet!"

I shrug. "I'm not happy with my audition choice. I need something more daring, modern. Every student tries to go the traditional route and I need to stand out. I bet they hear Bach and Rubenstein every day of the week!"

"You haven't even picked a school yet," my father says and I sense we're on the verge of having another drawn out argument about my choices and the future he's envisioned for me. I excuse myself from the breakfast table and disappear out of the house with my new suede coat as soon as they were busy in their respective studies.

At once, the cold hits my face. It's not usually wintery weather for Christmas in London, but Chelsea is alive with streetlights and richly decorated houses around our own. I walk quickly down our quiet street with perfectly painted large houses and pristinely kept hedges and gardens. I haven't been allowed to visit the Richtersons' house for many weeks, but I head down the fastest shortcut with a spring in my step.

For mid-morning, the sky darkens considerably for the forecast snow shower. I glance at the rose gold watch on my wrist. I draw the heavy coat around myself tighter and hurry on past the post office on the corner and turn into the street with the grey house in the middle of the row of houses.

The tall house is just as foreboding as the last time I'd come. The grey slat roof was missing a couple of tiles and the brickwork needs another lick of paint, or five. Before I can stop myself, I rap my gloved hand against the door. After two minutes of waiting, I do it again.

The door flies open, and a man stands there. He's older than I remember, but Mr. Richterson wears his frayed lab coat proudly over tweed jumper and corduroy trousers. He doesn't recognise me at first and it takes a moment for him to squint and place me.

"Ahh, Terin," he greets. "I did not recognise you with that serious expression on your face."

"Uh... what expression?" I trail off. He'd thrown me momentarily off my game and for stating all the reasons why I should be allowed to visit Jared today. The man smiles.

"The one that looks as if the entire world is on your shoulders. Would you like to come in? This stoop is awfully cold for a teenager to be hovering around on."

"I shouldn't," I hedge, well-aware that my impromptu visit will no doubt get back to my parents in a matter of minutes. "I'm here to see Jared for a second if he's free to come to the door?"

"I am afraid he is out shopping with Gina. Do your parents know you're here? Your father usually calls ahead to say when he wants to come down, so they don't miss one another."

This shocks me. Dad never gave any indication that he ever wanted to *see* Jared, let alone book frequent visits to come and see him. I want to press the doctor further for more details, but now wasn't the time.

"Do you know when they're coming back? I'm kind of in a hurry."

He peers down at me through his lenses, his eyes more withered and tired looking since we'd last met properly. He quiet for a second before he says, "Are you quite well, Terin? You look more troubled since the last time you visited."

"I... feel like I'm falling apart," I whisper, my hand clutches the plastic beads around my neck, suddenly suffocating me. I want to crawl into the squashy dog bed in the hall and just disappear into nothingness. In a world where I was a part of a normal family and superpowers were something in a nerdy comic book. The Doctor looks sympathetic as he leans unsteadily on the doorframe.

"I see, that does sound messy indeed."

I gesture wildly and nod, running a hand through my scalp. "I used to understand what my place was. Now, I feel like I don't know anything anymore."

"Do you want to come in and talk? I have some time now." He steps to the side of the doorway, the heat radiates to the stoop bringing along the smell of hot tea and biscuits. I want more than anything to step inside, sit down and come clean. About everything. From the cellar to the mild abuse to the strange energy that courses through me. I want to know I'm safe and I'm going to be OK. The thought causes my eyes to prickle.

"No," I say firmly. "But thanks."

He nods. "We are here, should you ever need to get that chip off your shoulder. It is not healthy to be feeling like you are falling apart, young miss, especially not at your age."

"I'm getting used to it," I mutter and say my goodbye.

I weep childishly at the end of the street and gaze back at the small, squat house that lays between the terraced seventies housing of London. I take a moment to calm myself and I see Jared's whitened face at the window. I can't tell if it's him or it's an illusion – but I swallow and focus my energy.

The silent streetlamps flicker and buzz quietly as they turn on and off again in unison. The Christmas lights on the surrounding houses do the same and suddenly, it's a sudden quiet chorus of electrical energy that plays only for him. The only sound that perforates it, are the sobs that come from my chest and the sound of the snow hitting the wet road.

It happens as soon as I reach the house, like I suspected it would.

Dad is the first to meet me as I calmly take off my coat and boots and place them on the side. He reaches forwards and grabs me roughly by the arm and shakes me.

"You do not go behind our backs and defy me," he snarls, breath hot in my face. He's still shaking me, and my mother appears somewhere behind him, shrieking something at the top of her voice. I don't hear the words. I'm focusing on my father's eyes and trying to send him every negative emotion he's ever made me feel. Fear, anger, isolation, despair, regret.

"You took away my brother!" I say, my voice shaking. "What did you expect?"

"Loyalty," he growls. "For god's sake girl – it's not *safe*. He will hurt you."

"No one will even bother to explain why!" I push him away with more force than intended and he retreats back a few steps. The anger was building in the pit of my belly and with every year that passes, it gets more difficult to swallow it down and ignore.

"What the hell is wrong with us?" I say quietly and look between the both of them. The captors. The primary agents of some kind of child abuse.

"We're trying to protect you. But you're as goddamn stubborn as that boy!"

"*That boy* is your son! Don't you give a single damn about him?" I'm sobbing again. It explodes outwards like a volcano. I can feel the energy in every molecule that surrounds us in the entry hall. I decide that I'm fed up with trying to reason with these people and beg for their acceptance when I was blind to their neglect for so many years. I leave them in the entrance hall and escape up the stairs on all fours, desperate to get away and ignore the roars of my father demanding my return.

I thunder around my bedroom like an angry bull. My breath comes out in short, gasps. I grow angrier with every exchange. The air around me changes. I can feel the tingle on the surface of my skin as it prickles. There's a charge build up somewhere – as if I've stuck my hand into a socket and I was feeling the current all over my body. My head burns all the way down to my fingertips to my toes and I need to release it. I need to get it out of me before it combusts inside.

My hand forms into a fist and I punch the nearest wall. In a flash, the wallpaper singes and crumbles at the edges as they curl into themselves to recede up the plaster.

My lips curl around my teeth and I breathe heavily. My fist draws back, and it happens again. The punch and the spark. Another punch. There's a burn on the wall that's not quite like a flame like Jared can conjure – but charred tendrils of electrical energy that start from the fist prints on the wall and have splayed outwards to reach the edges of the paintwork. The pattern is almost beautiful, it resembles a tree that's devoid of leaves in the dead of winter. But it stands tall and proud.

I turn to find there's someone standing in the doorway. It only takes a moment from my mother to glance at the charred wall and the strange burns – to me panting heavily in the semi-darkness of the soft fluttering of snow outside.

She knows there's a storm inside me now too.

-14-

I'm filled to the brim with anxiety. I haven't felt so small and vulnerable since Jared lived with us when I was always expecting the next big argument or drama to shake the household.

Strangely there's also an excitement from the consciousness in my brain as well. There's an air of tangible curiosity for a future not under this roof or sitting at the head of CoilerTech. I had never tried to force that weird energy into physical reality before, but I was now furious with everyone and myself for letting things get so out of control. In the moment, I felt like I'd broken out of my chains somehow.

Mum had disappeared pretty quickly that night and for the many sleepless evenings that followed. I wonder if she did really see something or if it were a mistake of my imagination. Still, I hid the burns on the wall with an old art project from school and try to rearrange the bedroom a little, so it wouldn't look so out of place.

It was a couple of days until my parents and I start talking normally again and thankfully, my father seems more than happy to put my outburst behind us and focus on my upcoming end of school exams.

Another isolated Christmas passes. Another New Year. Now my only shining beacon of hope was finishing school and getting out of this damn prison.

Ted Sanders is eating with us this morning out on the patio. He and Dad are talking animatedly about a newspaper article in *The Times* and my mother sits nearby on a sun lounger with her head in a book. She catches sight of me and smiles in greeting. I wave back.

"Why haven't you told anyone what I am yet?" I wonder. My paranoia leans into the idea that she's sitting on the information and waiting for a time she––or they––could exploit me. The consciousness within agrees and that anger flares along with it. I shake my head. It's ridiculous. I'm quickly becoming as paranoid as my brother.

Is this really how he felt all the time when living here? Teetering dangerously between reality and loss of control?

How I wish I could talk to him and explain everything. Did I even see his face at the window that night, or was it just another tick to the evidence that I am losing my mind?

"Terin's all set for her Skype interview next week with Julliard's talent scout." Ted Sanders grins. I wonder how much money he's set to make from the introduction if all goes his way. He rubs his hands together enthusiastically, his chins wobbling with belly laughter. My parents laugh along with him and discuss how exciting and wonderful everything was.

I decide I've never felt so alone in all my life.

It's around nine I decided to go to bed that night. Ted and my father had drunk themselves into a stupor in celebration after an afternoon of wine and cheese and my mother had excused herself hours ago. No one had noticed me slip upstairs and change out of my dress in favour of pyjamas to crawl under the covers and hide from the world in misery.

I'm staring into the corner of the open bathroom when there's a sudden movement at the window by my bed. The glass pane slides up effortlessly, juddering the frame.

"Jesus Christ!" I jump. The toothbrush falls from my mouth, but I catch it easily and wipe the residue of toothpaste off my chin. There's a figure now crouched on my windowsill like a gargoyle and he's grinning at me from across the room. I know the face instantly.

"Little sister," he says quietly. He sounds different since we'd last spoken face to face. It's deeper, wiser somehow––with an edge of permanent loneliness to it. I have to pull my eyes way from him for a few seconds to toss the toothbrush back into the sink and wash my face. When I return, he's still patiently there on the windowsill, having not moved a muscle.

I rush forwards and hug him before I'm too embarrassed to. He's bigger in build, but skinnier than I'd remembered––as if he'd grown into his own lanky body at last. I pull back. I have so many questions that I want to ask him but nothing sounds right for the moment. I cross the room to quietly push the door shut and turn to face him again, weirdly shy.

"They wouldn't know I'm here anyway," Jared says. "He's still on the bottle with the old fat guy. She's passed out in her room."

"Just habit. I haven't exactly been able to freely talk about you in ages," I whisper. "How are you here right now? I haven't been allowed to visit in months!" My eyes fill with tears, and it takes too much strength to hold them back, so I let them run free. My whole face feels tired from the effort in holding in so much emotion for so damn long. He lets me cry without interrupting for a few minutes.

"Managed to escape for the night," he says lightly and grins. He is a completely different Jared to who I'd dreamed about, he stands from the sill and stretches his long arms and legs out in front of him.

"I tried to visit you a few weeks ago. I don't know if they told you?"

"Oh?" he replies. "I didn't know. Doug and Gina keep me busy with research and stuff, but that's over now anyway. I wanted to say goodbye before I left. I'm headed to the US soon. Oregon, to be exact."

I blink stupidly for a few seconds and try to absorb what he's just said to me. "The US as in the United States? Why? Are they taking you on holiday?"

"No. They're staying here. I'm going by myself. My work here is done, Terin, and I want to live my life now," he swallows, his voice dries out like autumn leaves. "Listen to this, it'll blow your mind: I've heard rumours of a group of people who are *like me*. They live on the edge of society, away from everyone else."

"You're leaving your home to go and find a bunch of strangers you've never met before?" My eyebrows furrow together and my heart aches.

"Not strangers," he insists. His cheeks flush slightly with a mixture of excitement and something else. "Outcasts. Rejects. I've played test subject boy for so long, it's time for me to move on and find them."

"Hang on, I don't understand Jare. What do you mean people *like* you?"

He rolls his eyes. "Don't be slow. People with *abilities*. They can do things other people can't and they don't have to hide from each other. How cool would that be?" To accentuate his point, he lifts up a finger and orange and yellow flames rise up from the surface of his skin and a few inches above his hand. Even a few steps away, I can feel the heat.

"Jared stop – you'll hurt yourself!"

He just laughs airily, a sound I'd never really heard from him and dispels the flame. "I can't be hurt from it, I'm immune somehow. That's something I've been working on. Self-control and honing it."

I don't have any response I can give, without sounding incredulous and judgemental, so I nod politely. My head spins with the strangeness of the conversation.

"Can you imagine," he continues, "living somewhere where we don't need to hide who we are? Where people don't give a crap what we're capable of?"

"What do you mean *us*?" I ask hotly, faintly annoyed at the crypticism of everything.

"You can lie to yourself as much as you want, but there's a spark in your eye and a confidence in you that says otherwise," he insists and pulls me to him, so we're stood eye to eye. He is still so much taller, but I have grown too. "I wasn't sure before I arrived, but now I am. I can practically *sense* the gift on you. If we continue to play this game: we're going to end up in an underground base somewhere and will never see the light of day again."

"You don't know anything about me." I try to shrug him off.

"Oh yeah?" He cocks an eyebrow. "I've managed to reach you in your dreams every night this week. Regardless of what you think, I know who you really are."

I freeze. True enough, I'd been imagining weird and random conversations with my brother recently, but it'd been about menial things I don't even remember when I wake up, only that he'd been there.

My mouth drops open. "How the hell do you know that?"

"It's like a form of lucid dreaming of something. I've been working my skill on. it. You've been letting me into your head all these months and years I've been gone," he says softly. "You just don't remember a lot of our meetings. Plus, you're scared about drawing attention to yourself, it seems." He steps over to the artwork and neatly pulls it down off the wall, where the canvas lands heavily on the carpet. He stares at the ridges in the walls and runs his fingers over the damaged crevices and scorch marks while I burn quietly with shame.

"How did you--"

"You told me. In a dream, you told me you did this, and you were worried about it being found out." He continues to gaze at the wall like it was the next Da Vinci, looking strangely proud.

"I–I lost control."

He glances back. "You're gifted like me. That's nothing to be ashamed of."

"What even does this *gifted* mean? What kind of freaks are we?" I whisper. Hot tears cling to my eyelashes. I can feel the consciousness yearn to take over and lose control again. The more emotional and out of control I feel, the more I can sense a similar connection that emanates from Jared's body. He looks and me steadily and nods.

"You feel that don't you?"

"No," I snap.

"You're a liar. Look Ter, I can't waste any more time trying to convince you."

I shrug lightly. All I can think about how my brother is going to disappear on me again and I feel lost and abandoned. I try and wipe my eyes with the sleeve of my bed shirt without looking too pathetic and immature in my oversized pyjamas.

"They didn't torture *you* with the cellar. They didn't give you up to a pair of old doctors for testing. You're their little girl," he says. "I wasn't so lucky because I had the misfortune of being older and manifesting first. But believe me Terin, it'll happen. As soon as they find out, you'll be just as much as a problem for them, and you'll end up in the cellar."

Immediately I think of my mother illuminated by my window, stood in the doorway as she gazed at me. I remember her fearful face, her shaking hands, and the way she melted away into the darkness so quickly; it was as if she was never really there.

As much as I don't want to admit it, my days are probably numbered.

"There's something red on your neck," I say quickly to try and defuse the situation. He quickly brushes my hand away and rubs at his skin. "Is that blood?"

"Don't be stupid," he pushes me off. "When can I expect you to bag your bags then?" He grins at me expectantly with an air of triumph, no doubt from the defeated look on my face.

"You can't just run away and leave everything behind!"

He snorts. "Terin, I'm nineteen years old – it's a bit past running away now, isn't it? No, I'm off to start again somewhere else. I told you. The US. Other people like us. Keep up."

"Come home!" I plead.

"No way," he says. "Do you seriously want me to waltz through the front door of this *hellhole* and sit down with Mum and Dad over dinner and chat about how they don't love me? Don't be dim, Terin."

"I'm sure they thought they were acting for the best, deep down," I say half-heartedly. It's a weak, ancient, worn-out excuse and I know it. Jared stops and his mouth snaps shut. His face is rigid, and his jaw is tight. I knew I'd said the wrong thing before the words leave my mouth, but there's no way to take them back now.

"You're no better than me," he hisses. "Don't pretend I don't see that fear inside you – you're choosing to hide it and conform to what society wants from you. What our parents want from you."

"Jared, let go of my wrist. You're hurting me," I plead. He glances down to my arm and blinks, as if he doesn't even recall grabbing it. He drops it quickly and pulls his cap down further over his face.

"I don't suppose you're going to come with me?" he mutters. He says it quickly, but I can tell from his face that he's disappointed with me, he already knows the answer.

"I want to get out of here too," I reply. "But the right way. If we run away from this city – country or whatever, our problems are just going to follow us. I'm going to get out on my own steam and build my life, so I'll have something to go on to. And I'll happily forget about this place someday. I need to feel grounded and safe."

He half smiles faintly and sighs. He knows that he won't be able to change my mind with words, and I stand my ground. I realise with a plummet in my stomach that our restricted contact in the five years he'd been gone, has made us separate entities now.

"Maybe, I don't want to be grounded anymore," he says softly.

.

-15-

Three days have passed since my last conversation with Jared Coiler.

My mind is still reeling at the concept of my brother upping and moving to a country he's never been before to seek down a group of people he's never met. It is insane. Neither he nor I understand *what* we are, so how would he find these answers with a bunch of strangers? I want to know how he even found out about them if they were so secretive. What kind of powers do they have? What happened to them to make them that way? What happened to *us* to make us this way?

Jared doesn't know me as I am now. This unstable, emotional pit of angst and teenagerhood. He knows the sweet little Terin that had no choice but to obey and hope everything around her would settle and be normal. How could he even turn up and try and tell me who I was now?

But that little part of me hates myself for not taking his hands and just disappearing with him.

And now, it's too late and I am alone. Again.

"I can't believe we're due to sit our GCSE's in a few months," Georgia's voice pulls me out of my mind. I'm back in history with my notes scattered beneath me across the desk and my friend quietly freaking out next to me.

"Elizabethans – it's here." I calmly push the correct paper toward her. "You got the Tudors down?"

"More than the Great Depression. The only thing I liked about that was the Gatsby era."

I grin. "Gatsby is fiction. The Great Depression wasn't."

"Yes," she agrees. "But bead headdresses and flapper dresses are still in. That's the theme of prom for our year, if you haven't heard. The school council decided on the roaring twenties."

"Upon your recommendation?"

She smiles widely. "Maybe. I hope you have something nice picked out, we're going as friend dates."

"Next to you, I'll look like the physical embodiment of *Great Depression*," I mutter. Across the class, I see Alexa, Alice, and Sarah talking animatedly amongst themselves. Catching my gaze, they glance up at me in unison and fall silent, casually looking back down at their workbooks, all conversation ceased.

As much as I enjoy the fact they leave me alone now, it still bothers me. Are they actually *afraid* of what I will do next? If I would send Jared over to their houses with more pointy objects? Do they sense the power in me and cringe as far away as possibl??

"I might just leave the idea of a prom alone," I mutter. "Pretty sure I've got family stuff or something that day."

"Mhmm hmm," she says knowingly. "Here, take my WW2 notes. You're coming with me Terin, like it or not. You can come to my house on Friday to help me look at dresses online."

"I can't dance."

"We're not going to *dance*, per se. We're going to get up there and waves our arms around like we don't give a crap. Because we don't. We're heading to college in September and we're going to enjoy our last freedom as much as we can before uni applications begin.""I only have a year before I'm due to start at Julliard."

"Exactly!" She sighs, throwing more notes at me. "Which is why we have to make the most of what we have before everything changes and you're playing sold out halls in the US." She turns to me on her stool, eyebrows raised in expectation. I sigh and nod slowly, letting an awkward smile fill my face.

"You make a good argument."

"I know. Next Friday at 7. Bring your purse, we're shopping for you too," she says smugly and turns back to continue writing her flashcards.

True to Jared's revelation, I continue to dream about him. The deeper into the dreams I dig, the world becomes more and more twisted. Tonight is a little different however. I find myself just sitting at the kitchen table while I watch him gesture at me angrily. The details are perfect, down to the last kitchen utensil hung on the silver rack by the herb stand. The window above the sink is wide open but no breeze is blowing through like usual for a typical day in London. I watch him move erratically from one side of the kitchen to the other, but the whole scene was silent, save for my own breaths.

I want to be brave and stop telling him to contact me in my sleep if that was *really* what he was trying to do and that I am sorry that he probably feels so betrayed and unloved by everyone. I want to tell him just how much *I* love him and that I would always be his sister no matter what, regardless of who or what we were.

But the words don't come.

When he speaks, I can't hear his sentences. It's like someone had severed the special connection between us and I could only decipher his facial expressions in a pathetic game of charades. Sad, lonely, sarcastic, irritated, furious. My heart thrums inside my dream-like chest. The kitchen around us bursts into several colours of yellow, red and orange. The heat from the walls is intense, but he doesn't seem to notice, he still rages on.

"I can't hear you," I try to mouth, but no sound comes out of me either. He looks more and more frustrated and the colours deepen with their intensity. It eventually becomes so bright that he disappears into the light, my hands fly up to my face as I try to shield my own eyes from the onslaught.

I manage to drag myself into consciousness again, the flickering orange and yellow glow still present from my dream. Groggy and drowsy, I try to reach for the alarm clock on the bedside table. I don't even see what the time is, distracted by the reflection of flames on the plastic see through casing.

Now fully awake, I glance towards the open bedroom door and see flames dance across the ceiling of the hallway outside.

"Fire!" I snarl. Smoke crawls into the bedroom and my eyes burn with effort as I try to keep them open. My body protests with grogginess, however I somehow manage to leap across the room, slam the bedroom door closed against the wall of impenetrable flames spreading from along the landing. Grabbing my water bottle from the bedside table, I pour it over a pile of dirty clothes and stuff them at the bottom of the door in an effort to block out the smoke.

I'd learned about fire prevention at school years ago. I try to quell the panic, breathe easy and think as logically as possible. Are my parents still asleep? Can I reach them?

I had to try something.

Coughing, my throat protests. I try to catch my breath enough to cry out for my parents – anyone. The air scorches my airway and my head pounds with the effort of trying to get oxygen into my lungs.

I lumber forward to the window latch, which has been stiffened with time and months of wet cold English weather – perhaps it was even my weakened state. It's raining hard outside, the cold night-time March air pools in and sucks the heat out of the room. I hitch myself out onto the outer window ledge and try not to slip on the chipping paint with my body shaking all over. There are no streetlights in the distance, the world is dark and motionless – but I've got no time to figure out where everyone is or what time of night it is.

There's a short gap before the next window ledge starts outside my bathroom. I grit my teeth and take a wide leap before my brain catches up with me. I clear the first gap easily. The next one is a little larger. Silently thanking my PE instructor for prodding me towards gymnastics lessons when I was 11, I clear this one too, but the heat from inside the glowing house is starting to make the paint curl and flake off in my hands. My knees glue themselves to the surface where the plastic of the double-glazed windows is melting. I can feel the intense heat scorch my skin. Every window along the back of the building is aflame from here. I can see the double French doors in the distance of my parent's balcony. Inside, hues of colours dance thickly in the room and I see no signs of life from within.

"Mum, Dad!" I open my mouth to scream, but only smoky air rushes in to fill the emptiness. I'm having a hard time trying not to splutter and lose my grip on the sill.

There's a sickening crack that turns my stomach. The window ledge I'm crouching on, splits down the middle as easily as a hot knife through butter. My bleeding fingers scrabble for a new hold, but I'm falling below faster than I can react. My back explodes in pain, the little precious air I have is forced out of my lungs at the impact.

I lie on the floor of the ruined conservatory – dazed for a second. Above, the smashed glass roof rains down on me along with the actual rain which only provides a little cooling relief before the intense scorching of the inferno around me returns, determined to take me in its fiery grasp once and for all.

The room once housed the old piano my mother used to practice on before she went pro. It is an old thing, barely worth the wood it was built from as she used to say, the keys were still sound enough to play well. I would curl up on the wicker loveseat by her potted palms in the corner and watch her play during my summers off school, the doors wide open so that the music would spill into the garden and beyond. It's a weird memory to come back to me at such a time, perhaps I am so close to death I'm delusional.

Would I ever hear my mother play again?

Another sickening crunch. I barely roll out of way in time as the old balcony begins to crumble away from the brickwork above and debris smashes into what's left of the conservatory. My body screams in pain, somehow I manage to scramble to my feet and head through to the main room which peels off in separate directions to Mum's and Dad's respective living rooms. The main archway into the hallway is bending dangerously from the weight of the ceiling above.

"Mum.... Dad!" I try to scream again. I see my beautiful piano in the far end of the second lounge which is half crushed under the weight of the music shelves. My mother's concert paintings are tearing themselves from the walls and becoming black with soot. Where the hell are they? Had they already managed to escape?

Thinking about the worst-case scenario was not an option. I *have* to be as adult and logical as possible or I will definitely die here today.

My heart hammers painfully, but I ignore the stabbing sensation in my chest and head for the front door. As I approach the entrance hall, there's an almighty crash. I turn the corner to see that the imported chandelier from Paris sits on itself on the scorched carpet. Some of the plaster on the ceiling has fallen with it, partially blocked the front door. I try to tug the wood inwards, but the huge brass arms are too heavy to move out of the way. I scream in anguish and frustration. It's too late to go back the way I entered. I hear some of the upstairs rooms begin to creak with the immense heat of the fireball above.

My proverbial window of escape is getting thinner which each passing minute.

The windows and doors are a no go, and the ceilings didn't look as if they are going to hold for much longer. My lungs strain against my chest and gasp for air. I notice an old scarf over by the far side wall which hasn't quite fully caught aflame yet, so I snatch it up to waft the embers away, quickly tying it around my face. There's nothing I can use for my eyes that burned with the effort of straining against the smoke, but it will have to do for now.

Desperate, I head for the corridor that lines the kitchen and fling open the forbidden hardwood door to the side of the room. The stairs are dark, creaking with age on every step as I fly down them without much regard for the safety handrail. I can't help but habitually pause at the bottom of the steps as the intimidating steel of the cellar door stares back coolly at me.

The childhood fear grips me instantly. I hadn't even ventured down here since Jared had left years ago. It's ridiculous to still feel so *terrified*.

I reach forward and pull it open, wincing at the metallic scrape, that was always paired with my brother's angry screams during my childhood. If I was lucky, the fortified structure would hopefully hold up against the house's destruction.

Jesus, I hope my parents had managed to find a way out.

Surely they weren't... no... they couldn't be.

I clench my teeth together and summon whatever tired courage I have left. I know what I should do, but my heart wants to pull me upstairs to find them. I quickly glance up at the glowing house at the top of the stairs above me, guilt pooling in my stomach and I disappear beneath the door, which swings shut behind me with a final loud clang.

-16-

As the door swings closed, the fire, the whoosh, the groaning of wounded wood and struggling plaster completely disappears. There's no sound but the rising panic from my throat and thud of a tired heart in my chest. Am I alive or dead? Am I about to find my Mum and Dad on another plane of reality somewhere?

Thoughts buzz around loudly like a swarm in my brain. Everything hurts. Everything is pain. I can barely keep upright on my own feet, swaying from side to side, unconsciously clinging onto the door like it was going to save me. Crap, this cellar. Why did I have to come in *here*?

"Mum? Dad?" I try into the silence; a strangers' weak groan comes out of my own mouth. Even *if* they are down here by some miracle, there's no way they'd understand me. Am I burned beyond recognition?

The creeping, silent darkness sets in quickly. I succumb to it, passing out on the hard cold floor and letting it take me into a dreamless sleep. I don't know how long I'm actually unconscious for. I wake up again in the same total blackness.

There's no windows or source of natural light so it's difficult to tell what time of day it is or how much time has gone by. I assume the cellar must have some degree of sound proofing to it as I hear nothing from the burning inferno upstairs or if anyone is stumbling through the wreckage, calling my name. Would I even hear? My ears are ringing with the sounds of never ending destruction.

Oh my god – the fire.

I want to cry but there's no possible moisture left in my body that wasn't already used. I'm stiffened on the ground. Broken and burned, wondering if the dark was all that was waiting for me in the afterlife. It takes some minutes to let the memories slowly come back to me, which causes me to dry heave and cough onto the dusty floor. I wonder if the cellar has a built-in oxygen filtration or a generator system somewhere. Jared would have suffocated all those years ago considering the amount of time he spent down here if not, I suppose. I just hope it isn't pooling air from inside of the house, or else I have no chance of surviving.

I sniff, wincing at the rush of air through ruined tissue inside my nose. Aside from the smoky smell from my clothes, I can't smell anything else – maybe I am unable to. Even a steady breath sears my nose, causing me to need to open my mouth and cry out wordlessly.

"Ok, move. Get up," I try to say through cracked lips too sore to move properly. My voice sounds like hard leaves crushed underfoot in Autumn. It only makes me more emotional to hear myself so beaten and broken. More than anything I want my parents to hold me and tell me everything was going to be OK, regardless of our differences and views and our history. They are still my mum and dad. Deep down, I had to love them.

God – where are they?

I must have fallen back into unconsciousness again at some point. When I wake a second time, I feel a little more with it. My eyes adjust to the darkness a lot easier this time.

I notice a pull cord to the upper right-hand side of the door, and it takes a good few tries to try and move my exhausted body the way I want to. Finally with gritted teeth, I'm able to creep my fingers up the cool reinforced walls to tug on the light cord until it catches.

The room's suddenly bathed in a half dim glow and I burst into dry sobs. The room itself is decent size, I could see my brother's spare bed sheets and old teddy bears laying in the corner of the annexe. How can I reach him to let him know what's happened? Would he even care? Would he help me find our parents and figure out what to do next?

The cellar is a cross between an old wine store and a converted bunker; it's nowhere near as rusted as dilapidated as I imagined. Old metal racks stand solitary against the far wall, empty of any kegs or bottles they were once trusted to hold so now they stand silently, with some old books and food tins. The room itself was cased within a metal shell but didn't look as if it would withstand any kind of direct bombing, regardless of how good it appeared. All in all I was currently alive and not burned to a crisp yet, so it did the job well in my eyes.

The room is not as intricately decorated as the rest of the house was. Besides old pieces of furniture and the futon in the corner, there's a small incline in the alcove which I assume is where the toilet and sink are. Whether the plumbing still worked or not, I would soon find out.

There's no entertainment or fun activities bar a couple of old superhero comics that are yellowed from time and a pre-war HAM radio that sits under a cover of dust. We'd covered them briefly during a history lesson once.

With a strong swell of overwhelming despair, I conclude that my parents are obviously not down here either.

"Ok," I croak after a few minutes. It takes an immense effort to scrape myself together to stand shakily, but I manage to use a metal rack of old survival guides to hoist myself up and stay on my feet for more than a few seconds. I limp cautiously over to the incline and over to the sink and mirror, where thankfully, the taps turn on effortlessly and cool, fresh water spills out.

I cup my hands together and I slurp greedily from them. Mouthfuls of mouthfuls of water run down my scorched throat and cool down the ache in my belly until I can't physically take any more liquid. The last few mouthfuls I end up regurgitating back into the drain. More handfuls are splashed on my face to cool the burning of my eyes. Every inch of skin across my hands and arms is black and red with soot, cuts, and burns.

Once I take a few shaky breaths and allow the water to cool me down, I glance down to assess the damage. Nothing looks or feels broken. One of my shins is puffier than the other and I was peppered in shards of glass, plaster, and wood. My clothes are singed and ripped to pieces, barely hanging onto me. I still have the scarf wrapped around my neck from the makeshift facemask though. so I peer around the room for a new change of clothes and find nothing.

I'm want to sit and cry on the floor again from frustration. It takes a few moments for this to pass as I breathe deeply and swallow the panic attack that threatens to consume me.

"OK," I repeat to myself. It's the only word I can really manage and hearing the sound of my own voice helps, knowing I'm still alive. "OK."

The first step is to try and get myself as cleaned up as possible before infection had the chance to set in. I wonder if there was a medical kid down here and try to scour the shelves for supplies. The kit itself is easy to find, it's mostly empty except for a couple of bandages, plasters and ironically, a fire blanket. I grab everything I possibly could – including some Vaseline and long expired paracetamol from the shelves and quickly went to work.

I am pretty sure it was against the rules to pull sharp objects out of the body once they went in until I could get to a hospital – but there is no way I can rest or lie down and wait for help until then. *And* that was assuming someone would actually find me.

I have no choice to pull out the small shards of glass from my skin with some old eyebrow tweezers behind the mirror, almost passing out after the first one was free from my forearm. I lean against the sink as the cellar spins around me, just as out of control as I feel and wait for death or sickness to take me – whichever one wanted me first, I don't care. As soon as I come to, I splash a capful of expired peppermint mouthwash to disinfect the wound and scream as the burning sensation overcomes me.

My back still sears with pain, I can only see half of each side of my shoulders and waist turning each way in the mirror. I'd have to do the best I could for a while.

After the initial shard, I remove the rest – each one easier and easier to take out. I still wince and cry out, but it's mostly partly from exhaustion and sorrow at this point. There was a very real realisation settling in that I have no idea what I was going to do next.

I'm spent, sat against the toilet after heaving unsuccessfully a few times however many hours later. It's a slow, painful, and gruelling process but eventually the wounds are as treated and dressed as I could get them. The more serious burns are covered with the Vaseline and bandages. I feel my stomach gurgle with hunger. The rest of my body doesn't respond to the message, barely able to crawl around on my hands and knees, let alone daydream about a meal.

The fire blanket will have to do as a covering I decide, pulling it around me tightly. It's a good fit for a small duvet and mobile enough to contain at least *some* modesty. It would have to do until I can figure something else out.

I finally get the energy to stumble to my feet again and manage as far as the futon in the corner, before I topple down and cover myself with the material. It's not freezing, but I feel shivery and sick. At some point, I try to close my eyes again and succumb to the darkness. Pass the time. Regain some energy.

When I wake, I'm disappointed. As much as he was so *sure* he could step into my dream world, I tried to unsuccessfully to contact my brother. There's no real cool paranormal response or connection that I can latch onto. He must have been messing with me.

I remember my last dream about him – the fire and the anger than emanated from him. The absolute fury that overwhelmed me. My eyes fly open to meet with the half light of the cellar. I lie there, unmoving for a while.

It takes some effort, but I eventually turn my body to quietly peer around the room properly for the first time and try to imagine the many hours my brother had spent down here, alone. I wasn't sure what I had envisioned this place to be like but it was a far cry from the cold, smelly, wet, cobwebbed environment I was sure he suffered in.

By the bed, I notice that there are claw marks – no, *nail* marks. Years of indented scratches that run up the metal walls, the steel door, and the concrete ground. Hours of Jared screaming by himself, totally isolated. Abandoned in this silent, desolate space. There are pen drawings too. Most are immature little doodles, others are large well detailed murals that show Jared's growth as he spent more and more time down here over the years.

The more I notice, the more sketches I see that are engraved and drawn on the walls all around the cellar. The light's dim enough that I hadn't noticed them during my initial observation. They run around the backs of the furniture and equipment racks that line the far walls. It must have taken him hours upon hours to decorate.

Above the bed, there's a drawing on the wall that's bigger, more refined than all the other sketches. There's a small figure drawn at the side – a young boy with a sad face, who's curled up in the corner. Behind him, an older figure of a young man with his stick hand on the boy's shoulder. He has a thin line for a mouth, but there's two intricately detailed wings made of flames that from his shoulder blades and stretch across the wall.

I feel embarrassed just looking at it – like I was deliberately stumbling over the most private parts of himself without him knowing. Every line in the room is coloured with a rusty hue that flakes easily when I try to trace the outline with my fingers. I don't see any signs of pens, pencils, or any drawing paper. The penny takes a minute to drop.

"Ugh." My fingers retract and I rub them on the blanket in disgust. There's an overwhelming feeling that it's entirely possible he drew this mural and every other drawing, in his own blood.

My stomach lurches and I vomit everywhere. It's painful because of my scorched throat and I half vomit, half cry out as I grab the futon for support, heaving onto the floor, again and again. My stomach screams with the effort and for the thousandth time, I'm crying and feeling sorry for myself. Not only that, I'm feeling sorry for Jared.

I feel dirty in this room and the lack of windows only makes it worse. I feel trapped, as if *I* am the one who was thrown into the cellar and locked away with only my own pain for comfort. If I was the older one and manifested first, would this have been my fate too? It was my very worst nightmare come to light.

I curl up on the dirty futon and hug my knees to hide from the smell of my sick. I was just as lost as Jared had been all those years and no one was coming to save me either.

-17-

I scour the few scattered tins of food on the metal racks, trying to soothe my belly by rubbing it gently. Despite the years they'd been down here, the aluminium tins look in good enough shape. The hunger is almost unbearable, taking over every other logical thought in my brain. Despite's Mum's cooking, I'd have happily lapped down any vegetable soup or kale smoothie she put down on the table now. As soon as I think about her, the burn in my throat and every other part of my aching body flares up in pain. I should have tried harder. I should have tried to--

No, I wouldn't have made any difference. My stomach groans with the combined pain and guilt and I feel a wave of nausea wash over me. I feel pathetic.

The only tins left on the shelves contain fruits, vegetables, nuts, and some salted crackers. The labels are worn, obviously they hadn't been restocked in a while. I try to remember when our family moved into the house and hope these items hadn't been left behind from the previous tenants.

Picking up a can of salted peanuts, I try to hunt around the shelves for a tin opener or something. Once I realise there's literally nothing of any use, my eyes sting with the effort of keeping my emotion within – I am pretty sure that being a big baby wasn't going to get me anywhere. Now isn't the time to curl up and feel useless. I need to reserve moisture.

Seeing something shiny that sticks out under the futon, I pull the sheets and futon away from the wall to discover a what looks like a pocket knife or hunting tool partially hidden under an old tshirt of Jared's and clumps of hair and dust.

It helps the clothing situation, I suppose. Shaking off the motes and cobwebs from the hoodie, I slip it over my body and tie the fire blanket securely in a haphazard knot around my waist. The knife is rusted beyond belief, the blade sticking out was coated in the same flaked residue on the wall.

"This is how you did it, Jare," I croak.

Washing off the tool as best I could in the clean water and using a little of the ancient bottle of mouthwash to try and kill off any old bacteria, I carry it back to the futon and work to slip the serrated edge of the blade into the lid.

It's hard going, taking me a number of minutes to shove the blade into the aluminium. The overwhelming smell of salt wafts upwards to signify I am getting closer to reaching my goal. Spurred on by the breakthrough, I greedily work the knife faster and push it into the edges of the lid to guide it around to the opposite edge of the can as my stomach gurgles loudly in anticipation.

The blade suddenly slips and buries itself into my left palm, which takes a good few seconds to register before pain screams out of the surface. I yell loudly, dropping everything onto the bed. I stupidly remove the knife from the skin immediately before again, remembering the basic rule of first aid. I stop and laugh stupidly – who the hell would come to my aid now anyway? I could bleed to death down here and no one would know for a while.

Luckily––as I discover after a soak in the sink––the wound isn't too deep and the blood is darker than it usually is on television dramas, it only oozes from the skin rather than spurts – so it is likely nowhere near an arterial bleed. I've used most of the meagre medical supplies on the rest of my body, so I'm forced to cut off a small square from the fire blanket skirt and make use of a roll of black tape to secure it around my left palm.

Catching sight of myself in the bathroom mirror, I can barely recognise the beaten and bruised person that stares back at me. I resemble some kind of war victim, one who doesn't know the first thing about first aid and emergency care. Of all the things to learn growing up, basic survival skills would have been so much more useful over piano any day.

"It'll have to do," I croak, gritting my teeth to turn away in disgust.

I've totally lost track of time in the cellar. I wonder if it was safe to try and open the door – or if the movement would cause the house to totally collapse down on me and block the entrance. I can feel the slow, dark tendrils of cabin fever creep along my spine and shoulders – I don't want to die down here alone, with Jared's ghostly blood murals.

I opt to try to escape when I wake up from another long sleep, fuelled by the partially open can of peanuts that I pour needily into the mouth. The salt burns the sides of my sore throat – but I decide that I don't care and push through the pain, followed by a long drink of cool water and a chance to relieve myself, thanking whoever had the initiative to ensure the converted bunker still retained proper plumbing.

Awake and as refreshed as I was going to be, I move across the room to approach the door. My heart's beating with nerves; I'm really unsure what's going to be waiting for me on the other side.

I grab the handles with both hands, suppressing a wince at the pain from my palm but push the feeling downwards inside. I try to use all my strength on the door at once, but it doesn't budge. Another firm tug and the barrier stays put. A third and a fourth time – also using as much additional leg power as I can – it still doesn't move.

"No!" I yell and punch the metal. I'm panting, beads of sweat that run down my skin, irritating the many cuts, abrasions, and burns – putting me in more of a bad mood.

In my head, the consciousness is beginning to stir again – the first time in what feels like *days*. It's watching me closely and assessing the situation. I think about Jared trying to explain to me how special we are and as much as I want to deny his craziness, it was apparent we both possessed some kind of... *ability*. I wonder if that is what this consciousness was?

"Help me out," I say quietly. Nothing of course replies and I feel stupid. I'm feeling angrier and upset with each passing minute. I lash out, again and again at the stupid cellar entrance. Each contact feels easier and easier, I barely feel the bite of the metal grinding against my knuckles.

It's stupid – but I feel as if I can see the door welting slightly with each punch. No. That's impossible! The entire thing had been reinforced to withstand wars and bombs – it must be a placebo effect from letting out my anger on the thing.

At the height of my rage, I seize the handle again with both hands and try with all of my might to pull it towards me. It whines and scrapes against the brick work – but relents and eventually moves with me. Not expecting this, I fly from the handle and collapse onto the concrete floor. A burst of fresh smoke fills the air as soon as the seal is penetrated. I cough and splutter, waiting for it to pass.

The air is colder than I remember. It bursts down the concrete steps into the cellar and freezes me in seconds. There's no natural light at the top of the doorway into the house. The entrance is filled with charred wood and flakes of plaster that spill down to where I'm laying.

Drawing the hoodie and the fire blanket closer around me, I try to squint and peer into the inky darkness above. The smell of air is unexpectantly fresh – despite the scent of burnt embers. I realise it's the smell of the outside air that pools around me.

I swallow and begin to scramble up the debris as safely as I can – all residual anger washes away, the consciousness retreats to the back of my mind where I don't need it right now.

I'm forced to dig my way upwards with just my fingernails. I close my eyes to avoid the soot and falling materials which peppers my head and covers my irritated skin in more crap. As soon as I feel my hands meet no more resistance, I try to push myself upwards and free from debris. It's a painfully slow dance of scrabbling and pushing, stopping only to quickly pull splinters from under my nails and fingertips.

"Yes!" I say. An air pocket finally appears. Desperation for freedom gives me the extra boost to keep pushing. When I reach the top, I expect to see the doorway to the kitchen and the rest of the house. I can see the dim orange glow of the London night-time sky above. It confuses me momentarily for a second.

It takes one last hard push before I peer above the last steps, covered with charred wood, to see the rest of the neighbourhood sit quietly around me.

The house is completely gone. It's now a huge square of blackened debris spanning across the entire property to the tall bushes and entrance to the lake in the distance. The nearest houses aren't situated close enough for the fire to have spread to easily, but they sit in twilight and the only lights for miles, are the streetlamps that glow mournfully by the road against the jet black sky.

I'm not sure what I had expected, but the image of everything I'd grown up with completely destroyed and burned away was difficult. I barely feel the cold chill of the late-night air anymore. It's replaced with utter despair and sorrow for my home and everything in it. There's no crying parents in the distance or search party in full force. Someone had erected a taped off perimeter over by the road and around the property lines. Huge shadows of construction equipment have been left, having already started to clean up the mess.

My stomach lurches as I try to swallow down the peanuts that threaten to make their way back out. There wasn't any sense in losing energy now – especially when I had no goddamn idea what the *hell* was going to happen next.

Should I go to CoilerTech and ask for help? The doorman had seemed nice enough years ago, he would recognise me and let me in if he was working the night shift––maybe would even offer me a glass of water and help me figure out what to do next.

The Richterson's seemed nice enough. But I didn't want to be locked up like Jared.

I could go to Georgia's, I supposed. She lives closer to the wharf than I do – but it would definitely raise issues with her parents and neighbours if I turned up on the doorsteps, blackened with soot and wounded beyond recognition. Her house is in an upper-class gated community – there was no way I would be able to get through easily without the police called.

I stop, my heart in my mouth. I hadn't even considered the police. There would be a public investigation, news reports, detectives. Strangers combing every inch of the property to look for clues. I eye the construction equipment carefully. If they had started to move debris aside, maybe it'd already been concluded and was no longer a crime scene? I must have been down there for days rather than hours.

How could I even begin to explain what'd happened? The very real fact that I was worried *I'd* set the fire by accident in my dream?

It made sense. Jared could barely control himself at my age and growing up. Who knew what I was capable of? I'd been too emotional at seeing him in my dream and somehow, projected that energy outwards?

The thought makes me panic. Air doesn't seem to be travelling down my lungs as it should do. I'm feeling strangled, restrained by my own guilt and realisation that it might have been me, that'd killed my own parents.

"Need... to go," I choke. The police would find out about me sooner or later. I head in the direction of the construction vehicles to see if there's any PPE clothing lying around to borrow.

On reaching the digger in the far boundary near where my Dad's Mercedes once sat in the garage, I discover there's a small temporary hut that's been built around the other side. It's a tiny little structure that doesn't hold any food or drinking facilities. After kicking in the door quickly, I find a couple of protein bars leftover from someone's lunch and consume them quickly, dropping the wrappers back onto the table.

My heart leaps with joy, peering behind the door to find several sets of high vis gear. The trousers are way too big for me, the rainproof jacket swamps me in puffy material – but I'm so much warmer and a whole lot less inconspicuous than wandering the streets with a thick fire blanket for a skirt.

I'm about to turn and leave when I see there's a few slips of paper to the side of an old radio. One of which is a blueprint of my parent's estate, excluding the cellar/converted bunker – which was interesting – they hadn't yet reached or discovered my hiding place under the debris. I could have seriously died before they reached me.

But I am safe, and warmer now.

The other papers are permits to work on the property and a couple of police notes about the ongoing investigation. The very last slip of paper is some kind of information poster. I see my own face gaze back up at me. It's last year's school photo in which I'm wearing my blazer with a moody expression. The rough mock up displays my name in bold lettering and reads: MISSING. Underneath, two posters with my parent's faces read the same information.

This was it. It's definitive. They hadn't miraculously escaped to safety either.

The cool, wintery air leaves me as I struggle to breathe again. I continue to stare down at the mock-up in total shock. My fingers are shaking along with my knees. I can't seem to think properly.

Grabbing the paper from the table and balling it into my pocket, I race from the hut. Anywhere would be better than here. I need to get away. Think.

I decide to leave the neighbourhood by hurrying around the back of property rather than head down the silent pavement to the busier roads. I don't bother to glance back at the scorched husk that was once my life.

A childhood that'd officially ended.

-18-

I'm running through a small public park, trying to conceal the sound of sobs that escape from my chest. My mind whirs at a mile a minute. I'm missing. My parents and I are *missing*.

I hated them for everything they did to my brother including the awkwardness of their pushy love for me but they were still my *parents*. I wouldn't have wished *any* death on them, let alone burning to cinders in their own *home*.

And what about school? Have they announced to my year about my disappearance? Is Georgia sat at home wondering what had happened to our prom dress date? And even Sarah, Alexa, and Alice – were they feeling guilty for making my life a living hell all these years, unable to rectify it?

I lurch to my knees and vomit underneath a children's slide. The park is dark and empty, only bathed by a couple of streetlights. It is still either very late at night or very early in the morning, so I am incredibly lucky that there were very few people on the streets. The absence of merry singing and cheering from nearby pubs and clubs, tells me that it's most likely in the middle of the week and not a Friday or Saturday.

I try to rack my brain and remember what day the fire was. All I know is that I have never vomited so much in my life as I have in the past few days or so.

I need to keep going. Gather my thoughts somewhere. Get my story and my nerves straightened out before I approach the police with the story.

There is only one place nearby that I could easily reach without heading into the brighter areas of the city. It was a long shot, but I was sure I'd get help there. I had to.

The walk is easy enough – it wasn't a million miles away from the quietened and safe streets of my neighbourhood. I'd still need to be careful of late walkers or early morning commuters, listening to the news on the radio about the crazy sixteen-year-old arsonist who possibly killed her parents.

I wince involuntarily. It was all an awful nightmare, it had to be. This could not be real.

Coming to a low brick wall, I ignore the scream of my burns and injuries, climbing over to stand in the garden, ears straining for sounds. No dogs barking nearby at the intruder in the area, no police helicopter scouring overhead. The house looms above, obnoxiously modern in build, hosteing a private jacuzzi built into the decking under a finely constructed gazebo. I try the back doors which are predictably locked. There are no signs of life inside as I peer through the slats of the blinds, no lights shine within.

"Fine," I whisper. I know there's an electronic panel inside, situated just by the front door which controls the security of this house. It's another state-of-the-art invention, designed people who didn't want to bother checking all the doors and windows were locked with their own hands, so it did it automatically.

Trying desperately to calm the panic, I close my eyes and allow myself to reach out. It takes a few tries to stop myself biting my lip from sobbing pathetically. The energy – my energy, wants to be used. Eventually, I feel the pull of the electric panel that responds to my gentle mental stimulation. Of course, I have no idea what I'm doing or whether I'm imagining it all. I'm prodding around with my mind and stabbing randomly with no real intention. Still, a few minutes later, the back doors click quietly in time with my relief.

I waste no time seizing the handle and slipping through the blinds which sway back into me. The warmth of the inside makes me want to itch.

Suddenly, I'm momentarily blinded from the overhead lights that switch on as soon as I take two steps into the room.

Ted Sanders stands in nothing more than comically oversized silk boxer shorts, as he gazes at me from the doorway. He looks around quizzically, more furious than I could imagine and sees the open door I'd entered through. He's holding a bat in his hand that he's retrieved in panic.

"What the hell are you doing here?" he demands. He's shaking slightly – either from the cold, or fear, I don't know. I'm still covered in dried blood and soot, swamped in oversized high vis clothes that I keep pulling back up over my hips. I'm also barefoot on his expensive carpet.

"I... don't have a lot of time, Mr. Sanders," I say weakly. I can feel myself weary and tired. I'm about to faint but I try with all my might, to steady myself on the door frame and not let him see how weak I am. He's looking at me like a ghost and it's unnerving me.

"I need help," I suggest when he says nothing.

"And you think you can hide out here, is that it?" he demands.

"I… don't know what happened. My… house was on fire, and I couldn't escape or reach anyone. Have you heard from my parents?" I glance behind me worriedly, the street is still quiet however I was in front of the window bathed right under the lights. "Can we sit… down, somewhere?"

He nods stiffly, a strange expression on his face and gestures to the dining room table in the corner, wincing as he watches me track mud and wet grass over the cream carpet.

"Sit there," he instructs turning to disappear into one of the other rooms of the house. I have only been here once or twice; it's smaller than I originally envisioned, holding only one bedroom and bathroom. His musical producing trophies and accolades litter the walls and the neatly polished cabinets. Every piece of furniture was clean of any dust or dirt – aside from me darkening his abode.

I hear a murmur from the next room, I frown, wondering if he ever mentioned if he was married or seeing anyone. I close my eyes to try to tune into what he's saying, when I realise that he's actually speaking quietly on the phone.

It takes me less than a few steps to cross the room and burst into the kitchen, where he's leaning against the back door, mobile in hand. In panic, my hand smacks it across the room where it clatters loudly into the sink, breaking into several pieces.

"No!" I moan. "No police – please Mr. Sanders – I just need some time to figure out what the *hell* is happening."

"Do you understand what you've done?" he spits incredulously. "The police are looking for you! I always worried that you'd turn out just like your brother – and well. Here I am proved correct." His moustache bristles with anger and he turns to try and collect the smashed phone.

"How do you know about him?" I gape.

"Your parents aren't the only well-connected people in London," he bristles. Spit lines his facial hair. "We run in the same circles and, oh, I know just exactly what he and the Richtersons have been trying to do. The whole scientific community Is talking about it for Christ's sake."

I shake my head and try to lower my voice. Now was not the time to get into an argument about Jared.

"I came here because I thought you could help me as a friend of my father's."

"Sod your father!" Ted shouts. "He was a loose business connection – nothing more. You've just lost me a huge amount of money and investment. No one's going to want to teach a teenage pyromaniac who's murdered her own parents!" He runs his hand through the few loose hairs on his head, starting to pace back and forth, eyes crazy and frothing at the mouth. He's muttering something to himself that I can't figure out.

"Why would they even assume it *was* me!" I argue.

"Because I jolly well told them it was!" Ted snarls. "It doesn't take a *rocket scientist* to figure out that the apple doesn't fall far from its rotten sibling! When the police came calling, of course I pointed you out!"

"I don't understand––"

"Of course you wouldn't – you naïve little guttersnipe – you were *supposed* to make me thousands! You were supposed to be my ticket right back into the arms of so many contacts and opportunities your tiny little spoilt head couldn't even *dream* of."

I begin to back away from the kitchen, my back following the lines of the hallway and into the lounge. Ted becomes more and more erratic by the minute as he continues ranting. He throws the broken phone back into the sink.

"They're going to think I'm an accomplice..." he continues. "They'll investigate me. HMRC will look at my tax returns... they'll figure out the Cayman accounts...." He stops and glances at me, There's a wild, cold look in his eyes.

"Calm down," I say weakly. Fury crosses his face in a scowl. His hands feel for the bat leaning against the door.

"You've ruined this!" he whines, shaking his head. His chin wobbles in anger. "I can't afford another scandal."

"We can work it out. I'll go somewhere else. Maybe continue with those contacts in the US and––"

"It's over!" he roars, upturning a small table holding a cordless telephone and a stone statue. Whether unconsciously or not, he's coming towards me, hands flailing erratically with the weapon. "I took a chance on you. You're Helen's daughter after all! Now, you've ruined me," he finishes, spittle marking the bottom of his face. Never could I have imagined old lecherous Ted Sanders to have an anger problem like this.

Suddenly, I can barely feel my injuries, only the cold hand of fear clawing at my chest. I watch him slowly rub his temples with the fee hand, turning back to me with a mournful sigh.

He launches himself towards me – bat high –pushing me against the glass table. My already raw back explodes into pain as yet more glass shards penetrate the healing flesh. I'm crying uncontrollably by this point, a heap on the blood-speckled floor. There's a heavy blow on my shoulder marked by a crack of bone and Ted retracts the bat above for another clean chance at my head. As it flies towards my face with surprising dexterity from a middle-aged man, I roll out of the way and bring my bare foot up to connect with his breast bone. He exhales sharply with a moan and collides with the side of the doorframe.

The weapon is lost somewhere behind him. He manages to yank on my skinny ankle and drags me across the broken glass towards him. There's a scuffle. Pure desperation and anger makes him stronger than me. I yell and shriek in his grasp – his hands find their way around my neck and he's squeezing with all his might.

"They should have sent you away with your freak of a brother," he cries.

I choke. Bright spots are dancing in front of my eyes. My lungs – already broken and sore from smoke inhalation – are about ready to pack up and give in.

Randomly, I envision Jared's face the new bedroom of his surrogate guardians. He's looking at me, into my soul somehow. I remember something he once said very clearly and now, it rings through my mind.

I need to look after myself. Get out when the opportunity arises. I reach out to connect with the other consciousness in my mind. I push back the mental flood gate that I'd held at bay for so long. I let it flow through me. I can feel my blood boil from the centre of my chest, to the tips of my fingers and toes, until I *was* the unstoppable current of raw power.

There is a loud roar, a sizzle, the smell of burning flesh. Before me, sprawled on the floor Ted Sanders lays dead. He's motionless, burned almost beyond recognition. Around the room, various electrical appliances and outlets have sizzled and blown their circuits. The lights have gone out. A sickening silence is only disturbed by my panting on the floor.

There's no time to have another panic attack. I need to act quickly before my brain catches up to what I've just done. There's no sense in leaving further DNA in this place if possible. Using strength, I don't even know I had, I manage to drag his charred corpse into the kitchen and close the door behind him.

My newfound survival mode kicks in and I try to make a note of what I would need. Seeking out a spare backpack in the hallway, I pack several pairs of socks and clothing into it along with some snacks and bottles of water from the newly stocked fridge. My borrowed clothing is well too noticeable, so I elect to steal a pair of black jeans from a pile of clean washing along with a long-sleeved t-shirt – trying not to cringe about how much I smell like that disgusting old man.

My back screams and aches when the material pushes against the skin. There is no time to sit and nurse my wounds this time and get the shards of glass out. I bite my lip to stop myself from crying out and head around the house to try and cover up my tracks as much as possible.

The high vis jacket was incredibly warm, but I would be identified too easily. Ted had some light jackets hanging up by the front door, so I grab a thin sports coat and pull a fleece over my head to wear under it. A grey beanie and a pair of thick leather gloves sit atop the welcome dresser. I grab those too.

I think about taking his car keys and making off with his Lexus, but the police would easily put out an APB and I'd be caught on the roads in seconds – I'd seen the television criminal chase shows. Not to mention I had never driven more than up and down the driveway in my Mum's Mini.

Making up my mind to take my chances on foot, I head carefully out of the back door and try to strain my ears for the sounds of any curious neighbours. All I can hear is the heart hammering in my chest, below the stolen clothing of the late Ted Sanders.

There's no power in any of the surrounding streetlamps or traffic lights, let alone the houses. I wonder if I managed to take out the whole street with my performance. Either way, it's the best chance I would get and if I wanted to leave now, there would be no going back. No redos and certainly no police would want to listen to me now. Not after I'd just murdered a man, self-defence or not. I feel numb, nothingness.

For the second time that evening, I take off with a brisk run into the darkened neighbourhood with the knowledge that this time, I really *am* escaping for my life and my freedom.

-19-

I 'm a murderer.

I killed someone.

Hysteria sweeps up through my abdomen as I swing to and fro in time with the train. The bathroom cabin swims around me through my tears. My hand smacks across my own mouth to stop myself from screaming. I can't afford to mess this up now. I need to grow up.

What exactly I am trying not to mess up, I have no idea. I'm a good person, raised with the basics of right and wrong and I thought that I had a healthy regard for respect for people. Terin Coiler is not the sort of person to set house fires and sizzle their music teachers to death. I'm not a criminal, I'm a sixteen-year-old girl with the possibility of studying at Julliard or some other prestigious music academy. I'm supposed to be studying for my GCSE's, doing at least a year at college, and then moving over to the US to start a new life for myself.

How could everything have gone so wrong for me in the space of two weeks?

The train driver's voice echoes through the carriages in calm soothing tones. We were heading to some out of the way destination I didn't bother to focus on before jumping on the first train available. There must be at least twenty stops before the end of the line. Maybe half a day on the train would be enough time to calm myself down.

I stare down at the sink, which is papered in thick, dark auburn hair. Inches and inches of it cover the basin with an old pair of sharp garden shears on the top, stolen from one of Ted's neighbours. I'm blank and torn inside, along with my beaten and broken body. Every part of me hurts, but cutting my hair is one of the worst things I have ever had to do. I was looking down at my entire existence, not quite recognising the rough, cropped hair in the mirror staring back at me.

What am I missing? I have different hair, clothes, and a moody expression. There isn't anything I could do about my complexion or height, but the burns on the side of my upper forehead need to stay covered with the woollen hat--also courtesy of Mr. Sanders. I try to estimate how long it would take for authorities to find the man after I interrupted their call? Perhaps they would put his injuries down to spontaneous human combustion. Or a huge electrical surge through a faulty outlet that he was unlucky enough to be in the path of. No, it would have taken only seconds to explain there was an intruder in his house. They would put two and two together.

I have to go--get out of here and go far away--I decide. Ted Sanders was a horrible mistake I would never forgive myself for, but he definitely isn't going to be the reason for me going to prison.

I need answers.

I swallow, closing my eyes. I allow myself some time to push back the fear and tears and exhaustion downwards again. I need to be smart about this before I had another chance to totally fall apart. My priority was getting as far away as possible.

The shears are small enough so they can be concealed in the jacket, plus a little extra safety couldn't hurt. I just need to make sure I'm not stopped by anyone.

I grab the hair from the sink to shove into the toilet to flush, which takes a few slow tries. While the last strands are watered down the plug hole in the basin. I splash some water across my face, try and paste on my best 'I'm a moody teenager, don't approach me' look and leave the safety of the bathroom cabin behind.

The ticket inspector has already passed by and is making his way back down to the posterior end of the train. I turn and go in the opposite direction, selecting a quiet seat by a set of carriage doors. Just one or two other people were around me with headphones, their faces distracted by their phones. Perfect.

I sit, breathing slowly and evenly. In and out. I was going to be OK. In and out. Don't think about my parents.

What would Jared say if he were with me right now? *He would probably slap me on the back and congratulate me for getting rid of them.* I think dryly. He would be sickly proud, probably come out with some big speech about how we were special and that their will was holding us back from who we should be, rather than accepting and embracing who we were.

I wish he'd left a damn phone number to reach him. This dream theory is utterly useless.

The cityscape of outer London peels away to reveal a greener, fresher view of gardens, fields and long stretches of country road. I try to focus on the herds of cows and sheep we pass by, sometimes the odd horse stands grazing alone with a coat on, barely giving the loud tin can passing by another thought as he eats. I wonder what I would be doing at home now if things had only stayed the same.

My stomach groans loudly. I only have a little money on me, the last cash and change from Ted's pockets I could grab. I should have checked under his mattress for a little safe somewhere holding a stack of his savings – but there had been no time.

A sigh pushes its way out of my mouth. I was crazy. Did I actually believe I was going to bypass the police and be able to evade them for the rest of my life? They would have more than enough evidence and theoretical suspicion to try and pin everything on me. Ted had seen to that. He'd shoved me to the top of their suspect list.

They won't assume me missing for very long. Only until they find and check the cellar and put two and two together. Connecting me to Ted's death would be easy.

My heart rate increases along with my breaths. How long until they could identify his charred remains? Another panic attack is coming on. I can literally *feel* the electricity surge from the rails underneath us. The hum of raw power tingling and vibrating against the ground to the train wheels that glide along them. One small, concentrated movement, I could use that energy and project it outwards. I can potentially destroy this train and everyone on it if I want to.

No, I need to be strong. I need to be in control. Closing my eyes, I try to force down the power into a mental box and close a lid on it. It vibrates – protesting at being squashed away. It wants to be released, it *likes* to be used.

"Not today," I say firmly through gritted teeth, barely holding back the damn from bursting open. I would not kill all of these people. I will not be responsible for more blood on my hands. I can feel the power threatening to slip through my mental grasp, tendrils of electrical energy lashing out, trying to reach the environment around me.

And it stops. The mental box is closed. I'm spent, exhausted all over again. I can't keep doing this and pushing down the surge of power when I was too emotional. I would kill again unless I can figure out a way to control it properly. Christ. Did Jared have this much trouble too? Was there a graveyard of bodies somewhere courtesy of him?

I must have fallen asleep at some point during the train's journey. When my eyes flutter open to another driver announcement, we're pulling into a busy train station which is apparently the last stop before termination. Reluctantly, I leave the warmth of my seat behind and exit the train with the other residual passengers.

The air is fresh, but painfully cold. Even through my stolen woollen clothes, I can feel the bite of the evening air that pushes through the station. Strings of lights hang suspended from the roof's high arches, cascading downwards towards the swell of people beneath them.

"Cardiff Central," I recite. I've never been to Wales, let alone much further that the Outer strip of the Home Counties. There would be no way to tie me to a family member or anything out here because I don't know anyone who lives this far West. It would give me at least some time to work out what the hell to do next.

There's a burger joint on the platform opposite me -- nothing fancy, just a little kiosk with the scent of warm, fatty foods -- that makes me salivate at the thought of it. I set off to navigate my way up and around the platforms, being careful not to venture too close to wall cameras or security guards checking tickets at the barriers in the distance.

"Cheeseburger and chips please," I mumble, handing over the cash to the store clerk. He barely looks much older than me. He smiles briefly, taking the money to ring me up and hand over a receipt before turning to the grill.

"Travelling alone?" he asks casually. It takes me a moment to pause and try and understand the strong Welsh lilt to his voice. It was melodic and casual at the same time, every syllable having a different pitch between higher and lower. I was suddenly self-conscious, next to him, I sound too posh..

"I'm with my mum and aunt. Heading to Pontypridd." I roll my eyes to highlight the fake audacity at travelling with two imaginary high-strung women. The clerk grins again, eyebrows raising.

"You're lucky, I'm stuck here in the bare cold till eleven tonight. Do you want onions with this?" He gestures to the burger in his gloved hands. I shake my head.

"Try going shopping all day! My feet hurt," I grumble. It's slowly getting easier to lie, words just springing from my mouth like practised spider webs to trap my potential victims. I can hear the electric heaters in the back right hand side of the kiosk. I can feel the energy pulsing from the mains socket.

"I hear you, my Dad got the short straw today since I had to work. Unfortunately for him, one of my colleagues quit yesterday, so I had to do a double today. Killer, but the free food is fine."

"Killer," I mouth in agreement. "Hey, does that mean you're taking CVs for applications? My mum's keen on me getting a holiday job. A temp thing, you know."

He wraps the burger effortlessly and places it neatly beside a tray of fries and bags them altogether, tossing in a few sachets of salt and tomato sauce.

"We do but," he eyes me up and down quickly, "I'm sorry, we only take applicants eighteen and older. Fair working laws and all that." To his credit, he genuinely looks sympathetic. No doubt he'd be tired when he finishes his shift tonight, but he would be heading home to a real house with a real family and would have real dreams and aspirations. He would probably have a lot of friends at school, maybe even a girlfriend or boyfriend since he was so friendly and easy to talk to. I wish I was so lucky.

"It's fine, I was just thinking aloud anyway. Thank you for the burger." I take the bag gratefully from him, smiling and turn away to start heading back down the platform again.

"You can try local fishing docks and stuff!" he calls after me, leaning over the counter until his black shaggy hair peers over the threshold. "When my cousin was saving up for something, he ended up doing some odd jobs down at the docks. Nothing glamourous, just some carrying and fetching. It's cash in hand, but there's always people needing help with taking off fish and nets and stuff." I nod. "Thanks, I'll look into that."

The burger and chips are devoured quickly, instantly filling me with warm salty gratitude. Even my stomach rumbles pleasantly like a well fed predator. For the first time in two days, the feeling of the electrical currents all around me seemingly dies down into the background of my head, where it's easier to ignore. I allow myself to sit down on a nearby bench for a few minutes to rest and digest.

I need some kind of job, I decide. Asking about a position at the kiosk had been a spur of the moment decision, but unless I want to run out of money and die of starvation or cold very soon, I need a source of income from someone who wouldn't ask too many questions or care whether I have a national insurance ID or not. Claiming my stake to CoilerTech is out. Quieter trade places are definitely a good place to start.

Newly assured of myself, I toss my rubbish in a nearby bin and stand to stretch out my muscles and limbs that'd been asleep for hours. I notice there's a small television above a newsstand. The owner was busy talking to a friend in fluent Welsh just to the side, neither of them noticing me creeping closer to it.

"Seventy mile an hour winds prompt caution for the residents, the meteorological office strongly advises to only travel for necessary reason and to stay home if possible. Back to you in the studio." The weather presenter smiles at the camera and the scene changes back to the news anchor at her desk.

"In our main news today, esteemed entrepreneur and supporter of the arts; Richard Coiler, has been confirmed dead in his own home, along with his wife, Helen in a fatal house fire at their home in Chelsea. Richard was a popular name back in the nineties when he founded his technology empire under the name of CoilerTech. Since then, he has personally funded technological advancements in the industry, even going as far as to set up his very own educational programme for underprivileged children with a talent for computers and programming. At this point, an investigation has been launched to determine the cause of the blaze and if their currently missing daughter, Terin Coiler, also succumbed to the inferno or not. The Metropolitan police report that the situation is ongoing with forensic investigation at the scene. More on this story as it develops." The anchor arranges her notes in front of her, gazing into the camera. Gazing into me. The killer.

Frozen, in a state of numbness, I turn away from the television and head back down to the platforms where I board the train nearest to me, leaving behind the shell that was Terin Coiler.

-20-

The pub's not as tragic at the ones back in London, however it still holds the smell of ancient smoke and beer permeated into a threadbare rugs and faded curtains. The décor is dark, filled with old fashioned polished wooden booths with the scars of years of use. There's a modern jukebox in the corner that's crooning some old hits from the seventies mostly, providing a background noise under the chatter of a few dotted conversations of some of the locals. A wall of amber coloured bottles and alcohols is the brightest thing in the room and stood in front it, eyeing me suspiciously was the landlady as she wipes down glasses and stacks them behind the bar.

"We don't normally take girls," the fisherman grunts as he finishes the last few swigs of the ale I had bought him. I'm sat across the table in a dark corner in of a bar, right on the outskirts of a tiny village in Wales, wondering what the hell I'm thinking. Clearly everyone else here is wondering the same thing, because aside from the eagle-eyed land lady, I've attracted more curious glances my way. I run my hand over my cropped head sub consciously.

"As you've said about thirty times already. But I'm keen to get on the water as soon as possible," I sigh. I'm close to crying again for the millionth time since the journey begun. It's been at least a week or two after the struggle for my life with Ted Sanders.

Shuddering, I push his ruined face out of my mind as quickly as possible, swallowing down the revulsion. It must have shown on my face as my companion shoots me a weird look.

Since my run in with the devastating news report, I have deliberately been avoiding the national and local news outlets so far, but London is the most monitored city in the country with security cameras everywhere. It'd only be a matter of time before facial recognition paints my journey to the police.

If anything, I probably deserved it for what I did to Ted alone. But I will not go down without a fight. Not before I had a chance to find my answers.

"Go home," the fisherman says firmly. "The sea's no place for a young girl and you would be worth nothing to me."

"I can work," I say desperately, voice rising. "I can do any jobs you can assign your crew – I can help fish or cook or clean the deck – whatever you need. Look, I need this job.""And I don't need a teenage runaway." He coughs and drains the last of the glass, scraping his chair back to stumble to his feet. He's not a particularly very old man, but he moves across the room with an unsteady gait and nods his head in goodbye at the landlady. She inclines back at him and continues to watch me closely.

I grab my coat to follow him out quickly. Wales is notably a lot cooler than I was used to while growing up in the city––but Abersoch is only a tiny little village of about 800 residents. I'd travelled from

Cardiff Central to Bangor and then hitchhiked a ride from strangers until I hit the first coastal town I came across. Sure enough, there were hotels and some degree of idyllic holiday tourism – but nowhere near enough to rumble me before I had a chance to escape.

Despite his limp, I see the man amble quickly down the cobbled street away from the pub and towards the car park behind the building. I follow him eagerly to catch up.

"*Merch uffern waedlyd*," he mutters under his breath, exasperated. "Would you not take no for an answer, girlie? Go home to your mam and pap.""They're dead," I say. "I know they had some distant family in Brighton and Essex, but I have no one." I can't stop the tears that stream down my face. Horrified, I try to wipe them away with my sleeve, however the local fisherman known as Captain William Perry has already seen.

Perry rolls his eyes under the bushy peppered trim of his eyebrows. "I'm sorry to hear that, but this life's not a good one. I'm sure someone's looking for you."

How right he probably was.

"I'm sixteen years old. I'm of legal age to work and make my own decisions."

"You're legal to go out and get a bloody paper round!" he chortles and continues his walk. "Get back to where you belong, little miss. Look after yourself."

I stop following as he climbs into his beige and green jeep, he gives me a nod of his head as he starts up the engine and drives back down the gravel path to the road. Dejected, I head back to the cave by the beach and try to figure out my next move.

The cave itself isn't a huge formation of cavernous proportion, although it is enough to keep out the shrill wind that blew in from the sea. Curved inwards from the entrance, it's a good place to curl up in my borrowed sleeping bag and blankets from a local homeless shelter I'd passed through in a previous town.

Borrowed quickly however, before the shelter management could ascertain that I was now apparently an orphan. The lady was nice enough. Big and brunette and caring, also one step away from calling social services before I could get out of there quick enough.

"She's a murderer, miss," they would have said. "We'll take her straight to juvenile to await trial."

It hurts too much to think about my parents and what they would say if they could see me; unclean, bordering on starvation and living homeless on the coast with no further education, career or chance to clear my name. Their faces haunt me every time I try to distract myself. All I can do was sob into my sleeping bag at night and apologise for whatever role I played in their deaths.I try to conjure up what my brother would advise and stick to the quieter roads, only hitchhiking from people I was confident I'd be able to fight off if needed. I'd only been on the run a couple of weeks, but I was lonely and hungry. When asleep, I still try to contact him through the apparent dream connection we had, but it was as if something was missing. We were on different radio frequencies or something. He has at least three years ahead on his 'abilities' than I did to understand and perfect his control over them.

Still, even in his darkest moments he didn't burn down his own house while he slept.

I must have fallen asleep at some point during the afternoon, because I dream this time about Ted Sanders. It was the same nightmare that'd been plaguing me whenever I closed my eyes.

His throat is between my hands and no matter how hard I try, I can't release the pressure my fingers exert on his neck. I can feel his trachea and oesophagus collapse beneath my skin, his heartbeat is racing in my hands, pulsing greedily as his lungs try and scream for air.

I shake my head and try to pull my hands off, but he's turning purple, his eyes are dotted red from the effort of struggling so much. He's flailing and batting me with hands that barely touch my strong frame. I'm only holding him down with the sheer pressure of my left leg on his chest and my arms locked.

"Murderer," he's gasping. The dream ends and I find myself sitting up sweating in my sleeping bag. The material sticks to me, threatening to drag me back down into its depths as I struggle to climb free of the zip, getting more desperate as I'm trying to wriggle out. Finally, I land on the dry sand and carve my knee onto a jagged rock, but I barely feel it – I'm shaking too much.

It's now dark enough outside for me to venture out of the cave and onto the edge of the shore without the locals spotting me. I can barely see my hands in front of my face, but it's a quick walk to where the freezing water hits my borrowed boots and I lean down to splash it onto my warm face. The salt burns my eyes, but I keep washing and washing. Wash the guilt away. I need to scrub myself. Be clean of these sins.

"I'm a murderer," I sob quietly.

"Perry, byddai'n well ichi ddod I edrych ar hwn," someone mutters nearby in the darkness, cutting through the silent air and making me jump.

Frozen, I glance up to see the source a few metres away, illuminated only by a torch that someone's holding directly behind the guy, so I can't discern any recognisable features on their face. Behind them, there's a small canoe that's being gently pulled onto the beach, bathed in moonlight with several other large figures talking quietly among themselves.

I'm literally a deer stuck in the headlights. I hear a shuffle and a sharp intake of breath. My body wills itself to move – to do anything, but I'm unable to get my thoughts into order besides the very real suggestion that I'm probably about to die or be kidnapped.

"Uffern waedlyd," was the eventual reply. Someone else turns a torch on and blinds me as they step closer. "You again, girlie?"

"Perry?" I hold up my hand to squint. "Why are you here?"

"Fishing, you daft girl, question is - what are you doing down here?" He shines the beam quickly on himself and then turns it off and signals for his friends do to the same. I frown and glance at the cargo in the back of the canoe and wonder what kind of fishermen only go out in the dead of night.

"I, uhhh…" I wonder how to best explain the entire situation without the police being called. I'm saved by one of Perry's friends tapping his shoulder and hissing something urgently in Welsh, pointing towards the road in the distance, where there's a gleam of headlights slowly passing.

I wonder if I should take the opportunity to scream and flag down the car, but something tells me that it would the worst possible thing I could do, so I wait quietly while the fishermen crouch low on the sand and rocks, killing all lights and conversation. It's a few agonising silent minutes as the car passes in the distance, I can feel everyone letting out their breaths.

"Come on lads," Perry grunts and together, they haul the canoe from the water and slowly pull it inside the mouth of my cave. He shoves a torch at me on the way past and points into the darkened gloom of the interior so I can light the way as they drag the vessel against the far wall, covering it with a tarpaulin. The group immediately relaxes, they sit in the sand and open a pack of beer to share amongst themselves.

Perry frowns in my direction, now his apparent strange mission is over and marches over to me. "You need to go home girl. I've told you - you don't belong here."

"I'm not going anywhere," I say quietly. He watches me retreat to the entrance and pull my sleeping bag towards the outcropping of rocks and climb inside. I try to zip myself back in and curl up in a ball, but he walks over eventually and crouches down nearby.

"One of the blokes says he heard you say something about a murder?" His voice is surprisingly even, calm. His face isn't filled with mistrust or amusement. Despite the light covering of facial hair, there's an air of concern.

"I killed someone," I blurt out. I don't quite know why I feel like it's better to be honest with this man, it manages to throw him momentarily. William Perry patiently lets me finish without interrupting, calling me an idiot or trying to discredit me. "And I think I may have accidentally killed my parents too."

"Accidentally?" He frowns. "Either you did or you didn't – which is it?"

"I don't know, can't really tell you more than that. But I definitely killed a man. Someone is one hundred percent dead because of me." I swallow down the emotion and force myself to keep eye contact. His icy blue gaze was surprisingly hard to read, but he doesn't start immediately calling the authorities, which I took as a good sign.

"Why?" he says quietly.

That was easy. "He tried to hurt me. I think he might have killed me first if I wasn't lucky."

"So, in self-defence," he reasons and nods. "That's not the worst thing to commit a murder over."

"I still took a man's life, there's no excuse for that and I'll probably live with that guilt forever."

He nods and pauses for a moment, touching his peppered beard with a fingerless glove. "The principle of right and wrong is a funny thing. There are so many variables that can influence these decisions, these actions. Not all are as black and white as they seem. Is this why you want to leave with us?"

"Anyone really," I say quietly. "I came here randomly with no intent of finding anyone, just running. I heard about your crew from one of the locals. They mention you sail internationally so I thought it might benefit me. Be my ticket out of here."

"Occasionally," he hedges, and I see a slight shiftiness to his words. "Since you told me your secret and entrusted that to me, I'll be honest with you: I employ some shady characters and not everything we do is let's say – totally legal." His eye twitches, All I need to do is glance back at the semi-hidden canoe to work out that he's telling the truth.

"Right and wrong isn't black and white," I echo, shrugging. The little nagging voice in my head tries to remind me that I'm in a cave in the middle of nowhere with a bunch of possible criminals and dangerous men. I should be terrified and looking for an escape.

"You shouldn't be so trusting of strangers though," he reasons, as if reading my mind. "I could be anyone and you wouldn't stand a chance against me. I'm bigger and stronger than you."

"I don't care what happens to me," I whisper, semi-shocked at how calm and dark it sounded –– even more so because it was the truth. I really didn't care if I lived or died in this very moment. By as far as my definition, I'd committed the worst possible acts and sooner or later, would pay for it.

"Sixteen, you say. That's far beyond your years." He chuckles lightly.

I make a non-committal sound in my throat, tears pushed against the sides of my eyelids along with days of broken sleep. "Do you think I should turn myself in and face the music? It's what a decent person would do."

"I think even considering that idea tells me you aren't a stone-cold killer with no conscience," he replies. "The world isn't full of only strictly good and bad people. Which is why I have so many guys on my crew who I trust my life with, because I gave them an opportunity when no-one else would. In return, they give me their time and their loyalty."

I try to imagine what category of people I fit into. Perry shuffles uncomfortably from one foot to the other, stretching out his weakened leg.

"There's a tiny dock down Cilan Uchaf. We leave at 11 PM tomorrow night with or without you," he says eventually with a ghost of a smile under his grey peppered facial hair.

I'm stunned. My mouth opens and closes with no words to reply. I'm both sad and happy at the same time, my eyes fill with tears. I hide my face in the material of the sleeping bag to stop myself from collapsing at his kindness.

"I'll take that as a yes," Perry murmurs and rises to his feet. He looks back to his crew, who have finished their beers and are ensuring the canoe is offloaded and secured properly before heading out to the beach, sending curious and suspicious glances in my direction. The sheer fact none of them are concerned about a homeless person sharing a hiding place with them, makes me wonder how many times they've seen this.

"I'll be there," I whisper and nod.

"Good," he replies and turns on his heel. "A word of advice? You better stop your crying before somebody decides that you're too vulnerable not to exploit. The sea doesn't take kindly to cry babies."

-21-

I expect William Perry's fishing boat to be a medium to large vessel, but I stop and stare with a frown, at the small rib that's waiting for me. The canoe from the night before is tied on to the side, bobbing along gently to the rhythm of the waves that lap greedily at the edges.

"Is this it?" I ask. A couple of crew spurt quietly with laughter at me and I blush with shame at my apparent obvious stupidity.

"No," Perry shakes his head slowly, raising an eyebrow. "We need to travel out and collect her. Christ, this'd be a messy trip across the Atlantic otherwise."

I figure that *her* is an affectionate term for his real fishing boat and before I open my mouth and ask *who* she is, I swallow down the question and climb precariously into the canoe. I manage to slip, misjudging the sloshing water against the boat and land awkwardly on my ankle – causing another round of stifled giggles from the rest of the crew. Perry patiently hands me a life jacket and one stern look causes the sounds to die down.

"Pull this if you land in that water. Try to swim in the direction of land." Were all the safety instructions provided to me.

"*Os nad yw hi'n suddo ni yn gyntaf,*" someone mutters, but he ignores them.

There's a small engine on the back of the rib that he starts up effortlessly with a few tugs of the cord. After a few guarded glances up and down the shore, we begin to pull away from the makeshift dock.

I look down at my feet to see that the same bags in the canoe from the night before, are stashed carefully under the horizontal benches. I was so caught up with everything going on with me that I didn't stop to ask the captain exactly *what* alleged shady activities they got up to on the side, when fishing wasn't bringing in the big money.

The land falls away quickly as we disappear into the night. The conversation among the few crew members dies down so they can stay on full alert on every direction, scanning the horizon for signs of trouble. Late night fog clings to the top of the dark water as we pass through with the gentle humming of the engine. The whole thing feels ghostly and ethereal.

I try to make myself useful by using my own eyes and ears. The silence aside from the rib is both terrifying and calm. I want to ask more questions and get to know the people I'd no doubt have to work closely with for a while, but the looks on their faces dare me to try and distract them. This obviously wasn't the time for idle chit chat.

I lose track of the hours that tick by before I see a darkened structure that begins to appear on the horizon, only visible against the inkiness of the sky and sea by the lights in the windows. The boat itself is painted black and blue and looks as if it really *was* a large commercial fishing vessel, down to the metal structures and nets that were folded along the back.

It isn't until we pan around the circumference of the vessel to the other side, that I notice the tiny italic scrawl of *The Whittaker* down the edge of the bow. On the deck, a few silohuettes stare down at us in the boats. They toss a rope ladder over the side that unfurls neatly into the water.

With ladies first clearly not being a rule on the sea, someone tests the ladder and one by one, they scale the side of the large ship, dwarfing our tiny two boats in comparison. Perry nudges me when I'm the last to ascend, besides him.

"Don't look down, don't get tangled up, don't twist and cut off the blood supply to your ankles" he grunts in encouragement.

I glance up to see a couple of curious faces peer over the edge and gingerly, I place both feet on the bottom wedge to haul my body onto the rope. It tries to twist and buck me off as soon as I try to climb, like a wild animal. I struggle to cling on. A couple of titters from above cause me to blush deeply. I grit my teeth to stop from crying out.

My hands are frozen and stiff, the rope burns against them as I try desperately to hold on from falling back into the churning sea below. I hope that Perry doesn't climb up and push me.

"Come on," I whisper. One foot on the next rung and then again, and again, until I lose count. I'm too scared to look up or down at my slow progress for fear I'd get vertigo and fall backwards. Eventually I can peer over the top of the railings and, using what little arm strength I have left, I swing my body over the side to land on the deck.

It was a less than graceful dismount, the smirks around me note it too – but I don't care. I was back on somewhat dry land, hopefully soon to be far away from the country I called home.

The boat itself looks bigger on the inside than I initially thought it would. I'd never been sailing or even properly at sea before, so the compact interior surprises me when I follow Perry and his men into the main door. I notice that a few individuals remain remain outside on the deck, busying themselves with whatever jobs they had to do. With a minute gulp, I wonder how Perry was going to have me earn my keep on the ship.

We end up in a small hall that resembles a school canteen, nothing as special as the private school dining halls I'd experienced before, but it was snug and warm with the sweet aroma of something meaty cooking in the adjacent kitchen. The walls are adorned with crew photos over the years and what I imagine were trophies from some of their jobs – legal or otherwise.

My stomach rumbles, loudly announcing I haven't eaten since a small hotdog the night before. I scuttle over to the far side of the room and sit at an empty bench as the crew fills the seats in the room. Some of which were men arriving from other areas of the boat who greet each other merrily in what I imagine was still Welsh. There's a couple of curious glances thrown my way and I try my best to look tough and uncaring, even though I'm sitting alone. I count twenty-two men plus Perry and myself and any crew left working out on deck. Twenty-seven altogether at a push.

Perry takes the centre next to a table filled with an array of bottled drinks crated on top of kegs. He grins toothily and lifts up a bottle to his men.

"*I genhadaeth lwyddiannus arall!*" he booms and his men clap and cheer along with him. "Now your going be seeing a couple of new faces around here lads. First of which is young'in Darrell here." He rasies his bottle at a young man who's already seated among the crowd. They jeer and slap him repeatedly on the back. I notice him wincing, but his grin stays bravely on his face. I remember him from the journey across the bay – probably a few years older than me, taller and heftier in build.

"We also have our second female on board, so I expect you all to be on your best behaviour," he glances over at me with his piercing eyes and raises his bottle once again. I suddenly realise that he has no idea what my name is, letalone who I am – did he even ask? "We'd like to welcome you, *Morgan*."

"Morgan?" I whisper.

"*Mae hi'n edrych fel llygoden fawr gors wedi boddi!*" someone mutters rudely to comments and low laughter. I don't know what they're saying but the nasty look on the hairy face of the man closest, was enough for me to glare back and clench my fists.

"*Digon, byddwch chi'n barchus,*" Perry snaps and gives him a hard look that would put me in my place. The man mutters what I assume is an apology and falls silent. The captain then reels on to report on their latest job and what kind of work they have coming up and the timeframes they – or we, would all be working to.

I try desperately to listen to the English – I guess was for my benefit than anything else, but I'm too caught up in the name he presented me as. *Morgan*. Where did that even come from?

A plate of steaming food catches my attention as it's placed in front of me. I blink stupidly. The talk is over and the crew are already tucking into the dinner of beef and mash that's been served. Perry is nowhere in sight.

"You look a bit lost, little bird." A blonde woman smiles down at me, sliding a plate underneath my nose. She's older than her makeup would have her appear with bight red lips and purple eyeshadow, dressed in similar bright colours that move around her frame with a floaty movement. She sits down in front of me, effectively blocking the stares from the other crew members.

"You could say I'm out of my depth," I mumble before grabbing the knife and fork to dig into the food. I'm too staving to feel embarrassed to eat while someone watches. The woman waits patiently, head resting on her hands as I devour each bite greedily, polishing down the bottle of water with it.

"When was the last time you had a hearty meal in you?" She winks. "You know, I think we got seconds somewhere. Just don't let the captain know, mind. He'll think I'm playing favourites."

"It's delicious. Did you make it?"

She shrugs. "Would any of this bloody terrible lot be able to prepare a meal for the whole crew? Hell, half of them don't bother getting dressed properly in the morning!" She laughs big and loud, it's impossible not to smile along with her. She's every bit the exact opposite of my mother, who was demure and slender in every sense of the word. This strange Welsh woman commands the presence of the room, and she knew it.

"My name's Serene." She offers a neatly manicured hand and I take it quickly to shake.

"I'm uh--"

"Morgan," Serene confirms. "It's a typical Welsh name. William likes to give all our new crew their own names so they can take on new identities out here. Some people really take to it, some don't."

"Is Darrell a Welsh name too?"

"Maybe Darrell hasn't impressed him enough to have his own yet," she taps her head thoughtfully. "He's a hard one to impress at times, but you somehow managed. How old are you, pet? You look way too young to be out here. He wouldn't have brought you without good cause." The furrow and concern in her brow makes my stomach cramp with anxiety. I hope the mobile reception on international waters was patchy, so she couldn't call social services.

I killed a man and possibly my own parents with some sort of super-natural force I can't really explain but it comes out sometimes, I try in my head.

"I don't have anyone," I hedge. "I've been living rough for a bit."

She makes a sound in her throat and nods her head in understanding. "Well, let me get you that second helping. Let me know when you're done, and I'll show you to the ladies mess."

"The... mess?"

"The ladies' room, the quarters," she explains. "No way you are bunking with that rabble over there!" She disappears back into the kitchen with my empty plate and bottle. I'm left feeling alone and exposed again. A few of the men get to their feet and disappear out of the food hall, others stay to drink loudly with their friends, share stories that I can't understand a word of. At least they'd forgotten about the weird English girl in their midst, I supposed.

My view of the room is blocked again by a figure sitting down but this time, it's William Perry himself.

"Morgan," he says. "I see you've met Serene, my wife. She'll look after you."

"Why didn't you ask me for my name when we met?" I say quietly.

"It's of no consequence to me. Does it matter?" he says and I decide that it really doesn't – especially if I'm running away from the very person that was once Terin Coiler, only daughter of the late Helen and Richard. My heart pangs for my parents and my old life, regardless of how controlling it was. It's *my* normal, after all. Everything I've ever known and cared about.

What about Jared and Georgia? And CoilerTech? What would happen next? What about the fishbowl in the second living room? Would the RSCPA also be looking for my arrest along with the long line of others? I was a fish killer too.

"We'll be on the open sea soon," Perry says kindly, probably reading my change in mood. "Nothing will judge you out there and you'll only be defined by your actions and decisions on this crew, for as long as you want to sail with us."

-22-

The crew on *The Whittaker* are mostly Welsh, as I initially suspect. They sit in tight groups during meals, muttering together in their native tongue, mostly when I am nearby, continuously glancing back at me in a mixture of scepticism and mistrust. There's an old Texan called Bobby Dee that sits to himself most of the time, murmuring about the good old days and how in his country, he'd be permitted to carry his damn shotgun for protection. A small handful of others were from other parts of the UK and wider Europe.

True to our agreement, Perry puts me to work straight away. I'm sat in my usual seat at the side of the dining hall, peeling sacks of potatoes, carrots and parsnips for dinner. If not for the fact that I didn't know the first thing about life on a ship, I would have moaned about being assigned such a feminine task – but I zip my mouth and concentrate on the fact that with every passing sea mile, we're heading deeper into international waters and to freedom.

The women's quarters were nothing more than a few hammocks in a smaller room down from the kitchen and storage areas. Aside from Serene, who stayed with Perry, it's just me alone in the darkness with my thoughts and my guilt weighing down on me, threatening to plunge me through the boat and into the cold, unforgiving sea.

The first few days are the worst, and I am caught between playing the attentive role of new crewmate, desperate to stay away from the spotlight and letting out my feelings as soon as the door close behind me at night.

Grief consumes every being of me, every molecule, every crevice. It's the last thing I think about at night and the first thing when I wake, red eyed in the mornings. The only good thing I could really focus on was that being out in the middle of the water greatly reduced the amount of electrical flow I could feel all around me. It was more manageable, more breathable. I could think without concentrating most of my energy on pushing back the sing of the current and its constant call.

We move towards international waters mostly in the middle of the night at a slower pace than I would expect. When I ask Perry if it was a logistical fishing decision, he mumbles something and makes some excuse up, while asking me if I had been crying in my cabin.

The meaning was clear; if I don't interfere with his business, he won't interfere with mine. It's all I could ask for really.

A guy named Hamish is in charge of showing Darrell and I the ropes. Young Darrell looks more seasick than me, as he leans against the door of the men's bathrooms, a sheen of sweat across his face. When I appear next to him, he breathes deeply and tries to smile.

"Morgan," he says, probably the only one to address me directly aside from Perry and Serene. "What took you so long? I've been here for ages waiting."

"Eating breakfast," I reply. "There's still some left if you want. Egg, bacon, and sausages." A light smirk spreads across my face as he turns a light shade of green, no doubt thinking about the greasy breakfast baps Serene had made in advance of the morning rush. There is no time to prod him further however, because a medium build slim man opened one of the small cabin offices nearby and locked it quickly behind him. He gave us both the once over, betraying nothing on his face.

"Call me Hamish, I'm the quartermaster and the Captain's second in command," he says with a ghost of a European accent that catches the edge his words. "I'm here to make sure you both don't get lost around the ship and end up where you're not supposed to be. You're here to work and complete your assigned jobs. Morgan, Serene has you in hand. Darrell, you'll be graced with my presence." The look on his face suggests that it was anything but an enchanting experience. I feel Darrell try to stand up a little taller with a cocky grin, extending his hand. Hamish ignores it and moves his gaze to the clipboard in his hand.

"There are some rules we need go through first before we take the tour. Now as both of you probably know, this isn't a usual fishing vessel. It's our cover, and it's one we try to maintain very seriously. The fact both of you are even here makes it apparent that Captain Perry sees potential in you," he glares at both of us, moving from one to the other. "However, it doesn't mean we won't leave you marooned somewhere out to sea if you become a problem."

"Well. Not in the middle of the ocean though, right?" Darrell jokes. The look on Hamish's face says otherwise.

"Don't become a thorn in my side," the quartermaster responds. "You should see what we do to traitors."

Darrell pales and glances at me, I shrug nonchalantly in reply. Whether or not Hamish is elaborating to scare us, his face doesn't betray a thing. Once the initial threat is roused, he ticks off some health and safety checks on the clipboard and then leads the way to the deck.

I've only been aboard *The Whittaker* for a couple of days, but it's apparent that the crew is more like family to one another. They still gave me a wide berth, but they greet Hamish and Darrell and pound them on the back as we stream through the corridor that lines the engine room and crew mess areas.

I'm too sleep deprived to care, meeting their mistrusting looks with one of my own. Darrell natters on non-stop with bouts of verbal diarrhoea and Hamish looks as if he's one step from marooning the young man away on a dinghy himself.

We reach the deck through the door I'd come through to start my new life, only a couple of days prior. The fresh ocean air fills my nose with its salty scent and the surrounding environment is totally devoid of any human life for miles. The water churns softly beneath the hull and kisses the lightly clouded sky in the far distance. I'm surprised to find it's now late morning – the dim light of the interior paired with the lack of sleep was really throwing off my internal clock.

"Say hello to the big guns," Hamish says and points to the steel structures that stoop from the far side of the boat, attached to huge winches with a pile of netting sits at the side. "We are on a converted oceanic research vessel, so we modified some of the features to suit our cover. These machines here stop to lower the nets when we need to need to berth somewhere."

"So then we berth with fresh fish," I note.

Hamish nods. "Indeed. People tend to take less notice of us if we're stopping to trade or deliver an order. Our prices aren't bad, so folks won't look at us twice if we're working hard."

"But fishing isn't all we do?" Darrell pipes up.

"We travel mostly at night, as I'm sure you've noticed," Hamish says and points to several points around the deck. "You see those cameras there? Some high-tech kit that enables us to see infra-red images of the boats and vessels in the distance. We're connected into a radar network that will bounce any nearby transmission signals back to us, so we can disappear before any authorities happen to pass by."

"What about submarines?"

"Occasionally we cross paths. Some governments have real secret equipment that allows them to spy, so we scramble our own transmission signal so it's tougher for them to locate us without surfacing. If we know for sure we're being tailed by a sub, we might drop some cargo to disrupt their sonar and while we escape."

"Cool." Darrell breathes with his stupidly enthusiastic grin, as if he'd been dropped into the middle of a *James Bond* film. He looks like a young excited boy at Christmas.

"What's the likelihood of us getting caught and arrested?" I ask seriously. My shiny new future hangs in the balance.

Hamish meets my gaze, his amber eyes burn into mine for a few seconds. "There's no freedom without a little risk and a little risk is what keeps us all out of trouble," he says honestly. It's good enough for me.

He leads up back through the door, but this time we take a right and head down a narrow flight of steel steps into the belly of the ship. The steps twist downwards, and it grows hotter and humid but somehow, I manage to keep up with the pace. The smell of the air is saturated with engine oil and fumes. Some of the crew walk around in oily overalls and facemasks as they head to their tasks. Our walkway steers upwards and below the steely mesh under our feet, lies several pieces of heavy looking machinery with pipes and valves attached to the sides.

The noise is almost deafening, but we move on quickly to the other side of the hull and follow the walkway as it arches up a slope and peels around to reveal a white corridor.

"Cockpit's up there," Hamish indicates towards two or three steps that lead into a largely windowed room where a small group of men are pointing towards an electronic map on a screen. "You can thank the Captain's team for making sure that we don't die, get lost, or end up in a naval prison somewhere." He opens up a small cabinet barely concealed in the wall. Once he pulls the latch open and pulls the cover of the panel upwards, our mouths drop open. There's a pile of guns and ammo tucked neatly into the interior. I've never been this close to *one* real gun before, let alone stood in front of an entire cache. I take an involuntary step back.

"We get to use them, right?" Darrell says excitedly.

Hamish raises an eyebrow. "Only in the event our lives are in danger. Kids however, aren't allowed to play with guns."

"I'm nineteen," my companion groans. He's the same age as Jared.... "Come on, I went clay pigeon shooting a few times! I know how to handle a rifle."

"This isn't a country club, lad," Hamish deadpans. "And I'm not your daddy. I am however one of the only crew who holds the key to this stash however, so I'll be the judge of when you're good and ready to learn."

I shiver lightly and frown. There was no way I would wield a weapon knowingly and take a life, ever again. I was *enough* of a weapon.

Our guide continues the tour and concludes with the crew shower and bathrooms cubicles – insisting that all male members of the crew were under explicit instruction not to use the women's areas if they couldn't be bothered to wait their turn.

"Serene had to beat a few men into submission over that one," Hamish says darkly and I believe him immediately.

It's around lunchtime when we finally conclude, and Darrell's dragged off to his first assignment on his own, while I'm summoned directly back to the kitchens to check in with the matriarch herself.

Serene's back is to me as she works away at a batch of something cooking in a huge pot. It smells like the vegetables and potatoes I'd helped to cut earlier, mixed with a sweet fruity scent.

"Orange zest," the blonde woman turns and winks before I could ask. "My secret ingredient in most meat dishes. Your mam ever make something similar?"

I open my mouth to make a snide comment about my mother's home cooking and promptly close it, thinking about how strange it was that I'd never taste it again. My head swims, No more family meals, not playing the piano, not falling asleep in my beautiful four poster bed again.

On some level, I had weaved an elaborate lie for myself that this was all an elaborate holiday away from reality and somehow, things would go back to normal. One day.

The world is shaking. Serene must have noticed the expression on my face change. She abandons her stirring spoon and kneels down on the floor next to me, her black skirt pooling the both of us in its satin material.

"Breathe Morgan," she commands. My ears pound with a rushing sound. "You're having a panic attack."

The rushing sound is me. My lungs are screaming for air and my sobs pound against my diaphragm. My heart beats painfully. Everything hurts. Everything aches for oxygen. I'm going to die.

I must have said the last part verbally, because she shakes her head firmly and plants her manicured hands on my shoulders.

"You're OK, you're fine. Breathe deeply, there pet," she coos again and again until my breathing finally begins to slow. I let myself fall into the sweet smelling scent of her chest. The cotton fabric smells so much like home that if I close my eyes, I could be walking through the Chelsea house into my own bedroom.

"The stew's burning," I say weakly after some time has passed. How long had we even been on the floor for?

"It'll be fine," Serene says calmly. "I could feed week old turds to this lot, and they wouldn't notice the difference really."

I giggle weakly. The sound borders on hysterical to my ears. Serene continues to hold me, rocking me backwards and forwards, hushing me gently from crying. All I could do was sit and let her and hold the broken pieces of me together as best she could.

-23-

I'm playing the grand piano again. Not one as elaborately luxurious as the one my mum received from my father for one of their wedding anniversaries, however it's just as beautiful.

The old Steinway itches to be played and I can't ignore the impatiently tapping of my fingers as they seek to reach across the polished keys to find their starting places. I don't really know what I want to play exactly, so I let my fingers guide me and follow behind them. It's a sombre melody from a play my mother helped to orchestrate once. It wasn't West End worthy, not by a long shot but she loved her projects more than Jared or I.

I don't know where I am exactly in the world, but the soft white sand underneath my feet and the sound of gulls in the distance signify I'm on a coast. I try to rack the conscious part of my brain to remember if Perry docked us nearby, but my body was still in the middle of the ocean – so where exactly was my mind?

There's someone in the near distance, sitting on a grassy dune that overlooks a little beach hut and lifeguard chair. Nothing that looked like it would be on a UK beach, it was way too sunny and warm. I move from the leather stool, pulling my flowing dress around myself to try to head closer without starling them.

It's a boy – or a man, a young one. He has a head of brown thick hair with reddened tips at the very ends that shine in the sunlight, streaking through the longer grass which barely conceals him. He's staring out into the distance and not really paying attention to the grass that crunches under my bare feet. Propelled further by something I don't understand, I feel the consciousness inside me begin to rouse for the first time since I'd escaped on the train from London Every step becomes more desperate and I'm moving faster.

"Jared?" I breathe. A mixture of shock and relief. Hearing my voice, he turns – snapping to where I'm standing only a few metres away.

The look in his eyes isn't hard to read – he's just as shocked as I am. I wonder if he's been looking for me – trying to reach me on the dream plane just as much as I had, him.

I was so sure this was a real connection. It feels so different to other dreams, more vibrant somehow. If I concentrate, I could smell the rugged earthy scent from whatever deodorant he was wearing. God, he was *here*.

I try to speak and gush out absolutely everything to him – the whole truth. Our eyes meet for a few moments. The mental band snaps and he disappears into nothingness.

I'm alone again.

I wake up with the pillow wet from the corners of my eyes. I wipe them briefly and toss the thing out of my hammock. It's been days and the *one* time I manage to reach him – he's gone before I can open my mouth.

Something must have interrupted us, I decide. We aren't sailing through the middle of a storm, but the boat is rocking from side to side, the remnants of some winds that'd originated from France, Serene had explained. I suppose that my body could have roused my mind from REM or something. Broken the fragile connection somehow. I need to try and understand my own ability more and work on it.

"Crap," I say, and climb out of the hammock in my new fleece jumper and trousers.

Despite the rocky conditions, only Darrell sits at his breakfast table with a green hue on his face again while the rest of the crew bustles around the boat with their chores, well-practised in stepping to and fro to avoid knocking into one another. Serene and a couple of her kitchen staff move professionally around the canteen with trays and plates in their hands, not missing a beat. I try to follow their example and move with the ebb and flow of the waves that lash against the hull, but all I succeed in doing is dropping a couple of plates and a cup.

"Takes some time to get those sea legs in," she sings cheerfully as she sweeps past with hands filled with dirty dishes. I ignore the guffaws from some of the other crew members who watch me clear up the mess by myself and scuttle away back to the privacy of the kitchen.

"Everyone seems so busy this morning," I comment as one of the kitchen hands begins to wash the dishes next to me. He glances sideways and ignores the comment, looking down at what he's doing instead. It's the same look the rest of them give me.

"What's your problem?" I snap, surprising myself and glower at his shoulder. Days and weeks of sub-par sleep and constant worry are catching up with me and threatening to spill over the threshold of my patience. The Jared dream still has me teetering on the edge.

Wide eyed, the man stands still. I can feel that he wants to open his mouth and bark a retort at me but doesn't. Quietly he returns back to what he's doing. I stomp away from the kitchen and head to the pantry to start hauling out food for lunch.

It's the middle of the afternoon when I decide to head back to the makeshift cabin for my afternoon break. The two hours before the dinner rush begins would give me a hopeful good couple of hours rest. I could sense Serene had wanted to ask me about my bad mood all day, but skilfully decides to leave me alone to it.

I need to put my parents and my brother and Ted Sanders out of my head somehow. They are behind me in my recent, horrific past. For now, I need to try and find ways to control myself from hurting others – or I would never be able to trust myself around people ever again.

Before I could escape to my cabin, Perry appears from Hamish's office and grunts at my arrival.

"Morgan, I was hoping we could have a chat. Serene got you running around right now?"

"No, nothing," I reply, all hopes of my nap ebbing away. He nods in approval and inclines his head for me to follow him. Like everyone else on this damn ship, his footwork is effortless, not phased by the rocking from side to side or by the doors that try to swing shut into me when I try to open them myself.

We head back to the direction of the canteen and take the turn off that peels around the side of the bathrooms to head towards the back of the boat. I notice it's a faster route to some of the lesser known areas of the ship I haven't managed to explore yet and make the mental note to try and find some peaceful spaces to curl up and read a book in. I also make a resolve to actually try and find some books to read and try to take the edge off my mood.

Perry holds open a door for me, I head through to see that it's his and Serene's own private quarters. Alike the rest of the ship, the walls are adorned with various fishing memorabilia, including a novelty talking fish on the wall that turns and greets us with a song when we enter.

"A present from an old friend in the navy," Perry mutters and struggles to turn the switch off behind the plaque. "Bloody woman keeps switching it on to annoy me." He gestures to a couple of overly stuffed armchairs covered with knitted throws and takes the one closet to his little desk which boasts a mount of paperwork and a small, outdated computer. There's a newer-looking laptop that sits on the stuffed shelf behind him that's possibly being used as an expensive paperweight.

"Why did you give me my name?" I blurt when we both sit. "Serene says it's because I impressed you. But I'm a sixteen-year-old runaway, so I can't imagine I've done anything amazing. Even the crew seem to accept Darrell more than me!"

I can see it takes him a moment to decipher through the hasty muddle of words that spill out, but he leans back in his chair thoughtfully.

"Darrell's a puppy," he says. "Barely a man. Brought up sheltered – you can see it in his eyes, he's never known any kind of hardship like you and me. You battled to get where you are. Don't get me wrong, I don't make it a habit of taking on wayward teenagers, but you have something special in there. You'd be wasted in prison, I reckon. May as well make a decent person of you."

He didn't know how close he was to the mark there.

"I actually brought you up here for a little chat," he leans forward on his knees. "Nothing heart to heart mind, touchy feely things make me nervous. No, I think it's time we had a proper adult talk about our business here." He reaches across to the piles of paper on the desk that I realise are pages and pages of faxes. They were outdated machines for the modern world, however my father still liked to keep one in his old office for memorabilia more than anything else.

"I pick my crew very carefully. It wasn't until I saw you in that cave, I realised you had just as much to lose as the rest of us," his eyes flick to meet mine. "Which makes you trustworthy."

"I have nothing that I can offer," I say honestly. I try to look for the disappointment in his eyes to gauge what sort of longevity I was looking at on this boat. He continues without skipping a beat.

"And we don't want nothing from you, except your time and skill. In exchange for room and board of course. The same deal the rest of these lugs get."

"And what sort of deal I that?" I say carefully.

He passes the fax at the top of the pile across to me. It's nothing but a name of a location south of Portugal along with some coordinates that I assume made more sense to him than me. There's no sender or address aside from a range of randomly placed dots and symbols at the bottom that made no recognisable pattern or words.

"Morse code," Perry explains. "Little outdated but you'd be surprised how useful it still is, post war. What do you think you're looking at?"

"It doesn't look like anything. Like someone was testing out a pen or something."

He chuckles. "Think about it, we're a fishing vessel and we're sailing on the biggest weapon at our disposal. Where do you think we'd be heading next?"

I shrug. "Um. Not a holiday destination. A dock maybe?"

"A job," he says, a gleam of excitement in his icy eyes. "I have an old industry contact who tips me off about certain... stock that needs to be... liberated from certain international ports."

"OK. So stolen? We're stealing something?"

"It's more than simple thievery Morgan, it's mostly electronics from corporations too corrupt to regulate their profits versus their workers. We act mainly as the channel from A to B. We're paid on delivery."

I feel uneasy at the thought of *stealing*. I wasn't a perfect child in the long run, but I was still brought up with the basic idea of Heaven and Hell. It was laughable that I had such anxiety, considering what I'd done. Did I even have the *right* to think about good and evil?

"The principle of right and wrong... there are so many variables that can influence these decisions, these actions. Not all are as black and white as they seem," Perry had said before.

Maybe, this was one of those times.

"Keeps the wind in our sails. As so to speak. A lot of the guys on here are like just like you. Lost and needed a way out to start again. Took some time for the wife to get used to this way of living, but she's never felt better, I think."

"And what about you?" I say with more confidence than I feel.

"That's a story for another time, Morgan," he says cryptically, leaning back on his chair. To say I was entirely happy with the situation would be lying, but what other choice did I have? I was incredibly lucky to have been the chance for the new beginning with someone who didn't ask too many difficult questions and didn't care about my secret shame.

William Perry has been so open and entrusting from the beginning, that on some twisted level, I feel guilty for not telling him everything about me. What if we found ourselves in the middle of the ocean one day and I accidentally destroy the boat or electrocute everyone? With the thought, fear floods me. The energy leans in eagerly. The walls begin to close in. Jared was wrong. We are *abnormal*.

I need to come clean to someone.

"I'm a freak..." I begin but was cut abruptly by the shrill sound of a siren blasting throughout the boat. Around us, I can hear the sounds of the crew moving in the hallways in an orderly fashion and the hum of concerned murmurs reach us, ensconced in his rooms.

"What's that alarm sound for?" I say sharply. Perry's face is masked, his excited gleam gone but there's no hiding the hooded darkness in his eye.

"Police patrol," he grunts.

-24-

"Follow me. Do as I say and stay close," Perry instructs as we head down the winding hallways to the cockpit. I barely hear him over the sound of my pounding heart. I'm desperately looking around the ship like it's possibly the last chance I'll get to absorb every arched metal doorway, the biting scent of engine oil and warm aromas of cooking. I expect armed MI5 agents to jump at me from every darkened corner, aiming guns.

"What are we looking at?" Perry says and stops at the controls as soon as we barge through the door. Rows and rows of buttons and levers and lights twinkle quietly, unaware of the tension in the room. Hamish and the others don't look as worried as I imagine them to.

"Bit farther out for a patrol than usual," Hamish answers and points to the distance, handing the captain the binoculars. "You see? Hiding behind that rig there. Little thing. Hard to try and distinguish which police. Likely Spanish or Portuguese."

"There's been drug trafficking round these waters lately," one of the other navigators pops up. "Probably a random search of that facility. Abandoned rigs are gold mines for hoarding merch."

"If they're searching that rig, they'll see us soon if not already," Perry mutters. "Damn, we'll lose a night sailing."

Hamish turns to him with a grin. "Actually Captain, there's heavy fog due to roll in from the South West and it'll hit soon. From this angle, it's entirely possible they haven't seen us yet if the sun's behind them. The paintwork should hold us up in the dark horizon well enough. We can just kill the lights and wait till the fog rolls in to move past."

"And if they move before then?" a second crew mate asks.

"With these waves, I expect'll be docked for a while till the storm moves on. Those little boats have some decent tech, but they don't have the muscle behind it." Perry says thoughtfully and glances towards me. Up until now I decide to stay quiet, let them battle out the tactics and hope they don't notice how white I've gone.

"Play it safe?" Another crew member affirms. The others nod.

"There's no real confirmation they'll hail us down or even be bothered by our presence, but it's always good to play it safe, especially when the authorities are involved. Cutting through red tape is a pain."

"Won't they see us on their radar or anything?" I say shyly. The others glance at me as if only just registering my presence.

"Blocker," someone muttered by way off explanation. "Surface ships won't see us on their equipment if we don't want them to. If there's an under-water vessel, it's a different story."

"There's no way at all?"

"Not unless they're using live satellite feeds or perhaps acoustic pinging. There's been unconfirmed suggestions of high-tech trackers on the dark web over the years, but nothing concrete enough to get our knickers in a twist over."

"Does that dark web thing have anything we can harness?" Perry asks, scratching his chin thoughtfully.

"Not without being traced. There's some real crazies on those places."

"Well damn," the Captain mutters. "We'll stick to the fog and hope for the best. We'll lose some time but...." He glances out of the window. "It'll be safer for everyone."

Perry presses a red button next to a microphone that juts out from the control panel and calmly explains the situation to the rest of the ship. I want to move, but my eyes are glued to the police vessel on the horizon. I wonder what the possibility was that they could be looking at my wanted poster right now.

"Don't fret so much, Morgan. It's routine. We see this all the time; we're just preparing for the worst case scenario," he says quietly. He'd finished his announcement and was overseeing Hamish and the others as they manoeuvred the ship to a slow crawl. My eyes meet his and there was nothing guilty in them. Nothing that suggests he wants to pull the wool over my eyes.

But for all I knew being on a boat with complete strangers, he could have called ahead to drop in a hint.

"I'll believe it when I see it," I say finally.

When the fog finally rolls in and the sun sinks below the horizon, I'm stood precariously on deck with my rucksack. It's packed with what little possessions I have and despite the freezing air and undoubtedly, freezing waters – I was ready to go overboard if I needed to. The anorak did nothing for the cold winds that rattle across deck, nearly pinning me against the side of the winch. My fingers are cold and shaking, but I peer over the side to try and judge the drop. As the visibility fell, so did the signs of the enemy in the distance, but it didn't mean they were also using the weather to their advantage, just as we were planning to.

"Captain said you'd probably be out here," someone says. I turn quickly to see Hamish shake his head. "Must admit I didn't peg you for the dramatic type. That's more Darrell."

"I'm not being dramatic; I'm being realistic," I huff. The drop was maybe ten metres and the waves were choppy but were still the calmest they'd been in a few days, it could work. Maybe the foreign police would go easier on me if I swam over and surrendered.

"Mmm," he concedes and folds his arms against his woollen coat. "So how many people do you personally know, who've survived the swimming the Atlantic?"

"It can be done." I'm at least semi-confident. Surely I must be a little stronger than the average non-ability human?

"Yes. Until you drown or freeze or get dragged under the waves. How much do you know about the flight path of orcas or minke whales?

"There aren't sharks around here, right."

His stern, slim face breaks for a fraction of a second into a smile. He was mocking me. "And that Morgan, tells me just how much you value your life."

"I value it more than..." I gesture to the boat and the sea and generally, everything that lay before us. It was difficult to pinpoint *who* exactly I was angry at and *why*. Perry had a chance to flag down the police boat and hand me in, but he didn't, because the rest of the crew had the same chance as a second beginning as I did.

"You don't need to trust us or anyone if you don't want to," Hamish says. "But trust in the fact we know our craft and we do our jobs well." "It's not that I don't trust--"

"It is," he cuts me off. "You don't trust easily and it's not a bad thing. I wouldn't expect anything else from a little girl who's run away from home and whatever bugs you and makes you cry at night or whatever. But out here, you're a woman. Which means you need to make grown-up decisions and face the consequences."

"I'm sixteen."

He nods and steps aside to gesture to the dingy that's attached to the side of the boat. He holds out his arms. "So, you keep saying either through defence or offense. Now am I preparing madam for transport or no? Hurry and decide, I have things to do."

I look between Hamish and the dinghy with a scowl. He had me. I would undoubtedly be killed, starve, or drown to death out in the middle of the ocean. I did not go through my journey from the charred remains in Chelsea to be picked apart by bottlenose dolphins.

My bag slides from my back to land in the heap by my boots, which gives him his answer. Satisfied, he grabs the pack and slings it over his own shoulder and holds the door open while I moodily slink back into the welcoming warmth.

In my panic of the police boat, I miss the preparations for dinner and guilty, offer my mumbled apologies to Serene, who's rushed off her feet in the kitchen with one of the chefs.

"Yes yes, fine fine!" She waves me off quickly and whirls past with a steaming pan of soup. It does nothing for the guilt of my selfishness. The usual glares from the kitchen staff do nothing to help.

I grab the first bowls that make it to the warmed canteen tables and begin to serve them to the hungry crew, who mumble their thank yous and barely give me a second glance to see that my eyes were misted and blurry.

There's a swagger from the corner of my eyes as another comrade enters the canteen and hangs up his coat by the door. Aside from everyone else, Darrell's wearing at least two or three thick layers of clothing and a pair of gloves indoors, so he looks ridiculous. One improvement is that he's not green or looking sickly for the first time, so he may have gotten some sea legs after all.

"Darrell," I hiss and grab him by the shoulder as he wanders past me for dinner. He looks at me, aghast and quickly glances over his shoulder to see if anyone's looking in our direction. I roll my eyes and haul him into the alcove of the cleaning cupboard around the corner.

"Can't be seen talking with me to ruin your street cred, huh? You're just like the rest of them," I mutter.

He smiles sheepishly. If he wasn't such an arrogant, bumbling idiot, he would have been an OK person to hang out with. "It's just that they say it's bad luck to carry a *girl* on board a ship. I don't want people to think you're spreading all that bad luck on me."

"Is that why no one talks to me in English aside from Perry, Serene, and Hamish?" I spit incredulously, scowling. "Is that it? Some superstitious crap that means nothing?"

"These sailors really value their superstitions," he defends weakly. Despite our difference in height and probably few years in age, he's *definitely* more of a boy, more of a puppy than I was. I got what Perry was talking about.

"Plus, I don't understand Welsh either. I'm a *Mancunian*." He pushes his accent for effect.

"Well, tell them to stop it. Serene's a female and Perry's fine with having me aboard."

"The Captain and his wife are the pinnacle for *any* good crew. They don't count."

"OK, get out of my face," I snarl. "Before I actually punch you."

He holds up his hands and takes a step back, just not enough for the other crew to see us speaking together. "Hey hey – I'm in here by *your* request. Just answering your questions, alright? I don't have it as easy either, you know. Did you know that any new crew member is *initiated* before they're formally accepted by the others?"

I frown. "I'm already here with you all."

"Ahh," he says annoyingly, wagging a finger. "You're present Morgan and so am I, but are we *accepted* by the crew? The remains to be seen. At any rate, there's like a group of tasks or something. The guys are gonna talk to me more tonight about it."

"How juvenile."

"How brilliant," he cuts across. "I need to lay some ground here, lady, and get some street cred. You wanna be like that scary old Texan all by himself most nights?"

"I'd rather be a Bobby, any day," I say defiantly. He snorts, pats me on the shoulder and leaves me alone in the alcove before sliding out to join the rest of the hustle.

The ship begins gliding slowly across the waters again which means we're out of immediate danger. I should already have felt the sweet breath of relief, but I'm still feeling embarrassed and ashamed of my childish behaviour, so I head to bed after mumbling goodnight to Serene.

I don't know what I'm dreaming about. It's hot as hell and I'm writhing and twisting in the bed sheets that stick to me like tar. I'm muttering something incoherently, dropping in and out of consciousness. The boat had long stopped rocking with the ebb of the weather, but my whole cabin feels as if it were shaking – or is it me?

I feel a body next to me before I hear them. Their warm cinnamon smelling essence invades into my own aura, feeling alien and inhuman. I shove back as hard as I could and was rewarded with an 'oof' and a crash of things falling off shelves, like an almighty crack of thunder. When I come to, the room is half blackened and charred with streaks of energy cooling after the initial outburst of current from my sleeping self. Two, large eyes stare at me in horror from beside my hammock.

It's Darrell.

He's totally shocked, his hands still clutching onto a Whoopee Cushion that looks as if it spills from the top with leftover mashed potato from dinner. If it wasn't for the lightning shaped streaks that was burned across the sheets and to the very far corners of the cabin, I wouldn't have been worried.

His cheek is raw from where a lash of power had struck him clean across the face. Already, pinpricks of blood were appearing on the smooth tanned surface – but it doesn't look as if he's even noticed or registered the pain. He's still staring, frozen into place.

"I... I can explain!" I begin to gabble desperately, but he's already dropped the prank cushion on the floor and escapes from the room with surprising finesse, before I can stop him.

-25-

"We need you for a raid, Morgan," Hamish says one morning, slapping my back lightly with one of the captain's faxes from his mysterious contact. I choke on my bread roll and quickly snatch the paper from the bow ledge before it catches the wind and flies over the side of the ship.

"You're eating out here now?" The slender man nods to the wooden crate of ropes I'm precariously sitting on. His short brown hair tugs at the bottom of his neck, blowing around his face lightly.

"Fresh air helps with the headaches," I mutter and scan the paper.

"You're a terrible liar," he chides but the personal talk was over. "We're hitting the south of Portugal at a place called *Sagres.* There's a privately-owned dock and warehouse we need to gain access to. Should be fairly low key. A good first raid."

"So what do we actually do in a raid?"

"We're being paid to release a couple of shipments of some electronics and deliver it to the North African continent."

"Seems like a pretty long journey for just some old DVD players and televisions?" I frown. The fax confirmed nothing more really then what he'd explained anyway, plus a string of complicated looking coordinates and letters.

"We got some other jobs down that way, so the flight path's set-in stone. We got strict deadlines to meet."

"No tourist stops?"

"No tacky keychains for you," he says and takes the paper back from me, shredding it carefully in his hands, casting it over the side. I decide that although his tall, stern, and blank look is typically intimidating; he's an honest man and I respect that.

"Darrell feeling better?" I ask nonchalantly.

He shrugs. "I'm not his nanny. He'll come out of his bunk when he's well enough to get back to work again. That kid should come with a permanent sick note."

"Yeah," I say softly. It's been three days since the fateful night Darrell walked in to see me shoot electricity across the room. By sheer miracle, I was on my own in the female quarters – but disguising and explaining the scorch marks was definitely going to be a problem for another day. I was lucky enough I didn't ignite the whole ship and if anything, was a terrifying reminder that I need to work on my self-control. And fast

My problem is his big mouth and the habit of putting his even bigger foot inside it. True enough, my mother hadn't told a soul to my knowledge before she... passed. But the likelihood of being this lucky two times in a row was slim to nothing.

I thought about trying to track the boy down myself to threaten him within an inch of his life, but an announcement from one of the crew in the cockpit, confirms that we will be closing in on our designated job within a few hours.

"Meeting in 10 to discuss tactics," Hamish says finally and returns to the inside.

We don't officially dock until just after 11pm local time, so dinner was served a little later than usual to accommodate for the hunger pangs at the later hour, but not so close that we were all bloated and sluggish.

Serene let me off my duties for the day so I can prepare and be involved with the other crew members selected to go on land. A part of me wonders why the hell they trust me to not screw the operation for everyone, but maybe that's the point. Perhaps this was *my* initiation and the chance to proof myself.

Even now, the majority of the crew members look at me with uncertain worried glances and I remember Darrell insisting it was because of the old wives' tale that women were simply unlucky at sea.

I frown. I'd show them alright.

My family never holidayed outside of the UK, so I was hoping that Sangres was going to be a hot paradise of palm trees and beaches. Instead, outlined by the gloom of the warehouse against a crescent moon, it's a boring old port with concrete buildings and structures that line the side of the shore. Again, we leave the bigger ship farther out in the water where it's harder to be seen and ride the dingy closer to land.

The calm waves against the side of the boat were feeling more normalised now, I barely even feel the nausea anymore as we rock back and forth.

"Now everybody's got their tasks," Hamish says, voice low and barely audible against the wash of the water against the wooden berth. "If you got any questions or concerns – now better be the time. No? Off we go then." Quietly, he swings himself up from the boat and expertly pulls himself around the beams to slide onto the wooden planks, pausing to listen for any voices nearby.

Satisfied, he unfurls the rope ladder from the platform and one by one, we scuttle up onto the deck and crouch low. I expect the air to be humid for Portugal, but it's bitter and chilly. Still, the freshness is a welcome change from the ship.

Hamish tosses the aft dingy rope to one of the other crew mates, who ties it neatly against the berth. "Razor, Turnip, Caramel – you head left. Crow, Surrey, and Ghost – right. Morgan, you're the lookout," he whispers. "You got your tasks. Get to it!" As the rest of the crew shuffle off into the darkness, a hand falls on my shoulder and he points towards the corner of the back yard.

I turn to where he's pointing and see a small security office that's completely dark with no visible life within. There's a huge sign by the front door, warning criminals of the ramifications of breaking in and theft. I swallow. I can't read Portuguese, but the meaning is pretty clear, it wouldn't take long for the authorities to figure out that I wasn't a local if I was caught.

"You want me to guard it?" I ask lightly. He nods. "I can't get arrested, Hamish"

"Then don't get caught," he offers. "You probably won't find any trouble there, but it's wise to have a pair of eyes and ears, especially with the naval patrols getting more frequent. We'll only be a few metres away in the warehouse, so whistle if you see anything, OK?

I'm counting on you." He looks so confident in me, that I find myself nodding along. If this would literally be my only use in life from now on, so be it. I would be as useful as I possibly could.

"Good luck," he murmurs. "Keep yourself hidden and safe. We'll see you in a bit." He pulls his dark beanie down over his face, taking the other route down the deck which drops onto the wooden slats below. He disappears into the distance with the others and before I get too scared to move, I follow the route laid out for me.

The slats are worn and creak in places with the pressure of my shoes, but seems stable enough to sprint along. I head over to the left-hand side of the huge building and make my way over to the security unit. It's a lot darker without the moonlight to bounce off the sea as the clouds roll in overhead. It's so silent that I can hear my own heart drum away in my chest.

There must be a main road not too far away as cars race back and forth somewhere in the distance. The only streetlamps are over the front of the complex which highlight the slip road that leads down to the docks. I wonder if there's really no security here at night or if one of Perry's contacts had been somehow engineered the staff to take the night off.

I exhale. The temperature isn't too uncomfortable, but the darkness presses down on me and makes me feel alienated and small. The flickers of the streetlights are orange balls in my field of vision, and I'm suddenly transported back to *that* night.

"Breathe," I scold myself. "Get it together." How can I be a reliable part of the team when I was freaking out at the dark, for God's sake.

I crouch low, back against the rough surface of the brick behind me. There's a couple of bins that provide a lot of cover which churns my stomach with old smells. There are rat droppings on the floor and a small hole in the side of the plastic. If a rodent decides to appear, the jig is up for me.

I try to count the minutes in my head, but I quickly get bored and drop my eyes from the road and the other buildings around us. Instead, I think of Jared and where he was now. I try to imagine him happy, maybe with a girlfriend or a home even. I wish I had properly memorised his face as he balanced on the edge of my windowsill the evening that seemed so long ago.

I should have gone with him. They'd still be alive.

A jangle of keys startles me from my thoughts and my body presses itself further into the shadows, ears and eyes strained. There's nothing for a few moments, but a pair of boots approaches from the other side of the security building, from the main entrance that faced the road.

"No," I mutter. I try to push my lips together to whistle, but only air comes out. Exasperated, I try again and again. I'm red in the face and my heart is racing a mile a minute. The guard stops to unlock the door metres from me, humming a little tune to himself.

When he enters, I only have moments before he drops his belongings and get back to his job. Everyone's depending on me.

I drop the whistling attempt and push my hands to my face and give a loud seagull imitation. It's nowhere near believable, but it's just loud and ridiculous enough, I hoped, for someone to hear in the warehouse and raise a silent alarm.

Inside, I hear the guard mutter to himself, and I hoped to God that he wouldn't appear from the windows or doors. I can feel the change in energy in the air as he begins to turn on his electronic equipment, boost up his computer. In a few seconds, he will see us in his security feed, and it'd be over.

I move quickly away from the safety of the bins and the shadows as I race across the concrete towards the deck. My feet are slapping heavily against the old wooden slats and I'm making a huge racket, but I see the dingy slowly pulling away from the mooring and will them to run faster.

Hamish and the others are poised ready to help me with their arms outstretched. There's no time for questions and second guesses, so I run to the end of the pier, plant my feet on the rim and force my body outwards towards the boat.

Whether or not it was a normal jump that seemed to go on forever or aided by my abilities, no one says anything out of the ordinary. Five pairs of hands catch me easily, holding both arms and my waist so I don't fall backwards into the water.

It isn't until we move further out into the middle of the harbour that there's enthusiastic whoops and cheers from my peers.

The feeling is electric. Every person ruffles my hair and plants a kiss on the top of my head as I am passed from one to the next. Someone drapes an arm around my shoulders and another high fives me. The mission was an obvious success as a pile of small leather bags line the bottom of the boat.

"Not really the sort of electronics I was thinking." I laugh. I'm still in shock at the magnitude of what we've just accomplished and how close we were to getting caught.

Hamish smiles, he looks relieved and even pats me on the back. "These chips and computer disks are extremely valuable to certain parties. Payday will be good." More cheers meet the end of his sentence.

When we return to The Whittaker, Captain Perry and Serene are among a small crowd of people are gathered to meet us. Immediately she grabs me into a bone crushing hug with a murmur of; "I'd have *bloody* murdered that man if he let anything happen to you!"

"Ye of little faith, woman. I would never have left her behind." Hamish rolls his eyes. I smile at their exchange and try to crane my head through the small crowed to see if Darrell had left his bunk to join us, but saw no sign of the lanky, cockily grinning idiot that I expected.

I swallow and put him out of my mind as much as I can. Tonight will be cause for celebration, tomorrow we'll be back to work as we head towards the scheduled drop.

I'm carried around on the shoulders of my peers and clapped on the back in congratulations for an awesome first assignment. Someone hands me a bottle of beer and I happily bask in my newfound comfortable acceptance, wondering if this is what family and happiness is really supposed to be.

-26-

Feigning a stomach-ache, I wait until everyone's disappeared to breakfast the next day before exploring the ship for the men's quarters.

They're easy enough to find. It's a much larger cabin with two doors either side of the room that looked more like a man den more than a bedroom. Similar to mine, hammocks are strewn around the perimeter of the room with a few bunkbeds in the corner for the older sailors. In the middle, on an old rug, someone had pulled a coffee table and pillows with scattered playing cards and chess pieces around it. It matches the chaos and disorganisation as the rest of the cabin which was sparsely decorated in hanging clothes, bags, and shoes for drying. I wouldn't have even noticed the movement of covers from the hammock in the far corner if I didn't see the clothes swinging along with it.

Holding my breath, I move over to the pile and drag everything off in one fell swoop.

"Christ!" someone shouts and races to pull his blanket back over him. Darrell blearily peers through the gloom towards me, confused more than anything else. "What the hell are you doing in here?"

"I came to see if you were OK." I point towards the deep scratch on his cheek. He touches it, wincing and nods slowly.

"I'm fine. I didn't tell anyone either, if that's what you're coming to check," he adds as an afterthought, voice croaky from his latest cold. He wasn't lying to avoid me after all.

Slightly stung, I shake my head. "I was more worried about you than me. It must've been a shock."

"Is that a joke?" he asks, incredulous. "Because if so, it's pretty funny." His cracked lips pull up into a half smile, he sits up in his hammock a little straighter now that the initial tension was over and done with.

"I just want to say that I'm sorry. I was half asleep and then suddenly you were there and--"

"It's okay, no harm done. A cool scar hopefully to tell the girls back home, but we're good, you and me." He gestures between us. I try to look for a hint of mistrust or fear behind his clean expression, but don't find anything.

"Still," I reason. "I try not to make it a habit to hurt anyone," I smile gingerly, turning to leave the cabin and head down for some food. I hear him scramble out of his hammock with difficulty behind me.

"That was really you?" he says breathlessly, pulling on his many layers of clothing. "I didn't imagine it? The guys didn't put me up to it as part of their stupid initiation trial? I mean, I thought the potato Whoopee Cushion sounded kinda easy but...."

"All me." I shrug, the sudden feeling of exposure overwhelming me. Darrell is not acting at all like I thought he would, and it's making me nervous.

"Cool." He nods as if we were talking about someone completely mundane compared to this. Perplexed, I force a smile one last time and leave to retrace my steps back down to the canteen where the scent of bacon sandwiches are waiting for me.

Serene waves me over to my usual table where she'd already lain down my share along with a brimming mug of hot tea. The success of my first raid the night before must have spread, because there's a couple of people sitting at my bench and cheerfully greeting me good morning as I take my usual seat.

Feeling as if the entire world was upside down and wondering if I was still dreaming, I lean down to take the first bite out of my bacon sandwich, when a tall shadow crosses over the table.

"Move up buddy," Darrell says cheerfully to our comrade named Ghost. To his credit, he's braver than I would have thought – Ghost is a large built, very muscular man and regards Darrell with a brief glance of a raised eyebrow before returning back to his pile of bacon.

"Gotcha," Darrell mutters and slides in on the other side of me, still grinning from ear to ear.

"Wipe that stupid smile off your face," I say, cheeks flaming with embarrassment that I hoped no one would see and get the wrong idea over. He shrugs nonchalantly and takes a huge bite of his own sandwich, looking thoughtful.

"So can you control it?" Was his next question.

"Keep your voice down," I mutter. "No one else but you knows, and even *that* is further beyond my threshold than I wanted."

"Sure, but have you always been able to do things like that?"

"No," I snap. "Are you capable of restraining your verbal diarrhoea for five minutes to let me *eat* in peace?" Beside us, Ghost and the other guy finish their meals and rise to head off somewhere else. They both give us a nod goodbye, leaving me to the painful mercy of my rookie comrade.

"Not when my interest is piqued. I need to know more! Come on, Morg. Give up the gory details."

"There's nothing to tell."

He snorts. "I have never seen someone literally shoot electricity out of their body like that before. This cut right here – hasn't stopped tingling since!"

"Get yourself a plaster or something."

"No way, this is my battle scar. I'm telling the guys I got this fighting off some angry homeless man for our next shipment. Oh, don't look at me like that Morg, I said before – you're fine."

"I'm far from fine. And stop calling me *Morg*." I sigh and rise to toss my half-eaten food in the rubbish bin nearby. Predictably, he rises with me and slaps his tray on top of my own on the trolley rack. As I turn to head into the kitchen to start the day, he grabs my arm firmly until I turn back to face him. Shockingly, all traces of laughter and excitement are gone, replaced with an alien look of concern.

"What can I do to help?" he says.

That was easy. "I need you to stay away from me, Darrell. You'll get hurt and I can't always keep it inside where it belongs," I murmur and gently pull my arm away from him.

The kitchen staff are also acting a lot nicer to me than usual. They involve me in their banter back and forth, providing some background history of The Whittaker, when the main body of the crew was formed under Captain Perry and Serene's leadership almost a decade ago, after they decided to lump their life savings together and buy an old boat from a former navy colleague.

None of this did much to distract me from the very real fact that I had a human ticking time bomb walking around the ship, grinning as if I were the coolest thing in the whole world.

Leaving the smells of slow cooking ham hock and pea soup behind me, I have the afternoon to myself before I am needed again to help with the dinner rush. We dock tomorrow morning to offload our stock in a little fishing port in Safi, Morocco. Serene is going to write up a list of cooking supplies for me to pick up on land before we move off again.

"What's this?" I choke, opening my cabin door.

Darrell sits in the middle on one of the armchairs, casually lifting his feet off the shelving unit and turns to face me. Beside him on the table, are a couple of assorted bits and pieces. Random items of junk.

"Hear me out before you go flying off the handle and throw the door in my face," he warns, palms up. "I'm here to offer my assistance."

"And how are you going to help me exactly?"

"I'm going to help train you."

The thought was so ridiculous and out of place, I begin to giggle until my stomach hurt. Darrell stands patiently and waits for it to pass before attempting to say anything else.

"I'm sorry, it's just so––"

"Weird."

"Yeah. I didn't think you were going to be the next Professor X. You're what – nineteen?"

"Twenty. Almost. The point is, you're worried about hurting people and you clearly have no idea what you're doing. So here I am, dedicating my free afternoon to helping my young protégé achieve her greatest self." He opens his arms gesturing broadly to the items next to him, daring me to say otherwise. With a sigh, I let the door push to a close behind me.

"And what are your training credentials, may I ask?"

"I trained my mum's Shih Tzu to bring me her car keys once," he offers, deadpan. "And trust me, that Shih Tzu was a worse student than you."

"We'll see about that," I mutter. The confidence in his face makes me want to close my eyes and run. He honestly has no idea how much power I could possess, or how it would be so easy to use his body's own electrical current to stop his heart. He blindly trusts me without even knowing who I am or what I've done. Then again, I guess Captain Perry did too.

"Fine, fine. Whatever."

"That's the spirit," he says cheerfully and gestures to a couple of pillows he'd grabbed off my hammock for me to sit on. Obediently, I follow his lead and sit, trying not to let the swell of nerves grab me.

The assortment of random items Darrell had found around the ship consists of old batteries, lightbulbs, an alarm clock, an electric fan, and an old toaster. When I ask if Serene knew he was borrowing the kitchen appliances, he pretends he didn't hear the question.

"You'll be in trouble," I warn.

He rolls his eyes and moves to grab a lightbulb from his small pile of stolen goods.

I wave my hand away. "I don't know if I want to do this. This is useless."

"Are you crazy? Have you seen what you can do? Yeah, it's not perfect, but that's why you're training it. You think Spiderman *knew* how to web sling and wall crawl?"

"I'm not a superhero, I'm an accident, let's not forget about that. At least Spiderman knew where his powers came from, I can barely concentrate on getting my life together for God's sake."

"Ok so, concentrate on this then," he says as if it were the easiest thing in the world. "It's gotta be as natural as opening a book or taking a shower or *walking*, for you. It's inside, like a part of you."

"It's completely unnatural for a start and no, it's not that easy to concentrate," I hiss. "Not when one slip of concentration could easily kill you and everyone aboard or fry our electrics or even the navigational system!"

"Calm down, calm down. Look at me. You're not going to kill me; you aren't like that."

"It's a lightbulb." I sigh. "It's not even connected to anything. What are we even doing here?"

"We are making sure you don't become someone's weapon of mass destruction," he shrugs. "AKA the lightbulb test. In theory, you should be replacing the current – so it doesn't need to be connected to anything. It is literally your conduit."

"This is so stupid."

"Humour me." He presses and holds it firmly between his fingers. Treating him to an eye roll of my own, I lean forward to rest on my crossed legs and gaze at the thing. Nothing happens.

"See?"

"You're not even bothering to try."

Stung, I gaze harder at the bulb. Try to visualise a light turning on somewhere. It barely even changes hue. I can't feel any electrical residue from it.

"Again," he says simply.

"I'm trying."

"Not you're not."

I frown and my teeth grind together in annoyance. I would show him exactly what wasting an afternoon with me would give him. I move my body's energy inwards, grasping around for that lever of power hiding deep within. When I find it, the strange consciousness is ignited. It's pulsing quietly, unsure of itself.

The bulb sparks into life as soon as I project that energy outward. Just a quick burst that plunges the room back into a half-light quicker than it had illuminated. I try again, another burst I can't hold for very long before the mental band snaps back. On the third try, the lightbulb shines brighter and brighter. I manage to hold the current steady for about ten seconds before cracks fill the air and it explodes into hundreds of shards, peppering my companion.

"Next one," he says, shaking his hair and pulling out another.

"I don't think I can," I say, already feeling the pull of tiredness.

"Think about the angriest you've ever been. The times you literally had no one to support you, had a crappy day or week or year. All those times you've been alone."

I glance at the shards of lightbulb on the floor and shake my head. "I'm going to end up hurting you and that's not fair."

"I'm fine. I'm not hurt – see?" He holds up both palms. "I've even got gloves next to me if I need them, but I'm not feeling the whole 'I think you're about to kill me, Morg' vibe here yet."

"Stop calling me Morg. And you won't," I say hotly, anger flaring up and licking the edges of my brain. "If I wanted to kill you, you'd be dead before you even know it! I've killed before and I will definitely do it again if I get out of control so... just leave it alone."

Silence fills the room quicker than I realise what I've just said. Darrell's face stays neutral, as if I didn't just announce one of my biggest shames to him. After a few minutes, he shakes his head with a small grin and says, "Woah, hey. You won't be able to kill *The Darrell*, no matter how much you try."

I snort involuntarily. "That's your sailor name?"

"I haven't earned mine yet. I'm hoping for something preceding with 'The'. It sounds more powerful and cooler."

It's so ridiculous that I begin to laugh, really laugh, from the bottom of my abdomen to my brain. He chuckles along with me, not at all bothered this was at his expense. When I'm done, I wipe the moisture from my eyes – from fear or hilarity, I don't know.

"I will hurt you," I say again, becoming serious.

"You won't," he presses and jiggles the bulb. "Conduit, remember? Just focus on this object in my hands and I won't go back to my bunk a human glass dispenser."

"I can't."

"You can," he presses. "And I'll bet the more you try not to, the worse it gets to try and control. "You're practically shaking."

Sighing dramatically and with no other argument left in my weary body, I give in and follow every instruction. By the time three hours has passed, I've managed to charge at least two of the five batteries, which we tested by loading up the alarm clock. I wasted a few lightbulbs and saved the others successfully. I also managed to spin the electric fan for three cycles before the front of the grate blew off into the corner of the room and the toaster spluttered and fried before dying completely and filling the room with light smoke.

Sweating, I allow myself to lean back and catch my breath which was ragged with effort. Still sitting patiently in the same place, Darrell tries to save Serene's toaster one last time before calling time of death.

"Maybe we can blame it on Bobby?" he mutters, pushing it under one of the unused bunks.

-27-

My muscles strain under the weight of the rope that's tossed in my direction by Ghost. Just over the twenty-four months I'd been sailing with the crew now, and it has given my scrawny body a little definition, but my joints and tendons still cry with the dull aches they aren't used to. Mortifyingly, Serene provides me with heat patches at the end of the evenings so I can find sleep properly.

"It takes years to build up the muscle." She soothes nightly and slaps the next hot cloth on, straight from the side of the oven.

I finish with the rope. My knot's not perfect but it holds the dinghy securely and does the job. Hamish quickly glances as he passes and gives me a small nod and a grunt of approval.

"Is this how you thought you'd spend your last weeks being eighteen?" Darrell whispers and hands me a pack from the boat. I take it and shoulder it quickly, strapping the tools to me securely via the clips at the front of my chest. I give him a look.

"You know the answer to that."

"Wanted to see if you'd gone hardcore Morg yet." He grins at the sly comment, but I know better than to snipe at him in front of the others and he knew better than to push my buttons further.

My core strength isn't the only thing I'm still finding. Darrell and I hole up in my cabin most nights to continue to try and maintain some kind of composure over my power, with slow and frustrating results. We decided to make a truce and he wouldn't tell my secret in trade for a proper friendship with me. It was two years of mutual respect.

I was surprised at the time. Why would *anyone* want to befriend someone filthy and murderous like me? Sure enough after my first successful raid, the crew warmed to me significantly after that and we became a single unit of trust and kinmanship, but it still baffles me.

"What's the play?" Viper murmurs to Hamish as we skim the bottom of a concrete wall that peels and flicks paint off against our clothes. Our leader holds his fist high as he peers around the corner and we huddle together. It was just the five of us moving in a small group on this particular landing. I've never worked much with Viper before, but he and Ghost are solid mates already, even resembling brothers with their matching curly brown hair and roughly shaven faces––if not for Ghost's intimidating bicep muscles and Viper's arms adorned in tattoos from his home in Barbados.

"Quick mission," Hamish says. "Team One will go round the front and keep lookout, while Team Two here are in charge of the good stuff. You see that beautiful little yacht over there? Our client lost it during a high stakes game of poker and well... we're cleaning up."

It certainly looks as if it's been well looked after. The boat rocks quietly on the end of the private dock, surrounded by high, lush green hedges and the typical Spanish orange vineyard––looking straight out of a holiday magazine.

In the distance, a beautiful cream coloured villa sits barricaded by rows of perfect beds of flowers and a pool around the side, illuminated in a golden sunshine colour.

"Who the hell lives here?" I mutter. I'd seen a lot of expensive looking houses in my short time as a crew member, but it was one of the more illustrious places we'd hit.

"It's some billionaire's third holiday home," Viper mutters. "There's probably a lot of expensive shit in there. A theatre room I'll bet."

"And a home gym," Ghost interjects. "These millionaires always have home gyms they hardly use. It's almost a shame to leave it all behind. Good gym equipment is pricey."

Hamish indicates his hand towards the dock. "Forget about the house – let's get moving. Stay focused."

On his mark, we press ourselves against the stone slabs of the outer wall and follow the cobbled path around to where our feet meet the rows of wood. We pause, each assigned a direction and a job to keep an eye on. Nothing seems particularly out of the ordinary, except for a handsome male peacock that roams around the lower tier of the expanse of grass. He hears our quiet approach and glares, feathers rustling.

"Crap, do you think they bite?" Darrell asks.

"You're about to find out if you don't shut it," Hamish retorts. "Escort Morgan to the yacht since she's good with electronics. Turn off the satellite navigation and tracker. We'll patrol our here and keep watch. Give the signal when you're done, and we'll stay in two teams to sail back together."

"I'll make a sound if someone comes," Ghost affirms.

"Better not be a peacock or he'll have you." Darrell grins and nods towards the bird that ventures closer.

"*Darrell.*"

"We're going, we're going." He prods me in the shoulder to follow him and takes lead. I feel so exposed, losing the strength of the other three men around me, but it was just psychological. We'd done this at least twice a week for the past six months. We're one of most efficient units on the Whittaker and Perry knew it, only entrusting the higher stakes of jobs to our cell of five. Somehow, the job was always completed, one way or another.

Up close, the yacht is more extravagant than I'd initially realised. A good fifty or sixty feet of well-polished and scrubbed fibre glass down to the plush velvet seats that were down in the sheltered seating area. The cockpit itself was a separately doored compartment that was positioned just to the side of the neat steps that wound down to the cabin below.

"Only an asshat sails out in velvet chairs," Darrell mutters. I don't do him the justice of letting him see my grin but slap him lightly on the shoulders. "What? You don't see Perry all decked out in silk pyjamas and velvet slippers, do you?"

"I never want to think about Perry in silk pyjamas, thanks." The lock of the cockpit door was easy enough to work, Darrell was more skilled with bobby pins than I was, so I step aside and let him work on it while I keep watch. The night air is cool and still, chillier now we were on the water. I think I can sense the winds changing within the next day or two – a skill Perry himself taught me – but there wasn't supposed to be another storm for a couple of weeks, which allows us some work opportunities possibly around Italy next.

"Done," Darrell whispers and pushes the door open. We prepare for an alarm or a ringing, but the silence stretches on.

"I'll be quick," I promise and kneel down next to the controls, out of sight from anyone who might potentially stroll up the private docks or down the gardens of the surrounding estates. I feel him stir impatiently next to me, eager to be involved.

"Keep lookout, will you?" I hiss and concentrate on working the control panel. My light's suddenly blocked by a Darrell shaped shadow as he leans eagerly over me. "What the hell, do you *mind*?"

"Not at all. I love watching you do your thing."

"That's creepy and wrong on so many levels," I grumble, but I turn back to the equipment and try to unfurl the electrical currents with my imperfect and clumsy mental feelers. The next time a shadow falls over me, I full on curse him loudly, turning to punch him in the kneecap, but I'm met with a big scary man with a scar across his face.

Before I can react, I lose my concentration with the power – it falls away from me as he grabs my hair and yanks me to my feet. I begin to open my mouth to screech when he shoves a fistful of material in my mouth to muffle the sound and drags me out of the cockpit onto the bow of the yacht.

"Another," he says to four equally large gentleman on the dock, all each have one of us. Viper's shoulder is held at an odd angle, and he must be in agony, but he's trying with all his might not to show any weakness. Hamish simply looks bored, but I don't miss the pinch of his jaw either side of his face.

"Start walking!" my assailant commands and lifts me with him over the safety line onto the dock, as easily as a stuffed bear. Ghost purposely tries to drag his heels and earns himself several kicks to the backs of his legs.

I expect to be shot and killed straight away, but we're led across the darkened grass to a greenhouse looking structure that houses baskets of recently picked oranges on the shelves. The whole place reeks of the sickly-sweet citrus taste that's so strong and overpowering, I begin to feel sick.

One by one, we're tossed to the floor and deliberately separated at least a metre apart. Two guards are left with us, each of which has a smart leather holster on their hips with an equally smart pistol easily in hands reach.

"Go wake him," one disembodied voice says to another, just outside of the greenhouse door. "I don't *care* how late it is, he must be notified!"

"They're not Spanish," I whisper, mostly for my own benefit. The guard closest to me slaps the back of my head with the palm of his rock-hard hand and sends me reeling.

"Gustav, Raka," the first voice says. "Come out here for two seconds."

The two men obey after checking we were tied up efficiently enough and they both slough off to the outside of the greenhouse to speak with the others. Whoever they were trying to wake up, I assume would probably live in the amazingly large villa and probably an equally large temper, to employ guards so muscular and ham fisted in their execution of apprehending us.

We each had a set of expensive looking handcuffs pressing tightly on our wrists. Mine are prised painfully behind my back. I shuffle closer to study Darrell's closely, moving my head from side to side to get a good angle on the locking mechanism.

"Getting *real* close to your boyfriend there, Morgan." Viper smiles, wincing as his dislocated shoulder twitches.

"Shut up," Darrell mutters. "What do you think?" he directs towards me.

"Some sort of electronic lock," I conclude. Our eyes meet for just a moment, and I know what he's thinking.

"It's up to you," he says. "Or we wait for another opportunity when they return with Mr. Big Boss."

"There may not be one," I bite the sides of my lip and searching around the room to check for security cameras. I'd only cause more trouble if my next act was going to be filmed and passed around the dark side of the web with a bounty on my head.

"Hamish, Ghost, Viper. I'm gonna need you to close your eyes here and trust me," I whisper. Three confused looks shine at me and there's no time to explain properly, so Darrell hisses at them to shut up and listen to everything I say.

"I'm going to override the electronic locks on these handcuffs," I say hurriedly. "There's no time to explain how – but I need you all to keep quiet ease off on the questions."

More puzzled looks and frowns. But they're as trapped and hopeless as I am, so they wisely choose to close their mouths and let me focus on the tangible buzz of electrodes in the atmosphere so I could close my eyelids and shut off the world.

The handcuffs are easy enough to find, even with my eyes closed. The electrically charged molecules in the air all around us was attracted to them and greedily converged on the small charging pulses that kept the lock engaged. Not having direct contact with each piece of equipment was going to be tougher than usual, but I'd been trying to practice every opportunity I can.

I try my own handcuffs first to try and test the waters. I'm moving the electricity around within the equipment and trying to find the perfect range in which I could manipulate the release catch. I'm trying not to be too self-conscious at how crazy I must look, wiggling back and forth on my pile of dried soil.

The greenhouse is quiet as they hang on to my every movement. It feels like a thousand degrees, sweat pours from my forehead. I can feel the intensity of their eyes on me and I'm sure Darrell's beaming face is in amongst the shock and confusion. The handcuffs are warm around my wrists, and I triumphantly feel the click of sweet release. I project outwards to the other four sets of handcuffs and gently try to force the electrical currents in the opposite direction. Quicker now, I'd gotten the hang and feel for the frequency of pressure and charge I needed to pulse.

Four pairs of hands mirror mine as we rub our palms and our wrists to encourage blood flow again. Hamish and Ghost waste no time in taking each side of Viper, gingerly helping him to his feet.

"Not yet, man," Viper moans as his dislocated shoulder rocks to the side with the effort of being helped to his feet. "We'll reset it... later. No time."

"How did you do that?" Ghost gapes at me, a large grown man so muscled and strong that it looks almost comical for him to be in awe of a little woman like me. I shrug and mumble something about being good with electronics. My go to answer that said explained absolutely nothing but was the best they were all going to get.

"We can't fight with one man down," Hamish says. "But there's an open window over there. Too small for comfort. We only have a small gap to escape, so it's now or never."Darrell takes the rear as the other two men try their best to navigate Viper through the small horizontal opening in the glass. It must be excruciating work for Viper, who had a roll of Ghost's bandanas in his mouth and tears stream down his eyes with every jolt.

When they are clear. Darrell gives me a boost up so I can clear the ledge easily, leaning down to offer my hands to him while hooking my legs over the opposite side of the sill to anchor me. He's surprisingly lighter than I thought he would be, for someone who ate nothing but crisps and half-drank beer.

By a sheer stroke of luck, the guards are still discussing at the front of the structure and partially arguing at how best to handle their boss, who would no doubt be out to give them a bollocking for their lack security, to disturb his sleep.

We choose to keep to the shadows of the high slate wall and the shade of the orange trees as we make our way back down to the entrance to the private dock, where our own floating chariot floats close by in which to make our escape.

When the first three are boarded, Darrell grabs me lightly on the shoulder.

"What is it?" I spit, partly in frustration that I allowed us to get caught so stupidly and partly because I now had three other full-grown problems walking around with my secret, that I was really trying not to focus on.

"You're... uh, pretty awesome, you know," he says quickly. and turns around to head back into the boat before he could see the unsteady blush furl across my face.

-28-

There's an unsteady silence on the dingy back to The Whittaker only shattered by the intermittent groans of Viper, holding his wounded shoulder.

"Doesn't look too challenging to get back into place," Hamish grunts, scrutinising the joint with his piercing eyes. "A contained fracture and dislocation most likely."

"You're a lot more cheerful about that than I am," Viper grunts. With every rock of the boat against the cool waves, he winces, his face contorts. For a skinny guy he had a decent pain threshold, probably more than I would have.

"You want me to call your mama?" Ghost offers. "I have her on speed dial somewhere." He grins, lightly punching his friend's other shoulder, who rolls his eyes and grits his teeth. Darrell, a long way off from the conversation, glances back where we'd left the dock behind.

"That was a close one." He whispers.

"Too close," Hamish nods. "If not for Morgan, we'd probably be dead or enjoying torture right now. These are not people to be messed with. The Captain won't like this."

"What did we do wrong?" I ask, my voice killing all other murmurs of conversation.

Hamish takes a minute to analyse this. "We acted to what the specifications of the mission were: we infiltrated in a blind spot, played to the change of the guard shifts. We checked every corner, every dark spot. Sometimes, it happens and there's nothing we can do. Could have been a tip off, could have been bad luck."

"Won't they have our faces on CCTV to show the authorities?" Darrell says.

Hamish snorts, humourlessly. "These are not the kind of people who file police reports." He concentrates back on controlling the engine. Whether or not his words are meant to console us or scare us, we fall into a deep silence and don't glance at one another until we're back on the ship.

It's the middle of the night so there's no fanfare to join us this time. Just Captain Perry and Serene with grave looking faces after Hamish has radioed ahead to give them a head up. As soon as we hoist ourselves up the ladders and the dingy is back on the winch, Serene envelopes me in a quick hug and ushers me quickly inside.

"You don't need to meet me every time I go out," I protest. "I'll be fine."

"You're a young lady going out with a bunch of loud, smelly men," she says. "I'll be damned if I don't ensure they bring you back in one piece!"

I almost tell her that I'm probably the most well equipped of the whole crew, but the smile dies on my lips. Regardless, if everyone was distracted by the failed mission or not; they had seen and felt the effect of my power. I performed the impossible to save our lives sure, but I *had* performed the impossible.

Still, a small part of me wants to see this as the beginning of change. I managed to use and focus my energy for *good*. I did it. All me.

Maybe, I'm not as doomed as I thought I was going to be.

It doesn't take long for the hammock lightly tilting back and fro, to lull me into sleep. The dreams start out innocent enough. I'm playing with Georgia in her house when we were five years old and they'd brought home their puppy for the first time, rendering me hot with jealously. Then it changes to Jared and I playing at the beach when we were kids, eating ice cream. A dark shadow falls upon us and I glance up from our wonky sandcastle to see three men looming over with ropes in their hands. I'm screaming as they're tying me together and dragging me away from Jared, daring me to escape.

"Woah." Darrell moves out of the way to allow me to sit up straight in the hammock. My skin is peppered with beads of sweat, even though I'd kicked my covers onto the floor during the course of the night. I'm shaking. Every part of me is trembling.

"You OK?" he says. "I was just walking down to grab lunch, and I heard you screaming."

"I'm fine," I say quickly, holding up a hand to give me space. He moves across the room, leaning against one of the storage containers, still staring.

"What?" I snap. "You shouldn't even be in here – you know what happened last time."

He taps his cheek subconsciously. The wound was long gone, but there was still a hint of a scar from his ear to the middle of his cheekbone. Instantly, I feel the old stab of regret and shame.

"I'm sorry. Bad dream."

"It's OK," he says easily. "You want to get something to eat? You've been asleep near ten hours."

My stomach rolls hopefully but I don't want to think about sitting in a canteen surrounded by people staring at me. Was the secret out? Will they all know the moment I come face to face and parade me with questions I can't answer?

"No, I think I'll just hang here today. I have some crisps and peanuts in my bag."

"Nutritious," he says, making no move to go anywhere.

"I think I might sneak in another nap then," I say pointedly. "So, I'll see you later. Or something."

He grins. "Oh I get the hint, but I'm not going anywhere until you tell me what's on your mind. I can practically smell the shame-spiral from here, but I can't work out why.

Throwing myself back into my bunk with a deep sigh, I try to close my eyes to avoid him. A few moments later, I can feel his energy hovering nearby. I can feel the electrical signals direct his body's functions from his brain. Every nerve that fires, every autonomous movement, I can sense just as soundly as my own sight or touch or smell.

It's better to focus on it rather than facing up to him. Currents are easier to deal with, more dependable. I can almost premptively feel the impulses in my own body as my heart fires slightly out of time with his. Everything else melts away so I can concentrate. It was easier than breathing and one of the calmest feelings I'd had in a very long time. I liked the feel of Darrell's natural currents.

"Are you asleep?" he murmurs from somewhere to the left of me.

"No," I say. "Just trying to zone out everything. The sound of your heart is quite calming."

"You can hear it from over there?"

I smile. "Not quite, I can hear – or *feel* the electrical energy in your body. Like its own personal drumroll. Your heartbeat kind of magnifies that so it's like a really dull vibration."

"Dull," he nods out of the corner of my semi-closed eyes. "Hey, I've been called worse."

I take my pillow and aim it across the room where he's sitting on my stack of floor cushions. He laughs good naturedly, catching it easily.

"Anything but," I say with confidence and turn over to face his direction. He takes a moment and nods.

"Right back at you." I must have fallen back asleep soon after that, because I wake up again from a dreamless sleep at about four PM local time. Judging by the course tracker on one of the wall televisions in the hallway, we were heading for the Mediterranean coast next. With our yacht recovery failed, the next job would likely involve another team in the next raid. Maybe we'd even lie low for a bit when we reached Tunisia.

Still adamant I wasn't going to face anyone for as long as possible, I grab my snacks and fleece lined jacket and head up to the deck. Despite the warm air, the wind was chilly as it breezes over the length of the ship. As we were on the open sea, we were free to move during the daylight hours, provided that the path was quiet and there was little traffic.

I select my usual spot over at the far end of the ship by the buoys and nets, finding a dry pile of folded sheets to settle on. The air feels good through my shorter hair I'd decided to keep, blowing away all negative and scary images from my dream. The constant roar of sea against the boat and the soft turning of the waves beneath us, blocks out the other consciousness in my brain, so I can only focus on one thing. Me.

"Weather's holding up," someone says against the breeze. I open my eyes to find Hamish standing nearby, his hand on the winch, gazing out to the horizon.

"Sorry, I didn't know you were out here." This is it, I realise. The moment of truth I would need to face before I would be able to look him in the eyes again. I swallow nervously.

"No bother. I just like to check out a little daylight before I head downstairs to supervise the engine checks. It's nice to remind myself I'm not a mole in a tunnel."

"I come out here when I want my brain to shut off," I admit, glancing back out to the waves. "It drowns out every other insignificant thought."

He nods in agreement. "Truth be told Morgan, we were very close to not being able to feel this at all. What you did back there at the compound, you saved us. Whatever you did, that is."

I nod, the sound of the waves moving to the background. I try and judge his mood by his facial expression but he's typically just as stoic as always. I imagine if he wanted to throw me off the ship, he would look angrier about it.

"I've been in this game long enough not to ask too many questions, especially from people I trust," he says eventually, surprisingly. He turns to look at me and I hold his steady gaze with my own confusion. Hamish trusted me.

"Does everyone know?" I gulp, my airway was closing with anxiety.

"Darrell threatened Ghost and Viper with their lives – they laughed and patted him on the back, naturally. He knows better than to try that with me, so tried a more diplomatic approach," he unfurls his hands, and a crisp twenty-pound note sits on his palm, anchored by his fingers in the wind.

"He *bribed* you?" I say, incredulous.

Hamish breaks into a rare smile. "He didn't really need to. I know better than to oust one of my most useful team members. But the extra twenty quid was a nice bonus."

"Oh, Darrell." I shake my head.

"That boy is an idiot, but he wants to protect you," Hamish continues. "Those people can be hard to find. So let him do what makes him happy, what gives him purpose. It might make him more reliable checking his own damn equipment." With a roll of his eyes, the man gives me on last nod and pockets the note. Just like that in a few short sentences, the fear is pressed down to the bottom of my stomach and evaporated, for now.

"I told you that I gave you the day off," Serene barks when I enter the kitchen to grab my apron from the hooks. She's midway through preparing a fish curry for dinner, commanding the other two kitchen hands to balance the cooking rice and sauce without burning either.

"I had nothing to do, I'd rather be busy," I return.

Exasperated, she points with a wooden spoon over towards the grill where several layers of fish are sizzling quietly. The atmosphere in the kitchen is more tense than usual, the usual banter between the others was non-existent this evening.

"Is everything OK?" I mutter to one of them called Smirnoff, when we were washing our utensils at the sink. The curry was in the slow pot to continue cooking gently and Serene was eagerly flicking through her cookbooks for the next day's culinary inspiration. Smirnoff glances at her and back at me before murmuring, "I think she and Perry had a fight earlier."

My eyebrows raise. It was out of the ordinary for the patriarch and matriarch of The Whittaker to have a slight disagreement, let alone a full-blown argument. The other kitchen hand, Talon, brings his pans over to join us and nods enthusiastically.

"Perry got a tip from one of the navigation team that we were being tailed or something. They both disagree with what we should do next."

"Tailed?" I hiss. "As in followed? By who?" My newfound calmness disappears once again. My companions both shrug, looking at one another.

"We don't know," Smirnoff offers. "They could be just cops or something, or maybe someone else. They hang far enough back we can barely see them over the horizon, but they've been careful to steer back far enough we can't identify them properly."

"Serene thinks we should just dump our cargo and try and loose them around Greece," Talon adds. "Thing is, we're walled in by the Strait of Gibraltar, so there's only so far we can go before we need to turn around."

"We also need to refill at some point. What does Perry think?"

"The Captain says that we are probably just being overly paranoid. Lots of ships take a similar trade route, but their flight patterns match ours too much."

"That's why Hamish was outside," I whisper to myself. He was checking in on me, but his eyes were locked on the horizon. Me being so dense and self-absorbed – didn't even realise that there was another boat in the long stretch of distance. Some crew mate, I was.

Despite the delicious scents of cooking and the heat emanating from the hobs and ovens, I feel cold and numb inside. My companions continue to discuss and debate which course of action was better, but I can't hear a word they're saying. Despite what Perry thought, I'm more inclined to be paranoid and believe we were likely being followed by someone who wants something from us.

Or even *someone*.

-29-

"Happy nineteenth!" Captain Perry commends as he slaps me on the back, rendering me unable to swallow my mouthful of homemade cake, presented by his wife.

"Happy birthday sweet." She smiles and gives me a huge hug. Around the canteen, there's murmurs of *'to Morg!'* followed by the warm sounds of food being devoured by hungry men. Blushing, I get down from the raised crate that Perry pulled me up to join him on and escape to the corner with my own portion of food. Entering nineteen officially had earned Serene to disappear and come back with a crate of expensive looking beer from the last place we'd docked to trade. There's an uproar or appreciative conversation and the bottles are passed around.

Darrell hands me one, flicking the top off easily. I take it and have a long sip of my first real alcoholic experience. It's disgusting, I wasn't missing anything.

"Beer isn't for everyone." He laughs. "Maybe you're a wine and dine kind of lady."

"I'm not even sure I can be defined as a lady," I mutter. I'd gotten into the habit of keeping my hair shoulder length with just enough for tying up. My fingernails – although I try to keep as clean as possible – are always chipped and broken. I definitely have the body and frame of a young boy.

"We'll go onto the mainland and get you something to commemorate this occasion," Captain Perry promises and swings his arm around my shoulders like a proud father.

"We've only just docked," Ghost says. "God, give the girl a minute to appreciate a good hangover in the morning, would you?"

I open my mouth to retort, but whatever I'm about to say next is lost to the sudden explosion of chaos all around us.

Men begin to flood into the canteen. Not the usual guys from engineering or navigation or the rest of the crew, but strange men in balaclavas, wielding large guns at their chests. The flurry of sudden movement is hard to digest – hard to decipher. Is this one another of the Captain's planned celebrations? Another crew under the same banner?

"Get against wall!" A man splits off to command in broken English, gesturing his rifle at us as we back cautiously into the metal frame of the wall. His colleagues follow suit, all armed to the teeth and sporting the same blank uniform with no real insignia or named department to them. They herd all of us to the outer rim of the canteen. Others disappear to search the rest of the boat, bringing back crew stragglers from other areas. My hands claw at Darrell who stands next to me, finding his arm and holding on tightly.

Whoever these people are, it's evident they were trained personnel. There must have been twenty in total, all well built under their uniforms with sun kissed skin peeking out from the squares in the balaclavas. Their hands expertly hold the rifles pointing down – only breaking to aim them at someone to bark orders.

There's a screech and the sound of kitchen utensils banging together before Serene is brought out, aided by two militia on either side of her. Immediately, Perry tries to cross to her side, but is stopped by the guard in front of us, sizing each of us up.

My mind is reeling – they'd caught up and boarded us so quickly and silently – there'd been no pre-warning or plan in place. This must be those who were following us. They'd disappeared from our tail a whole week ago without a sighting since. They'd lured us into a false sense of security and found us.

We docked at the first opportunity and fell right into their hands.

The last man to enter the room is a little shorter than his colleagues, but his calm stroll commands power. He doesn't have a gun in his hands – he doesn't need one. The situation is under his control. He'd find no resistance against us. His own uniform is a similar colour, with brass-coloured shoulders and a black beret with a symbol of a gun and a swirled logo. Despite the salt and pepper coloured hair peeking from under the rim of the hat, he was just as burly as the rest of them, from his large shoulders down to the leather combat boots.

I glance fugitively to Darrell, who for the first time ever, looks angry. There's a crest of a frown in the middle of his forehead, no sign of his usual light façade. His grip tightens on me, and he mutters under his breath, "Do as they say."

I scowl and try to step a step forward.

"Back! Wall!" The nearest militia barks at me, spit sprays from his mouth and lands on my boot. I don't hide the revulsion on my face as his fingers are practically itching on the trigger. I can finish him right here... But I swallow it down and don't break eye contact as I take two steps back.

"Any more cargo of mine on this ship?" The leader demands of Perry, raising his voice for the benefit of the rest of us. He is well spoken enough with a middle eastern air to his words. He smiles as us calmly.

"Cargo right here," Spit Man indicates twice with his gun towards me and Serene across the room. There's a dark look in his eye, but it's nothing compared to the fury that crosses Perry's face. Spit Man grabs me by the arm with his dirty gloves and tugs me towards him, they all jeer in response.

"Don't you touch her!" Darrell – of all people – bellows and rushes forward to punch my assailant in the gut, who clearly doesn't expect the bumble handed boy to land it, but he does. Another enforcer moves quickly between them to restrain Darrell by the arms, punching him again and again, in the face, the stomach – laughing manically. Ghost and Viper on the other side of him are pushed back by their collar bones as they automatically move to cover their comrade.

"Off my men!" Captain Perry roars, bringing a handgun from his belt, Hamish mirroring him in practised unison. The sound of weapons unholstered rings through the air. There's more firepower in one room than a powder keg full of TNT.

"You screw with me only once, Englishman." The leader roars jeeringly, looking back at his comrades for his sick approval. There's not an ounce of worry on his face, just undiluted glee and amusement as he moves back and forth between our crew, hands lazily clasped behind his back.

"What do you want Abbas? " Perry hisses.

The man known as Abbas faces him and inclines his head. "Good, you have heard of me. Would you care to explain why you felt the need to try and relieve me of my yacht?"

The room swims under me. Mr. Spanish Villa himself. He'd managed to track us down no problem at all.

Captain Perry barely misses a beat, pistol still poised. "It's all business Amir. I'm sure you understand."

Amir or Abbas, smiles in response. "I understand quite well, Englishman. But it is a shame you have crossed the wrong person in this occasion. You are correct though, it is business," the grin widens. "I had the pleasure of reviewing my security footage after my men were... suitably punished for being so careless."

"Meaning he had them killed probably." Darrell mutters.

Hamish's eyes flicker to me. Darrell's grip tightens.

The leader holds out his hands to Perry. A move that would be considered as welcoming in any other situation. "You have a magician in your midst it seems Englishman."

"I'm Welsh you son of a bitch." Perry snaps, flicking the safety off and aiming it directly at Abbas's chest, who regards him with nothing but a raised eyebrow and a smirk. How could he not? Every one of them was fully armed, plus several boats probably nearby to assist at the drop of a hat.

He knows he had us.

I attempt to step forward again, a little shakily, but I'm too exhausted and drained to feel embarrassed and belitted by these men. Spit Man looks excited at the prospect of hitting me with the butt of his gun to send me flying back into my place, but his boss raises a hand to quell him and allows me to move. A couple of our guys try to follow to back me up, but they're subsequently stopped.

I stand between Perry and the leader, standing shoulder to shoulder. He's nothing more than a couple of inches taller than me, give or take. I can feel the electricity of his heart beating steadily, not a shred of worry emanating from him. I wonder how much energy I would need to pulse to reach the automatic nervous system and stop his whole crew in their places.

He recognises me instantly. "Ahh, the little witch from the video! It is an honour to come face to face with you after your disappearing act. I simply had to meet you."

"This meet and greet is over," Hamish says. "Leave in peace and we won't come back to these waters."

"Now is that any way to treat the authority in the area?" He jests, peering over my shoulder at the Captain. "I can offer to overlook this whole attempted theft... *Incident* for payment just as any business transaction as you are men of honour, clearly. She is fine, I will accept her."

I feel sick and disgusted. Half of me is terrified that the crew – and Perry, will agree. Could I even blame them? We're in the middle of a deadly situation, and they're one step away from blowing our heads off. Serene opens her mouth to stream a string of curses but is pulled back by Bobby, the Texan.

"Never," Perry says firmly, not two milliseconds later. "You'll have to fight us."

"Not a problem," the leader says calmly, still looking into Perry's eyes as he unholsters a golden pistol and unloads one shot into the nearest person.

The unlucky recipient was Smirnoff, the head kitchen hand. Originally from the midlands and settled in Wales after his wife upped and left him with the kids. I didn't know him well and we'd only ever spoken a few times, but I watch in horror as the bullet leaves the chamber and finds its path, embedded into the middle of poor Smirnoff's skull. Quick as a flash, he falls back, dead.

The violent crush of curses and yells follow. The militia bark orders, raising their guns at our crew, seething and terrified. Even Hamish looks uncharacteristically sick and white as a sheet. All he can do is stand next to his fallen friend, knuckles clenching and unclenching.

"That was a warning shot," the leader says. "It's a warning because the next time; three of you will be dead. Bang. Then six. Then all." He reholsters his gun, gently blowing the smoke from the tip. He certainly had everyone's attention now.

I take a deep breath and mentally outstretch my hand to my consciousness. It's becoming gradually easier for me to fall onto the same wavelength from one side of the brain to the other. I patiently let it consume me, fitting into my body like a glove only we were made for together. My DNA, my vessels, my cells, all moved aside to let it in happily.

This process never takes more than a split second, but it really feels like time has slowed down to make special arrangement for the conscious and I to bond. However, I'm shaking and scared. The bond keeps loosening, we aren't finding each other. It's like I'm grasping at nothingness and it's slipping further and further away, the more fear sets in.

"Fine. We'll take volunteers for our army," the boss shrugs and says after a few moments' thought. "Three able bodied men or one girl."

His gaze lingers on me for a little longer than necessary, which only serves to fuel my power and anger.

A hand lands on my shoulder. I snap round to face Perry, who no doubt sees the power beginning to spill from my eyes and disappear into the ether. His face is frozen, gazing at me. I wonder if he regrets his decision to pass the freak over to the enemy.

"Come now! Three men or this girl!" Their leader roams backwards and forwards – unaware of the silent exchange in front of him. His eyes roam from Serene over to me, I suspect, but I drop my face down to hide. The gathering energy inside me spurts, failing to ignite the way I need it to. The man's smile bores into me as if I'm an unattainable treasure he can't keep his eyes off. I can see it even in puddle of Smirnoff's pooling blood.

"Hey, woah there – I'll go. I'll go," Darrell says, calmly and steps forward to meet the militia, who regards him with a bored expression. He nods to a couple of his guys who take Darrell by the shoulder and stand either side of him. Despite his calm persona, I see the corners of his wide eyes. I can sense the fear running from his skin in waves. The increase in his heart and lung signals I'd grown so accustomed to.

The power slips away from my fingers as soon as they grab my unlikely idiot of a friend. It's almost as if my engine fails to start. I try again, and again to grasp it. But I can't quite reclaim that connection immediately after I've stalled it.

"No..." I say and shake my head violently. "Don't be so bloody stupid."

Crap. Work. Please work.

"It's decided," Darrell says. He's made up his mind and it's done the trick, the leader's moved on from me to turn towards him, sizing up his frame for his crew.

"I'll go too," Viper offers. He holds his head up high, moving to salute Perry before making his way to stand by the militia. "Captain, it's been an honour for you to take chance on a guy like me."

"Feeling's mutual," Perry whispers, never sounding so shaken and un-captain like in his life.

"No one's going..." I begin to say. Another one of the crew opts to sacrifice himself. A middle-aged man called Penny.

"You leave here with lives today," the leader shrugs. "We take these three as payment for your crossing and incentive, you not return to these waters without invitation." He indicates his hand and his man start to drag out their three hostages one by one.

"Where are you taking him you *bastards!*" I begin to yell, but someone's got their arms around me, pulling me back. I'm struggling against the Captain's chest to get free. I glance up at him in disbelief. "Perry – *do something!*"

Serene watches, hand over her mouth as tears stream down her beautifully made-up face. She tries to say something to me, but I shrug her off and continue to scream and pound Perry's chest with all my might. I can feel the electricity crackle around me – unstable and dangerous. I must have been burning him at least a little, but he makes no move to let me go.

"Sorry, Morgan," he whispers.

"You promised!" I sob. "You promised you'd keep us all safe, you *liar*! Perry – let me go. I can save him - *them*! I can do it! I can do things, Perry. Let me prove it – hurry!" I don't care that the militia can hear every word of what I'm saying. I don't care that their leader is staring at me with renewed interest as he departs with the others.

"Get her out of here," Perry commands. There's a split second of me sobbing uncontrollably before Ghost's large arms wrap around me to carefully move me away from him.

"You liar!" I continue to scream and beat my fists at the rock of the man who turns to carry me away from the room. I can hear the air crackle and hiss. My fists are almost white with electrical energy. I'm seething to let out the power. Destroy everything and everyone.

Abbas and his militia takes their hostages away with no goodbye, no nothing. The last memory I have of that night, is the look in Darrell's eyes as they lock on mine in desperation as we both break farther away from one another, disappearing into nothingness.

-30-

Darrell has finally earned his Whittaker name: Guardian.

Perry announces this the day after the militia leaves us marooned in the middle of the Mediterranean with minimal food and fuel resources. We were outgunned, all luxuries, weapons, everything taken. In truth, he'd earned his nickname way before yesterday, but the crew and Serene were in the habit of just referring to him by his given name. It suits him, whether he was a law-abiding citizen still living in Manchester or sailing on the sea. Darrell is a sweet, funny, innocent young man and he would never know anything else.

I feel like my parents just died all over again. Like I've just said goodbye to Jared for one final time. I hadn't given them much thought in the past few months, too wrapped up in my life now, too enveloped in moving on. The wounds have been ripped open overnight. I was figuratively haemorrhaging, too shaken to pick myself up from the floor of my cabin and move on.

Losing Darrell is like losing an arm. He's been a constant in my new life and always on my side, ready to take on the next challenge, the next port. The whole crew felt his presence and even Serene, shiny bright

Serene, can't bear to smile without tearing up and excusing herself from the kitchen.

We sit altogether from there on out. The benches were turned and pulled up in a row during mealtimes, so we were huddled as one unit. Aside from Darrell, Viper, Smirnoff and Penny were also an irreplaceable loss. In the space of one day, four of the crew – our makeshift family, were ripped from us so violently in a way none of us could have imagined.

"We're all hurting right now," Perry says one evening, standing from the head of the table and peering at each of us in turn. "We're also being tailed – just far enough away it's not obvious. But we're being watched, and we need to move on."

"What do you think they want?" Hamish asks.

Perry deliberately doesn't look at me. "I don't know. These groups are corrupt, they have no moral code, they're only concerned with money and power."

"We should go and rescue them," I whisper, but the words aren't audible enough to carry across the room. Ghost repeats my sentence on my behalf, louder. A few others nod in scattered agreement.

"That would be refusing the sacrifice they gave us," Perry says. "We'd be rolling into a situation where we'd all be killed. I've already lost four of my crew, no more now."

"We can't... tell anyone? Call anyone to help?" I murmur, my voice raspy and thick with the lack of sleep. It's Hamish who quietly slides over to Perry and places his hand on his shoulder in solidarity.

"Some countries are run by their own militia and in these waters, they *are* the authority. You won't get any UK embassies anywhere near here or anyone willing to take a call from an unregistered vessel with shady dealings. We would all be arrested and questioned, likely prison time."

"I'm happy to do time to save them!" I burst out, teetering on the edge of fear and anger and frustration. Ghost carefully pulls me down back beside him, I shrug off his protection with a hiss.

Hamish nods, more patient than I could imagine. "But by the time any kind of government or authority can look into their kidnapping, they would be long gone. So would their ship. It would be as if they never existed."

"That's crap," Ghost says. I nod along with him, finding no more words I could easily summon and wait quietly for the meeting to end. Before we conclude for the evening, a few photos are tacked to the corkboard over by the far wall. I get up and leave before I see Darrell's face shines accusatorily at me.

My room is silent when I return. Defeating almost. It's a frozen time capsule of my friend and I dedicating our time to training cross-legged on the floor when we were both on breaks. His little stash of electronic items sits in the corner, along with the coveted broken toaster.

One of his woollen jumpers is draped over my hammock. Another lies across a pile of spare pillows in the corner. That's right, how long had he'd been sleeping on my floor? I hadn't even realised. He was naturally there when I went to sleep and when I'd woken up. Why hadn't Ghost made fun of his own empty hammock in their mess area?

It didn't matter anyway. Nothing did.

I fall into my hammock, pressing his jumper against my face. It still has a woody warm and comforting smell. The scent that would cool my temper down and bring me back to myself again after a long day of mental training. Hot tears cling to the material.

"Get the hell out." I snap towards the door. The material over my face conceals to who's peered into my cabin, but I have a pretty good idea.

"It's been three days now," Perry's disembodied voice says. "Don't you think it's time you ate something, Morg?"

"It's *Terin*," I pull the pillow off and turn to face him. "You have no right to even address me right now with what happened. Three men are probably dead right now because of you. The fourth's decomposing in the ocean as we speak!"

His face falls but he hides it quickly. "The rest of us are alive," he tries to reason. "Including you."

"I'm not even worth saving."

"Don't be stupid, you need to be protected."

"Protected?" I snort and turn to face him. "You have a whole ship worth of people to *protect* aside from me!"

"You're a young woman, a scrap of a little thing that people will exploit if given half a bloody chance to. Like it or not, I saved your bacon in there. There's no telling what men like that would do to your spirit."

"Darrell was worth *ten* of me. He was pure. He wasn't tainted," I hiss."

He knowingly *made* his choice the minute he stepped forward. He knew exactly at that moment what was going to happen, and he chose, Morgan – he *chose* to let himself be taken so you'd be safe. Least you can do is not make a mockery of his sacrifice."

"He was an idiot. You're all goddam idiots." My voice cracks. It's angry tears more than anything. Angry at the world. The injustice of everything. The sheer bad luck that these people know me.

"You're being a child," he thunders, surprising me "You're just as much as important as the rest of us and surrendering to people like that... it wouldn't end well for you."

"Because I'm a girl?"

"Because there's... something about you." The pregnant hesitation in his voice wasn't from a place of malice or fear. There was a note of unspoken concern that fires between the two of us breathing heavily in defiance. Only the occasional metallic clang of the ship around us breaks the silence. It answers the question hanging above me, I supposed. He definitely saw something inside me try to escape.

"You possess something Amir Abbas will want. He's main leader of the militia in this area. He's notorious and powerful in these waters, I had no idea when we signed up for that job what we'd be getting ourselves into or who the mark was-.."

"Well, now you know," I say flatly, turning to face my bunk again.

"I don't quite know *how* or *why* you seem to have an... Ability. but I understand enough when not to push a person. If you don't want to talk about it, that's fine by me girl." Shame flares my cheeks and I have to look away from him. I feel like I'd let him down. The only adult who ever seemed to genuinely give a crap about my wellbeing and I couldn't bear to come clean.

"Don't... Make me talk about it *please*." It comes out as a whisper. Every word scorches as it leaves my mouth, burning like poison. The boat continues to sway around us, undoubtedly heaving as far away from the militia's vessel as possible but I wasn't sure of the destination. Aside from Perry and Serene bringing me meals, no one else had wanted to bother me.

"I don't know what else I could have done," Perry says quietly. I believe him, but it doesn't quieten the anger inside.

"I know."

"He knew about you, didn't he?"

There's no point clarifying who. I nod wordlessly. He sighs and I think in the past few days, he's aged a good ten years by the deepening on the wrinkles in his brow. The crow's feet etched the sides of his eyes, which could barely bring themselves to meet my own. When he finally does, I see the horror in his own eyes of the choice he had to make. Suddenly, I find myself feeling sorry for him.

"They were readily about to kill us all. You saw Smirnoff, God rest his soul."

"I should have done something more. I had the ability to, and I choked. I *lost* it when I got too emotional." My fist extends to smack against the side of the cabin for the thousandth time. A metallic clang resounds around the room, joining the rest of the fist dents. Another punch and another. Dry blood flakes from my knuckles, but Perry waits me out until I'm too tired and sore to continue.

"I can tell Hamish I found the source of that noise now. Damn lad thought a shark was trying to attack us," he jokes, but the mood is unlighten-able. I wonder if I'd ever be able to smile again or enjoy crappy stories and anecdotes with the rest of the crew. There is no crew without Darrell, no companionship, no pranks. Not really.

"You did all you could," he continues to murmur. "But being captain sometimes means I have to shoulder this blame myself and live with the decisions I need to make," he pauses. "Which is why I want to discuss with you your future on this ship and where you see yourself going next."

"Next?" I blanch. "You're kicking me off?"

"When they left, the hunger in Abbas's eyes was unfathomable that he wanted you. I'll bet they're the ones quietly tailing us for a bit to see what we're up to before they try and board again. Hamish filled me in on what he'd have seen on the security footage of you. You're in real danger, Morgan. He probably saw it again when they took Darrell away – you were seething with it. Whatever it is."

"For all he knew it was a trick of the light."

"Small women don't go standing up to firepower like that without knowing they got moves up their sleeve, and he knows it. It's something he can sell and exploit. People like that don't just forget in countries like this and they'll be back." He stops and lets his words settle for a few silent minutes. They leave a cold, damp feeling in my bones, my skin, my muscles. He was totally right. It happened all the time in movies. Everything was off the table now, who's to say where reality would kick in?

"It's safer for us to lie low," he continues. "They're bad people."

"I don't even understand who they are," I snap. Another chance at my fingers reaching around the militia leader's throat was tempting. I wouldn't misfire the next time.

"Bad people," he answers. "And that's all you need to know. That emblem is well known in certain circles, and you don't want to be involved. It was our own bad luck we ran into them, last I heard he was operating around South Africa."

He pauses for me to digest and continues. "I've discussed it with the rest of the crew. We're going to head back to the UK and disband indefinitely for the time being. Maybe find a different vessel and throw them off. I assume you don't want to make that journey back home with us?"

"No," I say, all fight deflating out of me.

"I thought so. Best we can do is drop you off along the flight path – we've got a couple of light cargo jobs on the Eastern US coast and refuel before we head back, make it seem like we're going about our business so they don't get spooked and attack. But you can't stay on here."

I inhale slowly. "I'm so sorry, Perry."

"What for?"

"Making trouble for everyone."

He shrugs. "Either we'd have been taken away by them or we'd be dead. We all chose this life and none of that's on you. People like that don't let people like us go so easily. We've seen their faces."

I nod and thinking about their leader's eyes raking up and down my body. The way Perry had barely paused a heartbeat before declining to hand me over to him to save everyone else. Would my own father have done the same for me, I wondered?

"Why did you save me?" I begin to sob. Great heaving sounds that burst from the pit of my stomach, reverberating the air of the tiny space that holds my entire life's possessions. It was the second time I'd survived an impending death without giving a thought to living after. Why did this keep happening to me? Why was I being spared death constantly?

"I hate him."

"Abbas?"

"Darrell," I whisper.

He doesn't know what to say and no further words could form from my mouth, so he shuffles closer and gently pats me on the shoulder while I cry into his chest. I expect him to shy away and run from this kind of emotion, but he sits still and patiently lets me get it all out.

-31-

It takes a few days to escape the Mediterranean Sea to make our way into the North Atlantic. There are no ships visibly following, but Hamish loyally heads to the deck every morning with a pair of binoculars and ensures some of the best navigators are working the nightshifts. Everyone pulls their weight without question, each more eager than the last to get moving as far away as possible.

The concealed gun locker lies empty, almost every member is armed with some sort of weapon besides myself, at my own request. I won't endanger the lives of anyone else by taking their only form of defence, not when I royally screwed this up for everyone by letting my damn emotions get out of check.

The evenings are quiet, no one opts to sit around the crew mess after meals and socialise. As soon as Serene and I bring the food out, everyone's sitting down and eating with only minimal conversation before returning back to whatever they were assigned to do. The anxiety is tangible in the air; a hot knife could cut easily through it.

I think about Amir Abbas's jagged hunting knife at his belt, and I decide I can't swallow another bite of dinner.

Serene tries to stay her usual cheery self by filling the silence with nonstop chatter about what she's planning to do when they land back in Wales.

"I'd like to open an art shop," she says one morning. "But nothing rubbish like that contemporary stuff you see sell for millions. Proper paintings and vases and sculptures. They're doing wonderful things with resin these days."

I try to nod politely and look interested, but my heart isn't in it. No one's is. Not even Serene herself entirely. But the sound of words – any words, are a lot better than the sound of my own guilty silence.

It's futile, but I try a few more attempts to contact Jared via my dreams and let him know I'm coming to the US, I'm in trouble, and need to be found ASAP. Unsure if they got through, I try to stay up all night to the point where I collapse from exhaustion and pass out.

True to Perry's words, there's a few loose ends that need to be tied up along the eastern US seaboard, taking us to various berths and docks along the way before the flight path would head back East to international waters again. I don't get to actually *see* much of the skyline though as Hamish and Serene keep me busy with menial job after job, determined to keep me active and away from curling up in my bunk and shutting out the world.

About a week later, Biddeford, Maine is the first glimpse of the US I'd seen up close. Bobby, the Texan, had rambled on the night before about how it was classed as a real up and coming city and that his sister was once mayor. Although I wasn't sure how much I believed that as he'd continued to detail her alleged underground alligator fighting ring in the same breath.

I help with the unloading of fruit crates we'd picked up down South, expertly teetering over the rim of the ship and down the ramp fixed specially to the side of the pier. Behind me, Ghost and Bobby haul the heavier stock between them.

"We need some supplies for the trip home," Hamish mutters, moving his fingers over a clipboard in his hand. I set down my crate next to him and allow myself a quick stretch while subtly checking out the area. We were on a small jetty that arches away from the mainland of trees and shrubbery. A small beach juts out from the rock line in which a few people with dogs walk along in the distance. Far behind them, a white light house sits partially hidden in the grey sky around it. I shiver and pull Serene's old swede coat tighter around me.

"Agreed," Perry says darkly. "I can't stand another night of stew." He catches me looking and winks conspiratorially. "Don't you dare tell my wife I said that."

"Where would we even go? There's nowhere around here," I complain.

"The City of Biddeford is that way." Hamish points and smirks. "There's some naval authority some ways South of here – no way was I going to take the Whittaker closer and risk a stop and search." He hands his clipboard to one of his navigators and directs a couple of other crew members coming down the plank.

"Who's the client?" I scour the treeline for signs of movement.

"Must be that guy. Old Hawaiian shirt over there," Ghost grunts and nod towards an old campervan parked on the beachfront. The driver is as portly as Ted Sanders and moves with a cheerful wave and waddle as he backs onto the end of the jetty and opens the back doors to make some room. Hamish wanders over to briefly shake hands with the man, they chat good naturedly, exchanging something between them––likely cash––and Hamish beckons for the crates to be brought over.

"Hawaiian shirts are only good for crooks and drug dealers," Bobby mutters, hauling a crate back into his arms. Ghost and I mirror him and begin our slow walk to the end of the jetty.

"You ever been this far East?" I say conversationally. The Texan glances up shyly, as if in disbelief that someone was engaging him in conversation, he shakes his head, coughing.

"I stuck more south, y'see."

"Aye," Ghost agrees and tosses me a small net of crabs. "I heard a pure Texan can't survive anything north of Oklahoma! Dunno how true that is though... argh!" he winces as Bobby throws a perch at his face and catches him across the cheek.

"Damn British always think y'know us."

"*Scottish*," Ghost corrects. "We can only learn through stereotypes my man! You're the one who constantly harps on about your shotgun collection."

Bobby made a noise in his throat that sounded like a wistful cry. "I'd give anythin' ter have my collection again. Got 'em confiscated back in '98. Huntin' accident that went wrong. Damn shot my little brother's toe clean off!" He laughs and wipes away a tear. Ghost chortles along with him, I smile politely.

"Why did you leave?" I ask.

"Why did *you*?" Bobby retorts and raises an eyebrow. "We ain't on slow dancin' terms yet."

"Because she's obviously a live wire," Ghost cracks, nudging me in the ribs. "Clearly she's a serial electrician on the run!"

"The sounds like a Darrell worthy joke." I push him back lightly and the words tumble out before I can think to stop them. Bobby's eyes move back down to his collection of perch. Ghost clears his throat, moving his eyes back down to his crate.

"Good mornin' all," Hawaiian Shirt greets us, sticking out his hand for everyone to shake in turn. "I'm mighty glad the weather held out long enough to get this shipment in. I've been running low on stock all week." Now that he's closer, I can make out the rosiness of his round cheeks and the earnest expression.

"Irvine here runs a market stall in the city," Hamish introduces. "He's been a steady client for a few years now. You have no boys to help you with that today?"

The man known as Irvine blows out his cheeks, pulling his bucket hat off and wipes the sweat from his brow. "No sir, we had to make some layoffs back in the spring. The wife and I have been balling it between us, but it's been real hard work."

"That's a shame, Irvine." Perry says.

"Now don't you all be going mushy on me. Is your boy tellin' me right, Perry? You out of the game for a while?" He glances between Hamish and the Captain, who nod in unison.

"A while," Perry replies but doesn't give any more timeframe than that. He excuses himself to check on the rest of the shipment to be brought over while Hamish hovers to oversee and make small talk. As burly and round as Irvine was, he's clearly well practiced on his feet, spinning the crates into the back of the Volkswagen with ease. He tries to include us in the conversation, asking each of us our names, how long we'd been with the crew, what sort of adventures we'd been on – we all wince a little on that subject.

It's been getting easier and easier to let Terin Coiler fade into the background and for Morgan Archer––I needed a surname after all––to take the reins on my life. In my head, she's this calm and confident entity, sure of herself and the weird energy in the back of her head that occasionally steps in when she's emotional. Ultimately, she's in control of her life. Knows exactly what she wants.

"*Morgan* is an unusual name," Irvine comments, taking a net of crabs from me. "Don't hold it against me. though – Irvine is a family name. My pop and my grandpap were Irvines too. Sergeant Senior and Lieutenant Junior."

"It's nice," I hedge. "Were you in the army too?"

"You don't need to go lyin' for my benefit. Do I look like I ever enlisted?" He gestures to himself, chortling. "The wife, Bree, and I grew up here and we'll probably die here. When the kids grow up, we might take a cruise or somethin'. Our hearts are in the stall, but good produce without all them fancy chemicals just isn't easy to come by."

"Which is where we come in. Usually." Hamish claps Irvine on the shoulder and quickly shakes his hand again in goodbye. Bobby, Ghost, and the few others on the jetty follow him back to the ship. Only Perry and I stay behind.

Irvine secures the crates and nets in the back with some bungee rope and rachet straps. Sweat glistens on his face once again, he blows out a large breath.

"Whew. Could use you guys all the time!" he jokes, closing the loading doors behind him. I begin to understand what the feeling inside me is. The uneasy feeling of change on the wind. I'd felt it that night I left my house for the last time. I felt it when I spent the first few days on The Whittaker. Sooner or later, I figured this time would be coming again and I would need to find another place for me in the world aside from the open sea. Why not now?

"I think I'm going to get off here, Captain," I murmur.

"As in leave?" Perry frowns, incredulous. "Sure enough it's a nice city but we got a few more stops to make before we head back home. Are you sure?"

"I didn't know any of you," I retort and head around to Irvine's driver's seat to ask him to wait a few more minutes. The man nods, flicking on a fan on the dashboard and fans himself with his baseball cap. I head further down the jetty, the captain fast on my heels.

"Now wait a minute--"

"I've got to get off the ship at some point. You said it yourself – we're being tracked. It's one of the last stops we needed to do anyway – so why wait?"

I watch as his face goes through several subtle changes. Confusion to concern to hurt to fear. It settles on something vaguely neutral, although the creases of worry are etched between his eyebrows.

"Are you even packed?"

"I have everything I need." I gesture. Darrell's jumper. Borrowed shirt, trousers and boots. There was nothing else on the ship I want to take with me. It would be too painful, too full of memories.

"Spread it among the guys, the rest of my stuff."

"I can't... I just don't know what to say, gal."

I sigh a fresh breath, letting it all out. "Say that you'll support me no matter what and if anyone asks, you never saw Terin Coiler. Or if you did, she's dead."

"You'll never be dead to me. Or Serene. Or any of the other guys who would lay down their lives for you right here and now."

"And I'm not asking them to anymore," I say gently and take his large rough hands in my smaller ones. "But I need you to do me one more favour if that's OK? I don't want to say goodbye to anyone or you know, make a big thing of it. I just... don't want to explain and face them all right now. Just, say something nice from me, OK?"

He nods, looking a little awkward and embarrassed at the emotion on his face he obviously was having issues controlling. "Three years goes by so fast, eh?"

"Yeah." I agree and fall silent because I don't know what else to say to someone who'd unofficially fostered me after I ran away from London, letting me join and participate in their illicit international activities.

"Serene's gonna miss having you around. Me too."

"Just get back home in one piece?" I suggest. "I know I have no right to ask anything of you, after all you've done for me – but would you be able to do something on my behalf?"

Perry nods, rolling his eyes. "Of course.

"I swallow, hesitating. Darrell's face fills my mind as it had done almost as often as Ted Sander's bloated, mutilated corpse. I can't bear to think of Darrell's olive complexion and inky dark hair tainted with any memory of hurt or pain, so he stays smiling in my mind. I can hear his voice still so clearly.

"Please try and see if you can track down Darrell's family for me? I want to... well, I want them to know he--"

"I will.""And that I'm sorry."

"If you insist."

"Thanks Captain." My hand extends out into an awkward salute slash handshake. He glances at it for a moment before raising and eyebrow and pulling me into a hug.

"You, er, take care of yourself now." He digs into his pocket and slips a wad of cash into the palm of my hand. I stare down at it in disbelief.

"There's hundreds of dollars here! I can't take it," I hiss and try to push it back at him, but he smartly steps back.

"Well earned pay for one of the best crew members I've sailed with. Certainly, one of the ballsiest. Wouldn't you agree?" His eyebrow raises.

"Thank you," I whisper, preparing to step back for the last time.

"I'm also a murderer," he blurts suddenly. I'm not sure if I hear right the first time, so he says it again.

"That's why I have never judged you for your actions," he explains. "Because a very long time ago, I had to make the same decision and it was a long time before I forgave myself for that indiscretion."

"Who?" I whisper.

He swallows, glancing back up the platform before returning to me. "Serene and I had a daughter. Nine years old. She was taken suddenly one day – it all happened so quick. We were never able to get her back but I found the monster who... well, I found him, and I took care of him. We left our home soon after that and tried to move on the right way. Eventually, we decided the conventional approach wasn't working and we bought an old fishing boat. Took our lives and our matters into our own hands."

"I just want to thank you for showing me there's still some surprises I still have to experience in the world. Meta powers – who would have known?" His cheeks puff out with his breath as he rubs the side of his head.

"I'm full of surprises," I manage to say, mind reeling with his revelation. "The sea doesn't take too kindly to cry babies, remember?"

"The student becomes the master," he says, inclining his head to salute me. I copy him and we stand with our heads and hands raised. Captain Perry turns to disappear onto the walkway that leads onto the deck of the Whittaker, only stopping for a brief wave. Then he turns to join the rest of the crew inside and sails away with the only house that's ever felt truly like home.

-32-

The chapel stretches up high above me, becoming just as transparent against the greying sky as the lighthouse was the first time I'd set eyes on it. Fear doesn't begin to set in until I've reached the precipice of the street entrance, arched either side by various banners on blood drives and upcoming charity events. The road veers off onto a long street with neat white buildings on either side. A street food seller across the way is grilling something that smells like beef and onions. It makes my mouth water on top of everything else.

"You sure this is the place?" I ask, swallowing down the hunger pangs of a missed breakfast. I can't think of food at a time like this. Food makes me think of kitchens, which made me think of Serene and my cowardice in not saying a proper goodbye to the crew. Those that looked after me the past few years after my life imploded and I couldn't face telling them how much they meant to me....

It's better like this, I resolve eventually. A clean break.

Irvine points to the Satnav sitting atop his dashboard between the stuck Lego *Star Wars* figures and a dancing hula girl. "Same address as the good Captain gave us. You want me to come in with you for some muscle?"

I crack a smile. "I can take care of myself, thanks."

Irvine nods but concern laces his features. "I ain't sure I'd feel right if someone left my kid in a place like this. Some unsavoury characters in the area, you know."

I'm one of them, I think and reply with, "I'll be absolutely fine."

He relents, still unsure. "I'll meet you over by that museum across the road in a couple hours. That OK with you?"

"Perfect, thanks." I climb out of the van and wave briefly as Irvine navigates his way down the long stretch of road, disappearing in the distance. I don't realise I'm watching the fading taillights until I can't see them anymore. Another figurative glance up at the chapel. I really hope that Perry gave us the right location.

Inside, the church is warm with portable heaters strategically placed every few rows of pews. Calm music blows out from the speaker system to an empty hall, despite an old organ that lays untouched on the stage. We were never churchgoers growing up, so the only experiences with a higher entity were through Religious Education lessons at school and the odd Christmas service. I don't know what I was expecting in truth. Perry had called me 'Meta' in powers. Surely, it would mean if I was God's creation, I won't burst into flames on entry. Still, I hold out some suspicion just in case, should he decide I'm an abomination instead.

"You look a little lost?" A petite woman with several sets of silver earrings appears from the next room with a couple of spare chairs. She flashes a wide smile that moves her nose ring in the middle of her nose. The metal contrasts beautifully with her mocha-coloured complexion.

"I... don't know if I'm in the right place," I say shyly.

"A Brit," she catches with interest. "We don't get too many of y'all stopping this far North before Canada. Can't imagine it's our sparkling tourism."

"I just... landed. Haven't seen too much of the place yet."

"Well," she flaps her arms outward after placing the spare chairs over by one of the heaters. "Can't promise I can give you the Disney World Tour, but feel free to ask away. I know a few mean coffee shops."

"I'm looking for someone." I glance at the crumpled paper in my hands that'd been shoved into my hands along with Perry's saved dollars. There was little to no explanation on the paper except the words; *Denny Parker* and the address of the chapel we were standing in. I wonder if he's been carrying it around with him since we spoke about disbanding.

"Denny?" the girl clarifies after I show her. "Sure thing, he's out back probably working on the arrangement for the next service, but I'll go get him." She turns on her white wedges and unveils a door behind a large purple drape over by the stage. When her footsteps disappear, it's just me sitting awkwardly in the Lord's house, wondering what I should do next.

"Yo, you wanted to see me?" The man known as Denny appears from the wing. He tosses a wad of paper on top of the organ, jogging down the few steps to meet me in the middle of the aisle. Immediately I could pick out the rough New York undertone. It matches his bad boy swagger from the leather jacket to the jagged hairstyle.

"My name is Morgan Archer," I begin stupidly, and my mind goes completely blank. What would I even say – how should I explain? How many lies were acceptable within church walls before I was struck down by lightning?

"Morgan," he tries and extends his hand. "Nice to meet ya, I'm Denny. Haven't seen you around in these parts before. There an English fair in town or something?"

"Just me. I was given your details by a friend."

His eyebrow arches. "I only got a handful of those, only one who's a Brit." Scanning the hall for the other girl, he indicates for me to follow him into a side room around the side entrance to the stage. It's a small, squat yellowed box with a scratched old desk in the corner, next to a rack of royal purple gowns.

"For the choir," he explains, seeing me gazing. "They meet up on Sundays and holidays. Pretty much any other day they see fit really."

"Do you work here?"

He makes a face, taking a seat next to his desk. "Organist. Yeah, I know, laugh it up. It started as a community service gig for an old, suspended sentence, but well... I like it here." The tough man act was up again, daring me to laugh.

"I used to play piano," I say. No, *Terin Coiler* used to spend hours chained to her piano, Morgan Archer would need to find more hobbies, passions, likes and dislikes completely different. She is the complete opposite of Terin; Confident, sure of herself, strong. She isn't going to be pushed around and controlled.

"If our mutual friend put us in touch, it wasn't by no accident," Denny says, all business now. "He care to mention to ya exactly what it is I specialise in?"

"Just that you could help me," I say carefully. Perry wouldn't have sent me blind to a stranger for no reason at all, but it was a great leap to trust this potentially dangerous man.

He sighs, seeing my hesitation and pulls up the sleeve of his hoodie to expose his right forearm. There's a naval looking symbol with an anchor, identical to the one on Perry's same arm. "You can trust me. I rode with the Captain when I was a teen for *years* before he even took to the water."

"He didn't mention."

"He wouldn't. It was before... well, it doesn't really matter now anyway." He looks suddenly uncomfortable, turning away to focus on something else in his eyeline. I wonder if he was about to say something about Perry's kid. Perhaps he knew her, maybe he was even an honorary uncle. Did he know what Perry had to resort to?

"I uh... can help you with a lot of things. A new identity, papers, insurance, anything that requires some skill of the imitation kind. Usually takes a couple of weeks and a lotta dough to make this kind of thing happen, but Perry's a pal."

"What kind of money would you need for a new identity?"

"Free of charge for you," he says. "But don't expect no redos."

"I only need the one."

"Fine." He nods, bringing a flipbook out of his leather jacket and an expensive-looking pen. "I'm going out on a limb here and saying you want Morgan Archer to exist officially?"

I say nothing, only nod. I'm expecting cops like those on American TV shows to pull back the pews or the organ and point guns at me, threatening arrest for fraud. I can feel the tops of my ears burning with shame along with a sense of renewed hope in the pit of my belly.

"Hm. You sure about the name? Seems a little...."

"I'm sure."

He nods a final time and extends his hand. I shake it just as firmly as he grips back. He retracts, looking a little surprised at the strength but doesn't voice it. "Couple of days time," he affirms. "Don't go anywhere."

"I have nowhere to go." I smile ruefully.

"I'm sorry to hear that." And to his credit, the tough persona comes down for another split second. I feel like he's telling the truth. No matter how shady his personal affairs here are. I can't judge after all, I'm just as shady.

I leave to follow the street down to where Irvine had pointed before he dropped me off. The red buildings on either side of the museum wear the same look and façade as one another. A blue wash of river in the background sits under a small bridge arching over it. I wander further over a small bank of neatly kept grass to cross to the other side of the pavement. There's an atypical American newsstand with today's paper inside. The kind in movies that runs on old change.

I'm about to continue walking when a headline catches my interest on the front page of the display paper. If not for the photo of a little boy that looks exactly like a young Darrell, it wouldn't have even stood out to me.

The picture is in black and white, but had the same infectious grin, same tone of eyes – although they could have been green or hazel instead of brown. His hair is a similar cut, shaggy in length but with the same effortless volume of soft curls on the top. It's as if I'm staring into the accusing gaze of my lost friend himself. That haunted, lingering last gaze of goodbye. This kid, whoever he was, had recently disappeared with no trace from his own home.

I turn away feeling the lump in the base of my throat that threatens to cut off my entire circulation, or so it feels. I can't be haunted like this. I can't let myself feel.

When Morgan Archer goes to pick up her new passport and documents in the next couple of days, she needs to be a confident naturalised citizen. She won't have any damning secrets or be too scared to sleep and face the ghosts that wait for her in her dreams. She needs to toughen up and leave everything behind that separates her from the sad remains of Terin Coiler that washed away at sea.

It's easier said than done, of course. Locking Darrell away behind the walls of my mind is going to be tough. It's crowded in there already with my parents and Ted Sanders and everything else I want to forget – but Darrell is the closest thing I had to a brother since....

I should try and communicate with Jared and let him know where I am. If he cares at all. If he gives a damn that I had endured a lifetime of pain in a few short years. Maybe he doesn't want to be found. Maybe he had to construct his *own* mental walls to hide everything behind in order to move on with life.

Letting go will be hard, but letting Terin disappear and wither away was the easiest thing in the world.

-33-

"Jesus kid, you been sleeping at all?" The mocha-skinned girl with the nose ring stares down through the church door at me. I think it was a bit rich seeing as she herself was still wearing hair rollers and pyjama bottoms underneath an intimidating looking band T-shirt. Noticing my lack of enthusiasm, she changes her tone and smiles, pulling the door aside to let me in.

"Isn't that blasphemous or whatever?" I say.

"What is?"

"Using Jesus's name like that."

"I like to think it as expressive." She shrugs and shuts the door behind us, pulling the lock bar across.

After the screech of metal shifting together, the hall was completely silent. Almost eerily still. The church smells of rosebud perfume and sweet incense burning on the plinth at the front of the room. A soft morning light pushes in the stained windows at the huge circular arrangement towards the back and down either side of the building in tandem, each pane of glass is individually decorated, designed to show various scenes from the bible. Jesus's birth, feeding the crowds, performing miracles and, finally, the crucifixion. Instead of the Easter rising in the next panel, an image of a man in a long robe is instead climbing down from the cross and leaving the silent crowd behind in his wakes of blue and purple hues.

"When did Jesus have a ladder to climb down from the cross?" I try to recall my religious education lessons from so long ago. He was supposed to die and rise at Easter.

The girl follows my gaze and suppresses a short laugh. "Denny had that made for me special. He knows I hate that story. I don't like the thought of someone being tortured for being different, you know?" She rubs her shoulders self-consciously with long lightly muscled arms. While I stare back and forth, agape.

"So you just changed the story?"

"Yep. You see Jesus here manages to conjure up a ladder, pushes out the nails with his power and leaves the crowd behind him."

"What does he do next?"

"Whatever he wants. That's the point. It ends there..." she trails off, staring at the picture with a slightly cocked head. It's a weird conversation that I have the feeling is about a lot more than a few pieces of coloured glass and an old bible story.

Above, dust motes dance softly in the escaped rays of directed sunlight from the shiny shell of the organ at the front. I glance around at a couple of pews where a few duvets and pillows were stacked together in a makeshift human nest.

"You sleep here?" I muse, changing the subject.

"It's peaceful." She shrugs, snapping out of her momentary daydream. *Even* her smile is as comforting as the room. I want nothing more than to curl up on the pew and let sleep take me, if not for the impending doom that I didn't deserve to be in such a holy place.

"It's beautiful but won't the owner mind you staying here?"

"The owner is my grandfather. He doesn't come around here much no more except for the Thanksgiving and Christmas services maybe. He lets me run the place, double checks the books every now and again."

"But you're so... young."

"Twenty-six," she affirms and holds out her hands that jangle with the bracelets still on her wrists. "We haven't officially been introduced and since this is our second meeting; my name is Hailey."

"Morgan. Nineteen."

"Hello Morgan Nineteen, are you here to see Denny again?"

"It's probably too early. I'll let you get back to..." I glance back at her makeshift bed.

She laughs airily and gestures down to the thin cloth trousers. "I don't sleep much either. Too many things to do with so little time, you know? Denny usually sleeps in the back when he's been working hard. I'll go get him."

"Sorry – I didn't realise I was disturbing––"

"You're not," she said. "We aren't together or anything like that. Strictly platonic. Den helps me out looking after the place and I turn a blind eye to his *businesses*. In the house of God, no less! Gram would be rolling in her grave right now if she knew." Hailey rolls her eyes and expertly navigates the pews with placed movements while she talks.

With nothing else to do but wait, I sink into the pew next to me, letting the silence drown out my thoughts. It was difficult not to get caught up in the grandeur of this place. Regardless of if you believe in a higher entity or some other cosmic purpose, the church is quiet, warm, and welcoming. It wasn't as homely as Irvine's house, which he and his wife had generously let me use their spare room, but I imagine some people find some kind of peace here.

Hailey's grandmother may be turning in her grave but at least she had a place somewhere. I wouldn't have even known what had happened with my parent's bodies. Nothing but ashes I guessed. Mixed up in the embers of the very house we were all mentally imprisoned within. It was a cruel but fitting end, in a way.

"If you're listening," I mumble, cheeks reddening with second-hand embarrassment for both myself and anyone who overheard. "I'm sorry and I didn't mean for it to happen." I'm not even sure who I'm saying this to. God? My parents? Darrell? Anyone who'd listen?

"If I had a dollar for every time I've said that." Someone chuckles from next to me. I wince, jumping and clutching my heart. Denny Parker holds out a palm. "Sorry, didn't mean to scare you,"

"It's not... Don't worry about it. Have you got my things?"

"Right here." He holds up the papers and moves backwards slightly when I move to take them. "Hold on though, some ground rules here. First of which: I'd appreciate it mighty fine if you didn't go telling the world about my establishment here. Second, don't draw attention to yourself. These documents are perfect to get you by but a proper federal investigation will flag them as forged. Which brings me to my last point."

"Don't cause trouble for you?"

"Don't cause trouble for me," he affirms, looking down under lidded eyes. "The singular most important one. After today, you and I have never met. Our business is concluded here."

"Denny, who?"

"That's the spirit, kid. Also word to the wise; you might wanna change that accent, princess."

"Is there something wrong with it?" I say, genuinely confused. Back home, I sounded a little more distinguished than the local state school kids, but sure enough I spoke eloquently enough for people to understand me.

"That's the point," Denny says. "These documents say you were born in Vegas. People will start asking uncomfortable questions you don't wanna answer."

"Right. OK, yes."

He raises an eyebrow. "Take some time to practice. Watch videos online, take lessons on speech. Learn some basic American history. Celebrate the 4th of July and Thanksgiving. Good luck kid, you're gonna need it," he hands over the wad of papers. "That it, or you got someone else who needs to disappear?"

"Just me."

Denny nods, taking another puff of his cigar and looks me up and down. "You, er, tell Perry that I owe him no more favours after this. It's one thing making people disappear, it's another doing it free."

"Well, I appreciate this, thank you."Denny snorts. "Lose some of those manners too."

I straighten, try to hold some of my weight on my hip and cross my arms. I open my mouth and try to emulate the husk of his brogue, with poor results. "Yeah whatever, thanks,"

He laughs loud, his accent tinging along with it, reaching up to the beams of the church ceiling. He waves me off. "Keep trying Morgan Archer. Are you staying local?"

"For now," I say carefully, mulling it over. "I think I'm going to find my brother." Should I even be telling strangers this story from now on? I need to stay incognito. Nothing I could say could now have any connection to exposing who I really was.

"Well, good luck." Denny nods, unaware of my inner turmoil and reaches into his pocket to flick open a silver-plated lighter. The flame rises up quickly to touch a cigarette he protrudes and sticks in his mouth, face now as neutral as that of stranger. "What are you still doing here? Better get moving!"

I step out into the sunlight, letting the small wispy tendrils of anxiety take me for the first time in forever. Regardless of the papers now held clutched to my chest, the only thing that's really going to save me now is nothing but my own intelligence, wit, and skill. What would Jared have said in this situation? *'Uh oh, the states are in trouble!'* or *'Crap, she's loose.'*

I turn down the corner of the street and try to remember the directions of the quickest way back to the main shopping area, deep thoughts continuing. Should I change my walk too? The way I hold myself? Skipping to shuffle to the other foot to lead, I try to relax my steps along with my heartbeat. It feels unnatural. Like I'm trying to hide something. No. Back to the normal walk.

The hair prickles on the back of my neck, alerting me to the sounds of huffing and puffing coming up fast from behind. I turn to spin quickly on the balls of my feet to come face to face with Hailey as she jogs to keep up with me.

"Woah, she laughs. Where's the fire?" She's still glowing in the early morning sunlight, despite her old pyjamas. "I just wanted to say good luck. It's not easy, starting again."

"Who told... I'm--"

"I know the kind of company Denny keeps and you ain't going to be the first young woman finding a new beginning. You sure won't be the last either. Den's tough at times, but he has a soft spot for people like you. He's a good guy."

"Well... um, thank you."

"Don't be afraid to try and fit in and make friends. If you here now, you belong here," Hailey finishes. She looks torn between staying to say more and heading back to the church. For a brief second, I think she's going to cry, but she spins on her heels and walks lightly back down the street.

"How do you know?" I call after her retreating figure.

"People like us are survivors," she calls back cryptically.

-34-

Irvine's wife is nice enough when he first introduces us. Bree is a quiet, unassuming woman with a pinched face, small features, and a mistrusting look when she initially shakes my hand. I get the feeling she rarely trusts anyone, especially when running a little market stall with all sorts of thieves and unsavoury people around. Regardless of whatever thoughts she has of me, she doesn't treat me unkindly or make me feel like an outsider. She feeds me along with her own children and lets me sleep in the neatly made up guest room--which smells like fresh lemons from the scent diffuser on top of the night-stand. For room and board, all I needed to do was help out with the market stall.

I take Denny's advice and began to think about my words and certain American mannerisms. Nightstand is a horrible word, it was a bedside table and would always be. There's also sidewalk, sneakers, patties, faucet, eggplant, highway. I feel like I'm learning a totally new language that doesn't make sense.

Whatever Irvine had explained to his wife, she wisely doesn't question me on my awful American accent or grill me to where I really came from. Tactfully, Irvine doesn't question too much either and gives me helpful tips now and again. Their children, three little boys, give me cheerful thumbs up at the breakfast table when I practise my speech under my breath.

"French fries." He points out one evening over dinner as soon as his wife had taken their kids up to bed.

"Chips," I affirm and shrug apologetically.

"Chips are different. Chips are these." He pulled out a bag of family size Lays from the pantry. A brand that looked suspiciously like Walkers, back home.

"Crisps?" He suppresses a polite smile. "There's clearly a lot of work to be done here. You're a young lady with a lot to learn."

"Don't even start on me with the whole cookie is a biscuit thing, again."

The small house they reside in is in a quiet neighbourhood that overlooks a local park and a small pond with geese in. It boasts three small, square bedrooms and is completely detached from the neighbouring buildings, meaning the boys could make as much noise as they wanted to and wouldn't ever hear a complaint from next door.

As the days wear into each other, I find myself quietly appreciating how Irvine's wife fondly cleans up the boys faces with a tissue after every meal, kisses them on top of their heads before they go fishing with their father, and pulls out a huge book of coloured pictures to read to them at night. I even begin to find myself curling up on one of their armchairs in the corner of the room and listening to her narrate *The Gruffalo* and spend time emulating their voices. The boys giggle with glee. They love it. I love it too, strangely enough.

After a week of settling into the house, Irvine begins to introduce me to the workings of the stall. Rather than chatting to the locals and trying to push stock and special offers, I am to be in charge of taking payments at the till – no, *register* – and helping with the administrative side of things.

He and his family work like dogs from dawn to dusk 6 days a week. The 7th day is reserved for staying home and going to church in the morning – although it was across town rather than Denny's and Hailey's building.

Once upon a time, Terin Coiler would have suffered through this. But my days as Morgan Archer at sea were more than enough to support me carrying crates of fruits and vegetables back and forth. No longer do my feet ache at the end of a long day or did my hands burn under the pressure of rough surfaces. They weave through rope and tape expertly, thumbing through cash and change to give to customers. Irvine has even drawn up a little cheat sheet under the register to break down US currency and the UK equivalent for my understanding.

My first official paycheck comes in just a week after living with the small American family. Irvine looks sheepish as he handed over the envelope with the cash inside. I ask him why he's apologising, and he admits that he couldn't afford to pay me the same wage as I would earn anywhere else in the market

I snort. "I'm living here in your house, eating with your family, and I'm wearing an old Hawaiian shirt of yours. It's fine, Irvine." And it is. Besides, without amenities like rent or a mortgage or bills, I'm free to head out by myself down to the nearest mall and pick out clothes for the first time in forever. My sailing gear and Darrell's jumper are too heavy and hot for this humid weather, the Hawaiian shirt and ladies' khakis are too out of place on my small, boyish frame. Not ideal in a land where I'd start sweating and going red in the face in minutes.

It isn't too hard to find by myself by following the usual footpath to the market square and then following the road down from the English style pub at the North-West corner. Street signs like $3^{rd}/4^{th}$ didn't help – why are the streets not named instead? I follow the apex of the architecture of the streets toward a large circular building in the distance, dusted by apple trees around the circumference in small cages. It was a mostly off-white building with huge square windows to boast the three or four floors inside that gazed out to a rectangle stretch of green grass over by the parking lot entrance. There's a market here too, but not like the one I'd spent the past week in.These stalls are decorated with hues of greens, yellows, browns, and oranges. A colourful banner with a cartoon cow reclining on a couch tells me that this is a Vegan food fair.

I move past the bustle of shoppers and make a beeline for one of the huge entrance arches and sigh in relief as a wave of cool air washes across my shoulders. The humidity here has been awful. Way worse than the Mediterranean ports we'd sailed to and past – at least I had the benefit of the cold ocean all around me. Inland was a hot, bustling hive of activity that was difficult to get used to again. I wonder if I were to move back into the heart of London again – would I feel the same? Perry sure as hell wouldn't have bet money on me becoming used to sailing.

Another odd throwback to my time on the crew only happened while sleeping in bed. Despite the firm ground underneath, I still experience the ghostly feeling of swaying back and forth in my hammock while the waves danced under the hull. It was weird, thinking about *The Whittaker* hurt. I swallow the lump in my throat, force my head high, and ascend the escalator to main shopping centre.

Brightly lit, huge shop displays and brands are splatted as far as the eye could see. Familiar logos and fonts--Hollister, McDonalds, Burger King, Pizza Hut, Staples, Gucci, Nike--all catch my eye. I also spot new ones I'd only ever seen in the media, such as the crimson and white of the Wendy's signage.

I have to stop in the middle of the marble patterned floor and gaze upwards at the three levels of the sheer mass of the building. Above, a hexagonal sunroof with ribbons cascades downwards, ever moving in a windless motorised fashion through bronze ceiling sculptures of abstract angels. Everything around me hisses with energy--with life. It would take little to no effort to reach out and take it for myself, maybe just a little. Hundreds of bodies are milling past every minute, taking no notice of the smallish woman standing motionless in the middle of the centre, mouth open.

A wetness slides down my cheek. Is there a leak in the ceiling? A bird nesting above? No, it's clear water. Jesus, why am I crying?

The answer's simple: I've never felt so far from home and utterly lonely. For the second time in my life, I realise that the world is so much bigger than I am. Perhaps, I'm not the main character in my story after all.

"You didn't buy much?" One of the kids bounds up to me as soon as I return to the market, with a second-hand old teddy bear in his hands. He points towards the singular paper bag I'm holding, containing a couple of items from the first shop I went into.

"Not a fan of crowds," I say. I let the accent slip a little with my mood. He doesn't seem to notice much, already used to my odd ways. I duck around him and slip behind the tables of our stall, tucking the bag moodily behind the rest of our belongings. Irvine's chatting to one of the locals about the best fishing spots in the area while the man patiently tries to leave the conversation.

His wife finishes up a sale and pockets the spare cash in her belt. She catches me hovering quietly by the fish, but I'm determined not to look up and engage with anyone else right now. My heart and throat ache for some unspoken need. I don't understand how this beautiful town with all its picturesque scenery and life is making me feel this way.

"Morgan," she says gently. "I need you to run this down to the diner down on the corner, think you remember where it is?" She waits for me to nod until handing me a bundle of neatly wrapped items in tissue papers. Layers of fresh fish upon layers cradled together with an old-fashioned string on the top along with an invoice. I quickly calculate the route in my mind and nod.

I take off my own money belt and fold it under the table where there is a small deposit box. Bree nods only once in approval and leaves me to it, turning to the next customer.

"Right," I say, grateful for the quick escape. I wish I had a proper home to run away to – a bedroom to slam the door to and escape everyone and everything, to exist only in my small bubble. Throat still heavy with emotion, I disappear from the stall quickly and out into the midst of the crowd.

I feel as if I have a panic attack coming on. The pressure of people's bodies pressing in all around me and squashing out of the life from my body. Oxygen feels sparse; I'm starting to see spots. Christ, what's wrong with me? My day started out fine, I *felt* fine. Now, I feel like I simply can't cope with anything. Broken in too many ways.

I go headfirst into someone's body, mortifyingly gabbling an apology in my broken accent, half-crying.

"Hey now, shh," someone says soothingly. Caramel arms wrap around my shoulders gently and pull me to my feet, holding me while I shakily get my balance. I can't see who they are until I manage to get the tidal wave of sobs under control. They patiently let me finish my episode and wordlessly hand me a tissue when there's nothing but sniffles left.

I'm able to study them for the first time. The piercing gaze of Hailey smiles back at me. She cocks her head and says, "You all OK now, chick?"

I nod, feeling like a fumbling baby.

"Oh no, no. Don't look away. We all got moments of weakness and you need to accept and wear them like a badge." She prods my shoulder with a slender hand.

"Breaking down in the middle of a crowd isn't exactly something to be proud of."

"No," she concedes. "But getting to your feet and deciding to stand up straight is something you can control here. My grammy would say the same thing, tell you to get off your butt and get moving. There's sunnier days ahead."

I hope she doesn't mean literally. The weather is hellish enough without the threat of a hotter inferno beating down on me in the middle of the square like this. I'm embarrassed, feeling sticky and sweaty in front of this poor young woman who's hugged me.

I change the painful awareness of the situation. "You're out shopping here too?"

"Technically I'm on an errand. I need sneakers I can work in all day," she says, daintily holding up her feet encased within old rubber flats. They've definitely seen better days, reminding me of the old black plimsols we used to wear at primary school. My own feet hurt just thinking about it.

Hailey looks as if she wants to say something but can't find the words. Her eyebrows flex and furrow over her brown warm eyes, the corners of her mouth slating from one side to the other in thought.

"I'd better get going, this heat is getting to me," I complain and break away first. She follows my lead, jumping back into the present and nods with her own excuses as to why she can't stick around. It's a shame we can't hang out together properly. Hailey emanates a calm likeableness about herself that makes my realm of chaos feel a million miles away back out to sea. Every molecule is drawn to her in a pleasantly serene way. All of the outside noise falls away.

Christ, what's wrong with me? What I suddenly in love with this girl? No. It's more deep rooted. Like she's my sun and I am a star floating around her existence. She's an entity that I want to join and be apart of. Just... be.

"You're not like..." I gesture to the muffled tones of shoppers billowing around us. I watch her eyes lazily move to follow me. A pearlescent flash behind the iris flashes for a split second. I understand in an instant. A zing of excitement moves through me, waking up every cell and nerve ending with a recognition I only ever felt once before.

She understands too. I can see it in her eyes as my expression changes. Her faces becomes painfully contorted to the point where

I almost feel in pain along with whatever she's feeling. The calmness wobbles, threatening to break. Somehow, she's affecting my emotional state. I'm sure of it.

She's like me.

-35-

I'd finally come face to face with someone who shared the same secret trauma as I did. Jared was different, I was used to his weird ways and in some regard, his powers seemed almost like something I dreamed up to escape my own childhood ghosts.

Hailey is here. She's real. This is a real-world encounter, a once-in-a-million opportunity to connect with someone else on this level to try to understand how we came to be. And why.

I don't expect to become overwhelmed with sadness. The tears appear without me registering they were there until my face was all wet.

"Can we talk?" I choke out. She looks uneasy, her smiley expression faltered for a fraction of a second. She peers around nonchalantly as the shoppers milling around us, pressing in closer.

"Not here. There are too many eyes and ears around." She indicates for me to follow her, however, my feet won't move from their rooted position, no matter how much I wanted them to.

"I'm sorry, I just haven't met another one of... well us." My lip quivers, face struggling to hold it together. It was a weird knee jerk reaction. Of course I knew there were more of us in the world from what Jared had said, but to meet another like this?

"OK, you need to calm down. We're being watched," she says sweetly. The calmness returns after a few nanoseconds, soaking me in a lavish smelling honey scent that reminded me of a long hot bath. It must have been her influence. I breathe her in, gratefully and the tears disappear. I barely even hear what she's saying.

"This way now," Hailey says, guiding me gently with her slim wrist. She picks up the pack of fish I'd dropped at some point, and I follow her shining light through a café lined alleyway to a street filled with multicoloured banners and shop facades. Whatever power she's using on me, it works. I would follow her into walls of flaming inferno.

At first I think she's going to take me towards her church, instead we head past the centre of town and quickly towards a quiet road filled with car mechanics and technology repair shops. An old bridge sits at the top of some stone steps that overlooks some of the older buildings in the more residential area. It would have been a pretty nice little town if I was literally any other human on the planet and the constant threat of imprisonment and murder didn't hang over me.

"I need... to slow... down," I huff. Hailey glances back, relinquishing her grip on my wrist, bracelets jangling together. We continut to head down a grassy slope that leans just under the bridge entrance, out of the way of the road.

"Sorry, I was a high school track star. Don't realise my own speed sometimes." Whatever power she possesses, the calm emotional aura around her disappears and was replaced by a neutral one. I don't understand how I didn't sense her sooner. I can practically feel the alien vibrations from her like a spidey sixth sense. Is this what Jared had talked about before when he sussed me out?

"Are we OK to talk?" I breathe. "Not for long," she says. "I can feel you just at the edge of your control by the way, you need to reel it in a bit, or you'll lose yourself."

"What does that even mean?" I ask incredulously. So many questions whirl around my brain, all demanding answers at once. Nothing seems right for the moment, especially if we only have limited time. Instead, I settle with saying; "Why didn't you tell me when we first met?"

"Why would I? I didn't know who you were or what you wanted. Sometimes it's difficult to sense another energy like ours unless we're very close together or there's emotional involvement. I didn't know until I caught you panicking in the crowd." To her credit, she looks as freaked out as I do.

I launch into my next round of questions. "How many of us are there?"

"Few and far between. No way to know for sure. You?"

"Ditto," I say. "Well no, I know there's an apparent group of people like us hiding away in Oregon somewhere. Aside from that, we're alone."

"Not alone. Denny is also exceptionally gifted per se."

"Anyone else?" I say flatly. "Irvine and his wife? Their kids?"

"Who are *they*?" She asks. "This is not a safe country to be in. Things are going on and people like us are beginning to straight up disappear. There was one girl in a brain clinic in Saco who I grew up with. Poof, gone."

"Hang on. They're just *vanishing*?"

"The few I knew, yeah seems so. It's happening around the region." She points to a typical American newspaper crumpled at the edge of the concrete. It was a similar report to the one I'd seen of the little boy, but a young girl this time. "That's her right there."

"How could that even be possible? Isn't anyone looking for them?"

"Their families and friends. The cops. I even heard the FBI's getting involved. Once they disappear, they don't come back. No one sees where they go, and no one finds any trace of them." She pauses, worry etches across her face. "I'm honestly worried me and Denny will go next."

"I'm sure it'll be fine," I lie quickly. There's no way this wasn't involved and connected to our abilities. Someone out there knows about our existence and for whatever reason, has the resources to make us disappear.

She rolls her eyes. "I can sense you don't believe that. It's fine – neither do we. Den's suggested we get out of town and try somewhere new and cover our tracks. Whoever is following us will hopefully be at a loss and move on."

"Which is why you said eyes and ears are everywhere."

"They are. I can *feel* their intent Morgan. Like hearing a dripping tap from across a hall. I just don't know who they are, what they want or when they'll strike."

"That sounds terrifying, Hailey."

She sighs, momentarily fumbling with her nose ring. "Yeah. Problem now is, if they're hunting us, you won't be far off on the list either."

"I've only been here just over a week!"

She shakes her head. "Doesn't matter. If they want us for what we are, they won't care if you have a tourist pass or not. You're as screwed as the rest of us."

The fear in her voice is palpable. It was silly of me to think I would with exempt from this apparent witch hunt just because I just arrived here. If Hailey and I can sense one another, it's almost guaranteed others can sense us too. Why not these *hunters* also?

"How do you know so much about these people, whoever they are?"

She pauses. "I've run into a couple of them in my time. They're called Hunters. Sent to seek us out by any means necessary." Her words turn bitter. I wonder if those she'd met lived to report back or not, but she didn't elaborate.

Christ, I'd jumped from the frying pan and into the fire.

"Are you OK?" She peers at my face.

"It's all just a little too much information. I really thought I'd have a new start in this town.""We're survivors remember."

I try to breathe deeply, control myself. Darrell and I had run through all the breathing drills together for every situation. Slow breathing for calm, fast and efficient for combat. There are no promises that they would move in to capture us and if so, I could protect myself at least.

"Why now though?" I ask. "Why would they suddenly try anything when you and Denny have been here a while?

She shrugs, arms jangling out to the side. "Something's changed. It's almost like they were only keeping tabs before. Now it feels like they're creeping closer." She shivers. Goosebumps speckle her caramel skin.

"Like they know I'm here."

She nods. "And their window of opportunity is closing to catch all three of us."

I hesitate and swallow, unsure of what to do next. On one hand, I totally believe Hailey and on the other, I wanted to pretend this isn't happening.

"I'm going to talk with Denny and my Grandfather," she hands me the now warm packet of fish. "If you would like to come along and get out of here, I want to leave tonight."

"And if I don't?"

It's her turn to swallow. "Then I will pray for you, Morgan. But I don't like your chances."

When I finally return back to the market stall, Irvine and his family had stopped for lunch. They wave me over with a homemade burrito, still lukewarm from being stored in the thermal bag.

"You find the place all right?" Irvine greets.

"I got lost along the way, the fish was a bit warmer when I delivered it, but the man was nice enough." I force a smile and take the burrito gratefully. Rice, peppers, chicken, and cheese. I take large bites, barely able to savour the flavour from the lump of worry in my throat. Everything tastes like cardboard.

My mind is still torn in two; though I manage to excuse myself for the rest of the afternoon by feigning a stomachache. I begin to walk slowly out of the town and back to the house. Although I didn't know Hailey very well at all, she seems so genuine and caring. Why am I feeling uneasy about leaving at a moment's notice?

Because it doesn't feel real, I decide. Regardless of whoever these Hunters are, they haven't given any indication they are hunting or wanted anything to do with me. It all seems like a crappy fairy tale. So *convenient* that I'd land in a town with an even bigger problem than on *The Whittaker*.

I shower quickly – who knew when I would get the luxury of washing again if I was about to escape yet another sticky situation? Without drying properly, I pull on my clothes, leaving the woollen jumper tied around my waist. My new bag is already packed and good go to. I left a small amount of cash and a rushed goodbye note already written and placed on the dining room table.

I can't believe that I'm already having to do this again not two weeks since I'd left the sea. No time to dwell on my horrendous luck, I rake a brush through my hair, checking quickly in the mirror at how awful I'd be looking for the next escape attempt.

I swipe my head away from the mirror just as a throwing knife embeds itself into the shocked reflection, sending thousands of glass shards raining downwards. My whole body moves backward instinctively, colliding with the side of the shower. My shoulder exploding with pain, I swear under my breath and hold it with the other hand, peering around the side of the bathroom door.

Another knife hits the wood with a thud. They are the real deal – the type professional military personnel would use. These guys––or Hunters, as Hailey called them––are no joke. I slam my foot into the wooden door and pull the deadbolt across it. It won't stop them but should slow them down a few seconds. Without Hailey's ability to sense emotion, I can't tell how many are in the house or roughly where they are.

I try to scrape my fingernails over the bathroom window latch, forcing it open despite the creaks of the wooden frame. It's one of those higher rectangular windows with a sharp jump onto the grassy verge outside. I brace one foot on the side of the sink and the other on top of the toilet – made only more difficult by the borrowed flip flops that tumble to the tiles.

I force my body upwards, straining with pain as the sill presses against my stomach. I can't quite work my shoulders through the frame properly without having to dislocate anything.

"Come on!" I curse, throwing my weight against it. Again and again. No budging.

I pause, ears pricked. Sounds of booted footsteps flood the downstairs living area and the kitchen next door as whoever they are ready themselves for another attack––a far cry from the safety of the family environment in this small house I've grown quickly accustomed to. I hope that Irvine and the others don't decide to come home anytime soon.

Everything goes eerily silent for a few seconds. Shaking, I'm still poised on top of the cistern tank with the window wide open and no hope of getting out. My heart pounds. Is this how it's really going to end? In someone's bathroom smack dab in the middle of a foreign country?

The door flies off its hinges and across the room into the sink. Behind, someone lowers their boot and wasted no time in breaching the room, quickly scanning the environment before locating me.

It all happens so quickly. I reach out to my other energy for help, all too happy to oblige. My body seems to move on its own as I feel myself leap from the top of the toilet before a rain of bullets can begin. I use the shower door railing to swing myself outwards and cut back to kick the stranger into the soaked shower drain. Despite the black balaclava and padded vest, I could tell he was a male by the 'ooph' sound that escapes his lips on impact. As his head collides with the drain, some residual water flies up from the tray and soaks his head. Before I realise what I'm doing, I summon some power to my free hand and smash it onto the exposed lower portion of his face, allowing the water droplets to act as a conduit to the flow.

The smell is instantaneous as is the seizure-like movements underneath my feet. Regardless of the water that also splashes over me, like Jared, it seems that electricity doesn't affect me, like fire doesn't affect him.

A muffled yell brings my attention to the doorway. Three more similar dressed figures with guns point towards me, moving in quickly to the doorway. I stretch upwards to seize the portable shower extension and flicked the dial across to full intensity. Water immediately shoots from the nozzle, covering the small crowd and buying me two or three more precious seconds.

Using the tide to spray all three of them, I force my power through my hands and into the steel surface of the showerhead. The water immediately sizzles, steam raising from the stream that transfers quickly onto my assailants. They scream, guttural and painful, falling onto the soaked carpet, writhing back and forth as the current continued to surge through their bodies. Once I no longer feel an electrical signal from any of the four strangers laying motionless on the floor around me, I quell the charge and turn off the shower.

Everything's a mess. The smell is atrocious--barbeque and melting plastic. I try to swallow down my panic attack. *They were going to kill me first*, I try to reason. I should not have to feel guilty. These were bad people. They'd have killed Irvine's family if they'd stood in the way.

Any hesitation I had by the thought of leaving is immediately quelled. There's no way I'm going to stay and risk these good people in any more danger.

Mind made up, I pick up my bag from the side of the toilet and sling it over my shoulders. Tredging carefully through the rest of the house for anymore armed surprises, I can't shake the feeling I'm being watched.

One last sweep across the house for Irvine's sake and I give up. I pull open the front door in preparation to meet Hailey and am stopped dead in my tracks.

Smiling in greeting and standing jovially with his hands in his pockets on the welcome mat is Amir Abbas.

-36-

The train rattles beneath me, shaking me from side to side with every movement of the storm outside. Flecks of water streams against the window, dangling only for a few moments before they're hurled off into the darkness to rejoin the rain. I'd heard storms were more common down south as were earthquakes but I'd grown up in London. The rain is second nature to me.

With every jolt, Denny mutters something under his breath. His face is still pale from the endless string of arguments it had taken to get him to ride one of the 'metal deathtraps' as he calls them. Another rattle through the carriage. He closes his eyes and murmurs a plethora of curse words, folding his arms.

At his side, Hailey sits demurely with today's *New Yorker* in her lap. Her face is neutrally calm and smooth, but her fingers flicking lightly on the paper tell a different story.

I yawn, stretching out my legs underneath the table as far as they allow. The trains here are seemingly roomier than back home – some even have double decker compartments, I still manage to brush against Denny who grunts moodily

305

"I'm worried about them," I whisper. None of us had spoken in a few hours, each taking solace in the fact the carriage was near devoid of people and silence was welcoming.

"You couldn't risk staying," Hailey says. "Based on what you'd told us about this guy, he knows people like us exist. Specifically, you anyway. He's a bad guy, maybe involved in this somehow.

"Yeah, maybe," I mutter. Don't think about him, Terin. Don't lose it in front of these people.

"How do we know you didn't lead this psychopath here to us?" Denny says, eyes narrowing.

"People have been disappearing long before Morgan showed up." Hailey says gently, placing her hand on the shoulder of his leather jacket.

Denny sighs. "I've actually heard of this guy myself. He's been on the FBI list for months according to an old army buddy. It's only speculation but word on the street is that he's a big player in the middle east. We're talking about overthrowing establishments, imprisonment, kidnapping, bribery."

"Murder." I whisper.

"Run through again what he said to you?" Denny shakes his hair. I'd recounted the story multiple times, from every angle. We've scrutinised Amir's possible movements, meanings, plans from beginning to end. My throat's beginning to strain from the effort.

I recall Amir's beady black eyes boring into my very soul the moment the front door opened. That smile was already on his face, knowing exactly where I'd be exiting the house from. He'd definitely glanced past the threshold to see the bodies of his men sticking out of the downstairs bathroom, but his face didn't betray any kind of emotion – negative or otherwise. He was just *calm*.

Hearing his voice sent me right back to that night on *The Whittaker*. He'd said, "Glad to make your acquaintance once again, my dear" with that dangerous lilt of an accent. Everything came flying back to me in that instant. Darrell's hopeless expression as he tried to look brave for my benefit as he was led away.

"Where is he?" I had demanded with more emotion than intended. He'd taken a moment to let me hang in my anxiety for a moment and nodded only once, "He's alive."

I thought I'd misheard him at first, too terrified to fall into his trap if it was a lie. The swell of happiness momentarily consumed me. Darrell was *alive*, as was the others hopefully. They weren't executed after all.

"Why are you here?" Was my next question. I felt raw and drained from my previous encounter, I could probably summon a little more power if need be but it wouldn't be nearly enough to kill the man. My fists had clenched along with my teeth. If anyone deserved to be bubbled and fried to death, it was Amir Abbas. I'd glanced up and down the street path behind him, there were no signs of anyone else hovering. Just a quiet, unassuming road.

"I have no one with me," he'd replied. "Only those you have killed today. I did not think you had it in you." He blew a low whistle, hands still comfortably rested in the pockets of his cargo trousers like we were engaging in small talk. I found myself unable to read his body language or voice. He was a mystery.

"I won't let you take me," I'd threatened, sending a little power down to my hands so that they illuminated a cerulean shade of blue.

My internal battery struggled and strained, I tried not to let it show on my face.

He exhaled and waved his hand. "My plans seem to have changed. I think I prefer watching you fight for your freedom. Like drowning camels when they're no longer be of use." He'd laughed to himself, giving his mercenaries another interested glance.

I didn't know what to do. One part of me wanted to take the opportunity and run – the other wanted to stay and fight. This man was clearly sick in the head.

He chortled for a few moments more and then stopped, his eyes cold and empty. "I suggest you escape little mouse, let me take care of the clean-up here."

"You're... letting me go?"

"Think of it as extending your leash. You are rather fortunate I am tired of hunting Strays and I happen to have business elsewhere. You and your friends are safe––until I return at least." He finished with another smile. Like a snake conducting a business transaction. I bit my lip, glancing at the clock by the door. Did I dare leave him alone in the house an hour before Irvine and his family were due to return home?

"Tick tock," he'd taunted. "Every minute counts. Your little pet family here are not worth my time to kill and dispose of. But I am not known for my patience."

I'd decided to go. I rushed past with my bag, narrowly missing his shoulder. His arm lashed out and grabbed mine to swing me around and face him. Regardless of if he was weaponless or not, his grip was vice like.

"The Activated are nature's next innovation for the new world. You cannot run forever from what you are made for," he hissed and released me. I stumbled backwards down the porch stairs and scrambled to my feet, leaving both the house I'd temporarily learned to call home and Amir Abbas behind.

I sigh, low and long. Denny and Hailey were still peering at me, unsure of what to say next.

"About that," Denny cranks one eye open. "You say you met him before around the Mediterranean and he let you and your crew go?"

"It wasn't without payment," I say darkly. "He killed one of us, took three more for his army. Then took our provisions and let us go." Deep down, I was glad he'd followed me here. It meant that Perry and the crew would get back to the UK safely and be able to disperse without further issue. It cheers me up slightly.

"You believe her?" Denny shoots at his companion.

"She's not lying, her energy would change."

"About that too," I interject. "We haven't addressed the elephant in the room. Who are you guys? You promised me we'd talk properly when we escape but...." I gesture to the train. The storm. Whatever backwater town of city we were travelling through. It's their turn to fall silent now, throwing cautious glances at one another. Once upon a time, I would have been shy to talk to near strangers like this, but Morgan was exhausted, in desperate need of a shower and not in the mood.

Hailey smiles tightly, moving the paper to the table and addresses me directly. "Believe it or not, we are just as normal as you. What's normal for us, anyway."

"We have powers," I clarify, repressing a shudder from such a ridiculous notion.

Denny groans, eyes closing again. "This is pointless."

She ignores him. "Before, I was actively influencing you, trying to – calm you down a bit. You were in a state of panic and fear and whatever else you were feeling. It was all messing with my head and my juju, so I just... helped a bit."

As if to illustrate her point, I feel the air change around our seats with the same warm scent of a summer's day, freshly cut grass, and slow breaths while watching lazy clouds in my mind's eye. I glance back to the window again. The dark storm rages on outside.

Denny groans. "Stop that. If I wanted to hear my mother again, I'd goddamn call her."

"You can make me see whatever you want?"

"It's more that I can influence your energies and rearrange them. I can't make things appear out of nowhere, but I can kind of pluck and pull." She motions her fingers in the air. The scent of summer turns to a wintery smell of cinnamon and fresh pine––the kind from a real Christmas tree in the corner of the entrance hall across the way from my father's study. Vanilla candles are lit in the dining room by my mother, humming her favourite Christmas songs.

"STOP!" I snap. My hands slap onto the plastic table. My fingers prickle with the effort of not expelling every electrical signal on this whole train. Somehow, breathing heavily, I manage to keep in inside and tucked down into the pit of my belly, where it bubbles unpleasantly. When my breathing slows, I glance up from my lap to see that the top of the

table had melted where my hands were. The smell of burned plastic takes over the scent of Christmas in the Coiler mansion.

"Holy shit," Denny says. "She can barely keep it in."Even Hailey looks mildly freaked out, which is saying something after talking about manipulating my emotions. "I–I'm sorry... I didn't know."

"What did you see?" I hiss.

"Nothing. You shut me down." She lifts up her hands to show me her fingers and arms. I gulp back horror. The metals of her rings and bracelets have been melted and fused to her skin.

"I did that?" I choke.

"You didn't mean to," she said, pretty calmly for someone who'd become a human wick. "I can feel that. It was an accident, you can't control yourself."

"N-No I can. I mean... I don't really have that much of a problem anymore it's just. Those memories you made me feel, they're painful."

"Cry me a river, kid." Denny frowns, gently extending Hailey's hands to face him. He says nothing more, but cups her palms and stares at them intently, inspecting every fingernail, skin cell, metallic fragment. Watching his hands, they begin to glow a soft hue of orange. I watch as Hailey's skin is literally repairing itself in front of me. The metal falls to the table fleck by fleck, followed by slightly bigger chunks that are begin pushed out of the surface of her caramel skin, followed by dead skin flakes. Everything crumbles as easily as a squashed pastry. He continues this until every fragment of metal, plastic, and damaged skin is removed entirely from her hands and arms. I stare quietly at the heap of metallic dust on the table.

"Yeah yeah," he says, answering my unspoken question. "Me too."

The overhead PA system blares into life. "Sorry folks, we did have some technical issues for a moment there, but it seems to have resolved itself. We're twenty-two minutes from the next stop. Our dining cart will be serving meals shortly."

I look between the both of them, incredulous. "Have you guys ever stopped to ask *why* we're like this? Why is it only us or if they––we––are everywhere?"

"Keep your voice down rookie," Denny hisses, eyes scouring the panelling above. He nudges Hailey. "One over there, one just behind us by the door."

"Morgan, how clueless are you about your power?" Hailey says quietly.

"Not clueless. Just... not well practiced. I've taken a few people down but I need to be in a certain emotional state. It like, takes over."

"Good enough. You wanna try giving those security cameras a little pat on the back? Fizzle them out maybe?"

"Rewiring or deleting the memory bank would be more effective," Denny suggests.

"She's new, Den. She probably doesn't know how to do something that advanced. We don't even know her limits yet."

"She doesn't know them either! You saw how she can throw down suddenly – we could be in danger here. We are literally travelling in a metal tin can, that she can turn into a conduit at any moment."

"Trust me, she's not going to kill us."

"It's on you." He throws his hands upwards and moodily tucks them across his chest, glaring at the melted handprints on the surface of the table. He's a far cry from the tough talking New Yorker I'd first met in the back of the church. He's scared. We all are.

I shrug. It shouldn't be that hard. During raids with *The Whittaker*, I'd dabbled in a few electrical experimental bits with basic security systems and hacking. Rewiring an entire CCTV system with a likely backup system somewhere? Piece of cake.

I've toyed with explaining my background and my manifestation to the two near strangers but something in the root of my gut warns me to keep things to myself. Whether it's a ghost of Darrell's voice floating in the back of my mind––or Jared's––I don't know. It's right whatever it was––I don't know who I could trust and how much I should let on.

Play dumb, Morgan. I breathe inwardly. I especially don't want Hailey to get any auras or feelings of my old life.

"How do I.... project it?" I ask with the precise amount of confusion and overwhelm that I would naturally be feeling. Denny rolls his eyes again and elects to say nothing. Hailey leans forward and kindly takes my hands. Calmness and positivity fills the air around me.

"Summoning should be as easy as taking in a breath," she says seriously. "Just like you've been doing all your life, girl. Let yourself be quiet inside and reach out. Not too sharp now."

I scrunch up my face in effort and shook my head after a few attempts. My power sits patiently beside my consciousness, easily within reach. I made a show of becoming frustrated and a little teary.

"It's OK. It's fine, Morgan," Hailey soothes, cupping my face in her long slender fingers. "Don't force it so much of you'll exhaust yourself and get irritated. It's like reaching out for a glass, or the morning newspaper, or your cell. It's a natural subconscious movement of your energy and nervous system."

I grab a tendril of power and let it bathe me in a low buzz until it fills me from the fingers to my toes. The switch flips in my brain and I can feel every separate current soaring within the metal walls and floors.

The tracks underneath hum and sing with every new section we ride over until the sounds become a constant buzz in the back of my head.

I feel connected to everything. Almost Godlike. Is this what Jared let himself think?

"Good, good. Now I can't feel what you feel but let yourself feel everything around you. Take your time to search for what you're looking for." Hailey gives a thumbs up and allows herself to recline back against the seat, hands still clasped together.

Denny watches with mild disinterest as my aura evaporates and transforms into something else entirely. In addition to the electrical pulses soaring around my body. I can tap into the electrical pulses of the nerves in their bodies. The constant thrum of neurological synapses firing messages to and from the brain. One little tug and I could change this in an instant. If I pull on the hind brain receptors, I would be able to shut down their bodies in minutes.

I could feel it. I'm stronger than both of them. I could take them easily if necessary.

A breath hitches in my throat, cold and rasping. The lights flickered momentarily, mirroring my sudden shock and interrupting my focus. Why are these thoughts pushing their way into my consciousness?

It's from being Godlike, I think again. It was too easy to get lost in these feelings. Too easy too give into the cold and calculated killer side of myself where it'd be so easy to shut off my feelings.

"Did you manage to get it?" Hailey presses.

I nod numbly. A quick tug at a few of the security memory hubs around the train and we were as good as untraceable. The loop would run about thirty minutes behind livestream before resuming to the current time. It's almost too easy to manipulate.

"I... think so," I breathe and let myself settle back into the seat, wiping my face with the back of my hand.

"You did it." She beams and elbows her companion who gave a sarcastic thumbs up, a glare of recognition still flares quietly in his eyes. They really did believe I'd only manifested recently. I need to let them continue to think that, really believe I was nothing but an inexperienced fledging with nowhere else to go.

Regardless of the miles we put between ourselves and Abbas, the hair on the back of my neck still prickles as if his beady eyes were still watching me.

Especially now knowing that Darrell was alive – wherever he was, I would be ready to take him down next time.

-37-

New York is the next destination.

Hailey insists that we aren't going to the usual tourist traps like Central Park, The Empire State Building, or the Statue of Liberty––although no one could sanely visit the big apple for the first time without stopping to check them out. It certainly isn't my idea of fun. I've hated crowds ever since I was forced to endure my old home being flooded with distant relations every year.

New York is renowned for the rabbit holes that allowed people to disappear and start again. It offers more beginnings than most places and insanely crowded enough that a person could try to be whoever they wanted to without fear that they'd be hunted down easily. On paper it's a romantic notion, but in real life as part of a trio of fugitives, it's a smelly, rotten, busy hell.

"Can she keep up?" Denny grunts as we head up the entrance steps to the subway station. In my defence I was sleep deprived, dehydrated, and confused with which stairs were up and down. Hailey patiently follows me to expertly weave me in and out of the morning commuter traffic like a child. People 'tsk' and mutter when we got in the way, earning a few sharp words from my older companion that would intimidate *me*.

"She's doing her best." Hailey says, emerging from the top of the steps just behind me. We move to the side, and I take a deep breath of my first glance of New York.

It's everything I expected and more--minus the Avengers swinging around with an army of aliens. The city around us was a continuous thrum of movement from the sounds of shoes on the pavement to the constant murmur of hundreds of conversations around us. It isn't quite the famous Times Square, but the tallish buildings around us are adorned with decorations, music, and event posters. *CNN* blasts away on one TV screen from the electronics outlet to the right of us while *Good Morning America* is on the other.

Suddenly, I am an excited teenage girl all over again, determined to try and run into famous names and faces, while shopping at the most famous brands in the city. I can barely even feel the thrum of electricity, which lies forgotten in my sub consciousness.

Denny nudges Hailey and softly drags her over to the TV through the shop window. When I am done gawking at everything, I join them, trying to figure out the most mature way of begging to go sightseeing without totally embarrassing myself.

"Another day, another kid." Den frowns.

Hailey tries to calm him. "There's no evidence that it's anything to worry about. We don't know these kids or what background they have. The Underground will figure it out--"

"The Underground can barely define their own asses from their heads," he snaps, pulling away from the conversation as soon as they noticed me listening. My eyes move to a photo of a little girl emblazoned across the screen. She was taken from somewhere near Missouri.

"Abbas said he was leaving for a while. You think he's still operating?" I say.

"There are other hunters doing his dirty work for him, I'm sure," Denny says drily.

"A conversation for another day," Hailey yawns, nonplussed by her friend's hostility. "We'd better pick a place to hole up and sleep. I'm running on fumes here."

"I agree. I have an old buddy with an apartment a couple of blocks away. He won't mind us crashing while he's out of the country." Denny gestures for us to follow him and neither of them say anything more. I focus on the passing street signs for anything familiar that I've have heard of, while trying to ignore the zing of electricity that buzzes beneath my feet every time a train goes by.

"You grow to ignore it," Hailey offers. "I barely focus on anyone's aura unless I'm doing it on purpose now."

I groan, feeling weak and childlike. "When? It's a constant buzz and it's annoying to push down."

She shrugs lightly. "I guess it's different for everyone. The longer you live with it, the more you get used to it. So, you manifested recently?"

"Uh, yeah," I hedge. I try to do the maths in my head. Five years is too long for me to still feel like a novice at this.

"I remember the first time I started feeling different. So my grams and gramps were harvesting some of their home grown vegetables from pop's patch––it wasn't anything big really but enough to help feed the family, kind of thing? We were a big bunch. Anyway, my grams comes in from the backyard and she's holding her face together in pain and I catch her in the kitchen. Something happened and she ended up catching her hip the wrong way. She must have been emotional because all of a sudden, she starts crying about one of my uncles who died the week before. Cancer, I think. I knew she was gonna start crying before it was gonna happen because I felt the wall of emotions coming through. I didn't know what to do with it at first, so I cried in the kitchen along with her. After a while, my gramps comes back in to see what all the fuss is about and somehow, I have her laughing at the stupidest things with me. I don't even know how I did it, I just wished she would cheer up and wouldn't be suffering no more."

"What did your gramps say?"

She smiled. "He came in and said, 'Ladies, I thought there was a goddamn ghost in here, hollerin' for the past twenty minutes, but it's just you both being crazy!' Damn, I miss that man so much sometimes, it hurts." A forlorn expression appears, I wonder if she's lonely, being able to control of emotional state of everyone around her, but not her own

"What do you think he'd say about all of this if you told him the truth?" I gesture between us.

"He'd tell me I'm a silly little girl with big dreams, a loud mouth and a dopey expression. Then he'd kiss my head and insist we'd find a way out of this mess. Not before he'd beat me with a slipper for not being entirely truthful though, not my finest moment."

"Or enlisting me to come on the run with you?"

She rolls her eyes. "You're free to go at anytime. But with Amir Abbas possibly on our tail and the kind of *people* we are, we shouldn't split yet."

"I just feel guilty for leaving the family I was staying with. They were kind and compassionate and helped me out."

"For now; it's best they forget about you," she says sternly. "I don't know fully what Amir is capable of, but it's safer for them to keep out of it. Does anyone else know, about you?" "No," I say. Jared and Darrell, provided he really was alive still, were complicated.

"Good, we're all on the same page," Denny murmurs. His face is stoic with his hands shoved in his jeans as we walked. I wondered quietly who else they'd lost.

"Chin up." Hailey smiles. I feel her power begin to cling to me with gentle tendrils of contentedness. Everything is going to be ok. Everything is going to work out.

"We're here." Denny cuts across us and pushes open a glass door of an apartment complex. It isn't anything fancy with a doorman or a carpet and canopy outside, nor is it overly run down. I can't complain, boring normalcy is what I crave right about now.

Checking we weren't followed, Denny closes the latch behind us and ignores the lift in the empty lobby, opting for the stairs in front of us. We must have cleared five or six floors by the time he gestures us to follow him through the hallway adorned with apartment doors either side. I feel for my power to try and gage how much activity was around us. Not much. A few buzzes from televisions and radios, exercise equipment and a soup maker. Human electrical signatures were harder to grasp beyond my own. Especially when I can feel sleep tugging impatiently beneath my eyes.

Denny's friend's apartment is medium sized but cosy. A TV is mounted on the wall, and a coffee table with a stack of post and newspapers sits in front of it. There are some questionable paintings and décor. There's a little kitchen, bedroom, and bathroom that are off the main room behind their own doors. His friend seems to have a real thing for potted plants and Broadway posters.

I'm half asleep before even hitting the sofa – Hailey already closing her eyes on the other one. Denny offers to take the first watch and pulls an old Otterman over to the blinds, helping himself to a chilled beer from the fridge. My eyes close fully and I let myself be pulled into a deep sleep.

I wake to the smell of bacon and eggs which momentarily confuses me as the room is almost pitch black. It takes a moment to even work out where I am and who the figure standing over by the window in the corner is.

"Morning, sleepy head. Or evening now," Hailey's voice greets. "Den's making breakfast. Or dinner, even."

"In the dark?"

"Can't risk blowing cover," Denny answers over the swill of sizzling in the other room.

"We've already passed countless public spaces, security cameras and people. Surely it would have been blown by now?" I mutter.

"We got ourselves a hangry sleeper over here!" Hailey calls.

"She'll stay hangry unless she shows a little thanks." Denny moves into the main room with a plate of hot food and slams it down on the coffee table along with a fork. "Try not to choke on it."

"He was so friendly when I was giving him my business." I mutter.

"Ignore him, we're all under a lot of stress. We all got crap we can lose." Hailey tucked into her own plate, balanced precariously on crossed knees. Even in the light of the city around us, I can see from the reflection of her face that her eyes never strays from the window.

Denny returns and takes up residence on the floor nearby, chewing slowly and savouring each bite as if he hasn't eaten for a month.

"The food's delicious," I try after a while. Two grunts of acknowledgement meet my attempt of conversation as they do their own thing. Hailey moves over to the CD and Blu-ray rack, using a spot of moonlight to read the cases. Denny continues to frown and sit quietly by himself in the corner.

Yet again, I muse, I'm in completely new territory with total strangers; running from something I didn't quite understand. I stare down at my hand. I'm my normal tone of pasty Caucasian, and there's a couple of scars here and there, dirty nails.

"Why do you think only some of us were born with these... powers? And why weren't they always there?"

"Who knows, kid," Denny says. "A cosmic practical joke. A serious screw up in evolution. Maybe we just aren't wired right."

"All we know is that some of us exist out there. We don't know where we came from, genetically speaking. We don't know why or how or if everyone has some type of untapped potential deep down and we were just lucky enough to––"

"Lucky isn't the word I'd use," Denny says.

"I would," she says hotly. "We've all been blessed with something really special that no one else can do––just think of what your healing power could achieve in a hospital? What I could do to defuse tensions in a war room? What Morgan could do in a third-world country without power? Think of how many people wish they were us right now."

"Delusions of grandeur," her companion spits. "Just listen to yourself. We're all being quietly hunted by powerful people, it's only a matter of time." I can see his scowl in the shadows of the office block across the street. He thumbs his hands together nervously.

"You'll see. One day they'll need us." Hailey slaps the blinds with her hand, her bracelets jangling loudly into the glass beneath. I feel a bit guilty for starting a clearly well-debated old fight between the two friends.

"Amir Abbas *did* mention that the Activated – whatever that means – are nature's next development and that we have a job to do," I say quietly.

"He's a tyrant and a war criminal. One Google search on him brings up ten pages of amateur sleuthing and news articles. He's probably talking crap for his own agenda," Denny mutters.

Hailey exhales sharply. "Or maybe he's talking about a better future where we don't need to be afraid."

No one says anything after that. Uneasiness fills me. Hailey is sweet, but frighteningly alike Jared to the point where if I squinted, I could imagine his own eyes gleaming across the dark room from me.

-38-

U nfortunately, we need cash to be able to decide what our next move is.

"We need to go find The Underground," Hailey tries again one morning. "They are literally the only people who could offer us safety right now." She's in a rare bad mood, likely brought on by the lack of proper nutrients and sleep. I feel it too. The constant dangerous tug of wanting to give into my mood and let my power run amok so my energy wasn't drained all the time. I can't speak for my two unlikely companions, but it's a constant battle for me to keep myself suppressed.

"No," Denny says flatly. "We'll regroup and figure something else out. Hunters and Abbas cannot be in all states at once, so I say we use this brief reprieve to work out what he's up to."

"He might not even be in the country, plus the guys I took down might have been the only hunters tailing us." I chime in.

"He still has spies at his disposal and countless piles of money. As Morgan clearly showed us, if he wanted to kill or kidnap us, he would have done easily," Hailey reasons. "It's the perfect time to fall back on

the Underground and hide out with them before he changes his mind.
"

"If he can practically walk up to her front door," he gestures to me, "In broad daylight and easily lose four or five men, he won't be bothered by a bunch of rag tag misfits of all ages and sizes."

"I'm just saying, safety in numbers."

"And I'm just saying, we don't know what kind of weapons he has in his arsenal. There are three superpowered people just running around Biddeford who happen to be in the exact same place he appears? Maybe he has something that tracks our energy or something. Kind of like a kinetic signature."

"Is that possible? Can machines exist to track our electrical readings or something?" Hailey breaks off and redirects towards me.

Wide-eyed, I shrug. "I'm not a scientist or certified electrician."

Denny sighs, running his hands through his dark hair that looked more woeful than trendy now on the run together. "We need to look at the facts here and act on what we know for definite: people like us are going missing. Hunters have been sighted and known in areas where these occurrences happen but haven't been caught––according to a subreddit."

"Sweaty keyboard warriors are classed as factual now?" Hailey snorts.

He ignores this. "The theory is that our people are being kidnapped and are never seen or heard from again. These disappearances are growing in numbers and are happening all across the country. If this man can make something of this scale happen, The Underground won't scare him and they know it."

"How do we even *know* all of these people if we're few and far between?" I frown.

"Word of mouth mostly. There's no MySpace or Facebook for our kind. A friend of a friend of a friend who heard it from The Underground directly. He's got them worried."

"Which is exactly why we should seek them out," Hailey says.

"It's makes them too big of a target. Who's to say Abbas isn't already aware of them and moving in with a team as we speak? He has armies at his disposal, the organisation probably only has a handful. There are no laws, no legislation, no official record that any of us exist. If we disappear, we're done." He gives us a hard look, one to the other. There's no denying he is right about that fact. One wrong move and this powerful middle-aged man is going to catch up with us.

"So... what do we do now?" I say quietly.

"We try and find some cash to get moving again. Put as much distance between us and him as we can. I'll try and see if I can rustle up some contacts who got connections in the Middle East, maybe we can get more of an idea of what we're dealing with."

We're left with a defeated feeling of hopelessness and worry––two emotions I'm already pretty used to by now but the look of nausea on Hailey's face makes my stomach do worried flips. How is it that I ended up slap bang in the middle of New York in my early twenties, running away from another impossible situation?

As easy as it would be to let myself fall deeper into hiding away, finding a job is easy enough wherever there was a help wanted sign in one of the windows of the local stores. I end up working in a tiny pizza parlour just off China town. The clientele are usual customers who didn't ask too many questions and I don't bring attention to the boss taking cash in the back alley from local thugs. I get my tips and my wage packet in hand, and he gets the security of knowing I'm unlikely to up and leave anytime soon. It's mutually beneficial and sturdy.

Walking the short commute to and from our borrowed apartment is a literal walk through every American movie and TV show I'd grown up with. Subway signs, giant slices of pizza, newspaper vending machines, yellow cabs flood my view. A bagel stand sits on the corner filled the street with the fresh aroma of bread, cheese, and herbs. It's enough to keep that tourist euphoria going within me, a welcome change to overthinking everything else. I let it eat me up and consume me.

Jared must have visited New York too at some point, I decide. It was the multicoloured backdrop for every superhero movie in his childhood. It's the pinnacle of every average traveller aspiration to visit. Dreams are supposedly made here. He would be narcissistic enough to not pass up an opportunity like that.

Maybe, he's still here. Was this mysterious Underground organisation any part of the group of people he wanted to seek out?

"What's *The Underground* exactly?" I have enough courage to ask Denny later on. We're hanging out in a local park with a couple of fruit teas, waiting for Hailey to finish up her shift in a clothing store a block away. Although we're seated on the cool grass under a tree, the slow burn of the sun could be felt on the wind blowing through the leaves like a gradual chorus hum.

He groans. "That's a long story and to be honest, they're all kind of jerks who think they're some great collective power together."

"They're like us?"

"All of 'em. Came around when I manifested about thirteen." He pauses. "They approached me once, you know. Promised they'd have all the answers for me and would be able to help me get a grip of my power, all I needed to do was say goodbye to my home and my family and they'd look after me."

"Did you go?"

"Hell no. My sister was sick. She needed me."

"You couldn't heal her?"

He winces. "I didn't know how. I couldn't leave her, in case she died and I couldn't heal her the way I needed to because I couldn't leave to train."

"And what happened?"

He shrugs. "She died anyway. I tried to figure it out myself, accelerated his disease and well.. she was in a lot of pain in the end." He makes a lot of effort to carefully keep his face neutral but his hands fidget. His nails dig into his skin.

I didn't know what to say. "It wasn't your––"

"Don't you dare finish that sentence if you know what's good for you kid. There's no used trying to slap a band aid and a kiss on it. I effectively euthanised her by accident. It was my fault. I made my peace with that."

"It doesn't sound like you made your peace with it."

"You my therapist now?" he growls. "We shouldn't exist. That's the end of it."

I don't disagree. Our existence was nothing but a burden on everyone and everything around us. "Where do you think we came from, and why?"

A few moments ticked by before he finally says, "Hell, probably."

We both fall silent, allowing our legs to hang from the rocks we were sat on. I'm bored trying to fill in the awkward silence, so I settle for taking in the scenery instead. A group of pigeons eye us from the corner of the bench they are sat on across the path. I break a piece of my sandwich to toss across to them. They look interested for a moment but bristle and move away.

"Animals don't like our kind. Don't you know anything?" Den mutters. I choose not to snap at him for his crappy mood, especially reliving what was obviously the worst moment of his life.

"Apparently not," I whisper.

Hailey appears a few minutes later with a fresh sheen of sweat across her cheeks and the back of her neck. She tugs unhappily at her uniform. "Can we go already? It's like 100 degrees in this."

"We've been out too long anyway," Denny says. "Best we keep a low profile."

"You know, I'd never thought I'd miss the old church so much. Sometimes I wonder if it was worth the risk." Hailey says. "I hope gramps is OK looking after the place."

"You're alive aren't you?" Denny points out.

Whether or not they'd been close friends for too long and were used to their own space or if they truly were getting on each others' nerves, the tension between my two companions has reached a new peak.

"Let's all go out for a drink later," I suggest gently. "What's the point in coming to New York and only leaving the apartment for work?"

Denny looks aghast. "We're laying low, we're not gonna draw attention to ourselves!"

"And we won't. Morgan's got a point, Den, we're holed up too long together. We need to blow off some steam."

"Are you both forgetting that we aren't normal human beings? What if someone bumps into Morgan and gets electrocuted by accident? What if you're unable to shut out all the energies, Hailes?"

She sighs and stops walking to turn and take her best friend's hands into her own. She breaths deeply and smiles. "Denny, you're overreacting. One night out won't hurt and we'll be home before midnight. If *any* one of us," she glances at me, "becomes unstable in any way, we will pull them out and leave. Does that sound like a deal to you?"

"Amir Abbas," he grunts, barely meeting her eyes.

"Amir Abbas isn't going to stroll into the middle of a dingy local nightclub. We haven't seen him since we left the East Coast. Is this how you want to spend your life now?" She sighs again. It's small non-committal sound that shakes with uncertainty. Denny digests this for a moment and eventually nods once.

"Only a couple of drinks," he warns. "You're lucky I made Morgan Archer twenty-one on her license."

True to his promise, Denny doesn't breathe another word of complaint about the night's agenda ahead. We hit the nearest Goodwill on the walk back to grab a fresh change of clothes. It feels good to slip on another pair of jeans and a shirt after having to leave the rest of my new purchases back at Irvine's place. Again, guilt eats away at me as I dress. I hoped neither he nor his family would hold my sudden departure against me or had the sense to report me as missing. I also hope that Abbas would have been thorough in his weird offer of crime scene clean up.

It's eight in the evening by the time we step out onto the street. We'd have left sooner but Denny had insisted we needed to eat first so the alcohol wouldn't rob us of our wits. Dejectedly, Hailey and I agree and eat his homecooked pasta without arguing.

He knew of a small place down by the village that was generally avoided by the bigger crowds but apparently still had a nice vibe to it. It isn't a cesspool of gang activity but isn't the cleanest place either. As we approached from the corner, there's an old Dairy Queen sign at the top of the entrance which had clearly been disconnected from the power a long time ago. The letter 'D' dangerously tilts from its axis and precariously hangs over the blackened door windows.

"I wouldn't take you guys anywhere unsafe," he says, answering our unspoken question. "I just know the bartender here and he owes me a couple of favours. Maybe I can get some intel on local rumours."

"Well I'm glad someone said it," Hailey snorts.

"At least we have little to no money to be robbed of," I mutter.

"You wanted drinks, kids? I delivered," he mutters, grabbing us by our hands and leading us confidently over to the door. Despite his warm hand enveloped in mine, I can't swallow down the feeling of anxiety and nausea of being watched. My other consciousness feels it too. The expectation of change is in the air.

-39-

Whatever feelings of foreboding and fear wash away as soon as the cocktail touches my lips. It's a sudden burst of flavours that trigger every nerve ending in my mouth, explosion after explosion. I try to grin; it feels more like a grimace. Hailey laughs, even Denny looks amused.

"This is your first cocktail?" she asks.

"Tried a little beer and ale here and there. I'm not much of a drinker." I had a tough time trying to imagine what Captain Perry would think of me if I asked for a Cosmopolitan or a Sex on the Beach during one of the post job drink ups.

"Oh honey," she says. "We need to change that right away. You remember that drink we got in Ohio that one time, Den?"

"The forbidden jungle juice," he recalls, looking pained. "God knows what they put in it––I was puking for weeks after that birthday party."

"It sounds wild," I laugh. Our voices trail away into the next DJ set. A mixture of some popular songs from the nineties and early 2000s lace together. Hailey claps her hands and pulls us both onto the dancefloor. I can't name the singer or the track's name, but they seem to know every word. I smile along.

Morgan Archer is out clubbing, I muse. My mother would hate this sort of scene. It's too bohemian for her. The sticky floors and the haze of cigarette smoke wafting from the exit door in the corner was everything she stood against. I wondered if she was always that way or if she allowed herself to let her own hair down when she was younger.

The song fades away into an electronic crescendo. I was having so much fun attempting to dance, I don't even feel the energy drain from quelling my power. It's easier like this, easier to be happy. Denny excuses himself to go and track down his bartender contact.

"Have you thought about what you want to do next?" I ask Hailey as soon as the next song ends. Covered in a sheen of light sweat, she pauses for a moment to think and shrugs.

"I'm pretty interested in surfing. Maybe I'll end up on a beach somewhere, with a nice cabin. And a husband."

"And lots of money."

"Definitely." She grins. "What about you?"

"Hm. I want to find my brother, I guess. From there, who knows? Do any of us really have a future?"

"You have a future," she says, grabbing my hand. "If it's any one of us that deserves a happy ending, it's you."

That surprises me. I'm careful not to get too sensitive when it comes to sharing stories or memories, and then I remember that Hailey had accidentally tapped into my emotions, seeing and feeling some of the worst parts of my existence.

"You don't know my full history, regardless of whatever flashbacks you got through."

"I don't need to. I see who you are now. You'll find your brother. You'll get home. Wherever you came from." She finished off her sentence with a British flair of an accent and a wink.

"Thank you," I gush, "for being my friend. I don't have too many of those anymore."

"Magical siblings," she smiles and intertwines our pinkie fingers. "I guess that's closer to the truth. All of us out there who are different the way we are; we're all connected. We may not understand it, but that's the God honest truth"

"By some large unknown cosmic force," I giggle.

"Don't cry," she says quietly, cupping my cheek with her long slender fingers. "You've always been crying inside but now's the time to be happy. You're free as a bird, chick. Well, as much as we can be."

I laugh; the wetness that spilled onto my cheeks doesn't register with me until the very last moment. Christ, how embarrassing. How many other people cried their eyes out during the middle of a nightclub?

"So why do I feel like you're saying goodbye?"

She sighs, moving her hand down to intertwine our fingers. "There will never be a goodbye between us." She looks so sincere, so sure that everything I was worried about peeled away into the ether. I want to believe it's my own confidence in my friend that led me to this realisation of happiness, rather than her power at work. Either way, I don't care. She's my people. Denny too, as difficult to like as he is.

"Go find Denny," she suggests, breaking apart from me. "Go tell him I want my dance he promised. I'm heading to the bathroom real quick." A strange expression appears as she breaks away.

I nod, half listening. The cocktails are beginning to take their hold on me, sending me into a euphoria of fruit juice-tasting heaven. I hold my arms in the air and allow myself to fall in with the rest of the crowd heaving and jumping around me to the tempo of the bass. With each thump I can taste my own heartbeat. Everything is moving – it all feels so alive. I allow a little power to reach my fingertips and sizzle quietly into the air. It feels good. Like blowing out a slow inhale.

Somehow, I make my way over to the other side of the room where the makeshift bar is set up behind the old Dairy Queen counter. The little fridges are filled with multi coloured bottles of off brand alcohols and local brews.

"I knew Hailey would corrupt you," Denny sighs in my ear. "And I had such high hopes."

"Is corrupt the right word for someone who has been walking on the dark side long before I met you guys?"

"Probably not. Come on, you need some water. Look at you." He leads me over to the side of the bar to wait for one of the bartenders to become free.

"Why don't you like me?" I blurt out. Along with my alcohol levels, apparently my confidence had risen through the roof. Denny stood motionless for a moment.

"I don't trust you," he says honestly. "Me and Hailey been on our own far too long. For people like us it's hard to let those walls down, you know?"

"I've been alone too."

He nods. "I know. I'm sorry you didn't have a friend along for the ride."

I open my mouth to correct him. I had a great friend and a wonderful protector. "His name was Darrell," I choke back a sob. The second time this night I was going to breakdown in public. Denny stands attentively to listen but suddenly I don't want to talk about my friend anymore.

Pain licks at the corners of my subconscious, burning with every memory and every smile.

"Water please," I direct at one of the bartenders who approachces us. He wears a white shirt under his hooded sweatshirt with a matching fedora. He nods and smiles at me, then he glances over at Denny and does a double take.

"Denny?" he says. Utter shock laces his features. My empty glass hangs in mid air before he pours it.

"Hey Mickey! It's been a while. One of your guys said you'd be working tonight." Denny nods.

Mickey stares back at him like a ghost. Incredulous, he shakes his head and places the glass back on the counter. "You know I actually heard a rumour you were dead." His eyes flicker to the entrance and exit doors. The drink has been long forgotten about.

"Woah," Den frowns. "I just moved out of the city for a while. Who told you I was dead?"

Mickey shakes his head fervently. "It's the word on the street – everyone's terrified. A few people went silent and everyone else is gone. Just... gone. Some dead, some disappeared."

The alcohol began to burn away in my system, replaced with confusion. "Is he talking about people like us, Denny?"

"There aren't many," my companion scowls. "Only a handful of us. How much danger are we in right now?"

"Enough that you need to get your asses out of New York and back to wherever you crawled out of," Mickey says soberly. It's enough of a warning for Denny to nod once, attaching himself to my bicep and pulling me away from the throng of people waiting.

The DJ changes to something darker and faster. The dancers filter into the middle of our path again, moving their limbs with practiced agility. Denny and I have to slow down but somehow manage to try and reach the far side of the floor.

Movement above distracts me; I have to squint to stare up at the ceiling through the streams of light.

"Oh look, I think they have dancers." I point to the catwalks that laced the length and breadth of the ceiling. Figures filtered in through the doors either side of the room in uniform swift motion and each lined faced both sides of the room. They're all dressed in identical black clothing. Nothing is identifiable but the ski masks on their faces with the lenses reflecting our faces gazing back up at them. They each hold something shiny in their hands, which glints from the strobe lights. I'm mesmerised, waiting impatiently for the show to begin––regardless of the very serious warning we just had. Perhaps I haven't sobered up as much as I thought. The music increases in intensity.

"Those aren't..." Denny begins to whisper.

The items in the dancer's hands were unveiled from the darkness above, pointing directly towards the waiting crowd beneath. The pause of people laughing and dancing around us alert me to the sound of Denny's hitched breath.

"GET DOWN!" he roars over the crowd.

The sounds of bullets hitting something solid and wet ring out over the music. Instinctively I bow my head and dive into a bench along the far wall along with several other clubbers. A chorus of screams fill the small venue, a sick backing track to an otherwise catchy song, which cuts out when the DJ disappears from the makeshift stage. The sounds of boots and shoes squeaking to escape deafens me.

Another round of bullets sprays down from the catwalks. With the darkness and strobe lights, it's hard to pinpoint how far in the line of fire we are. Denny slides to my side and pushes me back down to the ground as a further gunshot is triggered. Like a war veteran, he drags me under his armpit and hauls me under the benches for cover.

"Stay!" he commands, wrapping his arms around my torso to protect me. Another round of shots. Metallic clinks fill the air alongside the heavy bodies of dancers hitting the ground. Cries and shouts. The scent of blood rises.

"Did you see––" I can't finish. Hailey is nowhere to be seen and I have no idea how we are going to find her in this chaos.

"No," he huffs, scanning the shoes thundering around us. Someone catches the side of his face with their sole as they pass and he swore, holding his nose.

"Press yourself against the wall," he commands, muffled. Blood leaks and trickles from between his fingers. Seeing my horrified expression, he pulls it away. "Just a broken nose. I haven't been shot. It's fine."

"Who are these people?" I cry.

"Shh! I don't know. I don't know. Maybe that bastard double crossed us after all." He sniffs. Bubbles of blood gush from his nose and dribble onto his shirt. He grunts in annoyance, hovering his hand across his face. I watched the bridge of his nose realign itself with a sickening crunch, earning a pained whine from him.

"Are you OK?"

"We need to move," he says. We wait for a break in gunfire while they reload and use the opportunity to move out from the benches and run to the speakers behind the stage. I trip and fall on something hard and squashy. I land awkwardly on my elbow, a cry leaves my lips. Holding it together, I glance down to see I'd fallen on the DJ laying dead beneath me. His glassy eyes and bloodied face from a shot to the temple sent me right back to that night all those years ago.

Ted Sanders's withered corpse stares back.

-40-

"Come on!" Denny hisses, yanking my sore elbow towards him. He braces so we don't fall back onto the stage. We crouch together behind the soundbar like stuck pigs. When had I become so drenched in blood?

"Hailey said she needed to use the bathroom before I came and found you," I breathe. It's hard to concentrate on him when the sounds of screaming continue around us. Innocent people run for the exits, torn between the desperation of escaping and the risk of being mowed down by our masked assailants.

"Woah, focus on me Morgan. We'll have to start there. The bathrooms are on the left of the entrance over there. If I distract them, do you think you can get over there?"

"You think she's OK?"

"I think she better be OK," he growls. "Can you do it or not?"

"I'll do it. Is there a way out?"

He thinks for the second. Boots are beginning to move along the catwalk above as the crowd begins to thin and succumb. For a heart wrenching second, I think it's because someone managed to break open the fire escape. But there is a growing pile of bodies over by the green neon sign. The doors were still tightly shut.

This was our fault. This couldn't be a coincidence.

"You need to start healing everyone! We can't let them all die." I suppress a sob.

"Are you crazy? Even if I could heal every person here – we'd just be shot again," his voice crumbles. He shakes his head. "Whoever they are, they're here for us and it's damn pretty obvious they'll do anything."

"They're slaughtering everyone ..." I whisper, edging towards panic attack. The breath hitches in my throat. Nausea rises up my oesophagus. I can't get away from it. The constant stench of death and decay.

"There's an old subway tunnel that runs around under the area. Sometimes they have access hatches in the basements of buildings to access the tracks for emergencies. It's probably our best bet for escape," Denny says grimly.

His warmth leaves. He's using every ounce of energy to propel himself forward into the middle of the dancefloor, expertly dodging and leaping over the dead and dying of those we can't help.

"Hey – you missed one, shitheads!" he roars and waves his arms. Immediately someone above barks an order and guns are pointed and fired in his direction. I want to close my eyes and hide away. I want to find my cellar and hide away all over again and pretend none of this was happening.

I need to run, I realise. We only have a short bracket of time.

Shakily, I rise to my legs and stick to the corner walls where the upper level lips over the rim of the bottom just enough, I can get around without being easily seen. I can see half of the figures on the catwalk begin to head to the stairwell as they cautiously peer down through the gloom for survivors. Denny was doing a great job at antagonising them to shoot.

My foot crunches unpleasantly on something, but I don't dare to glance down to see if it was food, a plastic cup, or a human. The bathrooms are easy enough to navigate to – they still hold the original signs above from the building's retail days. They are my beacon.

A cry shocks me into stumbling. Instinctively, I turn to see Denny falling to his knees. Another wet sound cracks across the room. He's been shot in the back of the leg.

"Denny!" I scream. A couple of dark clothed men above hear me cry and turn to face me. I can see my face in their reflection. My body is bruised and bloodied and broken. My eyes are wild and electric blue.

Using my fury and pain, I leap across to Denny's side and place my hand on the metal pillar in the middle of the room. It isn't particularly load bearing but is attached to the metal catwalks that are arched in a star shape from one side of the room to another.

Inside, I concentrate and focus every molecule of energy and power I possess – from the darkest reach of my limbs to each beat of my heart. I allow this to build and reach a pinnacle to the point where if I don't release it, it's going to explode.

I wait until the last minute and direct this energy to my hand on the pilar. As soon as it leaves my body, it's a free radical energy of released chaos. It reverberates and vibrates through the metal surface – soaring up through the beam and along the catwalks quicker than I can control it. I feel the flesh of the men sizzle against my current. I discover there's fifteen of them. Fifteen pairs of steel toed boots absorb my power. Fifteen voices begin to scream in pain.

I'm screaming along with them – whether from anger or over exertion, I don't know. Burning flesh fills the air. Connected electrical appliances nearby begin to flare and sizzle to life. The sound system copies the very frequency of my energy current. The sound fills me with more power faster than it can leave my body.

"Stop!" Denny cries over the crackling of electricity. "They're all dead!"

I pull myself out of my reverie. Above, the charred human remains of our mysterious assailants' bubble away quietly as the flesh peels from the bone. I let myself power down, feeling sickly more satisfied than I had done in months to let myself go.

"We should... get going..." I whisper. The gore sitting before me doesn't feel real. I feel disconnected from this whole situation. Did I do this?

"Come on," he says urgently. His bullet wounds are already healed, save for the blotches of dark dried crimson on his clothes. Wordlessly, we turn back to where the bathrooms are and jog the rest of the way across the room. There are no sounds, no signs of life from anyone left in the room. Just a drum and bass beat to a sea of slack figures.

"Did I hurt anyone else?" I dare to ask.

He shakes his head. "Only the gunmen. Everyone else was already..." his words catch in his throat. Slumped against the bathroom door, our friend is leaning against the varnished wood. We race quicker, jumping and leaping over the barriers of the mezzanine railings to the raised platform stairs.

"Shit!" he roars and drags our friend out into the confines of the cloakroom by her armpits. I follow, trying not to slip on the trail of blood underfoot.

"No, no, no, no no!" he moans, sinking to his knees. "Crap Hailey, crap. Give me that scarf Morgan!" I obey and tossed it into his impatient hand. He immediately sets to work by securing a tourniquet around the lower half of Hailey's right arm that was splattered in the rich coloured fluid.

She's deathly pale and unresponsive. I watch her face in silent horror, wishing and begging with whatever deity that caught my prayer to show her mercy. Not Hailey, she doesn't deserve this end.

It looks like Denny has the same thought. Despite stopping the main bleed from the artery in her arm, she doesn't make any movements. Not even an eye flutter, like in the movies.

"W-why isn't she waking up?" I demand. "Come on Denny – what are you waiting for?"

His face is already contorted with effort. "What do you think I've been trying to do? She isn't waking up! Come on, Hales. Come on!" His palms connect with her body. Nothing happens. No fast action paranormal healing. No weird fast forward skin stitching together. No happy ending.

"We're missing something," he hisses, scrabbling through the pile of blood he's knelt in. "Help me find the bullets would ya? They must be laced with something. A suppressant, or toxin?

Something that's blocking me. Come on... Why isn't this working."

Or maybe he knows he can't cure death, a little voice says inside me.

Denny continues to mutter to himself. Getting louder and louder until he's yelling and shaking Hailey by the shoulders. Despite the situation, I think she looks weirdly at peace. Like she's simply fallen asleep on the sofa at our shared apartment as she waited for the sunrise.

"I can't locate her electrical signals, Denny…" I whisper. There were simply as if they never existed. Just, gone. My power recedes from her frame and pulls back towards me, empty handed and dull. I can't feel anything. I can't move.

Loud footsteps begin to ascend the stairs outside the door. They're in no hurry, they obviously know we're here and aren't fazed by the amount of destruction and death in the other room. They're calculated, slow steps of someone with time and power.

Not now, Abbas, I plead. *Not now.*

They turn the corner to face us in the middle of the room, standing over Hailey. They wear a similar uniform––now I could see it properly in the lights overhead. A black rounded ski mask with a pearlescent finish to it. A snug black bodysuit with arm and chest guards that were padded with Kevlar underneath. They wear heavy combat boots laced up to the mid-calf with knife holsters at the sides of the outer leg. Whoever they were, they stood calmly toe to toe with us. Beside me, I feel Denny get a hold of himself and rise to his feet.

"You stay back you son of a bitch or we're going to fry you.""Fry me?" the figure says. His voice is muffled by the mask. "*She* might. What are you going to to? Heal me to death?" he chuckles. The mask has a distorted element to his voice that sounds robotic and cold. His body language is loose and aloof. We are no threat.

"Show us who you really are," I demand. "Or are you a coward?"

He chuckles. "Drop that accent, girl. It's ridiculous."

I'm taken aback. He sighs dramatically and begins to remove his ski mask. Underneath is another layer of head gear made of a thin material that hugs the top of his head to the tip of his nose so that only his eyes were on view.

His hazel speckled eyes.

The last layer comes off.

The man is about a foot taller than me. Slightly freckled and more weathered than I remembered. There's light sunburn on the tips of his ears from where he refused to put sunscreen on for so many years. His hair was still a dark shade of red and brown. Most notably, the smirk is exactly the same as I'd remembered.

"Jared?" I whisper. My mouth contorts into a twisted grimace of something I don't fully recognise. Denny stiffens beside me. The world loses all colour and potency around me. It's just me and my older brother staring at one another on an even keel.

"You idiot," he says. "You just can't stay out of trouble, can you?"

"Trouble?" I breathe. "Have you not just seen what's happened here?"

Denny shakes his head, putting his hand on my elbow. "Look what this freak is wearing, Morgan." I follow his eyes. There's a military patch on his breast plate and his upper arms. Whoever they are, he was leading these men.

"Morgan," Jared tests. "Better than the similarity to Terrapin. Did she tell you that story, Chuckles? Oh, forgive me, you were the one who helped her become the fraud she is today." He smiles to himself at his own joke, moving his handgun softly from one hand to the other.

"How long have you been following us?" Denny snarls.

"Hm. It's always the downfall of the villain to reveal all of his secrets at the end. Just know that we've kept tabs. Here and there. There aren't too many of us out in the wild now."

"You're one of us!" I spit.

"Indeed. Although I'm glad to see you've really earned your wings little sis. Great job back there with the barbequed bodies and all. Little macabre for my tastes but..." he pauses and looks at me. "I've been known to hold a barbeque myself now and again."

It's a strange comment that comes out of left field. Something clicks into place inside me the more I thought about spending my evenings watching Jared in his room, melting his toys with the mere tips of his fingers. He had the same smile as he does now. I can almost hear the crackle and roar of fire. I can feel the glass shards penetrating every ounce of flesh. The coldness of the cellar floor beneath me.

"It was you?" I whisper.

"I'm surprised frankly that it took you this long," he says. "I'm sorry I caught you up in it. It was my mistake."

Denny looks from one to the other in turn. "Anyone going to tell me what the hell is going on here? Morgan?"

I'm speechless. Angry. Sad. Regretful. "Uh... he's my b-brother. Jared... you let me think it was all *my* fault. All of these years...." I shake my head hard, hoping to shake out this revelation. "You bastard."

"You didn't help yourself much with the music teacher thing, did you?" he shoots back. "Our parents deserved everything they got, including their crispy end. Obviously creepy Sanders did too. I always thought he was a pervert."

"No one deserves to *die* like that."

"Hm," he muses. "You want to tell my men that."

"Our parents were murdered!" I shriek. "By you. And you let me think it was me – that I was the murderer! Jared, you had no idea what I've had to go through!" Hysteria creeps into my voice. Despite how drained I am, I still have a little flicker of electricity left in me somewhere.

"Again," he says stiffly, "I'm sorry. I didn't mean for you to get hurt."

"Your apologies don't mean anything to me," I whisper. "I've tried to dreamwalk to contact you for so many years. I've imagined this moment so many times and never in my imagination was this the reunion for us."

"You've over romanticised it," he says flatly. "We were never the hug and kiss sort of family. More torture and degrade. I blocked you out of my brain, I didn't need any extra attachment."

"Jared," I say softly. "I needed help. I tried to dream walk to you so many times – I could have used... I needed someone."

"I wish you would hurry up and kill us already so I can leave this painful conversation," Denny says. "Go on and swing at me. I dare you."

Jared scowls. "As much as I'd love to flay Mr. New York there, there's been a change of plans. You aren't worth the air I would need to kill you."

"You could try––"

"You have five minutes," Jared speaks louder, "to get out of here before I come for you. I suggest you don't waste your time. I'm sure we'll meet again, *Morgan*." He moves his attention back to me, intent loud and clear. He could not care any less about what happens to me. Whether I live or die. I was nothing more than a loose family tie that probably only warrants these five minutes of cease fire before he'd happily destroy us.

"Come with us – what are you doing here with them?" I spit. "This isn't you! Don't work for people like Amir Abbas!"

Jared pauses. "You don't know me or what I'm capable of anymore. And I don't work for that old Turkish fool."

Denny grits his teeth, tearing himself away from Hailey's side with tears prickled at the corners of his eyes. He throws a deadly look to Jared and a similar one to me. "Come on – let's go."

I switch between them both in desperation. Despite the truth of the fire that ended my childhood, he's still my only family left. "No – Jared, come on – listen to me! Jare, it's *me*. We can talk about this."

"Get out of here," he swallows and cocks his gun, pointing it directly at my chest. "Or I'll use deadly force. Leave your friend right where she is, she isn't going anywhere." He adds, speaking to Denny as he crouches to reach for her.

"J-Jared...."

"Out!" he roars. The room grew hotter and the air thicker. The doorway behind him began to quietly smoulder and flake away under his influence.

Despite my protests, Denny seizes me around the waist and drags me screaming from the bathroom and out into the night. We keep going until the old Dairy Queen is nothing but a smoking husk in the distance.

-41-

I'm transported back to one of our arguments at home during childhood. Jared is standing by the dining room table staring accusatorily at me. He couldn't have been more than seven and I must have been about four or five. I remember watching his bottom lip tremble with all of the emotion he struggled to say.

"It's not my fault!" I'd said indignantly to my brother at the time.

"Before you came along, they loved me more!" Jared insisted angrily. He aimed his teddy bear in his hands towards me and hurled it in my direction. I didn't even feel the collision of the plastic eyeballs against my mouth as I wondered if this really was the case. My heart broke.

Now, the tears won't stop streaming down my face. I was numb – aside from the vice like grip of Denny's hand around my wrist as he pulled me after him.

It's all some terrible dream I would never wake up from. How could one person––especially a young woman––keep this much bad luck and misfortune inside them? Everyone around me got hurt or became burdened in some way. There's no escaping Terin Coiler as much as there was escaping my own karma. I am a curse. Hell, my entire family is.

"Leave me!" I moan and tried to pull my wrist free. I can't find the right words to continue to fight so I cry – half in frustration, half in anguish. Denny chooses to say nothing.

We slip into the nearest subway station and disappear into the crowd like rats among a flock of sheep. He doesn't communicate where we we're going, just that we were moving and there's no chance of slowing anytime soon. Our feet are a blur, the sound of shoes on the tiles all around us did little to quieten my anguish.

"Here, put this on. It'll cover the blood," he murmurs, pulling various coats from the rack outside of a discount kiosk and chucking me the closest size. He produces some cash and tosses it at the vendor, telling him to keep the change. We're moving again, weaving through the trickle of night-time tourists.

"We need to go back!" I choke, barely holding it together. Passersby barely glance in my direction, obviously immune to the fact that drama is common here. Back home, they'd have pointed and whispered.

"We don't," Denny hisses. He's on edge also, I can see it in his eyes. Torn between going back for Hailey's corpse and running with every flight movement in his body. Whatever drives him, the latter wins.

"Everything good here?" a cop approaches us cautiously, eyes flickering between me and Denny. Den slipped an arm around my shoulder, not missing a beat.

"Argument with her friend out drinking," he rolls his eyes. "Brotherly duties, huh?"

The cop peers at me under the cover of my hair, assessing me quietly. "You OK, miss?"

Just arrest me already, I want to say. *Get it over and done with.*

The lights above began to flicker on and off with the effort of keeping the residual energy inside me. The power is harder to swallow down when I was this over the edge emotional. We glance up for a few seconds.

"Need to get her home to Mom," Denny mutters and smiles tightly at the cop, who nods and continues to stare at the flickering lights with the frown.

"Do you think he noticed that was me?" I whisper.

"You're going to kill everyone if you continue like this," Denny whispers, yanking me into an alcove as soon as we get to the next platform. "Take a breath. Cool down. Ten in and out, can you do that?"

"No," I rasp, clawing at my throat. His hands take mine – equally clammy and cold – and he breathes deeply to begin with until I could follow along.

"If there was ever a time to keep your shit together, Morgan, Terin, or whoever you are; you need to do that now, OK? Your psychopath brother is out there and regardless of if he wants to kill you or not––he'll definitely kill me."

"This is all my fault," I rasp. "He killed all those people... Hailey––"

"I can't think about that right now," he pleads. "Because if I do, so help me I will throw your ass into those tracks, and I can't hurt someone like that." A dark look crosses his face as I recall our earlier conversation that evening. Denny is never going to be able to trust me. Not after my brother, not after my suggestion to roam into the lion's den and cost the life of his best friend.

The subway journey is pretty quiet after that. We ride to the very end, only getting off briefly to change trains and head out of the city as quickly as possible. I am too tired and drained to try to fiddle with security cameras. The gaunt expression and oversized coat if anything, took me away from the dream of Morgan's new, stress-free life.

"Jared said he wasn't working for Abbas. Do you think that was a lie?" I ask quietly as we boarded in Newark.

"If not for the cockroach directly, he'll be pulling the strings somewhere, I'm sure. That was pretty hardcore gear they were wearing. Shame about those steel toecap boots. They won't make the same mistake again if they come across you." His answer is almost robotic. Nothing seems like it belonged in his mouth. There's no sense of emotion or real interest. He isn't even angry. He's nothing.

"I'm so sorry about my brother."

"Families," he grunts, as if my brother had just beaten him to asking out a girl at prom.

The most disturbing thing was that despite his intent, I still love Jared and I always would. The excitement and thrill of seeing him after so many years was impossible to quell, he was alive. He was well. He was also a murderer, a liar, a manipulator, and a villain.

My brother was the villain. I was torn in two.

How could he have let himself fall so far? To get in with the wrong people? His escape from the UK to the US was supposed to show him another way of life with people like us, living together in harmony. Now, for some unknown reason – he was hunting and killing. Was he also behind all of those disappearances across the country too?

I feel sick.

Denny manages to hail us a ride out of New Brunswick heading West. The truck driver is called Al and tells us that typically doesn't like to chat or ask too many questions, which was just fine by us. He's heading to Harrisburg anyway for work and can take us as far as we needed to, provided we don't listen to anything but country rock radio.

I barely hear anything anyway. My ears are a constant rush of noise and merging of sound – I idly wonder if I'd blown my own eardrums out when I blasted the club. It's only later that I realise that rush was *me*, the sound of my own increased raspy breathing in accordance with being in a constant state of panic.

The truck rolls to a stop at a nearby bus station so Al can break for a leak. The place is a little run down aside from the coffee shop at the corner of the ticket kiosk. There are a few tables and chairs inside the waiting room and a few outside where a couple of homeless guys slept. Naturally, the area stinks of old cheap beer and stale urine.

I slide down from the front seat of the truck, tightening the coat around me, watching Denny slide over to my side and close the door. He rummages around in his pocket and hands a wad of cash out the window to me. I take slowly in bewilderment.

"What's this?"

"We need to go our separate ways," he says. "I've been thinking, and this is the best thing."

"You're not coming with me?" I say.

He glances down from the cab window, the corners of his eyes crinkle slowly but no emotion shows on his face. "I'm not."

"Right." I nod, incredulous. "OK." Of course, he was leaving me here. He could barely look at me. I reminded him of everything he'd lost. Every pillar torn down he'd built. When we'd first met, he told me his one golden rule was not to cause him any trouble. It was laughable.

"It's probably best if we don't see each other again," he says. "For your own safety. And for mine."

"Yeah. Sure." I wait for a few seconds to see if he will say anything more. Whether or not he wants to, his face was a stone mask of indifference and exhaustion.

Al comes back at that point, hoisting himself back up into his cab. He looks at me questioningly and starts up the truck.

"She's staying. Gonna make her own way," Denny swallows.

The vehicle pulls away from the bus station drop off and twists back around the traffic island to head back to the freeway in the distance. Denny doesn't turn to look at me or wave. I'm unable to do anything more than stay rooted to the spot. I expect to feel more emotional, maybe even miffed that he decided he didn't want to stick with me. All that's left inside is my empty shell filled with nothingness.

"Ticket kiosk's closing in five if you need to head out, ma'am," the clerk calls from inside the waiting room. I approach the counter and slam down a few bills, not bothering to look at the amount.

"Where to, ma'am?" She smiles. She's younger than me by probably a few years. Fresh out of high school perhaps. Her whole life is still ahead of her. A normal existence unmarred by the unnatural and paranormal.

Please let me come home with you, I thought. *Just take me somewhere normal.*

"The first bus out of here is fine. I don't care where it's to," I whisper.

I am utterly and totally alone, again.

To be continued in **Within the Woods–The Chrysalis Saga Book Two**.

About the author

Holly Jane an aspiring writer by night, Student Veterinary Nurse by day. Aside from tending to a house of animals that include many rabbits, two cats and two chihuahuas with the grace of Great Danes, she can usually be found hunched over her desk with a lukewarm forgotten tea in hand and a computer full of projects. "Beneath the Door" is her first independently published novel. Before this, she has had a few short stories published in journals and magazines.

She can also be found lurking on the below social medias:

Twitter: @hollyjwrites

Instagram: @hollyjwriterxo

Tiktok: @hollyjwriter

Facebook: Holly Jane - Writer

Acknowledgements

There's been a myriad of people who have helped me along the way with either expertise or their amazing support in general.

Firstly, to my family who have always supported me with a pen in my pudgy hand since childhood right up to now, staring the big 30 in the face.

To my other half and best friend, Ryan, who doesn't understand the persuasive allure of books but will sit patiently and listen to me ramble for hours about a scene I just can't get right.

To my Alpha and Beta readers; Sarah, Carys, Martina, Anna, Karen and Catherine.

To Kirsty Price; for my English to Welsh translation.

To Anna Velfman; who is my literal angel and is more than happy to answer whatever random writing/publishing question I have and give me her time when she's so very busy herself.

To my friends who continuously boost me through my days and inspire me to live my best self, unapologetically.

Lastly, to all of you reading and getting this far to start of The Chrysalis Saga journey with me.

Buckle up.

HJ x

Printed in Great Britain
by Amazon